LABELED

Jenni Linn

Copyright © 2021 Jenni Linn

All rights reserved

The characters and events portrayed in this book are fictitious. Any similarity to real persons, living or dead, is coincidental and not intended by the author.

No part of this book may be reproduced, or stored in a retrieval system, or transmitted in any form or by any means, electronic, mechanical, photocopying, recording, or otherwise, without express written permission of the publisher.

ISBN-13: 9798682842803
ISBN-10: 1477123456

Cover design by: Savage Hart Book Services
Cover Photograph by: Lauren Anders Photography
Editing by: Rhonda Hewitt, EP Editing Services
Library of Congress Control Number: 2018675309
Printed in the United States of America

CONTENTS

Title Page
Copyright
Exhaust Fumes   1
Off Limits   6
Chase   13
Home   19
Crush   24
Damn Shame   29
Conflustered   31
Feelings   35
Day by Day   39
Beautiful   42
Six Fifteen   50
Douche Nozzle   58
Make It Up to You   62
Like Dessert   67
Take A Picture   76
Not into Me   81
I'll Break Your Face   88

McSwoony	91
Flying Stapler	105
Girl's Night	115
Smitten	125
I'm Not Ten Anymore	132
Hit or Miss	139
Three Sugars	146
Date	157
Sliders	167
Intoxicating	171
What Ifs	179
Distraction	193
Stupid Over You	202
Good Surprise	207
You're Beautiful	214
Seven Twenty-Five	227
Like it or Not	251
Together	265
You're Mine	282
Best Day Ever	290
It'll Be Okay	301
Actions Speak Volume	305
To Family	318
Bar Brawls	331
Late Night	342
Three Down	349

Lucky	359
Let's Race	365
Cosmo	376
Fancy Schmancy	382
With You	401
Back to Reality	410
Hurt	419
When You're Gone	425
Epilogue	436
AUTHOR NOTE	441
Acknowledgement	443
About The Author	445

EXHAUST FUMES

Veronica

It's a Friday night, and there are only two places anyone under twenty-one would be in this small town...the Strip or the Field. The drag strip is my favorite place to be. There isn't a weekend that I'm not here, along with the other motorheads of Great Meadows. The Strip brings all ages to its local track, along with its wide range of vehicles. From old classics to new imports--you'll find it here. We all have that one thing in common; our love for cars.

My fingers wrap around a link in the metal fence separating me from the paved slab of asphalt about twenty feet away. Two cars go racing by. Exhaust fumes follow in their wake, along with the loud tune of their tailpipes. The excitement as they race towards the finish line is palpable, just watching gets my blood pumping. I know neither of the drivers, but the determination to win is contagious.

The maroon Ford Mustang is in the lead, but the further away the cars move down the track, it's harder to see who crossed the finish line first. Two large digital boards, standing tall above the drag strip on either side of the lanes, flash the racers' time confirming the Mustang beat its opponent by 0.2 seconds. It was a close race, but those 0.2 seconds mean *everything*.

My gaze moves back to the starting line as the next two opponents pull up. The black Mitsubishi Evolution roars, the driver revving its engine until it hits the red line causing the car to pop in multiple sessions. The car is done up nicely; lots of money put into that engine. I would know. The driver is Wes, my best friend's boyfriend. His opponent, a blue Subaru STI, revs his engine causing the same backfire. A communication between racers, a way of saying, 'It's on!'

"WHOOO! Let's go, baby!"

The unexpected scream comes from my left, making me jump. I grasp at my chest, and turn to look at my best friend.

"Jeez, Tay!" I yell.

Taylor laughs as she tucks a few blonde strands of her hair behind her ear. "Sorry V, didn't mean to scare you," she responds, but her attention is on the starting line.

"What the hell took you so long?" I ask her. She was gone for what felt like a century. "I almost called the police."

Even though she's not facing me, I can see the roll of her eyes and her thin lips pull back into a smirk. "The line was a mile long, it's like every single person had to pee at that *exact* moment. Oh!" She gasps as if remembering something, "I ran into Jessica too...apparently she's seeing Blake now."

Ah, Blake. We have some brief history, and it's only history because of my brothers. My four loud, very overbearing, and *very* protective brothers. Speaking of my brothers...I look over my shoulder at three of them, who are currently huddled together looking under the hood of a silver car. With the lot of them standing in front of the car I can't make out what it is, and what's so special about it that has them fascinated. My eyes squint together, hoping to make out an emblem or maybe even a headlight, but my brothers are as wide as they are tall. It's no use, I can't see anything. I turn my attention back to the race that's about to go down.

The cars buck as each driver revs its engine waiting for the tree, a tall light placed in the middle of the two lanes signifying when a racer can go, to light up. The flash of the light shines on the front of each car, showering their car in an orangish-yellowish color.

Amber.
Amber.
Amber.
Green.

Both cars take off, their front ends slightly lifting as they press on the gas. Wes is quick off the line, just a second faster than his opponent, giving him an amazing reaction time. Within seconds, they're racing past us and Wes is holding the lead. "Yeeaahhh! Go baby!" Taylor yells, while jumping up and down, shaking the fence with her movements. Her high-pitched scream nearly bursts my eardrum. Even though she knows he can't hear her, it doesn't stop her from being his cheerleader. It's almost sweet. My hands move to my ears, covering them, "Taylor, you're going to bust my eardrum!" I yell at her.

"Oh, shut up and put in some earplugs!" She pulls a pair out of her pocket, still in the wrapper, and throws them at me. They bounce off my chest and land in the grass.

"There's no way I'm louder than the cars!" *Point for Taylor.*

I shake my head in amusement before bending down to pluck the plugs from the grass, then shove them into my back pocket. She screams again and suddenly jumps on my back, completely taking me by surprise. My hands shoot forward, grabbing onto the fence for support before we both eat dirt. "Taylor!" I yell, "Are you insane?"

"He beat him!" she shouts, her legs clutching my sides, ignoring my grunts of protest.

"WHOOOO!"

She clings to my back like some kind of monkey. Despite the extra weight, my head shoots up to look at the times displayed on the board. He won, indeed.

"He had two hundred bucks on that race!" she squeals, this time, at a more reasonable volume. My breath hitches.

"Really?" I glance over my shoulder, her face hovering above mine. Her large almond-shaped blue eyes are wide with excitement, "Yep! Honey is taking his boo out to dinner!" She gestures to herself with a megawatt smile.

I slap my hand against her leg at my hip. "If he keeps taking you out, I might not be able to carry you!"

She mumbles as she slides down my back, and I finally stand up straight. "Well, that definitely sounds like a 'you' problem. My ass is getting some dinner, so you may want to lift some weights." Taylor shouts out in victory, pumping her fist up in the air, not caring people are giving her strange looks. A loud and deep rumble is quickly approaching our spot. Wes' Evo appears behind a line of cars, coming from the exit of the drag strip, pulling into the open space next to the silver car. The same silver car that my brothers are engrossed in.

"Okay Pauly D, let's go congratulate your man." I pull her hand down and drag her towards the group. As we

near them, I can hear my brothers speaking very loud and animatedly to whom I assume is the owner of the mystery car. I've never seen him before, which strikes me as odd considering I know most of the people who come here--even if not personally--by name. He's tall, broad, clean-shaven, with sharp features, nice lips, and just...really freakin' hot. He's almost too hot for me to notice his car. *Almost.*
Now I can see why this car has my brothers' attention. It's a Nissan Skyline. A car so rare, it only recently became legal to own in the United States. It's a very expensive beautiful art of machinery. Now I have a serious lady boner.
Taylor runs to Wes and jumps into his arms, giving him a huge congratulatory kiss. The commotion gets Vin's attention. "Yo, V! C'mere, you've got to see this!" he yells when he sees me standing near Wes and Taylor. Vance, Vaughn, and the new guy look up. I slowly walk toward them, the new guy's gaze never leaving me. Vance notices this immediately and he snaps at the guy. *Literally* snaps his fingers at him. "Nuh-uh!" he bellows, "That's my baby sister. Get your eyes off her!"
"Seriously Vance!?" I yell at him. The new guy puts his hands up in defeat, "Got it."
I squeeze in between Vance and Vin. "You're such a dick," I mumble. This earns a glare from him, and a chuckle from Vin. I finally look at the engine bay. It is definitely impressive. My gaze flickers upward, catching the eyes of the cute new guy. Despite my brother's warning, he's still watching me. He's risking his eyeballs, but I like it.

OFF LIMITS
Veronica

"You gonna run?" I ask the cute stranger. He's about to speak but some yelling pulls our attention elsewhere.

"Yo, Wes!" Everyone turns to the voice. A man, much shorter than my brothers, is stalking our way. He clearly isn't happy. His face is pinched tight, and his hands are in fists. My brothers stand to their full height. This is a defensive tactic. Vin is well over six feet tall. Vance and Vaughn are almost the same. The three of them are very intimidating alone, put them together, and they are downright scary. My brothers move towards Wes, standing at his back, a clear sign. Wes gently pushes Taylor behind him, and she glances at me, her brows furrowed together looking worried. It wouldn't be the first time a fight broke out over someone being a sore loser. The Strip is full of cocky assholes who think they're the shit, that their car is the fastest, best car around. Losing is a major slap to their ego.

"What's up, Chris? You got my money?" Wes asks, not caring that he's looking pissed.

Chris stops a couple feet away from Wes. His nose flares, but instead of going off, he lets out a sigh. "Yeah, I got your money." Wes puts out his hand, and Chris pulls out a wad of cash from his pocket, slapping it into Wes' open palm. "Fucking bullshit man! What the fuck you runnin'?"

My brother's stances change at Chris' question. Obviously, he's not a threat anymore. They all launch into 'car talk' about Wes' ride, and I feel myself relax, even though I didn't realize I had stiffened.

"V, I'm gonna tell Wes that we are going to get a drink. I'm parched." Taylor hollers over her shoulder as she walks over to her boyfriend, slipping her arm around his slim waist, and he pauses his conversation to give her attention. His lips widen in a smile when he looks at her, and it is the sweetest damn thing. I glance away, feeling slightly envious. Not that she has Wes, but that she has *that*. You can see how much he loves her... I'm envious of that. I'm eighteen, and I haven't had one serious relationship. My focus moves at that thought, scanning for the cute stranger's face. His Skyline, the hood now closed, is still parked in the same place, but the guy is regrettably nowhere in sight.

My brothers, however, haven't moved an inch. If I don't let them know I'm leaving, I'll never hear the end of it. Sometimes I feel like I have five fathers, rather than four brothers and one father. Vin is closest, so I yell out to him. "I'm going to get a drink!" I point towards the food vendors. Vin simply looks at me and nods then this attention is back to the conversation. Taylor returns to my side, wrapping her arm around mine and tugs me with her.

There is a decent line for this food truck, and many of the provided picnic tables are occupied. The whole area is pretty crowded, groups of teens standing around, and I take notice of the number of young girls and their attire. A majority are scantily clad, like the girls in front of us. Small skirt, even smaller tops.

"So, are we going to the field after this?" Taylor's question makes me forget about the underdressed girls around us.

"Meh," I scrunch my nose, "No, I gotta work in the morning."

"Just go for a little, Pleaseeee?" Taylor begs.

"Yeah, okay," Pure sarcasm. "A little always turns into hours. Plus, if I go, so will my brothers or at least Vance since a lot of his friends are home for break."

"Yeah but Vance's the cool one."

"No, he's not ... none of them are cool."

"We can say you're coming to my house."

"They'll know, Tay. They always find out, and they're going to give me shit. I just don't want to deal with them. We can go tomorrow."

"Finnee. You party pooper!"

"So, 'baby sister' is it?" a deep male voice cuts into our conversation. Taylor and I both turn around to find the hot owner of the Skyline standing directly behind us. His hazel eyes are raking over my face and down my body. I sigh, "Yes, that'd be me."

"Do you have a name? I don't really want to call you baby sister." He grins, causing a dimple to appear. Grin + Dimple = Danger.

"Oh pretty boy, you have a death wish," Taylor says bluntly, and I elbow her. She shrugs, turning to put her order in, leaving us alone.

"Veronica," I answer him.

"Veronica," he repeats like he's testing the name on his lips. "Beautiful name for a beautiful girl." He smiles showing near-perfect teeth. "I'd like to take you out, but I assume your brothers are pretty protective of you?"

"Was it that obvious?" I ask sarcastically.

He laughs. "Yeah. So, maybe you can give me your

number, and I'll give you a call sometime."

"I don't even know your name."

He chuckles and licks his lips before answering, "Ryan." Ah. No longer the cute stranger. His hand moves out towards me and I instantly notice how large it is. I tentatively put out my hand to meet his. His hand gently closes around mine; my soft to his rough. He moves our hands up and down. "So, now that we're friends, we should exchange numbers."

"Oh, is that how it goes?"

"Well, yeah. Friends hang out...I want to hang out with my new friend."

"Alright, Friend." I conclude. He smiles wide and pulls his phone out of his pocket. I begin to rattle off the first few numbers.

"Get. Lost!" a deep familiar voice cuts in.

Startled, I whip around and find Vance standing behind me, his mouth in a tight line and eyes narrowed at Ryan. He raises his hand and takes a step forward, jabbing a finger into Ryan's chest.

"You don't fuckin' listen. I told you this is my sister! She's off-limits!"

"Vance, stop!" I plead, completely mortified.

"No! He was all over some chick earlier tonight. I don't give two shits what he does in his spare time, but it won't be you!" He grabs my arm and pulls me away from Ryan who's standing there dumbfounded. When we're far enough away I rip my arm out of his grasp. "That was embarrassing!" I hiss.

He stops a few feet from me and turns around. "Look, I'm not sorry I embarrassed you. Sure, I could have done it in a better way. But he's a dick, and you're better than that!"

"You do realize that you can't protect me from every guy, right? I'd like to date; I want to fall in love."

"You will V....but guys your age, hell even my age, they only want what's in your pants. I know, I'm a guy! You don't want that! I don't want that for you! Focus on school, make a career for yourself, then settle down."

"You sound like dad, Vance. You're twenty-one, not fifty." He needs to lighten up.

"Good! Dad's an amazing man, I hope one day I can be half the man he is! You just gave me a huge compliment." He smiles big.

"It wasn't supposed to be." I huff and cross my arms. Vance wraps his arm around my shoulders and hugs me to him. "I did you a favor, V. Say thank you and move on."

I stay quiet because while he probably did save me from 'falling in lust' with Ryan and getting hurt, I don't want to admit it.

"Vernnn..." he drags out my childhood nickname.

"Don't you dare!" I smack his shoulder and try to move out of his hold. Vance looks extremely amused, his eyes crinkled at the corners, "Say it!"

"No!" I yell, still struggling to break free. He grabs my arms and pulls me into a headlock.

"Vance!" I scream.

"Vern..." he warns, "All you have to do is say 'thank you.'" I remain quiet, trying to pull out of his hold. A burning pain upon my head has me screaming out as he rubs his knuckles swiftly over my hair.

"Say it!" he yells.

I can only imagine the faces of those around us. The burning becomes unbearable and I give in, screaming out. "Thank you!" I yell, "Mercy!"

As soon as he lets me go, I smack him on his bicep that's the size of my thigh and rub my head, expecting to have a bald spot. "Asshole!" I spit out. He only laughs as he walks back to our brothers. I quickly try to fix the mess he made of my hair. Taylor strolls over to me, holding out a cup, "Here, I got you a Coke," she eyes me up and down, quietly, "Nice hair."
"Shut up! Why didn't you help me?!
She slowly looks at me, one eyebrow arched upward, "'Really? Vance is like a buck eighty. He's got like fifty-some pounds on me. What was I supposed to do?"
"I don't know ... pinch his butt?"
She laughs loudly.
"Yanno, like surprise," I say weakly.
"Yeah, I'm sure it would've surprised him, but I don't think Wes would've appreciated it."
"He'd understand. You gotta take one for your best-est!"
With all the yelling, my throat is dry and scratchy. I take a big sip of my Coke, my eyes water a little. Ahh, carbonation. "I'm ready to get out of here."
"Okay. I'm gonna stay with Wes. I'll see you tomorrow?"
I nod. "Yeah. I'll call you when I'm out of work."
She embraces me in a big hug, "Okay. See you." I squeeze her back, "Let my brothers know, please."
She releases me, "Will do. Drive safe, text me when you get home." We go our separate ways. Since I didn't plan to race, my car is parked in the back lot. I press the unlock button on my key fob, the amber lights flashing allowing me to see where exactly I'm parked. I slide into the driver's seat, press my key in the ignition turning the crank over. A loud rumble escapes from the ex-

haust, as the car idles, a nice steady purr fills the inside. Making sure no one is driving by or walking behind me, I push the clutch down and shift into reverse to back out of my spot. A few catcalls come from my right. I ignore them because a gentleman never calls out to a lady. Sometimes...I don't want a gentleman, or to be a lady.

CHASE
Veronica

Most teenagers get to sleep in on their Saturday mornings. I haven't been able to sleep in on a Saturday since I was old enough to get a work permit. My alarm is going off, but I'm so comfortable I don't want to leave my blanket cocoon. I start to doze off again when my door is thrown open.

"V!! Turn that shit off!"

I peek an eye open to see the back of Vance as he walks out. I only know it's him because of the large Egyptian tattoo on his back. I groan, stretch my arms out. I slap the top of the alarm and find the knob to shut it off. I get up, throw my 'Victor's Garage' tee over my tank, change into some jeans, and throw on some socks. I hit the bathroom before heading down the stairs, pulling my long hair into a ponytail. At the bottom of the stairs, I make a left into the kitchen. Vin is sitting at the middle island already, shoveling food into his mouth and Mom is facing the stove making breakfast.

"Morning!" I make my way over to Vin and hop up on the stool next to him. He's wearing his black fitted Victor's Auto Garage T-shirt too.

"Good morning, sweetie." My mom smiles back at me. Mom has always been an early riser, but I guess with five children, she got used to being up around the clock even though we're all old enough now.

"Where's Dad?" I'm curious.

"Your father is at the restaurant. There was an issue

with this morning's delivery." Our family owns an Italian restaurant, Russo's, that has been in our family for two generations. They also own an auto garage, Victor's, that my great grandfather opened. He named it after himself, then also named his son Victor, who named his son Victor...and so on. It became a family tradition, which in turn meant that family gatherings were always very confusing. My father is semi-retired but doesn't know how to relax even if his life depends on it. Vin has been running the garage for a year now. Victor--the Fourth Victor and my eldest brother--was supposed to take over the restaurant but decided to go into accounting, so even though he's not in the family business, he does the books for both. Vance kinda does whatever. Right now, he's getting deeper into the racing scene with Wes. Vaughn is now in line to become the owner of Russo's after he finishes his degree at the community college.

Mom scoops some eggs from the pan on the stove and turns to the island to put toast and bacon onto the plate before placing it in front of me.

"Thanks, mom!" I put the eggs and bacon onto the toast, making myself an egg sandwich and take a big bite.

"Hmmmm" I moan. Mom smiles wide as she places a glass of orange juice in front of me.

"You ready?" Vin asks.

I glare at him. Seriously? I just sat down. "Do I look ready?"

"You better eat that fast because your messy ass ain't eating in my car!" I take another large bite of my egg sandwich, and smile wide, allowing some of the food to show.

"You're gross."

"I luff yoouu brudder," I mumble with my mouth full. Vin pushes away from the table, then leaves the kitchen. I cackle loudly.

"Veronica Marie!" Mom scolds me, pulling out my middle name. I close my mouth and finish my sandwich without another word. Mom starts doing the dishes. I pick up my plate, take it to the counter, and drop it into the sink filled with soapy bubbles. "Okay Mom, I'll see you later. Thanks for the yummy breakfast."

I skip out of the kitchen, slip into my work boots at the front door, and grab my bag before walking out the door. Vin is already in his beamer, windows down, white sunglasses on, rock music blasting loud. I slide into the passenger seat, "The Guido look fits you, Vin." I grab my seat belt but get punched in the left arm, instinctively my right-hand goes to my arm letting the seat belt snap back.

"OW!" I yell. "What the hell!"

"Oh, c'mon, that didn't hurt!"

"Yeah, it did!" I rub my arm and look at it. There's a nice red mark. He laughs, "You better hope you never get into a street fight. You'll get your ass kicked."

"No way! I'll throw down any chick!" I throw up my arms like I'm Mike Tyson and punch the air.

"I hope you don't hit like that." His voice falls. I drop my arms and shrug. "If all else fails, I'll pull some hair and bite her ear."

This earns a burst of laughter from him. A short drive later, we pull up in front of the garage. It's about ten minutes before we open. Vin opens the front door, turns on the office lights, and I follow after him. Heading straight to the desk to boot up the computer, then into the lounge to start the coffee maker for the rest of the guys. I man the front desk, answering phone calls, keeping track of appointments, and putting together bills to mail out.

When it's really busy, I'll help with oil changes and tire rotations. To uphold our reputation, all our mechanics are certified, and I'm not...so, I can help out with the small things that don't require certification. The bells on the door jingle, signifying that someone opened the door. I peek around the corner from the little break room to see Jimmy walk in.

"Hey Jimmy," I yell and wave, smiling cheerfully.

"Hey, kiddo."

Jimmy's older, in his forties, and married with three kids. He's worked for my dad for the past seventeen years, and his wife makes the best cookies, muffins, pies, fudge...well, everything.

"Cindy made some chocolate chip cookies," he says. He holds up a circular tin and shakes it.

"I love your wife!" I tell him while taking it from his hands.

"Yeah, some days, I do too." He laughs as he walks away.

I place the cookies by the coffee pot, swiping one for myself, and walk back into the front to log into the computer. Saturday is our busiest day, considering that most people don't work, and think it's the best day to have their car done. Today is no different, by the looks of our schedule.

The office has a massive window that looks out into the garage. Vin has already pulled in a car and has started working. I see Craig around his toolbox. He must've snuck in. Craig is quiet and keeps to himself most of the time. Nice guy, ex-military. Mark is the only one missing...no surprise there. It's a minute until we're officially open by the time he finally waltzes in.

"Veronica, you're a sight for sore eyes."

"Maybe you should get your eyes checked if they're hurting."

"Why, when you're the cure?"

I groan. Mark is the definition of a player. He's the cliché. Hot, rides a motorcycle, sleeps with just about every willing woman, mom, wife in a fifty-mile radius. I shake my head and smile, "Oh Mark, save your lines for the dumb girls they actually work on." He chuckles and walks into the garage.

The morning and afternoon move relatively quickly. Thank goodness. I keep myself busy with the daunting tasks of an office assistant. Victor stops in to grab the books but doesn't stay long. He moved out of our parent's house about six months ago, and now lives with his long-time girlfriend, Melissa. We don't get to see him much. They come over for our Sunday dinners sometimes, but it's not the same.

I order food for the guys, a Saturday ritual, and before I know it, we're shy two hours until closing. At five-thirty, Vance comes bursting through the door.

"To what do we owe the pleasure, big brother?" I don't need to look at him to acknowledge him.

"Just wasting some time before I have to get Chase from the airport." This causes my head to snap in his direction.

"Chase is coming home? Why are you picking him up?"

Chase has been Vance's best friend since elementary school. He was always at our house growing up. He's an only child and always said that our house was 'full of life'. But in reality, I think he enjoyed coming over and helping Vance torture me endlessly.

Vance shrugs, "His parents are in Hawaii or some shit."

"What!? He's coming home from deployment, and they're on vacation?" I find myself irritated.

"I don't know. He just called me a couple of hours ago asking if I could pick him up. You going to the field tonight?" Guess that conversation is over.

"Yeah, I told Taylor I would."

"You want to ride with us?"

"I suppose." Vance plays on his phone, no doubt making plans for later, and I finish up my work for the day. It's silent for a while until he stands up, "Alright, I'm out! I'll meet you at home then."

"Are you bringing Chase over?"

"I don't know...whatever he wants to do." With that, he walks out the door and leaves me reeling. Chase is coming home!

HOME
Chase

I awake with a jolt as the plane drops from turbulence. I lift my hat off my face and look towards Geoff, who was in my unit overseas. We're both from the northeast. It's comforting to fly home with a brother.

"We're about to land," he informs me. I sit up and make sure my seat is in its upright position. I've been gone for about eight months, but it's been over a year since I've been in my hometown. Geoff is three years older than me and has a girl waiting for him. He plans to propose to her. I don't have anyone waiting for me, not even my parents. I called my mother a month ago to let her know that I was coming home. I guess a long vacation was more important.

I knew my boy, Vance, would be around. I called him a few times while deployed. He's my brother from another mother and his whole family is like my second home. The plane begins to descend, and I grip the armrests. I watch out the window as the airport slowly becomes bigger, and cars no longer look like little ants. The plane hits the landing strip, jumping around until it finally starts straighten' out, all wheels on the ground.

Once the airplane has stopped moving and connects to the gate, all passengers are immediately grabbing their belongings. I guess they're just as eager as I am. Geoff gets up and grabs our packs from the overhead compartment and tosses mine to me. People are beginning to exit the aircraft. We're still in uniform therefore men are shaking our hands, thanking us for our service while ladies are, not so discreetly, eye fucking us. It's a perk of the uniform. We walk straight to baggage claim where we know our parties are waiting for us.

Once Geoff's girlfriend sees him, she comes running and jumps into his arms. It's quite a scene. I notice Vance leaning against a beam, his head down focused on his phone. He looks up at the commotion and straightens when he sees me. He meets me halfway, putting his hand out. I smack it with mine, we pull each other into a hug including a pat on the back.

"Chase, my man! You bulked up!"

I laugh and pull away from him. "Yeah," I squeeze his arm, "Looks like you put some muscle on, too."

"Oh, these?" He flexes a muscle and then kisses it.

"Dude, seriously?"

He laughs. "Welcome home man." He pats me on the back again.

"Thanks, it's good to be back on American soil."

"I bet. Do you want to go home? Settle in? Or grab something to eat? I'm going out to the Field tonight if you want to come out and see everyone." This sounds like it's exactly what I need.

"Yeah man, that sounds good. I wanna grab a shower. Do you mind if we hit up my place first, then grab some food?"

"Sounds like a plan."

We head to my house where it's extremely empty...and quiet. I quickly shower and change into some civilian clothes, pull on some boots, put my wallet in my back pocket, and run down the stairs.

"Where you wanna go?" Vance asks me.

I only have to think for a second. "Big Woody's?"

"Hell yeah, best wings in town! Let's go!"

Woody's is a quaint place, a mixture of restaurant and bar. The tables are tall and scattered around the restaurant. A sign hangs on the hostess desk, 'Seat Yourself'. I scan the place, noticing a few people that occupy a couple of stools at the bar, and some couples at the high-top tables. I head towards a table in the back for privacy, but mainly I prefer to have my back facing the wall allowing me to see the whole restaurant.

Shortly after being seated, a really pretty brunette approaches our table, "Hey guys, what can I get you?" Her cleavage is on heavy display and by the looks of it, the rest is about to follow suit...not that I'm complaining. Vance orders us two beers, and she asks for our IDs.

"Don't worry, sweetheart, we're legal." Vance winks at her, and we both hand our licenses over.

She takes a look, "Well look at that, you are." She flirts and hands them back to us. She smiles then saunters off. We both can't help but watch her walk away. "Damn, it's been a long time," I groan.

"I bet, I'm sure your hand could use a break."

"It's not like there are a plethora of hot women in the sandbox, dude. My hand was all I had!" I exasperate.

"I know, man, just bustin' your balls." He lands a hard slap on my shoulder blade.

The pretty brunette brings our bottles to the table, and with a secret smile asks us if we are ready to order.

"Sure are, sweetheart," Vance orders some wings, and I get a burger with some fries.

    We watch her walk away, again. I can't help it, it's a *really* nice view.. When she's gone, we jump into all the bullshit I've missed the last year. Vance's twenty-first birthday was epic, and he insists we have a re-do to celebrate mine since I didn't get to. Vance is still single and doesn't seem to want to settle down. This doesn't come as a surprise to me. I was, however, surprised to hear that Victor found a girl and that it's getting pretty serious. He's a full-time accountant, and a totally 'yuppy'. I laugh because I can't see Victor, the charmer, being serious about anything.

"How's V?" I ask.

"She's doin' good. She's a senior this year. I can't believe she's going to be graduating."

"Damn. I remember chasing her around the house with daddy long-leg spiders while she screamed like a banshee!"

"She hated us."

"Nah. She loves you, dude."

"I've had to beat the guys off her. Literally. I almost don't want to take her to the Strip anymore. Every time we go, there's some douchebag trying to get into her pants."

"She doesn't have a boyfriend?"

"Hell no. There's no one good enough for her. Maybe that choir boy, Daniel. I mean I'm sure he's saving himself till marriage or something."

I laugh, "Oh man, poor V."

"I told you...she hates me."

"I'm sure she knows you care about her."

"She was pissed at me last night. That fucker Ryan Wittman...she was about to give her number to him. I wanted to knock him out. He's as big as a manwhore as Mark!"

"She'll understand, one day." It felt nice to sit back,

drink beers, relax, and spend a couple of hours at Woody's. At close to eight o'clock when we're ready to leave, I pull out my wallet but Vance pushes my hand away.

"I got this," he says as he pays, leaving our waitress a nice tip.

"Thanks," I tell him as we walk out.

"Thank you, man. What you do, out there, that's brave. It's the least I can do." Those words mean a lot, especially coming from Vance.

"You want to head out to the field?" he asks me.

"Do you mind dropping me off? I wanna drive myself."

"No man, that's fine. I gotta swing home to grab Vaughn and V." Vance drops me off and I head inside. The house is dark, quiet, and it's almost too much. I haven't been alone in over a year, there was always someone around. I sit on the white couch, in the dark, and take it all in.

I'm home.

CRUSH

Veronica

The Field, as we call it, is a massive open area that's surrounded on three sides by a large thicket of trees. A huge lake sits on the edge of the north side; it's serene. From what I know, this has been around since our parents were teenagers. The dirt road to get back here is about a mile long.

The property is supposedly owned by an old man by the name of Cletus. He owns acres of land and is the creator of this 'little' area. His house is a couple of miles away, far enough to turn a blind eye about the shenanigans going on. I'd like to think we're an okay group and that most of us get along with each other. I think because we all know that if there are problems, they'll shut it down. If someone gets out of control, we find a way to get that person away before we involve the law. Tents are set up along the perimeter, and a bonfire is raging near the lake. There are huge logs situated around the fire, and that's where I find Tay with Wes.

As soon as I approach them Tay slurs out a sloppy "V" that sounds more like B.

"Taylor," I respond dryly.

She continues, "Yanno what you should do?"

"No, what should I do?" I watch as she sways towards me. Wes wraps his arm around her, keeping her upright. It makes me laugh. She looks so funny. "I love you, Wes," she says. She's looking at me but talking to him. He chuckles, "Love you too."

Wes continues his conversation with those sitting around us. Everyone has a cup in their hands; their faces illuminated by the fire. Some kids are home from college that graduated with Wes and Vaughn and some of our football players, including Bobby, are all standing in a circle. Bobby is looking in my direction and has yet to take his eyes off of me. It seems that since Vaughn has graduated, guys at school are a bit more forward. But my two brothers are around here somewhere.

"B." This time she definitely said B. "I think you should...go...get us...some more beers."

"Baby, I think you've had enough," Wes cuts in. She pouts, "No, you husssh," and puts her finger to his lips. The corners of his lips twist upwards, and he gently removes her hand, placing it in her lap.

I stand up, and Taylor yells, "YAY!" Wes is right, she's had enough, but I think I'm good for one. Taylor cheers. I giggle as she claps her hands; the clapping continues as I move towards the keg and start to fill a cup. I scan around keeping an eye out for my brothers. Half the people here are underage, but they still give me shit about drinking. What they don't know won't hurt them right?

"V, what are you doing?" A very deep voice asks eerily close to my right, causing me to jump and spill beer all over my hand. I skirt back as it just misses my shoes.

"Dammit, you just made me spill my beer," I pout, staring longingly at my empty cup. I look over at the dick who I now hear laughing. Laughing. The nerve. I drop my cup when I take in his handsome face, recognizing him instantly, and without thinking, I throw myself at him. I manage to form a half gurgled, "OHMYGOSHCHASE!" My arms wrap around his neck and squeeze him in a massive hug. I feel his arms wrap around my back, embracing me. I'm instantly warm, his chuckle in my ear.

"Now you really spilled your beer."

We both pull away after embracing for a bit longer than normal. I take him all in. *Really* take him all in. He looks older...maybe not older, but more filled out. His skin is golden, and his dirty blond hair is buzzed. It fits him. The Army was definitely good on his body. He's bigger, broader, and his arms are straining against his T-shirt. Holy crap, Chase is fucking *hot*. I mean, he was always good looking and now I am blatantly checking him out.

"Since when do you drink beer?" He asks me, thus snapping me out of my ogling.

"Oh. I'm not. I don't. This is for Taylor," I quickly lie. Afraid he's going to tell my brothers.

"Uh, huh. So why isn't she getting her own drink?" He asks. Oh, he knows.

"She can't walk." That sounded bad, and I cringe. Shit.

"Are her legs broken?"

"She's just... tipsy."

"So, let me get this straight...your friend is drunk. She can't walk, and you're getting her more beer?" He easily raises an eyebrow because he knows he's got me cornered. "Damn you, Chase Daniels!" I raise my voice, frustrated. He only laughs, grabs a new cup, and fills it up for me. "Here, I'm just kidding."

"What? Is this a trick?" I look around for my brothers.

"No, I swear. But don't let your brothers know I did this. I may not be a fool to think you don't drink but..." He trails off.

I just stare at him and take the cup from his hand. "Thank you?" It's more of a question than a statement. He laughs and smiles exposing a dimple in his cheek. Have I mentioned that I *love* dimples?

"Heeyy, what's going on here?" An arm wraps around my shoulders, jolting me, causing me to spill my new and freshly poured beer. I look at the drunken douche.

"What the hell Bobby?!" I push his arm off my shoulder. I officially smell like Bud Light.

"Damn V, you're so hot! Let's go to my truck." Bobby places his arm back around my shoulder.

"Um, no thanks." I push his arm off me once again.

"C'mon, don't be a prude!" This time he grabs me and crushes me against his chest; dropping my cup at our feet. *Damn it.*

"That's enough Bobby. You're drunk, and she said no." Chase cuts in, a clear warning in his tone, but I don't think Bobby gets it. "Chase, buddy! When did you get here?" Bobby stumbles towards Chase, causing me to stumble because his arm is still around my shoulders. Chase removes Bobby's arm from around me, pulls me to him.

"Oh c'mon. We were just about to go to my truck."

Chase doesn't try to pull away as I continue to hang onto his arm. "No, Bobby, Veronica's not going with you," he warns.

"Don't be a cock block, Chase."

"You need to go back to your friends and leave her alone. Drink some water, and sober up before getting in your truck."

"Man, you used to be fun!" He's swaying on his feet like a little kid that just got off the tilt-a-whirl. "What's going on here?" Vance asks as he joins us with a girl on his arm and a couple of girls behind them.

"Vance!" Bobby shouts at the appearance of my brother, "I was just telling your friend here, he needs to be more fun. He used to be fun," he shifts his attention back to Chase, "You changed man." He shakes his head, almost falling as he turns away, then stumbles off. I feel Chase physically relax, but keep a hold on his arm.

"V, I think Chase would like his arm back," Vance says.

"Oh. Yeah. Right. Well, here." I push Chase's arm to him, "That's yours."

He chuckles. "Thanks."

"You drinkin' V?" Vance eyes me.

"Me? No." I shake my head back and forth. "Not, I."

"She was just grabbing Taylor a beer...which is now on the ground," He grabs another cup and fills it up. Again. "Here, before she comes looking for you." He gives me the cup with a wink.

"Thanks." I quickly turn and rush away from them before Vance stops me. When I approach the log, Taylor is fast asleep on Wes. I shake my head, a smile on my lips, and sit down next to her. I can finally focus on my thoughts about what just occurred. I raise the cup to my lips and take a sip. Was Chase flirting with me? No way, right? There's no way. Chase used to run after me with gross bugs in his hands while I ran away screaming. Vance and Chase use to *torture* me. Mom made them stop after they'd officially traumatized me. When I was thirteen my little crush on him grew to epic proportions. My heart broke when I met his girlfriend for the first time. I hated him that summer and finally realized he would be nothing more than another brother. That childhood crush seems to be rearing its head again.

DAMN SHAME
Chase

Whoa. What. The. Fuck. In my time away, Veronica has turned into a goddamn supermodel. She was always pretty, but in a 'cute little sister' way, not a 'I want to fuck you seven ways from Sunday' type of way. I wasn't even sure that it was her standing at the keg. I watched her concentrating on pouring the beer into the sideways cup; keeping the foam to a minimum. This knowledge confirms she comes out here a lot. Pulling beer from a keg takes practice. I approached slowly, taking in all her features. Her dark brown hair was always long, but now it nearly reaches her waist. Her legs looked a mile long, even in jeans, which led to an amazing ass. Yes, I checked out her ass, and I don't even feel slightly sorry for it. It's an ass that deserves to be looked at.

When she turned to face me, it was almost like I was seeing her for the first time. I guess I was because I was seeing her in a completely different way. She was slightly taller, reaching my chin, now. Her shirt dipped low in the front, showing a small amount of cleavage. It wasn't until she tried to come up with a lie about the beer, forcing her to look away that I was able to *notice* her. This has taken me by surprise, and I'm barely listening as Vance is introducing me to this blonde chick standing next to me. I grab a cup, fill it up, and take a hefty chug.

"Whoa dude, you okay?" Vance asks me.

"Yeah, man. I'm good, just thirsty."
I'm totally hot for your sister.

I steal a look towards the way Veronica went. She's sitting with a group of friends, and a guy on her left with his arm around her shoulders. I'm feeling a bit possessive. I almost want to walk over and wrap *my* arm around her; protect her and twist that guys arm around his back...which is something I have no right doing.

After all, this guy could be a boyfriend that her brothers have failed to notice. The revelation stings more than it should. This would be a good thing--for me. I don't mess with another guy's girl.

I feel cold hands crawl up my arm, which snaps my attention to a blonde with her tits pushed up against me. She reaches my bicep and caresses my skin. I vaguely remember being introduced to her earlier in the night. Sharon? Shannon?

"Me too," she says in a voice a little too high for my liking, then grabs my cup out of my hand, immediately taking a drink. She licks her lips suggestively. She's pretty, but in a 'Hollywood Glamour' way that's not exactly *my* thing. She has glitter all over her eyes and I know it won't look like that in the early hours of the morning, after a late night with me. It's been *so* damn long that I consider the possibility that I won't care what she looks like in the morning, or that she's not my type. I can't help but also think it's a shame she's not a brunette.

A real damn shame.

CONFLUSTERED

Veronica

On Friday, I'm clocking in some hours working at the garage, and only have a half hour left before closing time. Right as I'm finishing up some invoices; I hear it. A very deep, distinguishing rumble that echoes louder and louder the closer it gets. I jump up from my seat and hurry into the garage to get a look at the approaching car.

A silver Nissan 350Z rolls to a stop at the open bay door with tint so dark I can't make out the driver. The car is as beautiful as it sounds. It sits so low to the ground it'd scrape roadkill off the streets. I anxiously wait for the driver to get out; silently hoping it isn't a car chick, but maybe a possible friend of Vance's instead. I am practically drooling, and if I had a penis I'd surely have a hard on right now.

The car shuts off; killing the deep idling. Shortly after, the door opens, and my breath hitches when the driver appears. They're wearing a black hat and shades and I notice the very broad muscular chest right away. I hang back, waiting for the driver to reveal themselves.

He finally looks into the garage bays, and the butterflies immediately take flight in my belly. My heart frantically beats faster at the sight of him. It's Chase. A big smile takes over his face, nearly knocking me on my ass when he looks my way.

"Vern!" he shouts as he removes his sunglasses. Damn. That *one* nickname. I sigh. The butterflies just died. I release the doorframe and saunter towards him.

When I was a baby, Vance couldn't say 'Veronica', so it came out as 'Vern'. After that, for years, I was Vern. They teased me relentlessly in middle school...them being the cool high schoolers and all. He pulls me into an embrace, leaving my arms to my side while he squeezes me to his chest. My face is smashed to his pecs--very nice pecs, I might add. I breathe him in, taking in his distinctive scent.

"Dingleberry," I retort, and I feel his chest vibrate in laughter.

"How original, *Vern*." He releases me, and I take a step back.

"Well, you know..." I rub my nails on my shoulder. "I'm a pretty original girl."

He flashes another megawatt beautiful smile. "That you are."

I purse my lips. I'm not quite sure if he means that in a good way, so, instead of prying I brush it off. "Whose car is this?" I walk around him and towards the silver beauty.

"Mine."

"When did you get this?"

"Right before I left. Vance found it online and it was too good of a deal to pass up."

"It's beautiful!" I move over to the driver's side door. "May I?" I ask while gesturing to the door handle. When he doesn't respond instantly, I glance up and find him staring at me.

"What?" I question self-consciously. Do I have something on my face? He shakes his head and smiles. "Nothing. Yeah, sure, check her out!"

I open the door and sit inside. The leather's a little

warm yet, lingering from the body heat he's emitting. It smells like him, mixed in with the leather. I inhale deeply, wishing I could bottle this scent. I could call it 'Leathered Chase'. HA!

I take in the interior. There's a gauge pod with four gauges that line the frame by the windshield, and a touch screen that was installed nicely. The trim on the dash is all carbon fiber, and very clean. It is *very* well done. "Nice work." I tilt my head up in his direction but instead find him kneeling close to my side.

"Thanks." He is staring at me again, and I can't bring myself to look away this time. It feels intimate. Maybe it is just me, but the way he is looking at me is like I am something more than his friend's little sister. I like it. A lot. It's this exact moment when Vance decides to make his appearance.

"Yo Chase!" He jogs over, and Chase stands up to greet him with a smack of their hands. "Hey man."

"Let me pull out this van, and you can bring her on in." Vance turns and walks to the van, climbing inside.

"What are you guys doing?" I remove myself from the car. Chase remains where he was, which puts us very close together.

"I want to go bigger!"

"That's what she said," I snort.

"Ah!" He laughs. "That was a good one."

I giggle and do a slight curtsy, "Why thank you."

Suddenly Chase is real serious; stepping forward into my space. "But you know..." he takes another step. Then another. His chest brushes mine and causes my body to break out in goosebumps. He grins while cocking his head to the side--then steals a quick glance at my lips. His blue eyes find mine. "That's something you won't ever say to me...."

I suck in a breath. He, ever so slowly, moves away--never taking his eyes off me--a sexy smirk playing on his lips.

"Pull her in!" Vance's yell snaps me out of whatever trance I was in. I move away from Chase with shaky legs, exhaling deeply. *Whoa.* I quickly walk into the bay, the sound of the engine starting up behind me, and keep moving into the office. I am completely speechless, and my brain is all over the place. What was *that*? What did that mean? I mean, obviously, he thinks he has a big... package. Is that information he wants me to know? Holy balls. I'm flustered and confused. *I'm conflustered!*

The clock on the office wall tells me it's well after closing now. I quickly turn off the outside lights and lock the door and everything else follows. Grabbing my purse from the desk drawer before hitting the office lights, I lock up the door leading to the bay and close the door behind me. Taking a breath I slowly turn around. The hood of the Z is open. Vance's hands are moving above the engine bay, and Chase is nodding with whatever he's saying.

"Hey, I'm leaving," I call across the bays. Vance glances up and waves, "Yeah, okay!" then continues talking, but Chase's intense gaze is on me. He's giving me attention I find unnerving and, yet, extremely wanted. His body is facing my way, and his arms are crossed over his chest, making his biceps bulge. A wicked grin forms on his beautiful lips, and then he winks. It's a simple gesture that hits me in my core and spreads warmth throughout my body. *Good lord.* I need to get out of here. As soon as I'm in my car I dial Taylor. I need to talk to my best friend about this.

FEELINGS
Chase

I've avoided Veronica all week. I told myself I couldn't let anything happen between us. I cannot--*should not*--have a thing for my best friend's little sister. That's *definitely* some kind of unspoken rule. I even went out with a redhead Vance was pushin' my way. He was claiming she was so hot and down to get in between my sheets. I wouldn't know...I couldn't focus on her. A particular brunette has been running amuck in my thoughts. I made plans to meet up with Vance this week to look over my car. I wasn't sure if Veronica would be there. If I *really* didn't want to see her I would've asked if she would be working. I decided to leave it up to fate.

As it seems, fate might be on my side-- or not. Depends on how you look at it. When I pull up and Veronica comes out of the office, I can't stop the smile that forms on my face. The fact that she's so into cars is extremely sexy. She was always a bit of a tomboy, but that would happen with four brothers. She may still be that tomboy, but she definitely grew into her own. Her face is lit up in awe, over my car, and I can't help but feel proud. *That's right! This beast is mine. Love me now.*

When she catches me staring the first time, I admit, I'm a little embarrassed. When I do it a second time-- not at all. During our little chat-- and her little 'that's what she said' dig--I can't push aside my instincts to flirt with her. I want to pin her against my car and ravage her mouth. Just thinking about it makes my jeans feel tighter. When she leaves, I'm bummed, yet relieved. Such conflicting reactions, but I can't focus with her around. I keep watching the office door, wanting to see her. She is becoming one of my favorite things to look at. When she is here, it's like nothing else is happening. All I see is her. My mind is still on V while Vance prattles on about something or other, and an idea pops into my head.

"Yo," I interrupt Vance, "We should hit the lake next weekend!" He looks at me quizzically because it seems to come out of nowhere. "Yeah, sure," His response seems more like a question rather than a response. "The whole gang!"

I'm getting excited at the possibility to be around Veronica. In a bathing suit. "Invite the brothers. V, even."

"Okay. I'm in. I'll let everyone know."

A rumble is heard from down the street and shortly Vin's black beamer pulls up in front of the open bay door, where he joins us at the front, "What's good?"

After some small chit chat, we spend the next hour planning out what parts I need to make this overhaul happen. "Dude, I'm excited! This is going to turn out nice!" Vin praises the car.

"I know man, me too! Thanks for helping out!"

"Anytime dude. You planning on comin' out to the track tomorrow night with us?"

"Yeah, definitely! I want to get a good run in before we do this overhaul."

He nods, "Yeah, that's a good idea."

"You wanna hit up the field then afterward?" Vance yells from the basin, washing his hands. I slightly cringe. Going back there the night I came home wasn't quite the same. While we were in school, it wasn't a question. We were always at the track, and then partying at the field. The track is for everyone of all ages. Young, old, parents, teachers, grandparents; it didn't matter. The field was a little different. It seemed that there weren't too many people our age at the field that night. I didn't realize how much things can change in a year, but V's a prime example. The crowd was a bit young; some too young. Being there again..it made me feel old, which is depressing because I'm not old!

"Man you gotta come. No pun intended. I gotta keep an eye on V."

"How? You spend most of the night with your tongue down some chick's throat."

He laughs, "Yeah, well me just being there scares them."

"She's gotta hate you," I joke, he responds with a grunt.

"Probably, but man...the guys here are scum."

I instantly look at him hard. "Speak for yourself dude."

"Not you, you don't count. But remember how we were in school? We fucked anything with a skirt."

"You still do, man." Even though Vance is my best friend, we are completely different when it comes to women. He assumes I've slept with every girl I talk to, because that's what he does and...that's just so far from the truth. He shrugs and remains quiet for a second. "She's a good girl with goals, and I don't want any guy messing that up for her."

"She's smart Vance, I don't think she'd allow that to happen. I mean, what happens when she goes off to college? You can't be at every party. Plus, I think guys are even worse there."

Even the thought of some guy putting his hands on her irritates me.

"Fuck, man! It looks like I'm going to college then." He laughs, and I just shake my head and sigh, "Yeah, man I'll go with you."

I'd be lying if I said I didn't want to go to the field just to hang out with Veronica a little or even help Vance keep the little peckers away from her. I feel incredibly guilty after the crap he just spewed to me, but I just *can't* turn these feelings off.

DAY BY DAY

Veronica

I dial Taylor as soon as I pull away from the shop. The only place I have privacy is the inside of my car. It's a short drive home.

"Hiya, doll face," Taylor's voice fills my car.

"Hey, gorgeous. What are you doing?"

"I just got out of work, about to go to Wes'. Why what's up?"

"Chase stopped in at the garage," I pause. Taylor purrs into the phone. Literally. We once spent a solid hour of her trying to teach me how to purr. My tongue just doesn't roll like that.

"Hmm, and what did that hot piece of man candy want?"

I fill Taylor in on every detail because it keeps replaying in my head. Over and over.

I sigh, "He was flirting right?" I need confirmation that I'm not imagining things, even if she wasn't there to verify it.

"Hmmm, girl...I think he was fucking you with his mind."

I laugh out loud. "What?"

"He was fucking you in his head. I wonder if he really does have a big penis."

"You always wonder about *every* guy's penis!"

"Hey, I've only experienced one! I'm curious! Though, Wes' is pretty nice."

"*SO* don't need to know that, Tay!"

"I have a picture, I can show you!"

"TAYLOR! NO! I won't be able to look at him in the eye again!"

She bursts out laughing, "Are you sure? You're my bestie. My almost sister. I don't mind sharing his third leg with you."

"Oh my--how did we get this far off-topic? No, I don't want to see Wes' penis but thank you for being *such* a good friend."

"Anytime," She pauses, "So. He's definitely into you."

I sigh loudly.

"Why are you being so dramatic? This is good!"

"Because it would never work! There's no way."

"You don't know that! And, besides, maybe no one would have to know," A squeal erupts from her throat. "Oh, that would be so exciting! Like a big secret Romeo and Juliet...minus the whole family feud and suicide thing. Though, not far from a family feud with you being the hot, off-limits, little sister."

"You're too much Tay."

"I know, but you loovveee me. But seriously, I think this might be a good thing."

"Sneaking behind my brothers' back with their friend? I don't know."

"Chase is a good guy, and I think they might be okay with it."

I snort, "I don't know about that. Chase has a reputation too. Maybe not as bad as my brothers, but still a reputation. I don't think they'd be okay with it," I pinch the bridge of my nose and shut my eyes, "I might as well become a nun."

"No way, even though you'd rock the shit out of their nun-attire. We have a couple of months, and then it's off to college! You can let your 'freak flag' fly without the big bad brothers being around!"

I laugh loudly. This girl is too much, and she's right. I love her like a sister from another mister. We've planned forever to go away to the same college and be roomies.

"Yeah, I can't wait to get away from here. I won't be labeled as the off-limits little Russo sister anymore. Maybe we should look into going to a school across the country."

Taylor gasps mockingly, "And move away from Mama Russo's amazing cooking? I don't think so. State college will be fine. We'll be a two-hour drive away. That's far enough from your brothers, but close enough to home." I sigh again.

"Cut that sighing shit out! You'll be fine. Go find Chase and get some penis!"

"Riiight," I say, sarcastically.

"Okay girlfriend, I'm at Wes'. Keep me updated with lover boy."

"Will do. See you tomorrow."

"See yaaa!" she sings. The only thing I can do is take this day by day. I like Chase, and by the way he's acting, he seems to return those feelings. I don't like to assume things, especially when it's not spoken outright, but I can only hope that he is into me the way I'm into him.

Day. By. Day.

BEAUTIFUL
Chase

Working for my father is not fun, even when he's not around. My parents have yet to arrive back from their Caribbean vacation. A part of me is pissed, but a part of me could care less. Not having them home is peaceful. I often think about taking Vance's offer to go work at the garage, but I don't know how any work would get done with Veronica nearby. Not to mention, my father would have a shit storm. He feels that since I'm his son and his only son, I should take over his business even though I've told him it's not something I want to do.

As soon as four o'clock comes around, I'm out. Once home, I take a quick shower and throw on a shirt and some jeans. I grab my keys from my dresser and jump into the Z.

Vance sent me a text earlier in the day, they were gonna wash up the cars before heading down to the track. A pointless thing to do since by the end of the night they're all dirty again but...you just *don't* roll in with a dirty car. It's been a long time since I've gotten to do this, and I'm pretty stoked. I wasn't planning on doing more than a couple runs tonight, but you never know what will go down.

Halfway down the Russo's driveway, I hear Def Leppard's, 'Pour Some Sugar on Me', blasting from the garage. That's Vin's doing. He's always liked his old school rock. I put the car in neutral and coast towards the entrance of the garage. The sight before me is like dying and going to heaven. Veronica--bent over--washing the rear end of her blue RSX. Her shorts are so short I don't think they'd even be classified as shorts. You can see the curve of her ass cheeks. She stands up, and it seems almost like in slow motion. Her brown hair is up in a messy bun that's allowing her neck to be exposed. The tank top she has on is wet in areas that shows parts of her turquoise bikini and toned stomach. I feel like that cartoon wolf--my eyes bulging out of my head--and I may be forming a puddle of drool on my pants.

She must have heard my car approaching, because her head whips in my direction. I catch the smile forming on her lips. I cut the engine and get out. Taylor comes from the front of Veronica's car, wearing something similar, holding a sponge. Beyond them, the guys are in the garage. Vance is buffing his BMW, nodding his head to the music. Wes' car is next to Vance's, but the hood is up. No doubt they're making sure his car is up to par.

I make my way over to the girls. "Aren't you ladies a sight for sore eyes?"

"Oh Chase, aren't you such a flirt. But, sadly, I'm very much taken. V here is totally available though." *Subtle.* V smacks Taylor in the shoulder.

"Our little V can be so shy." She looks between the two of us, "Well I'm gonna go grab a Coke. I'll be back." Taylor drops her sponge in the bucket and skips off towards the garage. Veronica watches her skip away and shakes her head. I put my hands in my pockets because I desperately want to touch her.

"Hey," she says simply, a slight grin playing on her face. Damn. She is adorable.

"Hey. Car looks good, but you missed a spot." I nod towards the back of her car. Her eyebrows furrow as she turns to look at her car covered in suds, "Where?"

I point towards the very bottom of her bumper, "Down there..."

She leans down to look and starts scrubbing furiously. The motion causes her ass to wiggle back and forth. I didn't really see a missed spot. I said it for my own dickish motives, and I'm not gonna apologize for it. The view of her rear is stunning. It would be better with my hands on it. I bite my bottom lip to keep a groan from escaping me.

"Yo, man!" *Shit.*

Vance's voice startles me, snapping me from my fantasizing. I quickly turn to face him. "What up?" He approaches me as I play it cool. *Dude, I was NOT just fantasizing about my hands on your sister's ass. I swear.*

"About time you got here!"

"Yeah, Yeah."

"Looks good V, but you missed a spot," Vance tells her, pointing towards the side of her door. She glowers at him as he laughs. She flips him the middle finger. He nods towards the garage, as he starts walking, "Wes and Vin are looking over the Evo." Wes and Vin glance up. Vin holds out his hand, and I smack it in greeting.

Wes walks around Vin to greet me, "Hey man, it's good to see you back!"

"Yeah, it's good to be back."

He laughs, "I bet.

I nod at his engine bay, "Dude this thing is sick!" Because it is. The turbo is enormous, massive down piping, a racing intercooler. It's beautiful.

"Wait until you see her run!" Vance says.

"What's she timing now?" I ask.

"High eleven's." Wes answers.

I whistle.

"Yeah, I dumped a lot of money in her."

"Yeah, too much," Taylor chimes in, walking into the garage. V is slowly trailing behind her. I watch as she walks towards us and puts the bucket on the table next to me. She turns around and leans back against the table, her elbows resting on top causing her chest to push outward. She knows I'm watching her. I can't help but think she's doing this on purpose. She smiles while reaching up to pull the band from her hair and shakes her head, her long brown hair falling around her.

Fuck, she's beautiful.

"What time are we leaving?" She asks the group.

"Six," Vin answers her but keeps his back to her.

"K, I'm going to go get ready." She turns and leaves the garage. Taylor kisses Wes and follows behind V, letting the door close behind her. My attention snaps back to the engine bay, glancing around to make sure I wasn't that obvious. Of course, no one's paying attention because Wes' engine is more important, and they would never expect me to be checking out V.

Vance moves back to stand next to me in the spot that V just stood, "Wes has got some cash runs tonight."

"Nice, more than one?"

"Yeah, three." Wes throws out.

"Three?" My shock must've been apparent.

Vance looks my way. "Yeah dude, this is big."

"And you're going to do all three?" I ask Wes.

"Not sure yet. Dude is driving a hatched Civic but being quiet about his set up."

"That's some shady shit."

"I know, he wants to put way too much money down. He's either really cocky or really sure of himself."

"How much?" I inquire.

"A grand," Vance cuts in.

"Damn!"

"I know. The other two are under five hundred. Chump change." I had no idea Wes had gotten so deep into the scene. When Wes moves his car out of the garage, I ask Vance more about it.

"When did he get so much attention?"

"A couple of months ago. He wasn't kidding when he said he put a lot of money into that car. He took it up to the track just to get a good time in, pulled a clean twelve. Then bored out his engine and got it down to eleven point eight seconds. People took notice. He's gotten really good with his reaction time. He's determined to get it down to eleven seconds."

"That's pretty impressive!"

Vin claps a hand on my shoulder and nods toward my car. "Dude, wait till we get your car hooked up!" He rubs his hands together mischievously. A deep low rumble grabs all our attention as another car pulls into the driveway. Just like that, the sun has set and it's now dark outside. I can only really make out the shape of the headlights, but I know it's Vaughn's VW. He swaggers in, "Yo my dude, what's up?" Vaughn got tall, and his hair is longer than it has ever been. Our palms slap together in greeting then he strolls over to the fridge, grabs a soda, pops open the tab, and takes a huge gulp. He lets out a massive burp and laughs at himself. He has the goofiest laugh, which, in turn, makes me laugh. I shake my head, he's still the same kid.

This guy.

"Where's Victor?" I ask no one in particular. He's the only missing brother. Vaughn, who's looking at his phone, his fingers moving quickly over the screen, is the one to answer. "Victor's too whipped. He barely comes out with us anymore."

"Damn."

"Yeah, damn shame."

His phone chimes a second later. He looks up, "Nice. Tracy's gonna be there, and bringing some honeys."

"Really Vaughn? 'Honeys'? You're *so* lame." Taylor speaks from behind us. I look over my shoulder as she walks further into the garage, wearing something completely different from ten minutes ago.

"What are you worried about? Wes' so whipped, he won't even notice them."

"Oh, I know that," she stops next to me crossing her arms, "I'm just worried about you, Vaughn," Tracy is a succubus. She sinks her teeth into different guys, then tosses them out; it's her thrill, "I heard she's not always...*safe*."

I look back at Vaughn, and he just laughs, "That's what condoms are for."

"That's nasty, Vaughn!" Veronica yells from behind us, and my head whips in her direction. Her hair is in a braid that hangs over her shoulder laying right atop her chest, so of course, that's where my eyes land. Her black top is ripped all over the place, showing some of her stomach and hangs off her other shoulder. Her jeans look like they mold to her skin. My eyes are glued to her as she walks to Taylor. I quickly glance at her ass. *Oh yes...*

Vaughn's distinguishing laugh grows louder, causing me to tear my eyes away from V. He's hunched over hands on his knees, trying to get his breathing under control. Vin joins us, looking around at everyone, his eyes on Vaughn, "What's so funny?"

"Vaughn's VD," Veronica says flatly, her hands upon her hips, displaying her attitude.

"Ew, dude, you get your shit checked?"

He stands up straight, , "I don't have any diseases, shut up V."

Vance and Wes join us. Wes comes up behind Taylor, wrapping his arms around her shoulders.

"You gonna run tonight?" Wes looks at me.

"Yeah, probably just a few. I wanna get a running time before I do any mods."

We all stand around just joking and talking in the Russo's garage. It feels like I haven't missed a thing.

"Hey Tay, you gonna try and run one?" Vaughn asks, trying to keep a straight face. She sticks her tongue out at him, and everyone starts laughing. I look around lost. Vaughn fills me in, "Tay wanted to give it a try."

"Shut up Vaughn!" Taylor starts to move towards him, but Wes holds her back.

"So, Wes let her try before he put in the new clutch." Vaughn continues trying to contain his laughter, "She got up to the line but went over and had to back up but when the light hit green she went backward." Everyone laughs, even Veronica, Taylor smacks her in the arm and huffs, "It's not that funny." She looks at me, "I forgot to put it back into first. I was nervous!"

"We know baby," Wes says kissing atop her head, rubbing his hands down her arms.

"It was fucking hilarious!"

I smile because it is pretty funny, I'm sad I missed it.

"Vaughn, you have no room to talk," Veronica interjects, "your little Jetta can't keep up with anything. You let a *stock* GSX beat you." Multiple 'ohh's' went around the garage.

"Burrrnnn," Vance yells.

"Okay V, you're on!" Vaughn points at Veronica. "I bet my GTI will wreck your RSX."

Everyone looks to Veronica for a response, she walks over to him with her hand out, "Sure thing, 'VD'!"

"Oh, shit," Vin mumbles as we all watch them shake hands. My thoughts exactly, but I can't wait to watch Veronica race. The thought alone turns me on.

SIX FIFTEEN
Veronica

"**Y**our ass is grass, little sister."

I smile sweetly, "Your ass must get jealous of all the *shit* that comes out of your mouth."

The laughter around us erupts to a roar, and Vaughn glares at me. Good ol' sibling rivalry. A clap sounds behind us. "Let's roll!" Vin yells.

"I'm gonna tell Ma we're leaving." I run into the house. "Ma!" I yell and walk into the living room where both my parents are. My mom is knitting, and dad is in his recliner passed out with the paper on his chest. She looks up as I enter. "Why you yellin'?"

"Sorry, I didn't think he'd be asleep. We're leaving." I walk over to her and kiss her on the cheek. "Be careful baby girl. I love you," Her voice is soft.

"I will, promise. I love you too." I run back out into the garage and grab my helmet off the shelf. Taylor is jogging away from Wes' car and she climbs into the passenger seat of my car as I get into the driver's seat. One by one, the guys are starting up their cars. The combining sounds of each car's exhaust are deafening. I love it! Goosebumps spread across my skin. I startup my car; my exhaust adds to the loudness. No doubt Dad is awake now. The guys are turning around in the driveway, and I put my car in reverse as Tay puts on some music. I roll down my windows to let the cool nights weather in.

It takes a good thirty minutes to get down to the

track. Pulling off the freeway when we reach the first light, I downshift and roll up behind Chase's car. Just the thought of Chase makes me smile. I'm jolted out of my little reverie when Taylor's loud off-pitch singing scares me. I burst out laughing and glance over at her. She looks awfully comfortable with her legs tucked up and aside of her on the seat. Her shoes, which she removed two minutes into the drive, are on the floor. The red light illuminates her face as she tosses her head back and forth continuing to sing...loudly...*horribly*...and she could care less.

Green light floods the car, then, and I pull my attention back towards the road. Instinctively, I put the car in first and drive. We reach the small town that's right before the track. I love the feel of this town; it's like something out of a movie. The main street is full of family-owned businesses on either side--A deli, florist, a laundry mat, clothing boutique and, at the end, a diner with amazing homemade food and pies. The town locals are all big racing fans, and the track is their money maker. It brings people in from all around, even people out of state!

As our line of cars drives through the little town, the rumble from our exhausts bounces off the buildings, creating a loud hum. It's almost deafening but it makes me giddy. The entrance is not far off from the main road, and as we approach, there's already a decent line of cars. Thankfully, the line moves steadily and within minutes I'm pulling up to the pay booth. Taylor hands me her money and turns down the music for me. The older man leans out of the booth, wearing a shirt with the track name on it, and glances into the car. "Racers?"

"One."

"Need a helmet?" he asks me.

"Nope." If you don't have your own helmet they will rent you one. With how many times we are here, it's just smart to invest in one. I hand him my helmet, so he can inspect it, making sure it's up to standards. He hands it back to me, along with a paper filled with information about the track and rules. "That'll be thirty," he informs me. I hand him the money, and he puts it in the drawer, then exits the booth with a marker in his hand, "Number?"

"Six Fifteen," I tell him and watch as he writes the number, my birthday, on the top of my windshield, then on my back window. He taps on the roof of my car. "All good. Drive safe!" The man gets back in his booth. I shift into gear and creep away slowly. The road isn't the smoothest and goes about half a mile before opening into a massive parking lot. The track is beyond the lot behind an eight-foot chain-link fence. Metal bleachers, similar to ones you find at a high school football field are to the right, in front of the starting line. There are a few concession stands behind the bleachers, with porta-potties not too far away from the picnic tables. The back of the parking lot is already getting full. I drive slowly through the lot, watching for people walking around when Taylor calls my name.

"Yeah?" I answer her but keep my eyes focused ahead.

"I love you, you know that right?"

"Uh. Yeah?" I glance at her, confused at where she's going with this. I hear her sigh and she continues, "You're my sister from another mister, and I know I told you I'd share Wes' penis with you, but I *lied*."

I burst out laughing. It's loud, and obnoxious.

"I love you but his peen is mine."

"Oh my gosh, Tay..no worries. His peen is *all* yours."
I pull in next to Wes' car, his number written on his window, which happens to be his and Taylor's anniversary date. Did I ever mention how grossly, disgustingly adorable they are? I pull the e-brake and look over at Taylor. She wipes the back of her hand across her forehead and blows out a large breath. Dramatic much?
"Well whew, I am so glad we had this talk."
Her door is opened, and Wes helps her out of the car. I just shake my head, silently laughing to myself, and cut the engine. I get out, round the front of my car, and lean against the fender. The hood is open on Wes' car, as a couple of different racers wanted to see what he's got going on under there. It's shady if you don't want to show what you're running, and most likely people won't want to race you, especially when dealing with cash races. He talks while his arm is draped around Taylor's shoulders.

I tune out their talk and take in the surroundings. The bleachers are filling up, and I twist to look down by the finish line where some trucks are parked with people sitting on the tailgates. I bring my attention back to the racing lanes, people are already lining up. I'm watching them prep the track when I feel heat all along my right side. It's startling. I whip my head to find the cause of the sudden warmth. Chase is standing extremely close. So close, that if he moved another inch we'd be touching. He must notice my attention is now on him because he looks down at me, a wide smile breaking out over his face. That smile and his proximity turn my legs to jelly, but thankfully my car is helping me manage to stay on my feet.

He leans in a little and says, "Hi," His voice is low

and intimate like this 'Hi' is for me, and me only. His beautiful blue eyes are staring into mine, making me lose myself even more than I already am. I take in a deep breath, and out comes a breathy, "Hey," His face is closer now. I don't recall him moving in, but I can see his pupils dilate. I remember Taylor telling me--she is always reading these magazines--this little tidbit about the pupils dilating when someone is looking at someone they find attractive.

I bite the inside of my cheek to fight the giggle that wants to erupt from my mouth, which will no doubt make me look like a bumbling idiot. I wonder if he knows this fact; there's no doubt my pupils are the size of a quarter. I'm warm all over as his eyes move all across my face. The whole exchange lasted seconds, but it's something that will replay in my head for the rest of the night. Maybe even my life.

He moves away, the smile slowly vanishing, and looks back at the group. I'm still staring at his strong beautiful profile, taking in his appearance. His buzzed hair. His fitted T-shirt, snuggling against his muscles. Is it weird to be jealous of a shirt? I shake my head to clear myself of my lust and glance back at the group.

Thankfully no one is paying us any attention. Not to mention, Wes' body is practically hiding me. In the short time we've been here, more people have gathered around, including a few race groupies. One girl is pressed up to Vance's side. Ugh. Gross. Vaughn's arm is slung around some girl--that girl is *not* Tracy. I shake my head.

A loud and high pitched revving breaks the conversation and causes everyone's head to turn. A handful of bikes--crotch rockets--go driving by. It is by far the most obnoxious thing in the entire world, but this particular group is *just that*. They are insane, rude and just bad news. It's unfortunate because their leader, if you want to call him that, is one guy who's not afraid of going head to head with my brothers. Dixon continues to harass me after I've turned him down every time. I think it's more to bother my brothers than anything. Rumor has it is that he deals drugs to afford parts for his bike. They continue to rev as they drive by. Chase leans into me but keeps his attention on the bikes. "Who are those clowns?"

"Dixon, and his crew."

He laughs and just shakes his head. I'm not sure what he's thinking. The bikes have passed and park down the lot. Everyone is back to talking to whoever they were before being interrupted. "Hellooo spectators!" the announcer comes over the loudspeaker. People in the bleachers scream, whistle, and cheer. "Let's get this show on the road!"

Two cars, both Mustangs, roll up to the starting line. I look at everyone, and their attention is on the cars. The loud revving snaps my attention back to the line, rightfully so. The older Stang is loud; louder than its opponent. You can see the car shake as its owner is giving it some gas. The newer Mustang is revving back. Seconds later they're flying down the track. It's over almost as soon as it started. The scores flash up on the boards near the end of the track. The older Mustang wins with a slightly better time. Cheering from the stands erupts, most likely the driver's friends or family. Suddenly Dixon is next to me, pulling me to his side.

"Hey, baby," he says.

"Dixon," I roll my eyes, "get *off* me." I try to push his

arm off, but he just squeezes me to him.

"Awe, babe. Don't be like that." This is exhausting.

"For the millionth time, don't call me that." I turn and duck under his arm. He doesn't try to grab me again, but he's smiling because it's just fun to him. I feel Chase at my back, and my brothers are rounding Wes' car.

"Dixon, get your ugly ass outta here," Vance says as he stops two feet in front of Dixon, my brothers, and Wes at his back. Dixon looks at me and back at my brothers, "Hey Vance, nice to see you too! Your sister happens to like my ugly ass."

"Shut up Dixon, and move along," Vin cuts in. Dixon puts his hands up in submission. "Okay. Okay. I'm going." He looks at me and winks, "I'll see you later doll face."

"Not happenin' dickface," Vance spits out. I wave goodbye as he turns and walks away. I watch him go, as do my brothers. Dixon is really attractive and, worse yet, he knows it. He has this 'James Dean' look to him. He's an asshole and has probably slept with more girls than my brothers combined...not to mention his chosen profession. It's a shame. My brothers move away, but I can still feel Chase at my back. I turn to face him.

"He do that often?" His eyes still on Dixon.

"Yeah, unfortunately. I think he does it to bother my brothers."

"I don't think so."

"I mean, in the beginning, I think he might have been serious. He would get to me when I wasn't around my brothers. I'd turn him down every time. I am one of the very few girls he hasn't slept with...all I am is a challenge to him. Now he does it right in front of them." Chase doesn't say anything, just nods. We go back to leaning against the car, listening to the guys talk. Two more cars go zooming down the track. I feel something curl around my pinky, confused, I glance down. Chase's pinky is wrapped around mine. I look up and try to act normal. My eyes are bugging out of my head. The butterflies are swarming my stomach.

"You alright back there V?" Vaughn yells to me. I yank my hand away from Chase's and cross my arms over my chest. My heart is pounding; *of course* they ruin a moment. Even though Vaughn had no idea, I still blame him. I look at Vaughn. He has a shit-eating grin on his face. I collect myself, bring out the sass, and give him my smug smile. "Peachy."

Vaughn laughs, "You look like you're about to shit yourself." Chase laughs beside me, and of course, Vaughn feeds on that, "Right? She looks like she's about to drop a load." I glare at Vaughn. Chase starts to say something, but I shove my finger against his lips to shut him up.

"No dear brother, I'm not scared."

"Well then...let's do this."

I smile. "Let's..."

DOUCHE NOZZLE
Veronica

Vaughn rubs his hands together like one of those evil cartoon characters, smiles wide, and runs to his car. I turn and glare at Chase, "What is so funny?"

"I'm sorry, you look freaked out."

"Yeah, just a bit." I put my hands on my hips. "You have some big balls doing that!"

He laughs again. "Maybe one day you'll see for yourself."

I stiffen. *Holy crap!* He did not just say that!

He gets in my face, "I'm kidding, V. Let's go...you have a race to win." Chase walks me to my car. I open the door and get into the driver's side and leave the door open because Chase is standing in between my door and the car. He kneels, stares at me, and looks like he wants to say something but remains quiet. He stands and looks down—"Kickass, V"—then walks away without another world, or waiting for me to say anything back. I close the door and start my car.

Putting the car in reverse, I back out and drive to the lineup. Vaughn is waiting for me and I pull up next to him. There's a couple of cars ahead of us, so the wait time is a bit longer than I'd like. No matter how many times I've done this, or plan to do this, it never fails to get my blood pumping and my heart racing. It's a feeling like no other. I'm starting to sweat, even though the windows are wide open. With the number of cars around us the air is mostly hot exhaust fumes.

For a couple minutes, we coast forward until we're up next. I look over at Vaughn, who is putting on his face mask while bopping around to his music. I shake my head. *He's such a dork.* He looks over and stops what he's doing to slice his pointer finger across his neck, the universal sign for 'you're dead'. I laugh, make a fist and smash it into my palm, then point to him. He puts on his helmet. I follow suit, first with my mask, then with my helmet.

The cars in front us take off and two minutes later we're motioned forward. I move the car up, slowly, lining up until the light on the tree shines bright. "I got this," I chant to myself, "Kickass." My sole focus is on the tree. My feet are ready to shift, and I have both hands on the steering wheel. My heart is pounding. I take in a deep breath and exhale.

Amber.
Boom. Boom.
Amber.
Boom. Boom.
Amber.
Deep Breath.
Green!

My right foot presses down on the gas pedal as my left foot relieves it's pressure on the clutch and *zoom--* my car shoots forward, propelling my body back into the seat. The speedometer pushing towards the rev line.

Shift.

My surroundings blur by me, I can see Vaughn's car in my peripheral vision, he's slightly ahead. I press down on the gas pedal.

Rev Line.
Shift.
The exhaust is loud, filling the car with nothing but a loud hum.
Rev Line.
Shift.
The nose of my car is passing his. "Yes!" I whisper, my lips split in a smile wide.
Rev Line.
Shift.
All of a sudden, his car disappears, and I pass the finish line. I begin the process of downshifting and braking, glancing in my rearview as I do. Vaughn is pretty far behind. Obviously, something happened. I slow down and pull up next to the time booth and the guy hands me my time slip. "Nice job!" he says. I give him a thumbs-up as I pull away from the booth. I take the 'U' and drive towards our spot, parking next to Wes' car. The crew comes over shouting and hollering. I pull off my helmet and mask. Vaughn pulls up shortly after and he rips off his helmet. He jumps out of his car before I've even opened my door.

"What the hell happened dude?" Vance yells to Vaughn, busting his balls.

"Redo, V!" He completely ignores everyone and stalks to my driver's side.

"What?!" I toss my helmet in my passenger seat.

"I missed a gear."

I burst out laughing and open my door. "This just proves who the better driver is," I point to myself and put my arms over the top of my door.

"Bullshit. We need to do it over."

I move away from my door, walking until I'm standing in front of him, and put my hands on my hips. "I don't think we do."

He huffs, "I fucked up. Hardy har har. It wasn't a fair race. I had you!"

I sigh because he's right. It wasn't exactly a fair race. "Fine."

He jumps back in his car.

"Wait, now?!" I yell.

"Hell yeah!"

I huff loudly in frustration. He backs out before I'm even in my car. I should've just told him to suck it up-...that he's a crap driver, and leave it at that. "Douche Nozzle," I mumble to myself while climbing back into my car. I shift into reverse and meet him at the lineup.

MAKE IT UP TO YOU
Chase

I watch Veronica get back into her car with annoyance and smile to myself. Watching her race is the sexiest thing I've ever witnessed. Better than porn. I follow the rest of the gang to our spot at the fence, standing next to Vance. "If V can get a better reaction time off the line, she could beat him." I just nod. Two cars zoom down the track. Their exhausts so loud as they pass that Vance has to shout, "They're pretty evenly matched. *But*"—at the word point he points his finger out—"what Vaughn doesn't know, we did some small mods to V's car recently."

I laugh and shake my head. "That's hilarious."

"I hope she can get him. Vaughn can be such a shit stain sometimes. He needs to be taken down a notch."

"That's funny coming from you."

"What?" He turns to me, "I may talk shit, but I speak the truth."

I laugh. The Russo brothers sure are cocky motherfuckers.

"They're up! WHOOO!" Taylor yells.

Vaughn's charcoal gray VW pulls up and Veronica's dark blue RSX follows. I'm nervous for her. Vaughn is a sore loser and winner.

From my view, you can't see the lights. It's only seconds...both their cars slightly lift as they take off, their exhausts whining out as they hit the rev line. V managed to get an awesome time off the line, but so did

Vaughn. They're neck and neck. Vaughn's car is backfiring. *Pop. Pop. Pop.*

"Go. Go. Go," I whisper to myself, bouncing on my feet. They speed past us, and they are right on top of each other. This shit is intense. My heart is pounding.

"GO, V!" Taylor yells out.

"WHOOOOO!" Vance yells. "This shit is close!" The farther they move down the track, the harder it is to see who's leading. Veronica's car swivels a bit, and my heart drops.

"Oh no!" I hear Taylor gasp.

"Shit!" Vance says, "Shit!"

"No!" Vin yells.

White smoke is pouring out of V's car. Her car loses speed and stops dead at the end of the track. Vance pushes off the fence and runs down towards the time slip booth and the rest of us follow. The tow truck races on the track to remove her car. Track officials run onto the track. Veronica throws them a thumbs up, indicating that she's okay. She did awesome keeping the car straight and on the road. This is a huge blow for any car enthusiast, but it happens all the time.

There's a trail of fluid left behind as the tow truck removes her car. The track scrubber is already on the task of cleaning up the fluids. The tow truck pulls her car to the lot at the back of the track and has her unhooked and off by the time we get down there. Vaughn is standing there with his hands on his head. He runs to her as she gets out. Vaughn squeezes her, "Are you okay? I am so sorry, V."

V's face is bright red, either from the heat or anger. He holds her at arm's length. "I'm fine, Vaughn. This is your fault, you--" She stumbles on her words, "--fart sucker!"

Taylor runs to her side and wraps her arms around her shoulders, hugging her from the side.

"Dammit!" Veronica yells. Taylor squeezes her.

"We'll fix it!" Vaughn tells her. I want to go to her, comfort her somehow. I want to wrap my arms around her and hold her, but I can't. "I'll call Triple A," Vin says as he pulls out his phone, walking away from the commotion. My feet are moving me forward before my head is registering what I'm doing. I grab her, pulling her away from Taylor and crush her to my body. Her arms wrap around my waist, her head nuzzles into my chest, and I lower my head next to her ear. I hear her sniffle. "It'll be okay, V. This is fixable. You did so awesome out there," I whisper.

I look up and all eyes are on us. Well, not everyone's. Vance and Wes are at the front of Veronica's car, Vin is on the phone with his back to us, but Taylor and Vaughn are watching us thoroughly. I pull her away quickly. "It'll be okay!" I tell her, pat her head, and walk away. Vaughn's eyeing me carefully. I look at him.

"What?" I ask, "She looked like she needed a hug, and not from an asshat like you." I laugh, nervously. I head over to Vance and Wes at the front of the car. "What're you thinking?" I ask both of them.

"It's hard to tell, and it's too hot to open the hood yet." He lays down on the ground about a foot away from the bumper. I look up. Vaughn is standing in front of Veronica blocking her from my view, but Taylor is staring at me, her eyebrow arched up with a wide smile. She winks and then turns her attention to V. Vin joins us, "They say the tow truck will be here in about an hour, so I'm guessing we have two." He nods at Veronica's car. "What you thinkin', Vance?"

He shrugs, "Radiator. Probably more. Definitely radiator fluid leaking. We'll take a good look at it tomorrow."

"V!" Vin shouts. She peeks around Vaughn, but they all look our way. "Have the driver take it right to the garage. We'll take a look at it in the morning." V nods. Vaughn puts his arm around her and guides her to his car. They get in and drive up towards our spot. The rest of us walk. A sleek black lowered Honda drives up next to us, "Yo! Wes! We gonna do this or what?"

"Yeah, as soon as you pop your hood," Wes tells this kid, who I've never seen before.

"Nah, we don't have time for that shit."

"No-go then." Wes' composure is calm as he walks with his arm around Taylor.

"Don't be a pussy, man!"

Wes shakes his head. "Don't be a dick, Ryder."

"You're just scared you're gonna get your ass handed to you."

"Move along now." Wes waves his hand in front of himself. Ryder revs his engine and peels off, kicking up dirt and rocks from aside the pavement. We all jump out of the way.

"Fuckin' prick!" Vance yells. Ryder's hand goes up, along with his middle finger. "Fuckin' prick." Vance mumbles again, under his breath this time. We all keep walking in the grassy area until we reach our spot. Veronica is sitting on Vance's trunk. Vaughn is nowhere in sight.

"Where's Vaughn?" Vin asks.

"He went to get me 'I'm sorry' food," Veronica smiles wide and kicks her feet out. The move makes me smile and I can't help but think how cute she is. Taylor jumps up next to her and moves her legs open as Wes stands in between them. They do it without thinking, just something so natural to them and I find myself...*envious*. Wes is animatedly talking to Vin and Vance. Taylor wraps her arms around his shoulders, resting her head on the top of his.

My eyes move to Veronica. She's listening to them talk, yet her eyes are also on her best friend and boyfriend. She bites her lip, as her face softens. Her eyes flicker to me like she knows I'm staring at her. She releases her lip from her teeth, "What?" she mouths. I shake my head.

Vaughn walks up at this moment, carrying a tray full of food. As the guys crowd him, all attention on the food, I make my move. Nonchalantly moving towards Veronica, I lean against the back fender facing my body towards hers.

I hear, "No!" followed by a loud whack, "Get your own, you leeches!" Vaughn yells. Vin shoves a pile of fries into his mouth, as Vance rubs his hand. Vaughn moves to place the tray in between V and me, causing me to move back. He grabs the burger off the tray and takes a large bite and with his mouth full he says something completely incoherent. Somehow, V seems to know exactly what he says. "Thanks, bro!"

I spot deep-fried Oreos and quick swipe one from the little carton they sit in.

"Hey!" Veronica protests. I take a bite and wink, "I'll make it up to you."

LIKE DESSERT
Veronica

If we weren't surrounded by people, in the middle of the track's parking lot, I would *so* jump Chase right now. My stomach is swirling with butterflies. I don't know why, but when he throws me a wink, it just does something to me. I find it incredibly sexy. I'm still staring at him as he eats my deep-fried Oreo. If it were one of my brothers that shanked one I'd smack it right out of their hand, but I'm sitting here just watching his beautiful mouth chew MY Oreo. I'd give him another one just to watch his mouth if I didn't love food so much.

I've been silently questioning his actions. He hasn't come out and told me he's into me, but there's no doubt about it. He wants me as much as I want him. I think back to his embrace, and supportive words after my car broke down. I was so consumed with my car, his actions didn't seem like much until now. All this fills me with joy and anxiety. Chase has been Vance's friend since middle school. He's seen me in my awkward stages, so I can't fathom why he would be interested in me. I used to follow them around all the time. They'd tell me to get lost and I'd cry, then mom would make them hang out with me.

I have no idea how this would even work...there's no way it could. He's friends with all of my brothers but being Vance's best friend is the worst. He would never let me date his friend. He doesn't even want me to date at all! All these things are ping-ponging inside my head.

I had zoned out, staring at Chase, but not quite looking at him. Chase waves his hand in front of my face. "Hello? V?" I focus my eyes on him, "Ah, there you are. What's going on in that head of yours?" he asks with a wicked grin on his face.

I focus on him, shaking the fog from my brain. *Quick! Think of something to say.* "I can't believe you just swiped an Oreo!" I blurt out. He chuckles and opens his mouth to say something, but is interrupted.

"Chase!" Vance is coming towards us. "You ready to take the Z out?" Chase stands up straight which gives some distance between us. He crosses his arms over his chest, his muscles bulging. *Yum.*

"Yep."

"Let's do this!" Vance whoops. Chase moves away from Vaughn's car and makes his way to his car parked on the other side of Wes'. He looks at me before getting in, winks, and follows it up with a white smile. Well, just stick a fork in me.

I. Am. *Done.*

Wes moves from between Taylor's legs and kisses her, then jogs to his car. Vaughn is walking to me, "I'm gonna go run again, hop-off V."

"Well, must be nice," I say sliding down his fender until my feet hit the ground.

"Don't be salty, V. I'm sorry your car broke. Maybe you should trade her in for a dub."

"Ew. No way in hell."

He laughs. I pick up the tray of food that managed to disappear, taking it to the nearest garbage can. Taylor comes bouncing up next to me, her arm looping through mine, "Well, well, well ... someone is definitely smitten with my bestie." She bumps her hip into mine.

"Tay, I'm in so much trouble."

"Oh *yes*, you are! You don't see the way he looks at you, my friend."

I look at her. "And what way would that be?"

"Like you're dessert. Like the last dessert on earth."

I sigh, "Oh nooo."

"Yesss."

"What do I do?"

"What do you want to do?"

I throw away the garbage and place the tray on top. I turn around to look at Taylor. "I'm terrified!" I confess, "I like him. What's not to like? He's freakin' hot as hell. He's into cars. But I have no experience what-so-ever, and he does! Just thinking about that makes me nervous and jealous. I shouldn't be jealous. He's best friends with my brother. There's no way anything can happen between us. They'd never allow it." Taylor grasps my shoulders stopping me mid-rant.

"I don't think he'd risk being castrated if he didn't care about you."

"So you don't think I'm just some challenge for him?" I ask what I'm really afraid of. I've been surrounded by guys my whole life. I know how they talk. I know what they really want. But I can't help but want to be wanted--truly wanted. Victor is the only one of my brothers to settle down even if it was a surprise to us all. No one knows how Melissa managed to get him to settle, we just kind of chalked it up to him getting older.

"What? V! No Way!" Tay pulls me towards the fence. "Is that what you think?" She's watching me carefully. Taylor knows me better than anyone, but this is the first time I've confessed my fear out loud. I have gone my whole life being off-limits, the little sister of the infamous badass Russo brothers. It honestly didn't phase me until around the seventh or eighth grade. All the girls and boys holding hands, becoming boyfriend and girlfriend. I was so excited to possibly have my first boyfriend. Guys in my school either look up to my brothers or they're afraid of them.

My first kiss was under the bleachers at a football game. He was from the rival school, so he had no idea who I was. It sounds so awful, but I just wanted to kiss someone. To experience what everyone was experiencing and at that point everyone in my school knew not to even touch me. I was the Russos' little sister.

I went on my first date last year. I had to beg my mom to keep it a secret, and yet, somehow, Vance got wind of it and showed up at the movie theater with Vin and Vaughn in tow. That was my first and last date *ever*. Why would anyone take the risk to even remotely try to date me, unless it was challenging, or to just get into my pants? Not that it would be easy. I may have had my first kiss with a kid I barely knew, but my lady bits are not open for business to just *anyone*. I sigh, "Yeah."

"Oh V, I can't predict the future, but I don't think you're a challenge for any guy. Okay, I lie, but only because you know more about cars than most guys. So, then, you need a guy more your speed. Your brothers care about you, and if any guy is willing to defy them for you, that's the guy you need. Not some pansy who's afraid of a little brotherly love." She makes sense,"So, with that said," she continues talking, "just take things slow. That's all you can do until he puts all his cards on the table. Which by the way, I think will be soon. You guys can figure it out then." I nod. She's right. I've told myself the same thing but sometimes hearing it from someone else helps.

"Tay, I am so nervous though."

"You think I wasn't nervous when I started dating Wes? Because I was. Completely."

"You were?"

"Hell yeah. I liked him *so* much, but he's older than us. I knew he was no angel."

"You never mentioned anything about it?"

"To you? No way. You have this air about yourself, V. You're strong and confident." I look at her, completely confused. "Don't look at me like that. Until now, I had no idea that you felt that way, and honestly, it shocks me. I didn't express my nerves to you because I didn't think you'd understand."

I couldn't hide my cringe. She continues, "Not in a bad way, don't make that face. It makes you look like a troll." This makes me laugh. "Anyway"—she waves her hand—"The more time I spent with Wes, the less nervous I was. He's kind and sweet. He never pushed me to do anything, but somehow, he just knew what and when I wanted. So, if you and Chase do get together, you'll know if it's right, and he won't make you nervous."

"Jeez Tay, when the hell did you get so freakin' insightful?"

"Shut up, it's always been there."

I wrap my arm around her. "I love you," I squeeze her.

"I know. You can't help but love me. I'm *awesome*." This makes me laugh. She wraps her arm around my waist and puts her head on my shoulder. "You know I love you too."

"Oh! Wes is up!" Tay's head pops up, her hand drops from around my waist, she moves forward to grab the chain-link fence. Mushy girl time over. "Is that Chase's Z?" I squint.

"It is! Oh, this is so exciting! Our men...racing!"

I laugh. "He's not my man."

"Yet," she coos. This makes me smile. Seconds later, they're off. Their cars are slightly lifting as they give the cars' gas. Wes easily takes the lead. Tay is jumping up and down. It's not exactly a competitive race--we all know Wes' Evo is hooked up to the nines. Chase's Z is still pretty stock. They zoom down the track. The scoreboards flashing their times. Wes got an eleven point six, and Chase's Z came in at fourteen point five. A loud rev pulls my attention back to the starting line. Vaughn and Vance are pulling up. The rev comes from Vaughn because Vance's car is a little quieter; deeper. They lineup and then they're off. Vance is easily pulling away from Vaughn. They zoom past us, with Vance blowing Vaughn's VW out of the water. I smile wide.

Wes and Chase pull up behind us. Chase is a sight getting out of his car. He's tall, lean, and tan. They continue walking to us, my eyes following Chase as he comes to stand on my left while Wes is coming up behind Taylor and wrapping his arms around her. Chase doesn't look at me but has a wicked grin on his face.

"Not bad."

"Nope, not bad at all." He rocks back and forth on his toes. I decide to mess with him a little.

"I can do better," I say looking forward, fighting the grin that's trying to form on my lips watching the next two cars pulling up to the starting line.

"Oh, you think so?" Chase asks.

"Yep," I say, popping the 'p'.

"I'd like to see that."

"Hmm, I bet you would."

I hear a jingling of keys. I look his way, slightly shocked at him holding out his keys. He's facing me now, leaning on one of the poles of the fence. He nods behind me. "Show me." My eyes are bugging out of my head. *Holy crap, he's going to let me race his car?! What?* I'm about to grab the keys from him when Vin heads our way, the phone to his ear.

"Yeah, okay. It's towards the back of the parking lot." He removes the phone from his ear, presses a button, and slips it into his back pocket. "Tow truck's here," He informs us.

Vaughn and Vance just pull up, parking aside Chase's car. Vin jogs over to them, as they get out of the car, I assume he's telling them what he just told us. Our little group joins the rest of them just as I hear Vaughn asking, "We calling it a night?"

I glance around at everyone, Vin's nodding, while Vance voices his agreement.

"You guys don't have to leave, I'll go with the driver...you guys stay," I tell them.

"You're not going by yourself, are you crazy?" Vance is looking at me like I've lost my mind. I shrug, "Wasn't sure if you guys would want to cut your night short just because my car took a crap."

He laughs and looks around at the group. "Is she serious?"

"Stop being a dick, Vance." Taylor puts her hands on her hips.

"I have no problems heading out early," Chase cuts in.

"Yeah, we all got some runs in. We can hit up the Field

after we drop the car off at the garage," Vaughn volunteers.

"I'm gonna skip the Field tonight," Vin cuts in.

"What else you gonna do?" Vaughn elbows him.

"I'm gonna hit up Sliders," Vin answers while his fingers move around on his phone.

"Damn, you been goin' there a lot lately. What girl got her hooks in you now?" Vance hollers to him because Vin has started walking towards his car. Vin turns around, walking backward while answering, "Ain't no girls there buddy--women. Lots of women. You have fun hanging with the little girls at the Field. I'll be surrounded by women."

"Damn," Vaughn whispers, "I can't wait until I'm twenty-one."

I slap Vaughn in the head. "Shut up, you perv."

"What?" Vaughn rubs the spot I just smacked him, "Why'd you hit me?" I roll my eyes and start walking towards my car at the back of the lot. Chase jogs up next to me, as everyone else hops in their car.

"Whatcha doin?" I ask him.

"Accompanying you."

"You don't have to do that," I tell him.

"I know I don't have to, I want to."

Well. That is nice. *Really* nice. I can't keep my smile from spreading. It's so big and taking over my whole face, it almost hurts. "Thank you," I whisper. He returns the smile, but he is incredible. *Breathtaking.* He leans into me. "No problem," he whispers back, placing his hands in his front pockets. He elbows me then winks as he moves away. Good lord! He needs to stop doing that! My steps pick up a bit, putting some space between Chase and myself.

Not far ahead, the tow truck driver has already parked in front of my car and is lowering the rollback. He crawls under the front of my car, hooking it to his truck, and he stands up wiping the dirt from his already dirty jeans. The tow truck driver cranks the gear, which is loud, but slowly pulls my car up onto the rollback, then leveling it. The driver goes about making sure the car is secure and jumps off the rollback, approaching us while putting a toothpick in his mouth. "Where we headed?" He looks at Chase for an answer.

"A town over, about thirty minutes. We're going to Victor's Auto, on Fifth street. We're going that way, so you can follow us there." The driver walks back to his truck and hops in.

"You still up for driving?" Chase asks me.

"For real?" I turn to face him. Walking backward, he nods.

"Hell yeah!" I shout. He pulls out his keys and tosses them to me. I take off before I lose the chance to drive his car again. I can hear him laughing behind me. Everyone's already in their cars, waiting for us. I jump into the Z before anyone can say anything and start her up. It rumbles as she comes to life. I am so giddy I'm shaking. Chase falls into the passenger seat, his presence completely overwhelming me. My giddiness has now turned into nervousness. I hope I don't make an ass out of myself. I put the car into reverse and pray I don't stall his car. What the hell are we going to talk about for the next thirty minutes?

TAKE A PICTURE
Chase

Okay, I lied. Watching Veronica race is the second-best thing I've ever seen. The first? Watching her drive *my* car. She's sexy doing just about everything, but there's something primal about her being behind the wheel of my car. The radio is on...but it's low, like background noise. I watch her drive the car with ease--like driving is second nature to her, and I guess in a way, it is. I'm comfortable just sitting here, watching her, but it's clear she's not when she speaks.

"Take a picture, it'll last longer," she quips, her eyes flashing to me, then back to the road. Good idea. I whip out my phone and quickly snap a picture.

"Seriously? I was joking, you better delete that."

"No way. This moment is one to remember. I may just hire you to be my chauffeur." I watch her mouth as a smile plays on it. Those lips. I want to taste them so badly. I bet they're like little puffy pillows; soft and inviting. I clear my throat and look out the window. I need to think of something else before I have a noticeable tent in my jeans.

"Is it good to be home?" she asks quietly. I drum my fingers on my pants, taking in her question. I inhale deeply, then slowly release it. "Yes, it's good to be home. Sleeping in my bed, and not a cot. It's an adjustment, for sure, but knowing that I won't be shot at while walking around is relieving." I hear her breath hike.

"You were shot at?" her eyes are big.

"Well yeah, there's a war going on V," I tell her gently.

"I mean, I know, but I just didn't realize."

"I wasn't out in the field much, I'm a tech. We still train for battle, but it doesn't compare to actually being shot at."

"Jeez. Do you have to go back?"

"Yes, eventually. I don't know if they'll call me back, or when. It could be a year or a month."

"A month? Seriously? You just got back."

I shrug, even though she can't really see me. "It's how it works." She's gone quiet, chewing her bottom lip, brows furrowed showing her worry. That pulls at my heart. I like that she's worried about me, but I don't want to be that burden on her. I lean over the console, reach out, and pull her bottom lip from her mouth. My hand lingers there, then slowly moves to her chin and down her neck. Her eyes widen. I've startled her, or she's having some kind of reaction to my touch. By the way her breathing has become rapid, that seems like the most plausible possibility. I like that. I reluctantly move my hand to the center console, but I don't move away. I need to change the conversation to something a little lighter.

"How's your senior year going? Do you have any college plans?" It's ame, but it's a safe topic. She clears her throat. "It's going," she says simply. "We plan on going to state."

"We?"

"Yeah, Taylor and I."

"Watch out now, the double trouble on the loose at State. Takin' names and breakin' hearts." I laugh.

She lightly backhands me on the shoulder. "We are

not trouble!"

"You and Taylor? Oh yes, you are! Walking, talking, double trouble!"

"Whatever." She shakes her head. "You're one to talk!"

"OOH! What does that mean?"

"You and Vance? Takin' names and breakin' hearts."

"That's all Vance," I say and look out the window.

"Uh-huh," she hums.

I decide, *'fuck it'*. I lean back in my seat, "You jealous?"

She quickly looks at me, then back at the road, "What?"

"You heard me, sounds like jealousy." I sigh and place my arms behind my head.

"Jealous of what? The," she takes her one hand off the wheel to air quote the next word, "'lucky' ladies that get to hook up with you? The same ones you guys don't have the decency to call back?"

"Ouch." I wince. "I don't care how you view your brother, but you really think that of me?"

She shrugs.

"Don't get me wrong, I like women." She makes a face. "What?"

"Nothing."

"Why did you make that face then?"

She sighs, then shifts gears. "You sound like such a womanizer."

"Just because I like women? It doesn't mean I've slept with as many as you may think. It's the same with your brother."

"TMI, dude."

"No, you went there, so we're goin' there. You like men, right?"

She glances at me and purses her lips.

"Yes?" I prompt.

"Yeah."

"Okay, so just because you like men, doesn't mean you're going to sleep with every one of them," She says nothing, "right?" Finally, she nods. "That's all I meant by it. I love women. But cut me some slack, I have some standards. When I'm really into someone, that's the only person I see. So whatever prejudice you have of me, forget it, because it's wrong."

"I'm sorry," she says quietly.

"It's important you know this."

"Why?"

"As I said, when I'm into someone, they're the only person I see."

She glances at me, the confusion written all over her face. "So you're into someone?" It's a question.

"Yes."

"Okayyy. Well then, I guess it's good that she's all you see, then."

"You have no idea," I say looking at her. She's completely oblivious as she turns into the parking lot of Victor's Garage. I have no idea what I'm doing here. For the first time, I'm way out of my league. The more time I spend around her, the more attracted I become. This shouldn't come as a surprise; she's absolutely amazing. The smart thing to do would be to keep my distance, but I don't know if I'm smart enough for that anymore. I have to be careful, Vance would kill me, but I'll deal with that when it comes. Veronica pulls into a spot near the front office of the garage, then she pulls the e-brake. She looks at me, giving me a weak smile. "Thanks for letting me drive."

"No problem. I told you I'd make it up to you." I return her smile. Vance pulls up next to us, and Veronica is out of my car without another word. I take a deep breath, get out, and walk around the back of my car. Wes and Vaughn pull up behind us but remain inside with the windows down. Vance says something to Veronica then jogs over to the tow truck driver, directing him where to put V's car. He unloads it and waves as he drives out of the lot. Veronica gets into the passenger side of Vance's car, and I'm a little bummed. I guess I just assumed we'd ride over to the Field together. Vance walks back to his car, and whirls his finger around. "Let's roll."

I glance at the passenger side, but the window is up, and I can't see through his tint. So I just get in my car and follow behind everyone to the Field, trying to think where things went wrong in my conversation with Veronica.

NOT INTO ME
Veronica

"What the hell was that?" Vance starts *immediately* grilling me as soon as we pull out of the garage's lot. I can't help but roll my eyes, "What the hell was what?"

"You and Chase, what the hell were you driving his car for?"

"He asked. I think he was trying to cheer me up with my car being down."

"He didn't try anything, did he?"

I look at him like he's the one who lost his mind now and laugh. He doesn't say anything, so I have to follow up, "You're serious?"

"Fuck yeah, I'm serious."

"No Vance, he didn't try anything."

"He better fucking not. I'll fucking kill him."

"Vance, he's your best friend. We've known him forever. I can tell you he thinks of me as a little sister. In fact, he told me he's into someone."

"He told you that? Who the fuck is he into? He cannot be serious about that chick he hooked up with."

Whoa. All that crap he was talking in the car makes sense now. He's seeing' this girl, and anything that may have come off as flirting was just the opposite. He was making it clear tonight that he's into her. Ugh. I *knew* he wasn't into me! How could he be! But why the hell did he touch me like that? That wasn't nothing. I'm getting some serious whiplash on Chase's words and actions.

"That dog." Vance's whole demeanor has changed now that he knows Chase wasn't trying to put the moves on me. He's visibly relaxed and drops the whole subject. He leans forward and turns up his music. The car becomes engulfed in some techno rap and I can barely hear myself think. This is going to suck. I don't want to see Chase with this girl. Dammit, I should've just told Vance to take me home. Maybe I can find a ride home with someone who's leaving early. I have to get up for work in the morning, anyway, and I need to get a start on finding out what the hell happened to my car. I wonder if I can get Vin to go in early. He shouldn't be out too late because he has to be up, too.

I pull out my phone and send him a text. He responds quickly, which surprises me. It's one word. 'Maybe'.

Ugh.

Vance slows as we come to the entrance, his car bouncing because of the dirt road until he finds a place to park. I open my door but don't get out right away. Vance slams his door, "Let's go V, I need to lock it." I stand up and close my door. It beeps, and I walk around, leaning against the back to wait for Taylor. Chase is lingering until Vance calls him over, where they wander off. Taylor's smile is taking over her whole face. I shake my head, and her smile falls. Taylor hangs behind with me, Wes looks back at her. She tells him, "I'm gonna girl talk with V, I'll be up there in a minute." He just nods, he and Vaughn keep walking.

"What happened?" she asks.

"We were so far off Tay," I tell her.

"What? Off about what?"

"He's not into me. After Vance had a fit, and I told him that Chase told me he's into someone, Vance filled in the pieces a bit."

"Explain."

"It was nice. We were just talking. I asked about his deployment, and he asked about my plans for school...he called us trouble." I smiled. Taylor put her hands on her hips, "Double Trouble." She throws me a wink. I laugh, "Yeah, that's what he said."

"Okay...so..." She waves her hand for me to continue.

"It somehow got a bit personal. I kind of called him a whore, and he just went off, saying he likes women, but it's not like he sleeps with a ton, though he can't speak for Vance." She makes a face. "I know. I did the same thing. Anyway, I felt like crap for judging him. He said when he's into someone, that's all he sees. He made that specific. I wasn't quite sure how to take it until Vance said he hooked up with this chick."

She looked taken aback, exactly how I felt. "What?"

"Yessss."

"Wait, so he came home, hooked up with some girl, and is now seeing her? I'm not buying it. I *see* the way he looks at you."

"Then why tell me all this? I mean he says he doesn't sleep around but did just that?" This is starting to piss me off. I groan. "Yanno what? It doesn't matter. Vance was PISSED that we even drove together. That whole conversation was scary. I can't even imagine how we'd manage to get away with dating. I don't know why I'd think otherwise. Let's go..." I grab her hand and pull her towards the open field.

A bunch of our classmates greet us as we make our way to our usual spot at the log near the fire. I have to force myself not to look around. Someone takes a seat next to me, wrapping their arm around my shoulder, I startle and look over at the person. "Jerry!" I yell as soon as I see my very good friend. I snake my arm around his waist and squeeze him.

"Hi, my love!" he says laughing. Seeing Jerry brightens my mood immediately. He is one of the most attractive and charismatic guys I've had the pleasure of knowing. It's a shame for the female population because he does not see us in the same way they see him.

"How are you, baby?" he asks.

"Better now." I wink at him.

"You little flirt." He laughs.

"Is it working?"

"Oh baby doll, if I were to try to be straight for any girl, it'd be you." I grab at my chest, above my heart, and I sigh loudly, "If dreams could come true!"

"Stoppp, you're going to make me blush."

"Hey, Jer!" Taylor leans over me.

"Hey Tay Tay, how you doin' love?"

"Just peachy," she throws back.

"How was the track?" He asks.

"Ugh! My car broke."

"No way!" Jerry shouts.

"Yes, way."

"Oh honey, I'm sorry. You want a drink?"

"Yes, Please!"

"K, I'll be right back!" He gets up and walks away.

"He is too hot for his own good," Taylor swoons.

"Right here," Wes says, staring at her.

She turns to him, "He's gay baby, it's okay." She kisses his cheek, then pushes his face away. Jerry returns juggling with three plastic cups. He hands one to Taylor, then one to me, and takes his seat next to me. I take a sip of my beer.

"Giirrrlll. That *fine* specimen over there is staring at you," he says in my ear, causing me to choke on the beer. I start coughing like crazy. Jerry is patting my back. "Oh my gosh! You okay?"

I continue hacking up a lung. "I'm good. Wrong tube." I pat my chest.

"V, It's Chase," Taylor whispers.

"I can't look," I tell them, finally getting the coughing under control.

"What is going on?" Jerry asks.

"Nothing." I give Tay a warning, then glance at Wes.

"He won't say anything. I'll make him promise." Tay whispers. She moves closer to us,

"They're hot for each other," Taylor offers. I smack her on the thigh.

"Ow!" She rubs her leg, "You hoe!"

"I'd say! Damn, the way he's watching you."

"How is he watching me?" I question, looking between them.

"With the way he's glaring at me...I don't think he knows. That's *jealousy*," He pauses, "Should I be scared?" Jerry's panic makes me laugh.

"No worries, honey. I will protect you," I tell him. Jerry grabs my thigh, "Good, I can't have him messing up my face. It's too pretty." We're all laughing hard and only when the heat from the fire disappears, my eyes flash open. Chase is hovering over us, forcing me to crane my neck up. His eyes are hard and his arms are crossed over his chest. The laughter dies on my lips.

"Hey Chase," Taylor says. "What brings you this way?" she asks sweetly.

"I don't think we've met." He ignores Taylor, lowering into a crouch in front of us. Jerry grips my thigh tighter, and I place my hand on his. Chase doesn't miss it, his eyes move from Jerry's face to his hand, then glances at me before looking back at Jerry. The hand on my thigh disappears instantly, "Hey, we haven't met, that is. I'm Jerry."

"Chase," his response is simple; to the point. He looks at me, and then back at Jerry again. This is weird.

"Well girlies, it was fun catching up. I see a hottie over there, and my gaydar is going off." He points to the complete opposite side. I smile, "Go get em' tiger."

"Oh, I will honey." He winks at me and looks at Tay. "Bye love." Then whispers to Chase, "Nice to meet you, handsome." Chase coughs and clears his throat. "Yeah, you too."

We all watch as Jerry struts off. Chase takes Jerry's place next to me, resting his arms on his knees.

"He seems...nice."

"Jerry? Yeah, he's great," I say back. He tips my cup and looks into it. "Brave girl. Your brother's right over there." He nods across the way. I look up, but Vance is too consumed with some girl. A blonde within their group glances our way, crosses her arms, and takes a sip from her cup. She looks back at some guy, and laughs, but focuses her eyes back at us again. I wonder if this girl is who he's seeing. I silently shake my thoughts away. "Yeah, I don't think he cares. His attention is elsewhere."

Chase laughs, "I guess you're right."

I take a sip. "I think that girl wants your attention," I bump my shoulder with his. He catches a glimpse of the blonde, and she smiles wide at his attention. He sighs loudly; clearly annoyed, which confuses the heck out of me. Vance has finally noticed that Chase is missing, he's looking around the area but doesn't look this way. He says something to the female companion, who then points our way. I quickly hide my cup, hoping he doesn't see. He squints, his jaw clenches, then waves Chase over.

"You're being summoned."

"I can see." He sighs, "I better go see what he wants."

"Yeah, you better," I tell him.

"Have a good night girls," he grunts, and then he's gone.

"Giiiirrrllllll," Taylor drags out, "I think the only girl he's into is *you*."

I looked at her baffled; silent.

"He was about to beat up Jerry!"

"He was not!" I dismiss Chase's odd behavior. "I'm sure he was protecting me like my brothers would."

She shakes her head violently, "Nope, not buying it."

"Well," I clap my hands together,"you don't have to. He has a hot little number over there." I nod to where Chase is standing next to my brother, the blonde now on his right pawing at him. I look away. I feel a little pang in my heart, and I berate myself. *This is so stupid.* "He clearly could care less. He's barely acknowledging her," Taylor battles. I know I shouldn't, but I can't help but look. He's put some distance between him and the blonde.

"I need to go for a walk, this is driving me crazy."

"Want me to come with you?" she yells as I start walking away.

I just wave my hand at her, and walk towards the isolated area of the lake--away from the noise--away from everyone and, mostly, away from Chase.

I'LL BREAK YOUR FACE
Chase

"Dude. What the hell were you doing over there?" Vance grills me as I make my way to him. I shrug. "I saw some dude hitting on V. You were too busy with Brittany to notice."

"Jerry? He's gay." Vance laughs.

"Yeah, well, I didn't know that! I never met the dude." He thinks my argument is hilarious.

"I saw him," He pauses and looks at me, "You sure that's all it was? You into my sister?" He asks, the laughter gone. His mouth is in a tight line. It completely takes me off guard. I'm stunned and silent as he stares me down. Finally, I scoff and laugh nervously. "What? No!"

He bursts out laughing. "I'm fucking with you dude, you should've seen your face!" He smacks my shoulder and continues talking to me, "V, told me you're into someone." He nods his head to my right, I don't have time to process what Vance just said when I suddenly felt hands on my arm. I look at the delicate fingers with pink nail polish wrapping around my arm, and into blue eyes, "Hey, Chase."

Great.

"Hey, Shannon."

"You never called," she pouts, and it makes her look stupid. I cross my arms over my chest, which causes her to remove her hand from my arm. "I'm sorry, I've been busy." I know. I sound like a jerk; something Veronica called me out on earlier. I guess I *am* a jerk.

"You're not busy now," she points out. "But we can change that." I keep myself from sighing out loud. It's crazy how your feelings about someone can change and grow so rapidly, that the thought of doing anything with another girl disgusts me. This can't be normal. I need to somehow get her off my back, and not make it so obvious to Vance. He won't leave this alone.

"I need a drink. You want a drink?" I ask her in my lame attempt to get away.

She smiles. "Sure."

I turn away from her quickly and walk towards the keg, which passes the firepit where V is sitting... or was supposed to be sitting. I couldn't stop myself from looking around for her. *Where the hell did she go?* I grab a cup and fill it, chug it, and fill it up again. Taylor comes up next to me, doesn't say anything...just fills up her cup. She looks at me, a sneaky smile on her face.

"What?" I ask her.

She shakes her head. "Nothing."

"Why are you smiling at me like that?"

She takes a sip from her cup, then lowers it. "You break her heart, and I'll break your face."

"What the hell are you talking about?"

"V," She points at my chest. "I'm not blind. I see how you look at her."

Shit. *Fuck*. I remain quiet and look beyond her. She takes my silence as an invitation to continue on.

"You *like* her. It's painfully obvious...to me anyway, I'm just awesome like that. You need to stop fucking around with other girls," She nods her head to the area behind me. "V has the biggest heart of anyone I know. It's fragile and it needs to be treated with gentle hands.

So, like I said, you break it, I break your face."

I look at Taylor. "I know this, and that's the last thing I would ever want to do." It's the truth.

"I know, cause you would have a shit storm on your ass--not from just me but-- from her brothers."

"Plus, I like my face."

She laughs, "Yeah, it's not a bad face." I glance at the empty log.

"She's down by the lake." She turns and walks away leaving me standing at the keg. I don't even think twice, I leave the keg and head towards the lake.

MCSWOONY
Veronica

I walk along the pebbled edge of the lake; away from all the noise and commotion, though it could still be heard. I stop and pick up a flat rock and flip it around in my hand before throwing it sideways. I can barely see it as it skips out. I take a deep breath. A slight fishy scent lingers; it's nothing too intense, but somewhat relaxing. The yelling, music, and talking all behind me fades away. It is peaceful out here.

I find a large rock--large enough to sit on--and sit down. I hear footsteps behind me, along with the sound of crunching sand and rocks. I glance over my shoulder to see who is walking my way. His broad shoulders block out the fire, darkening his features, and create an orange glow around his body. I know it's Chase. *What the hell is he doing?*

"What are you doing?" I ask when he gets closer.

"What are *you* doing?" he shoots back. I look out at the calm dark water. Neither of us say anything but I can feel his eyes on me.

"You hungry?"

I look at him, incredulously, "What?"

"You hungry? I'm hungry. Wanna go grab some food?"

"What about my brothers? And your girlfriend?"

He kicks his foot around the little pebbles, his hands in his front pockets, "Vance is occupied, and actually, I haven't seen Vaughn at all," He looks at me, his eyebrows furrowed, "I don't have a girlfriend." We were silent again as I pondered his invitation to go get food.

"I don't know."

"C'mon. It's just food, and I'll drop you off right after."

"Okay...Can we not tell Vance?" I ask standing up, dusting the dirt off my butt. Even standing I have to look up at him. He grimaces.

"I don't know if that's a smart idea."

"And telling him we're leaving to grab food is?"

He sighs, "I feel like if he finds out we lied to him, then we're hiding something from him." He makes a good point because we're not hiding anything.

"We're not lying..."

"Lying by omission is pretty much the same thing, especially to Vance."

I sigh, "I know, I just don't need him giving me shit. He won't be home until late if he even comes home. So if I'm home before him, which, I most likely will be, he'll never even know."

"Okay," He relents, "I'll let him know I'm leaving."

I nod. "Okay. I'll let Taylor know." He turns to walk, but I remain where I am. He must realize that I didn't move because he pauses and turns towards me. "You comin?" I look at him for a second, taking him all in. He just stares at me, waiting for my response. I have no idea what I'm getting into, but I remind myself it's just some food with a friend. "Yeah."

He doesn't move until I'm next to him, and we both make our way back to the group. We split off, him going over to Vance, and me heading to Taylor. She wags her eyebrows at me as I approach her, and I take the seat next to her. "What kinda trouble you two getting into down there?"

I laugh. "Nothing. I'm gonna head out."

"And how are you getting home?" she asks with a smirk.

"Chase."

"Ooh la la," she sings.

"You're crazy." I laugh. I don't know why I'm not spilling that he's not just taking me home..that we're also going to grab some food. I don't need her to make something out of nothing. Right? Because it is nothing. I look up to see Chase and Vance smacking hands. Shannon is at his side and their gestures suggest Chase is telling Vance he's heading out. I watch as she says something to him, grabbing his arm. He says something and I watch her smile drop, her confidence deflate, and she watches as he walks away.

"I'll text you tomorrow," I tell Taylor and make my way to Chase, who's now reaching the dirt road that connects to the Field.

"You better!" I hear her yell back. I take my phone out and text Vance, telling him I'm hitching a ride with Chase, explaining that I want to get an early start on my car in the morning. I jog up to Chase.

"Ready?" he asks as I come up next to him.

"Yep." We walk in the dark, the sounds of the nightlife surrounding us. I don't quite remember where we all parked, until the headlights of his car flash and light up the road, making it a little easier to navigate. My nerves begin to get the best of me as I pull open his passenger door and slide onto the cool leather seats. We both buckle up, and I place my shaky hands between my thighs. I arrived thinking nothing would happen between us, and I'm leaving with conflicting thoughts.

"Cold? He asks, reaching towards his dash, turning on the heat. I smile weakly. I didn't even notice my arms covered in goosebumps-- I'm too wrapped up in my thoughts. "Thanks." The little bit of heat pumps from the vents help.

"Where to?"

"Hmm?" I hum looking out the window, watching him maneuver the car.

"It's been a while, what's open? Is Chrissy's Diner still open all night?"

"Yep."

"Perfect."

He exits the dirt road, pulling onto the main paved street. What are we doing? What am *I* doing? I want this...but am I setting myself up for disappointment? My mind is so occupied with my thoughts that I must miss what Chase has said because he nudges me, pulling me from said thoughts. "What?" I ask turning towards him. His handsome face is illuminated by his dash. He laughs, quickly glancing at me and then back at the road. "You're eerily quiet over there, what are you thinking about?"

I'm not about to tell him what I was really thinking about. "Soup or Pie?" I blurt out.

"What?"

"What to order...soup or pie."

"Do they still serve the best shoofly pie?"

"Uh...Yeah!"

"Damn, I've missed Chrissy's shoofly pie!"

"Oh, man. I don't think I could go a year without her pies." Because Chrissy makes the best pie I've ever had, but you'll never hear me say that in front of my mom, even if they go way back.

I see him shrug. "'Ts not like I could get pies in care packages."

"Yeah, I guess not. Oh! Her French onion soup is killer!" I tell him.

"Hmm, that sounds good too."

"See my dilemma?" I ask smiling at our stupid conversation, the nerves easing away.

"Yeah, first world problems," he jokes.

"Yeah, Yeah."

"We'll order both," he says simply.

"Hmm...yeah, that sounds perfect!" The diner isn't far from town, so it's not long until Chase pulls into the parking lot of Chrissy's.

"Wow, it looks so different!" he says looking out the windshield at the remodeled diner.

"Yeah, it was closed for a couple of weeks and redone..as you can see. Neat, right?" Chrissy's looks like an old fashion diner straight out of the fifties. It's shiny, with mirror-like siding. The name, 'Chrissy's Diner', is brightly displayed in red fluorescent lights high above the front doors.

"Yeah, wow."

"Let's go! Maybe Chrissy is still here!" I say and jump out of the car, closing the door, and rounding the front. Chase follows behind me as we walk up the steps and into the foyer of the diner, then opening the next set of doors. A young girl is at the register, and looks up at us, a wide smile forming. "Hey guys, how many?"

"Just two," Chase says from behind me. She grabs two menus and comes out from behind the counter. "Okay, follow me please." We follow her as she leads us past the pie and dessert case. I can't help but take a peek at the yummy goodness inside. She then stops in front of a small booth, placing the menus on the table. "Your waitress will be right with you. Enjoy!" she says and leaves us.

We both slide into the booth across from each other and don't bother looking at the menu because we already know what we're getting. I look around the diner and take in the late-night customers spread out. The waitress comes to our table and says, "Look at you two. You guys are the cutest couple I've ever set my eyes on."

I look up at the waitress, totally dumbfounded, and I hear Chase laughing which causes me to look at him. I know my eyes are bugging out of my sockets. He tells the waitress, "Thanks."

"No problem, doll. What can I get you cutie pies to drink?" Chase nods at me, referring me to go first. "Uh, a Coke is fine."

"Sure thing, sweetheart, and for you?" She looks to Chase, and I take in her features. Her blonde hair is proofed out and built up with lots of hair spray. It reminds me of a picture I once saw of my mom before I was born. If I had to guess her age, I'd say somewhere in her late forties, early fifties. She's pretty even with the crow's feet that crinkle when she smiles. It just tells me she's smiled a lot in her lifetime. It's a pretty smile, a mouth that showcases her perfect white teeth. She's wearing a cute pink top with her name sewed above her breast, something you'd see in a fifties diner. Beverly. She looks like a Beverly. I've always wondered if my name fits me. Do I look like a Veronica? A black modest skirt with an apron tied around her wide hips completes her uniform. It's been a while since I've been to Chrissy's. Beverly is someone I don't recognize, so she must be fairly new.

"I'll be right back with your drinks," she says and twirls on her feet towards the kitchen.

I look at Chase. "She thought we were a couple!"

He smiles wide, forcing me to look at his mouth, but I quickly avert my eyes. "Yeah, I was here."

"We're not a couple," I point out, stupidly.

"That, I'm also aware of."

"Why would she think we're a couple?" I ask, again, stupidly.

"I don't know. Maybe because we're a guy and a girl, out late, together?"

"Yeah, maybe."

"But we are the cutest couple she's ever set her eyes on," He says, making his voice high and feminine like hers. It makes me laugh. Beverly is back with our drinks, placing them in front of us, and taking her pad out of her apron. "Are you two love birds ready to order?" she asks.

"Two French onion soups, please," Chase simply tells her.

"Oh my goodness, you two are too much! Sure thing!" She writes down our order. "Is that all?" I cover my mouth to stifle my laughter.

"Yes, Ma'am." Chase scoops our menus up, handing them to her, his beautiful smile on full display. She takes them from him and starts fanning herself with them. "Oh sugar, I can see why she likes you. Whoo Honey, that smile would swoon any lady, especially this old lady."

Chase laughs. "You can't be a day over thirty."

"Oh, I need to walk away. You're trouble." She points at Chase and laughs. "Let me go put in your order."

She walks away, and I give Chase an incredulous look. "Oh my gosh!" I whisper-shout at him. She's halfway to the kitchen when we hear her shout, "Chrissy, we have a young 'McSwoony' out here!" I look at Chase, but I see some commotion towards the end of the bar. Chrissy comes from the swinging door connecting to the kitchen. She speaks to Beverly, looks our way, and her face breaks into a huge smile. Chrissy is all country Dutch-- her family goes back generations in this town. Chrissy is also blonde, but bottled-blonde, as her roots are a bit darker than the rest. The front of her hair is teased, somewhat like Beverly's, but the rest is pulled back into a low pony. She has a square-shaped face, with big blue eyes, and a sprinkle of freckles on the bridge of her slender nose. My mother and Chrissy grew up together, graduated together, and have remained friends throughout the years. Therefore, she's been around my whole childhood and Chase's.

"Well what do we have here?" she asks as she approaches our booth. I slide out and go into her open arms.

"Hey, Chrissy."

"Hello, my beautiful girl." She squeezes me. "And who do we have here?" She releases me from her embrace and looks at Chase. "Well, I'll be! Chase Daniels!" Chase slips out of the booth while I slide back into my side of the booth and watch them.

"Hi Chrissy!" he says while returning her hug. He moves back, but she grabs his face. "It's sure good to see you back boy!"

"Thank you, ma'am."

"Oh please! Don't ma'am me!" she spits out releasing his face, and he sits back down chuckling. "I didn't know you were back!"

"Yeah, just got back last week."

She smiles wide, pure pride. "This meal is on me.

Don't you dare think of paying for it!"

Chase starts to say something, but she cuts him off, "No. It's the least I can do for a soldier fighting for our country." She looks at me, "How's your mama baby doll?" Clearly ending that.

"She's good."

Beverly is walking our way with two steaming bowls. Yummy, gooey cheese drips onto the plate they're sitting on. Chrissy moves out of her way, so she can set them down, "They're hot, be careful," Beverly warns us.

"Bev, this is Vivian's daughter, Veronica!" Chrissy says to her, "And this fine young man is Chase. Lacey and Richard Daniels' son. He just returned from the service. Their check is on me!"

"Oh my goodness! Look at you!" She says to me, but I don't recall ever meeting her, other than just tonight. "You were a little thing the last time I saw you, I just moved back. Your mama, Chrissy, and I were the three amigos back in the day."

"Ohh boy!" I say. I'm sure they wreaked havoc.

She swats her hand. "We were perfectly behaved young ladies!"

"I'm sure."

They both laugh. "Alright, we'll let you eat in some peace," Chrissy says, "Make sure you two come see me before you leave!"

"Will do," Chase tells her. I dig my spoon into the melted cheesy goodness, the steam rising, and I blow on the food. Chase is groaning across from me, "This"—he points at his bowl—"is so good!"

"I told you!" I say to him and take another bite. SO. GOOD! We're both silent as we enjoy our soup.

"Man, it feels so good to be here," Chase says.

"Home?" I ask and take another bite.

"Yeah, home. Here, at Chrissy's. Somewhere familiar."

"You're brave," I tell him. He is. He is the bravest person I know. He smirks. "Thank you."

"You're welcome." We both finish up our soups and push the bowls to the end of the table. "You have room for some pie?" he asks.

"Hell yeah...but not a whole slice, maybe we can share?" I suggest.

"Sure."

Beverly comes over and takes the empty bowls, "You two thinkin' about having some dessert?"

"Yeah, a slice of shoofly!" Chase tells her.

"Sure thing, honey!"

She walks away.

"You may have a cougar on your hands," I tell him. He bursts out laughing which in turn makes me laugh. "Oh man, V. You are too much!"

"What's so funny?"

"A cougar? Seriously?"

"Yeah. I hear some young guys are into that type of thing...and she's a pretty older lady."

"Yeah, maybe some, but definitely not this guy. "

"Poor Beverly. Don't break her heart 'McSwoony'," I emphasize on her nickname for him. He sighs dramatically. "Don't even! 'McSwoony'? What the hell?"

I laugh, "What? I think it's fitting. Swooning one woman at a time," I say it like a newspaper article headline.

"Oh jeez. I do not swoon anyone."

I arch my eyebrows as I take a sip of my soda. Chase's

eyes quickly glance at my mouth, then, just as quickly, his eyes shift away. His posture becomes stiff as he adjusts himself. I use my straw to swish around my soda, "Soooo 'McSwoony.'" I can't stop the smile from forming, and I hear him groan.

"You're not going to let that drop, are you?"

"Hell no!"

"Greeaattt!"

Beverly places the overly large slice of molasses goodness in between us including new forks. She winks at me and returns to the kitchen. We both grab a fork. "Go ahead," he says to me. "No, No. You haven't had her pie in a year, you can have the first bite." He smiles and forks a big piece, and I watch him as he puts it in his mouth. His eyes close, and he moans. Well, I felt all the way down to my core. Holy...mother Mary.

"It's better than I remember."

"You totally had a foodgasm," I tell him.

He chuckles. "Yeah, I guess I did." He gestures to me to take a piece, so I do. We continue to go back and forth until the slice is completely gone. I finish my soda and rub my belly as I lean back in the booth. "I'm about to fall into a food coma."

"Well we can't have that, let's get you home."

"Thank you for taking me for food. I had a good time just hanging with you." It was simple, fun, and seemed so natural. We've never hung out like this before, it's always been with my brothers; never deliberately alone together. I really enjoyed myself, and I can't help but want to do this again. He throws a twenty down on the table. "Me too. We'll have to do it again." He says to me as we both slide out from the booth.

"Really?" I ask, surprised.

"Yeah, really. You're fun to be around. I haven't laughed like that in a long time," he says casually, and I remind myself, that's all it really can be.

"You need to get out more," I tell him joking as we walk toward the front.

"What are your plans for tomorrow?" he asks, and it surprises me again.

"Um. I work. I need to find out what exactly is wrong with my car and get it fixed. I need it to get to school, otherwise, I gotta bum a ride with Tay." Beverly clocks us. "Oh sweet thangs, you headin' out?"

"Yep." I turn to her. She moves to the swinging door, opening it a bit, and yells for Chrissy. A couple of seconds later Chrissy comes out of the back, heading to us as soon as she sees us standing there. She gives each of us a big hug. "I sure hope to see you both again soon!"

"Of course!" I tell her.

"Tell both your mamas I said hello!"

"Will do!" I tell her.

We both move to the door, but Chase opens it for me, letting me walk through and opening the next door for me as well. Such a gentleman. We get into his car, and he drives to my house.

"Oh hey, did Vance tell you about this weekend?" he asks.

I look at him. "Ermmm. No."

"Figured as much. I'll talk to him tomorrow. I invited you all out on the boat."

"Oh, nice!" I've only been on Chase's boat a couple of times. I was rarely invited; I guess having the little sister tag along wasn't always fun for them. I'm not sure I wanted to be on the boat with them anyways, especially if they brought their girlfriends. Chase's parents are wealthy, and their house is enormous. My thoughts wander to his parents because it's obviously not his boat we're going to be using.

"Your parents don't mind you just taking it out?" I ask

"No, but it's not like they're home to say anything about it. My father taught me everything about boating and driving a boat when I was twelve. I got my boating license when I was sixteen."

"Oh wow. Twelve?"

"Yeah. It's not that hard. It was a good bonding time with my father. He was actually a good teacher."

"Have you heard from them?" I ask hesitantly.

He sighs. "No."

I'm not quite sure what to say. I feel bad because...that's horrible. My parents have always been actively into our lives, all five of us, and Chase is an only child.

"I'm sorry," I say.

"It's fine."

"It's really not. I'm sorry, I can't make up for them, but I'm glad you're home!" I tell him. "Believe me, that means more than anything they'd say." I smile because his response brings me warm fuzzies. But I know I need to change the subject to something lighter.

"Can I drive the boat?" I ask, expecting him to tell me 'no way'.

"Sure"

"Really?" I turn towards him, totally excited at the thought of learning to drive a boat.

"Yeah." He shrugs like driving a boat that costs-- I don't even know how much boats cost, but I'm sure they're more than your average car--is no big deal.

"So cool!" I do a little dance in my seat, excited. I'm going to learn to drive a boat! He laughs, and his beautiful smile is on display. I like that I'm the reason behind it. He turns into my driveway, putting his car in neutral, and lets the car coast to the front of my house. It's completely dark and none of my brothers' cars are in the driveway, so I know I'm good. I pull my keys out of my bag and without really thinking much about it, I lean over the console to hug Chase. It's something I would do with any of my friends. I know I surprised him; it was more of me hugging his side until he turns...and then our chests are pressed together. I squeeze him, and he returns the squeeze. "Thank you. I had fun!"

"Anytime. I did too."

I loosen my hold, but his arm remains tight around me, then he moves back. I like it.

"See you tomorrow?" I ask.

"Yeah. I'll be around." I smile at him before getting out of the car and bounce to my front door. Chase remains out front until I'm safely inside, closing the door behind me. I rush to the front window and watch as his car maneuvers quietly down the driveway. I'm high on happiness, my smile remaining plastered to my face as I get ready for bed. I crawl under the covers and stare at the ceiling, the night replaying in my head until sleep overcomes me.

FLYING STAPLER
Chase

I wake up in a really good mood but, then again, I went to bed that way. Veronica is the first thing that comes into my mind, and I can't wait to see her again. Hanging out with her was so refreshing; it was fun, and it seemed so natural. All I know is I want to try and spend as much time with her as I can. I want to get to know everything about her. I know without a doubt that I want another night out with her. I just have to figure out how to make it happen. I throw my covers off and sit up, rubbing my eyes with the palm of my hands. I glance at the clock. Damn, I slept in. It felt amazing.

Excited to start my day, for once, I hurry in showering and getting ready. I want to drive right over to the garage, but I don't want to seem too eager. Grabbing my things off my dresser, I head downstairs to make some breakfast. Eight minutes later, I'm carrying my plate of three eggs and toast in one hand, and a glass of orange juice in the other to the dining room. The room is pretentious, to say the least. The walls are a deep red and the massive cherry wood table is placed directly under a huge crystal chandelier hanging above. It's so quiet I can hear the grandfather clock ticking from my father's study two rooms over. I devour my breakfast, knowing I need to get out of the house. The silence getting under my skin. I leave the room and place my plate in the sink before I beeline for the door.

I stop to fill up my car before going to the garage, so by the time I arrive, it's almost noon. The garage closes in two hours. I have no plans for tonight, and Vance hasn't mentioned anything else. All the bay doors are open, a car in each, but I notice V's car is still parked off to the side. I wonder if they were able to look at it yet. I park my car closest to the office door and stroll inside. The bell above the door announces my arrival, but there's no one in the room. I can vaguely hear that the radio is on; it's low. It's then that V comes bouncing from around the corner. She's wearing a Victor's Auto T-shirt, some tight black leggings, and her hair pulled up into a ponytail. She looks...perfect. Her eyes widen in surprise but quickly masks it, her lips breaking into a smile. "'McSwoony!'" she yells.

"Seriously?" I deadpan.

"Oh yeah. Sorry, it's not going away."

I laugh. I don't care.

"I looked the reference up this morning."

"And..."

She sits in the chair and pulls herself towards the desk. I grab a chair from the makeshift waiting area and pull it so it's right across from her, and lean forward, resting my arms on my knees. "There's a bunch of stuff on twitter, which leads to a guy named Derek, who happens to be on a TV show," she says this in one breath. "But they call him McDreamy. So I don't understand where 'McSwoony' comes in. I was curious, so I typed in McDreamy and google delivered! There's apparently a McSteamy too, he's a hot older guy. Total DILF."

"Alright, then."

She laughs, "Chrissy and Beverly are obviously fans of the show. I may have to check it out. Hot doctors..."

she trails off, looking up and nodding. "Oh yeahhh."

"Guess it hasn't been too busy this morning, huh?"

"Not too bad." She shrugs.

"Did Vin look at your car?" She rolls her eyes and sighs, "No, he promised he'd look after our last appointment. I wanted to be able to order any parts I needed this morning so they could be here Wednesday. His stupid ass didn't get here until five after eight."

I shake my head, a small laugh comes out. "Are you surprised?"

"I texted him last night. He knew I wanted to get a jump start on it...asshole. Where's Vance?" Huh. I didn't even bother to text him. "I actually don't know," I pull my phone from my pocket, "Did he come home last night?" I ask while shooting him a text.

I look up and catch an odd look upon V's face, but she looks towards her computer screen and starts typing. "Yeah, his car was in the driveway. I didn't hear him come home though, so I have no idea what time."

"So wait, how did you get here?"

"Borrowed Mom's car."

The door opens to the garage, and Mark waltzes through. He looks at me then at Veronica. "Hey sweetheart, you wanna call Mrs. Schultz and let her know her car is ready?"

"Sure." V turns and picks up the phone that's located on the other side of the computer, her back now facing Mark. Mark calling Veronica sweetheart bothers me, I know it shouldn't because it's coming from Mark. He gives pet names to every woman. But that's his boss' daughter, and he's much older than her. He's staring at me, trying to place me, I don't think he realizes who I am. It's been a while since he's seen me, but I haven't changed that much. I don't try to move or introduce myself.

"Who're you?" he barks. Veronica has the phone to her ear and looks over her shoulder at him. It's obvious he doesn't like me being here. I'm about to stand up and introduce myself; well, *reintroduce* myself, when Vin comes through and hits Mark with the door, pushing him forward.

"What the hell dude?" Mark turns to Vin.

"You're standing in front of the door asshole," Vin responds, then notices me sitting here.

"Chase! What's up!" Mark leaves the office, not caring who I am. He became an even bigger dick since I left.

"Nothing man, I told V I'd help out with her car." I see her chair turn my way in my peripheral vision because I never said it.

Vin cringes, and whispers, "Yeah, she's pretty pissed at me."

"Yeah, she is." Veronica's voice pipes up. We both look her way, she's off the phone now, her arms are crossed above the desk, and a cocky grin on her face.

"I'm almost done with this car, and I'll pull in your car right after."

She nods, the cocky grin still upon her face.

Vin looks at me. "Women."

It makes me chuckle, and V's eyes narrow at us.

"Where's Vance, is he coming to help?" Vin asks.

"I just texted him," I pull out my phone, with all the commotion I forgot to see if he responded. "He says he'll be here in an hour."

Veronica throws her hands up. "This is awesome. You guys are so helpful!" her tone drips with sarcasm.

"Shut it, we'll figure it out," Vin retorts.

"I wanted to have parts ordered already!" she complains.

"We'll go to the junkyard tomorrow morning," he compromises.

"And what if they don't have any RSX's?"

"Jeez V, call em."

She huffs and starts tapping on the computer before picking up the phone. "I'm gonna go finish this car, so I can get started on hers," Vin says pointing his thumb at Veronica. "Soon her head will be spinning, and she'll be spewing green shit out of her mouth like the Exorcist girl."

V throws her middle finger up making me laugh.

"You gonna wait around?" Vin asks me.

"Yeah, might as well." I shrug.

"Okay," He nods and then leans in. "Be careful, maybe you should go get a cross." he says low and moves back. Something black whizzes by our faces then clatter loudly to the floor.

"What the fuck?" Vin whispers, eyes wide. A stapler lays in pieces near the front door.

Holy shit! She threw a fucking stapler at our heads! "See!? She's fucking crazy." Vin backs up and runs out the door connecting to the garage. Veronica hangs up the phone. "I'm sorry. I wasn't aiming for you," she tells me.

"Well, I fucking hope not but that was inches from my face!"

"You would've survived. I'd nurse you to health out of pure guilt."

I liked that. It brought thoughts of Veronica, of the dirty genre, in a short nurse's outfit. "Would you wear the naughty nurse's outfit too?"

She laughs, and it's beautiful. "Would that help?" She purses her lips, and a black eyebrow arches upward. I nod, "Definitely." I walk to the door and pick up the stapler, snapping it back together easily. So, it's not technically broken. Impressive stapler. I walk back to the desk, stretch my arm out to her, putting the stapler in her face.

"Here, let's try it."

She smiles wide, grabbing the stapler from my hand. She shakes her head and puts the stapler down on the desk. She sighs before telling me, "They have a couple."

My thoughts are still on her in the nurse's uniform, "What?"

"At Harry's, they have a couple RSX's, but there's not much left of them."

She's pretty bummed, and this upsets me. "No worries. It'll work out, you'll see." I give her a reassuring half-smile.

"I hope so." She sighs. The front door opens, and Vance bursts through. I glance at the clock thinking 'shit an hour went by that fast?', but it was only about forty minutes. He pulls his sunglasses up and places them on top of his head. We can all see he just woke up.

"Good morning, Sleeping Beauty," Veronica says to her brother. He grunts. Then looks at me, "What the fuck you doing here so early?"

I shrug. "I thought you'd be here already."

"Why didn't you just stop by the house?" he questions. It didn't even occur to me. Veronica was the only thing on my mind, and I knew where she was.

"Did you not just hear what I said? You sure you're awake?"

"Shut up." He walks past us and into the little lunchroom behind V's desk. I look at her, and she's laughing. "He's never been a morning person."

"It's almost one," I point out, and she shrugs. I get up and walk into the break room. Vance is making himself a cup of coffee. I lean against the doorframe and cross my arms.

"What's your deal?" I ask him. He's pouring cream into his cup, and grunts. "Nothing." I watch him as he stirs his coffee--he's tense. He looks at me, and I'm afraid he knows I'm catching feelings for his sister. I've already decided this, but I'm not ready to confront her brothers about it yet. I have to approach her about it first. Vin pops up behind me. I didn't even hear him come in.

"Oh good, you're here. I'm gonna start on V's car," he tells Vance and taps my arm. "You comin?" he asks.

"Yeah." I move away from the door and follow Vin out into the garage.

"Alright. I'm done, Vin." Mark comes up to us, wiping his hands on a rag. He looks at me, "I didn't realize that was you, Chase. Sorry, I didn't shake your hand, I would now but..." He lifts his grease-covered hands.

"No worries," I tell him. I don't care if he wants to shake my hand or not.

"Welcome Home."

"Thanks."

"Sounds good, Mark," Vin says. "I'll move this out." Mark nods and walks over to the sink. "Here," Vin throws me some keys, "open V's doors. When Vance comes out we'll push it in." Vin jumps into the sedan, starting it up and backing it out of the bay. I walk out to V's car parked off to the side of the garage, and open up the doors, letting the hot stale air out. I sit in the driver's seat and turn the ignition, so I can roll the windows down. Vance strolls over, he doesn't look as moody anymore.

"You better now?" I ask, glancing at him and leaving the keys in the ignition.

"Yeah." He doesn't say anything else, and I don't press it. We've been friends long enough to know that if he wanted to tell me what's bugging him, he would. I get out of the car and close the door, leaning against it until Vin jogs over. "I'll get them back." Vance goes to the passenger side, and I turn to help steer and push. "Push on three...one...two...three!"

We all push, and it gives until it gets some momentum. I turn the wheel, and we line it up to the bay, pushing forward until we have it inside. I open the door and pull on the e-brake, then pull the lever to release the hood latch. Vin opens the hood, pulling on the rod to keep the hood up. "Alright, let's see what we got."

We've been at it for forty-five minutes now. I'm drenched in sweat. Vance lost his shirt about a half-hour ago, and I decide I need to do the same. I pull off my shirt and wipe my forehead with it then toss it on a nearby table. Everyone has left, except us and V, who's still in the office finishing up...whatever it is that she does here. We've got the radiator out which revealed a nice gash from a bolt. It must have flown off the chassis of a belt and completely snapped off. It could have been a whole lot worse. If it had been her timing belt, her engine could've been destroyed and this would cost her *so* much more. Vin has it all pulled out and set up on his workstation.

Footsteps approach us, "So what's the damage?" V comes into view but falters when she sees me. I catch her eying my naked chest then quickly dart her eyes towards her brother. A faint pink appears upon her cheeks, and it makes me smile. V is *blushing!*

Vin pops out from underneath the car and sits upon the creeper. He stands up and grabs the rag from his back pocket and wipes his hands on it. "Well, your radiator is shot, the serpentine belt toast, and you need new pulleys. You're lucky it was only that. I don't know how, but a bolt lodged into your radiator. We have the belt, but you need specific pulleys. Hopefully, the junk yard will have what we need. It'll have to get you by. I suggest getting a new set up though."

V nods, "Okay, I called Harry's earlier, and they have a couple at the yard. Tomorrow right?"

"Yeah, we can go tomorrow," Vin confirms. I grab my shirt and wrap it around my neck, "Mind if I tag along?"

"Nah, the more the merrier," Vin slaps my back, "Let's get the fuck outta here. I need a shower."

"Alright, I'll ride home with you," V tells Vin then heads back into the office. Vin starts to gather his tools and cleans up. I glance at Vance, "What are your plans for tonight?"

"Not sure, maybe hit up Sliders." Honestly, I rather hang out with V but I know that won't be happening, so Slider's it is. "Sounds good, I'll head home, clean up and meet up with you at your house."

"Alright," He holds out his hand and I connect mine with his, "I'll see you later." He heads out of the garage and hops into his car, then drives off.

"See you later?" I ask Vin. He nods once, "Yeah, I'll be there."

"Alright, I'm out."

"See ya man." Just as I exit the garage, V comes out of the office door with her bag over her shoulder. I pause and watch as she locks up. When she turns to see me standing there, she freezes but then seems to get her composure together. "All done?" I ask her.

"Yep," she's eying my chest and then glancing away quickly. Caught her again. My grin reappears. I'll help distract her. "You have any fun plans for tonight?"

"Oh yes!" she pauses, then leans in, "Going to a frat party! Shh don't tell my brothers." she whispers then a mischievous grin spreads upon her lips.

"An frat party, eh?"

"Yeah, lots of sex, drugs, and rock and roll."

"Oh shit." My eyes widen playfully because I know there's no way she's going to a frat party. "Those can get pretty wild, you better make sure you're prepared."

"Oh, I'm prepared." She winks and fuck if that doesn't hold all kinds of innuendos. That sends my mind reeling. Vin strolls up to us, eyeing us curiously, "You ready?"

"Yep." She giggles and Vin continues walking to his car, mumbling, "Not even gonna ask." She smiles wide and follows behind him. I walk over to my car, not far from where we stood, and glance over at her before opening my door. She does the same, throwing me a wink, then opens Vin's passenger door to get in. I think about that quick-witted girl my whole drive home.

GIRL'S NIGHT
Veronica

Chase is standing before me shirtless, and he's covered in a sheen of sweat, looking delectable. My body is humming. He takes a step closer, a cocky smile spreading upon his lips. He opens his mouth, and while I'm waiting to hear his soothing voice, a song blasts out of it. *What?* I jump at the intrusion of the song playing loudly and wildly look around my room. I am momentarily confused. The towel on my head unravels the more I move my head. I pull it off, and throw it. Damn it, I fell asleep. My heart's hammering in my chest at both the unexpected invasion and the realistic dream. My best friend's picture lights up on my phone that's situated next to my pillow. I quickly grab it, sliding the little green icon over, and put it to my ear.

"Hello," my voice is raspy from my nap.

"Bitch, are you sleeping?"

"Well, I was."

"It's freakin' six-thirty on a Saturday, and you're sleeping? You are SO lame."

She makes me smile. "It was just a nap. Shut up. You comin' over now?"

"Yeah, sorry it's a bit later than I thought. I went home to pack a bag, and Wes stopped by for a bit." Saturday is mine and Tay's. We do see each other at school every day, but we promised each other that we reserved Saturday night for us. Plans always vary; sometimes they include Wes, sometimes not. Seems like tonight is just us.

"What do you feel like doing?"

"I'm good with just hanging out, watching some movies, and stuffing our faces. I'm feeling lazy. I think my period is coming."

I laugh. "Well, I got chocolate."

"Thank goodness! I got the pizza! I'll be over in a bit."

"Kay. See you."

"Bye."

I hang up and throw my phone down on the bed next to me. My hair is still damp, and now it's a wavy mess. My stomach growls, and I am so looking forward to pizza. Loud laughter booms from downstairs; my interest is piqued. I grab my phone and hop off my bed. I toss on a cardigan over my ensemble of a tank top and shorts before heading down to see what's going on. The living room is empty; the voices seem to be coming from the kitchen. I pause just at the threshold and notice that there's a male body in every available space. The center island is covered in trays and bowls of finger foods. My brothers--minus Victor--Chase, and a few other guys are conversing. Pregaming, as they call it. They're all dressed nice minus Vaughn, who's in a tee and mesh shorts. Our mom has always enjoyed entertaining people, even if it's just our friends. But Mom is nowhere in sight. I snatch a piece of ring bologna from the tray and dip it in some spicy mustard.

Vance is the first one to notice me. "What up, V?" Everyone looks my way at Vance's greeting. I hug my sweater to me and take a bite of my bologna. "Nothing. Where's Mom?" I ask as I hop up on the stool in front of the kitchen island, right by the food.

"Her and Dad just left to go out for dinner," Vin answers. I nod, swinging my legs back and forth. They resume talking about whatever they were discussing before I came in. Chase comes to stand across from the kitchen island, leans down, and rests his arms on the countertop. "You don't look like you're going to a party," He says low enough so only I hear him. He looks good...real good. He's wearing a dark gray shirt that strains against his tan arms. His dirty blond hair is messy; well, the little bit that has grown in. His blue eyes seem more blue than usual. They're a weapon-- a girl could get lost in those.

"Yeahhh," I sigh. "not feelin' it. Doesn't sound all that appealing anymore."

He laughs, "So what are your *real* plans for tonight?" he takes a sip from his beer bottle.

"Tay's on her way over, gonna have a girls night."

"Girls Night," He rubs his chin. "does that include a sexy pillow fight?" he asks with a smile.

"Oh yeah, in nothing but our underwear."

He pauses, and I see his Adam's apple bob. I don't think he was expecting *that* response.

"You look nice," I tell him because it's the truth. He looks better than nice, and I'm a little annoyed at that. He's going to be the hottest guy in the bar, and no doubt the barflies are going to be all over him.

"You do too. I especially like the shorts." He winks.

"Pizza's here!" a loud voice booms from the front of the house. Taylor comes into the kitchen holding a pizza box in her right hand, above her shoulder. All the guys look her way.

"Pizza?" Vance repeats looking towards Tay. I point at him and say, "NOT for you!"

Tay moves through the kitchen, putting the pizza on the stovetop. I hop off the stool and walk around the island, grabbing plates from the cabinet above.

"Oh c'mon!" Vance says coming up behind us.

"No! You're going out, go get your own food."

When Tay opens the box, the fresh smell of hot peppers wafts upward. I love hot peppers on my pizza, as does Taylor. We're truly a match made in heaven. There's also steak, onion, and mushrooms. German pizza is the shit. Vance snatches a piece of meat off the pie. I smack his hand as he pulls away.

"Ow," he mumbles.

"Get outta here," I tell him, and bump him out of the way. I grab a slice and plop it on my plate. Tay does the same and closes the box. "Jerry's on his way over. He called me when I was picking up the pizza."

"Yay!" We both stand with our backs against the stove, protecting the pie. The moans coming from us have all the guys watching us.

"You two do not play fair," Vance tells us, "Now I want fucking pizza." He finishes his beer then throws the empty bottle in the recycling. "You guys ready?"

"You driving?" I ask him.

He shakes his head and says, "Chase is".

"How'd you get stuck being the DD?" I ask him and catch this mischievous smile on his face. That's when I notice my cell right in front of him. I cock my head to the side, and his smile widens. *Alright Chase, what are you up to?* My goodness, he looks so good.

He shrugs. "I don't drink to get drunk."

"Well then, have fun with those guys." I devour my slice and move onto the next. The guys all leave, except Vaughn, since he's not old enough to legally drink.

"What are your plans?" I ask him. He shrugs.
"You want pizza?" I offer, as sweet as I can.
"Yeah, thanks," He says as he grabs a slice, sans plate, and devours his slice in like four bites.
"Jeez. Hungry much?" I laugh.
"I guess. I'm gonna be out in the garage." He grabs another slice and walks out of the kitchen. Yeah, he was hungry. It's quiet now that it's just Tay and me.
"Who were those other guys?"
"I'm not sure, I haven't seen them before."
"They're cute."
I hum my approval, but Chase was the only one who held my eyes. When Taylor's phone dings, she picks it up. "Oh. Jerry's here!" She runs out of the kitchen to the front door. I hear them greet each other, then she returns with him in tow. "I brought goodies!" he announces holding up a grocery bag.
"Jerrryyyy!" I yell and go to him, wrapping my arms around his waist. He wraps his arms around my shoulders, squeezing me to him.
"I hope it's okay that I'm crashing your girl's night." He releases me and puts the bag on the counter.
"Jerry, you are the exception!"
Taylor peeks into his bag, "Whatcha bring us?" He pulls out a bag of chocolate bites, Twizzlers, Swedish Fish, and a two-liter of cream soda. He wags his eyebrows at us. I grab the package of Twizzlers; my favorite. We take our party of three into the living room. I flip on the TV and plop down onto the sofa. Jerry takes a seat next to me, leaving Tay on the other end of the sofa. I rip open the Twizzlers package and scroll through the premium channels. Sixteen Candles is on, so I immediately turn it on.

"Again? Seriously?" Taylor whines.

"Yes, shut up. One does not skip Sixteen Candles."

"Jake Ryan is boss," Jerry chimes in.

"See! Jerry knows what's up."

"I don't know how you can watch this over and over again."

"It is the best movie ever, *that's* how. Now shut up, you're killing my mood." I throw a Twizzlers at her. I can see her in the corner of my eye, she picks up the Twizzlers and takes a bite, then twirls it around. Jerry and I are watching intently. I can see Taylor is restless, checking her phone, bouncing her knee. Taylor is weird when it comes to movies. If she's seen it too many times, she can't watch it. I've made her watch this probably a million and one times.

"Taylor, I swear, go take a walk."

She puffs, "I'm gonna go make some brownies."

"YES!" I shout and throw my hands up. Sixteen Candles AND brownies? This night just turned epic!

"I'm picking the next movie," she says walking out of the room.

"Sure thing, now get to baking!" I yell after her. Seconds later, I hear pans banging, cabinets closing, and Tay talking to herself. Jerry and I have fun repeating the words to the movie. Taylor re-enters the room and sits back down on the couch ten minutes later. "They'll be ready in twenty minutes," she announces while playing on her phone. We continue to watch the movie, quoting words, and laughing. I hear a door open and then close; Vaughn comes into the living room a second later and crashes on Dad's recliner. He doesn't say anything but joins in on our little movie night.

"What's baking?" Vaughn asks a couple of minutes

later.

"Brownies," Taylor says, still fiddling with her phone.

"Niccce," He hisses.

"No plans?" I look towards Vaughn.

"Waiting for John to call me," He answers but doesn't bother to look at me. Vaughn only has a couple more months until he's legal to go to the bars. I know once that happens, he won't be home as much. It happened with each of my brothers until the excitement wore off. I ponder what I'll be allowed to do when I turn twenty-one.

Vaughn's phone starts ringing, and he quickly says, "Yo." A second later, he gets up and goes upstairs. The oven timer starts beeping in the kitchen and Taylor shoots up and runs out of the room. All the commotion is taking away from my favorite movie.

"Can't people just sit and enjoy a freakin' movie?" I mumble.

"For real! Hello! Jake Ryan is on TV," Jerry agrees.

"I'm so glad you're here!" I rest my head on Jerry's shoulder, and wrap my arm around his, snuggling into him. He pats my leg with his hand. Vaughn comes down the stairs, wearing something completely different from just a few minutes ago. He disappears into the kitchen and I hear voices but can't make out what they're saying. "Save me some!" he yells before going out the door.

I laugh out loud and say, "I can eat a whole pan of brownies by myself, and he wants three of us to save him some? He's crazy." Jerry laughs too. Taylor walks back in with a plate full of brownies. The aroma is mouthwatering, and I grab one before she can even sit. Jerry doesn't wait either.

"Ohmygod," I say with a full mouth. They're warm, chocolatey goodness.

"I know, they're amazing. I'm awesome," Taylor says, taking a bite of the brownie in her hand. "You are! These are delicious!" Jerry agrees. We all finish watching the movie; our mouths too busy chewing to do anything else. The credits are scrolling when Taylor holds out her hand and demands, "My turn."

I place the remote in her open palm and she pulls up the guide searching for our next movie. My phone dings, and I look at it curiously, wondering who would be texting me. I immediately assume it's one of my brothers. I let out a breath, wondering if any of them landed themselves in jail. It hasn't happened yet, surprisingly. I swipe open my phone and see a message from 'McSwoony'. What in the world? My mouth breaks into a huge grin, and I can't help but feel giddy.

McSwoony: You have that pillow fight yet?

I straight up giggle. It just bubbles out.

"What the hell are you giggling about?" Taylor asks.

I can't wipe the smile from my face. He managed to program his number into my phone. He's at a bar, and he's texting *me*.

Me: Oh yeah ;) Worked up quite an appetite, so we're eating yummy warm brownies.

"Uh, Hello? Who's got you smiling like that? Are you texting Chase?" Taylor yells. I can't help but laugh as I tell her, "Yeah."

"When in the world did you guys exchange numbers?"

"We didn't. He did it himself."

"Shut up!"

I nodded excitedly. Like a freakin' bobblehead.

"When?"

"I honestly have no idea, I'm assuming when you came with the pizza. I left it on the counter, and he had this mischievous expression. I knew he was up to something, but I didn't expect this."

"Hmm. I wish a hot guy would text me," Jerry pouts. My phone pings.

"What is he saying? What are you saying?" Taylor bounces on the couch. I wave my hand at her and say, "Aren't you supposed to be picking a movie?"

"This is so much more interesting!"

I shake my head. Jerry leans into me, and I look over at him. He's leaning into me because Taylor is leaning into him. "Oh my--what the hell is he saying about a pillow fight?! Are you guys sexting?!"

I tell her, "No! It was a joke." I can't stop laughing at her trying to figure out what we are saying.

"Send him a picture of your boobs!" Taylor suggests.

"Taylor! No way!"

"Why? I send them to Wes all the time."

"Yes, he's your boyfriend."

"Does he send you dick pics?" Jerry asks.

Taylor purrs, "All the time."

"Giirrrllll," Jerry drags out the word. She laughs and pulls out her phone, then I'm sure showing Jerry the pics. "Oh, *Giirrrlllll!*"Jerry says again.

She laughs, "Oh *yeah.*"

I ignore them and swipe my phone open to read Chase's text.

McSwoony: Damn, I'm coming back.

Me: Oh, Jerry would love it if you'd come back.
McSwoony: I wouldn't be coming back for Jerry.

I pause and reread his last text. A smile overtakes my face. I decide to keep teasing him.

Me: What? Why? Jerry is hot!
McSwoony: No, no. I prefer the female anatomy.

A small laugh escapes from me.

"What's so funny?"

I look over at my friends, and for a minute I forgot they were here. They're silently watching me, and I'm not sure how I feel about that. "Sorry, Jerry. I was trying to talk you up, but apparently, he likes the female body more."

"That's okay, He couldn't handle me anyway," he declares as he waves his hand like it's no big deal. He takes the remote from Taylor and starts scrolling through the guide on the TV. Taylor is looking at me with a large smile on her face, she tells me, "I like this."

This makes me smile because I like this too.

SMITTEN
Chase

The bar is crowded and there's a live band playing. So not only is it crowded, but it's also loud. Very loud. We grabbed a couple of hightop tables towards the back, pulling two together to accommodate us. It's a little less noisy, but it still requires us to shout.

"I'm gonna go get the first round!" Vance shouts and walks to the bar on our left.

I take in the band at the front of the place. They set up on a raised stage, and honestly, they're not half bad. They're currently playing a cover of a widely popular song right now--smart move. I drum my fingers on the table, enjoying the music. Vance returns with our first round of beers. He shouts among us, "Check out the table straight ahead." I lean around him and spot the table he's talking about. A table of beautiful women. The brunette holds my attention, her long hair almost reaching her waist. It immediately reminds me of Veronica. *Fuck!* I just nod my head in acceptance.

"Dude, the blonde...." He makes a gesture with his hands in front of his chest. "Nice." I laugh and take a sip from the bottle Vance set in front of me. "Wonder if the redhead is a natural. I can take her home and find out," Nate says next to me, then nudges me with his elbow.

"Thinking mighty high of yourself Nate," Shawn digs.

Nate smiles wide. "I'll let y'all know tomorrow."

"Not if I find out first." Vin smiles.

"Alright. Okay," Nate agrees, "Game on."

"Watch this junior," Vin says, stands up, taking a sip of his beer, and walks over to the table. We're all quiet as we watch him talk to the four women, chatting them up for a bit. The ladies are eating up whatever he's saying, and they all glance our way. The redhead nods then stands up, her friends doing the same. They grab their drinks and belongings and head our way.

"Damn," Shawn says.

"It's in our genes," Vance says, smirking and stands as Vin and the girls approach our table.

"Guys," Vin says and turns to the girls, "Say hello to Kylie, Erin, Raquel, and Jenna." He gestures to the two blondes, the redhead, then the brunette. I don't know how he remembers their names so quickly; I've already forgotten.

"Ladies, this is my brother Vance," he points to Vance as he continues to introduce everyone, "and our friends Chase, Nate, and Shawn." We all exchange hellos. Vin pulls another table up, making more room for our new company. The girls sit near each other, and Vin goes right into chatting up the redhead.

"What are you ladies drinking? Let me buy you each a drink." Nate waves over a server, and he flashes his cash. They rattle off some weird drinks to the server, and I see the one blonde eyeing him up. The redhead is still chatting with Vin. I don't think Nate is gonna be taking her home tonight.

An hour later the band has vacated the stage, and there's some rock music coming from the jukebox. It's easier to talk without live music. The whole table is still chatting, seats have been switched, and they're in small personal groups of two. Vance and the bleach blonde are getting chummy, and I won't be surprised if they cut out early. Vin has surprisingly moved onto the other blonde, and Nate with the brunette. Shawn and the redhead have seemed to hit it off, and it may be him who lets them know if she's a natural.

The brunette, Jenna-- I think--was trying to pull me into a conversation. I wasn't feeling it. I was polite and answered her questions but didn't make it out to be anything more. I think she got it and moved on to Nate. I finish my third beer and go to the bar to get water. I'm not even close to being buzzed, but I'm responsible for getting these guys home. Well, the ones that plan to go home. I may just be driving to my house alone. I approach the bar and take an open stool.

Only one bartender is working at the moment. She is a petite, tan little thing. Her black hair is long and thick with a red bandanna wrapped around her head. She has on a black shirt, that says Sliders across her chest, with ripped slits above the bar name, showcasing a nice chest in a neon green bra. The sleeves are ripped off, showing a full sleeve tattoo covering her right arm. It is too dim to make out what it is exactly-- looks like flowers and some swirls. She comes right up to get my order. That's when I really can see her face. Black makeup lines her brown eyes, and she has a piercing above her plump, red lips. I ask for a glass of water. She smiles and says, "Sure thing, handsome."

If I wasn't so hung up on another brunette, I'd be trying to get this girl's number, but V has me under some damn spell. *Speaking of...* I pull out my phone and shoot a text to V. While she was focusing on the pizza that Taylor brought, I quickly programmed my number in her phone, sent myself a text, then deleted it. Was it smart? Probably not. I've lost all common sense when it comes to her. The bartender drops the water on a coaster in front of me. "Thank you."

My phone pings. "Need anything else?" she asks.

"No, I'm good," I tell her while unlocking my phone to read V's message. She taps the bar top and saunters to the other end of the bar. That's when I notice the back of her top also has slits all down the back. I unlock my phone to read V's message.

Nic: Jerry's sad. :(

For obvious reasons, I couldn't put her in my phone under her actual name or nicknames. The chances of the guys seeing my messages, or her name popping up on my screen isn't one I'm willing to take quite just yet.

Me: Jerry will get over it.

I find myself smiling at our conversation.

"Water already?" A voice comes from my right, I glance over my shoulder as Vin strolls up to the open spot next to me.

"Yeah, Yeah," I say to his teasing, putting my phone down, and giving him my attention.

"You may just get off the hook on taking us all home."

I laugh. "I kind of figured, but I still gotta get my ass home."

"True," He pauses, "So what's up with you? I saw that chick trying to get you to talk. "

"Yeah, I don't know. She's pretty, seems nice but I wasn't feeling it." He nods. My phone pings, and it makes me smile. I'm anxious to see her response. I feel like a teenager again.

"Ahh. I see" He taps my arm with the back of his hand.

"You got someone waitin' for you?"

I rub the back of my neck, not quite sure what to say, and I have to be careful with what I do say, "No, not really."

"Well damn, that smile on your face ain't nothin."

I laugh, I guess I have to give him something. "Yeah, just talking to someone."

"No shit. Who is she, do I know her?"

"I don't think so." Lies.

He says, "Tell her to come here."

"She's out with friends." She's also not legal and...your sister, bro.

"Tell her to bring them along, dude."

"I don't know, man, seeing y'all may just scare her off."

"Or she might just ditch you for one of us." He ribs.

"Not likely." I say, "It's new, we haven't gone out yet, just talking." My phone pings again.

"Ah shit. Chase are you smitten?" he jokes. I can't help but laugh.

"You must really like her."

"Yeah, I think I do." I nod.

"My dude!" He pats my back. The hot bartender comes back and stops in front of Vin.

"Hey there, stranger," she purrs.

"Well if it isn't my favorite bartender," Vin replies.

"The one and only. Guinness?" she asks.

He winks at her. "You know it. Oh, and a Bay Breeze."

She pulls out a glass, putting it under the spout and pulling the handle to release the beer from the tap. She moves on to the Bay Breeze while she lets the Guinness settle. Once it's been a couple minutes, she places both drinks in front of Vin.

"Anything else?" she asks Vin, then me.

I shake my head, as Vin says, "That's all baby doll." He hands her a couple of bills, and she smiles, taking them from him and putting them in her top as she saunters away.

"You guys have a thing?" I ask curiously.

"Me and Jade? Nah. We went to school together, dated briefly. She's a cool chick, it just....didn't click," He takes a drink from his glass. "Well, I better get back to someone who I *do* click with." He pats me on the back, grabs the other drink, and walks towards the table. I know I have to join them, but I take the time to read the texts from V.

> **Nic:** I suppose he'll have to.
> **Nic:** I don't mean to be rude, but why are you texting me?

I sigh. *Good question.* I should be talking up a girl. Any other girl but V. But she's the one on my mind, and I enjoy talking to her.

> **Me:** I like talking to you.

There's silence for a bit. I glance at the TV hanging in the corner of the bar; a baseball game is on. I watch it for a bit until I hear the ping.

> **Nic**: Where are my brothers?

Well, I wasn't expecting her to ask about her brothers when I just told her I like talking to her, even though I told her that last night.

> **Me**: Busy.
> **Nic:** And you're not?
> **Me:** No.

Another pause in messages.

Nic: Because you rather text me?

A hand clamps down on my shoulder. "Dude what are you doing over here?" Vance says standing at my side. "Who ya texting?" He leans in, "Who's Nic?" I press the side of my phone, making my phone go dark. I turn to him, "No one, just a girl I'm talking to."

"She hot?" is all he asks.

I laugh. "Yeah, she's hot."

"Nice."

This is *so* fucked. He doesn't even know.

"Come back to the table and join the festivities!"

"Okay, I'll be right there."

As soon as Vance walks away, I unlock my phone and respond to V's message.

I'M NOT TEN ANYMORE

Veronica

It's almost midnight. Jerry went home claiming that he has a big bed he can sprawl out on, rather than sharing a bed with two girls or sleeping on the floor. Taylor is passed out next to me. We came up to my room after watching the last movie they picked. Some freaky ass shit that has me looking to my open closet in fear. *Assholes.*

None of my brothers are home yet, and I'm going to be pissed if they're not up and ready to go to Harry's tomorrow morning. I sent both Vin and Vance a text telling them so, but not too surprising; I haven't heard back from them. My phone buzzes and my heart picks up. Chase and I have been texting almost all night. It has me completely reeling and so, so confused. I hate to assume that he likes me, but it seems obvious at this point. Why else would he be at a bar, where I'm sure there are tons of girls, texting me? Not to mention he put his number in my phone like he had this planned already. *Ugh..* I hate overthinking shit, and I feel like that's what I'm doing. I look at Taylor. Her blonde hair is all over, mouth parted, and her breathing even.

"Taylor, am I overthinking this?" I ask her. I put my pointer finger on her chin then move it like she's speaking, making my voice a little higher, "Yes, yes you are bitch." I move my finger away and reply, "I knew it! Thanks, Tay." I laugh at myself. Taylor lets out a snore and rolls on her side facing away from me.

"Good chat," I mutter. My phone vibrates, and I pick it up off my chest, swiping it open.

McSwoony: Yes.

And there it is, ladies and gentlemen. He would rather be texting me than be 'busy'. Okay. Alright. No problem. My palms are sweating. What do I say back? I look at Tay's back. "What do I say?" I whisper. My phone vibrates in my hand, but Chase hasn't sent another text. I go back into my messages and see Vin has. A simple text telling me to be ready by nine am. I set an alarm for eight-thirty am and send him a quick one-word response.

Me: I'm flattered, glad I can keep you out of trouble and disease-free.

That's playful, right? I don't want him to know how much his response really meant. I put my phone on my chest and wait.

I'm startled awake by the vibrating on my chest, and the loud ringing. Shit. I grab my phone and turn off my alarm. Taylor groans next to me.
"What the fuck was that?" she mumbles.
"My alarm. Sorry."
She mumbles something incoherent.
"I'm going to the junkyard, I'll be back."
"O-Kay," she whispers, then she's snoring. I rub my face and open my phone to see if Chase messaged back. I must have passed out before he responded. He did, and more than once.

McSwoony: Haha real cute.
McSwoony: You fall asleep?

That was sent about seven minutes after a winky face.

McSwoony: You fell asleep.
McSwoony: I must be boring.

Three minutes later.

McSwoony: Sweet dreams.

I smile wide and clutch my phone to my chest. I hear lots of movement out in the hallway--doors opening, and closing, and the toilet flushing. I jump up from my bed and quickly get dressed in jeans and a tank. I throw my hair up in a messy bun. My door whips open.

"You ready?"

"Shhh!" I glance around my closet door at my brother and point to Tay who's still sleeping. "Yeah, I'll be right down," I whisper. Vin ducks out but leaves the door open. *Jerk.* I grab my boots from the closet and leave my room, trying to close my door as quietly as possible. At the bottom of the stairs, I place my boots on the last step before entering the kitchen. I find myself pausing again at the threshold taking in the scene. Vin and Vance's backs are facing away from the entrance. They're eating and too busy with their phones to notice me. My eyes collide with Chase's as he's leaning against the counter, and I watch as a smile slowly spreads upon his lips. The butterflies are flapping in my stomach. I don't know how long we stand there looking at each other until one of my brothers lets out a loud fart, completely breaking our trance.

"Ew, You nasty!" I yell. Vance looks over his shoulder,

"Oh hey V, didn't see you there."

"Like that would matter." I move into the kitchen to grab a cup from the cabinet.

"Nope." He laughs in agreement.

"Vin, you seriously need to knock before coming into my room."

He rolls his eyes, "You ain't got nothing to see."

"I hate to break it to you, I'm not ten anymore."

Vin puts his phone down and walks to me in two strides. He scoops me into a hug and squeezes, then proceeds to run his hand all over my head making a *huge* mess of my hair. I try to push away from him, but it's useless-- he's much bigger and much stronger.

"You'll always be ten to me, but I'll knock." He kisses me on the head, and releases me, walking back to the table. I don't even look at Chase. I'm totally embarrassed.

"Asshole," I mutter. I bend over, pulling the hair tie out of my hair and redo my bun. I stand up and put my hands on my hips.

"Alright, we ready?" Vance asks. Vin is grinning over his cup. *Ass. Hole.*

"Yup!" I skip out of the kitchen and sit on the steps to put my boots on. The guys walk past, Chase being the last. He pauses, and I look up at him, then at my brothers who are walking out the front door.

"Sleep well?" he asks with a smile.

"Yep." I slip my feet into my boots and start tying the laces.

"How was your night?" I ask curiously.

"Okay. Got bored once the girl I was talking to fell asleep on me."

Oh.

"Ouch. You must've bored her to sleep. I'm sure you had others to occupy you though." I stand up, and he moves closer to me causing my breath to hitch. I have to tilt my head up to look into his blue eyes. His hands go to my hips, holding me in place...*What is he doing?*

"The only girl I wanted to occupy me"—he scans my face—"was you." He winks then turns, walks out the door, leaving me completely speechless. He's left me a puddle in more than one way. I gather myself the best I can and rush out the door, grabbing my sunglasses and slipping them on top of my head. Chase's truck is parked out front, and I can see them sitting inside the cab. It would make sense to take his truck, as we all have smaller cars. The truck gives us more room. Surprisingly, my brothers are in the back, leaving the passenger seat open for me. I open the door and heft myself up. Chase has his sunglasses on, but his smile is wide.

"You okay?" he asks. "You look a bit flushed."

Jerk!

"Yeah, I'm good," I mumble and close the door. I slide my sunglasses down onto my nose. We start driving. It's awfully quiet so I turn to see what my brothers are doing in the back. Vance's head is tilted up towards the ceiling of the truck, his sunglasses covering his eyes, and his mouth is slightly open. He's fast asleep. If I was sitting next to him, I'd pick on him hardcore. I turn to look at Vin who is on his phone.

"What time did you guys get in last night?" I ask Vin.

"Later than I wanted to."

"And him?" I point to Vance.

Vin laughs, "I think he came in shortly after I woke up this morning." I shake my head. Vin leans forward between the front seats. He taps Chase and asks, "Yo, did you meet up with Nic then?"

I stiffen and very slowly look over at Chase. Are you fucking *kidding* me right now? He did NOT just touch me in the house and say what he said when he was with someone else last night. I can feel the anger rising; the warmth is spreading and my body is shaking. I look away from him, watching the world zoom by outside the window. I'm clenching my jaw so hard, it's hurting. I don't even want to hear his fucking reply.

Chase laughs. He fucking laughs. "No, I told you she was with her friends."

"Dude," Vin says, his tone sarcastic.

"Actually..." Chase pauses, and it forces me to look at him. He puts his hand in his front pocket and pulls out his phone then hands it to me. What? "V, can you send Nic a text for me? Just send something nice, like, 'good morning beautiful'."

I glare at him. He may not be able to see it, but if looks could kill, he'd be dead. He's lucky. Not only would my look kill him--if it were possible--but he's also lucky my brothers are in the cab with us. It is the only thing that stops me from telling him what he can do with his fucking phone. I school my expression and my temper the best I can, forcing a smile on my face as sweetly as I can.

"Sure. I'm sure Nic is SO lucky," I respond with as much sarcasm as possible. Chase smiles so wide, I can see his molars. I can't fucking believe this--or him. I want to scream. I want to cry. Fuck that, I want to punch him. My brothers are right. Men are fucking pigs. I swipe open his phone and push on the little envelope icon. 'Nic' is the first name in his messages. I don't even see my name...and we were texting last night, too. I should text her and tell her that Chase is a dickhead. I smile to myself. I am such a bitch. I don't even try to read what they talked about even though part of me wants to--I just can't.

Chase is a dick, and you should run far, far away from him.

I stare at what I wrote in the message box, hesitate for a second, and press 'send'. I smile and hand it back to him without even looking his way.

My phone vibrates and pings a minute later, the only person I can think of that would be texting me right now is Tay. I open my bag and pull my phone out of the front pocket. I have a message from 'McSwoony'. *What the hell?* I swipe my phone open, go into my messages, and find that the text I just sent 'Nic' sits in my inbox.

It takes me a second to register what just happened. I can't help the smile from spreading, and I laugh. The anger I just felt is replaced with relief and happiness. I am 'Nic', and he told my brothers about her--well, me. I laugh a bit more and take a deep breath while holding my phone to my chest. I guess it's a good thing I don't have a superpower that can kill with one look; I'd be pretty sorry right now. Vin isn't even paying any attention, he's still talking to Chase, but I feel Chase's eyes on me. I rest my head against the seat, a smile on my face, watching the trees blur by.

HIT OR MISS
Chase

V's face when Vin mentioned Nic was so apparent. She was *pissed*. It may have been mean for me to mess with her like that, but I obviously couldn't tell her that she IS 'Nic'. I think I made it obvious that I'm into her, so the ball is pretty much in her court. After a twenty-minute drive, I pull onto the gravel road of 'Harry's U-Pull It' and pull the truck into a makeshift spot. I put the truck in park and cut the engine. Vance shoots up. "I'm awake!" he shouts. We all face him and bust out laughing.

"Shut up," he mumbles as he grabs for the door handle. He gets out of the truck pulling his small tool bag out with him. Once we're all out of the cab, I lock the doors from my key fob. No one speaks as we approach the pay booth.

"Oh my gosh!" V whispers to my left. I look at her, taking in her facial expression. Her eyebrows are arched up above her sunglasses, and her mouth is parted in surprise or shock. I follow her line of sight to the area next to the booth. A beat-up car sits just on the left of it towards the back of the chain-link fence. It's almost too hard to determine exactly what kind of car it is, but the distinctive 'SS' in the grill is a dead giveaway. The yellow Camaro has seen better days, for sure, and a 'For Sale' sign sits in the front window. Veronica rushes toward it. "Look at this!" she yells to us, jumping in place. "Oh my gosh!" Her excitement is adorable. Vin and Vance move towards the car, and I follow behind them. I tear my eyes away, reluctantly, from Veronica and look back at the car. The tires are flat, the paint is non-existent, there's rust around the wheel wells, the headlights are missing, and the seats are ripped. With some TLC, the Camaro would look beastly. Vin whistles, "Damn."

"This car is beat!" Vance waves his hand at it, then walks to the booth.

"It's beautiful," V says to no one in particular. Watching Veronica get this excited over an old car like this is beautiful. There's no information on the sign in the window, just a number. I snap a quick picture of it with my phone.

"Even if it's beat, it's gonna be pricey," Vin says. "They don't come cheap, these classics." He kicks the flat tire.

"C'mon, let's go, " Vance yells impatiently. I watch Veronica's shoulders drop, and I see her excitement disappear as she rounds the front of the car. I put my arm around her and squeeze.

"It's so pretty," she whispers like a sad little girl who is parting with something special.

"It is," I agree.

"I want it."

"I know." I rub her shoulder, then release her as we move towards the booth where Vin and Vance are waiting for us. My instinct is to pay for her, but it'd look weird...so I pay for myself. He stamps my hand, and I move out of the way for Veronica to pay next. Once she's settled, we all make our way into the yard. Harry's is organized by make, which makes finding what we want much easier. Vance is walking ahead and at one point he turns around, and walks backward to tell us,

"I'm gonna go over to the beamer's. I'll meet up back up with you guys then." The three of us keep walking towards the Acura area, the make of Veronica's car. Normally you'd get a map, but we've all been here too many times to count. Enough times to remember where the parts we need are.

It's a bit of a trek, but we finally reach the area. Acura is a very popular import car, so it's no surprise that the cars are almost bare--any and everything that can be removed has been. Vin moves towards the right, Veronica goes to the left. As much as I want to follow V I don't, so I continue walking forward. While Harry's is separated into sections of make, they are not separated by model. This requires you to pay more attention to the body, especially when most of them are stripped bare.

"Found one!" Vin yells from my right. I turn towards Vin's voice, just as Veronica goes jogging by. I catch up with her easily. We round a car and walk between a row to where Vin is standing in front of an RSX that is still somewhat intact. Veronica drops her bag off to the side, and Vin moves to the driver's door, opening it, then disappearing inside. The hood pops open, and Veronica goes about lifting it up. Unfortunately, it's not as intact as we thought, the engine bay is pretty empty. Veronica sighs. "Dammit."

"Awe man," Vin says when he joins us. V lets the hood drop--which causes a loud bang--picks up her bag, and walks off. Vin runs his hands through his black hair. "If Vaughn didn't have classes so early in the morning, I'd make him take her to school." I think about it for a second. I drive towards their house on my way to work...I'd just have to take a slight detour but nothing that would make me late if I left a couple of minutes earlier than normal. It wouldn't be a bad way to start my mornings either.

"I could pick her up." I offer.

"I think Taylor is going to get her." I nod because as much as I'd love this new morning routine, I can't make it seem like I *really* want this.

"Okay, well the offer is there."

Vin pats my back as he walks by me and tells me, "Thanks man, I'm sure she'd appreciate it."

"I drive by on my way to work, so it really wouldn't be a big deal."

"Well, if we don't find anything today, you can let her know," Vin pauses and scopes out the area, "I'm gonna go look over here." He points towards the back nearing the fence.

"Alright, I'll check out over there." I point back towards where I came from.

After exploring the yard further I find another RSX, but the front passenger side is smashed. It doesn't look promising. Junkyards are a hit or miss. Sadly, car accidents happen daily, and insurance companies scrap cars all the time. We could come tomorrow, and THE car you need has been put in. The RSX, in particular, is a popular car. Not to mention, they're older cars and no longer made. There's probably not many left as it is, so car enthusiasts just like Veronica are always out scavenging and buying parts they don't even need but to turn a profit from it. The hood is already popped, probably from the crash, I lift it to find the engine bay completely bare. I sigh in relief....and sadness. If we don't find the parts she needs today, she'll be without her car for a couple of weeks or even longer. It will depend on where the parts are coming from. I almost--

dare I admit--desperately want the chance to take her to school. I keep looking around the area but don't find anything.

Without realizing it I walk right to where Veronica is. My footsteps aren't quiet, due to the glass and scrap laying on the ground, so I'm not surprised when she looks over her shoulder at me. I am surprised, though, to see the large smile displayed on her features. I like it. A lot.

"Find anything?" I ask her as I come to stand next to her.

She shakes her head, at the same time she says," No".

"I think I have an old bicycle you can borrow."

She laughs and it's music to my ears. I think I could listen to her laugh for the rest of my life. *Fuck. That's deep.* I'm taken aback at the thought.

"How generous of you."

"Yeah, well I'm just that kind of guy."

She licks her lips and it doesn't go unnoticed-- whether she meant for me to notice or not. It's fucking hot because she has these lips I'm dying to taste. There are sounds of footsteps coming our way and we both look in the direction of the noise. Vance is approaching us with some things in his hands that I can't quite make out. Fuck, if I'm not pissed at his timing. Of course, as much as I want to taste her pretty mouth, it won't happen now.

"Dude. Look at what I found!" He holds up his hands with excitement shown on his face. Seems Vance made out pretty well. He lays down the grill on the hood of the car next to us, along with some other parts. First one looks like a short shifter that's including the boot. He digs into his pocket and pulls out a shift knob. "I can't believe they just left all this in the car, these alone are like sixty bucks!"

"Nice!"

"Well at least *someone* made out okay," V mutters, annoyed, putting her hands on her hips. Vance's excitement slowly dissipates. "Oh, man. Nothing?"

"Nothing," V repeats, kicking a rock that also kicks up some dirt.

"Damn. I'm sorry V."

She shrugs like it's not a big deal, though we all know it is. Vin jogs over joining us, "Didn't find anything, you guys?"

V shakes her head and stares off into the distance.

"Nah," I respond. He sighs loudly, "You guys ready to head out then?"

There's some various yeahs that echo. Vance gathers his goods, and we all start walking towards the exit. Vance veers off to the booth to pay for his parts, while the rest of us continue to my truck. I peek at Veronica, who is looking behind her, at the old beat-up car. My truck beeps as I unlock it and the three of us climb into the cab. Veronica crosses her arms. "Looks like I may need to borrow that bike after all," she says to me.

I laugh and start the truck. "I'll do you one better...I travel your way every morning for work. I can just swing by and pick you up," I tell her. She looks at me and shifts her body to face me, putting her leg on the seat, then pulling her foot towards her. "You'd do that?" she asks. I'm kind of surprised. Doesn't she think I'd do something as simple as this for her? I guess I have to make myself more apparent. The back door opens as Vance climbs into the cab, putting his parts in the middle of him and Vin, before closing the door.

"Yeah, it's not a problem." What I really want to say is, 'Of course, I would, just to spend some time with you.'

"What's not a problem?" Vance butts in.

Veronica looks back at Vance and tells him, "Chase taking me to school."

I look at Vance in the rearview mirror. He makes a face. "Why not take the bus?" he asks Veronica. *Damn, Vance.* I look at Veronica as her face pinches. "Seriously, Vance? No. I'm a senior, there is NO way I'm taking the freakin' bus."

"What about Taylor?" Vance asks.

"Taylor would have to pass the school to get me. It's kind of counterproductive. Besides, if Chase passes our house and the school, I won't feel so bad as I would making Taylor drive all over. It works out this way for everyone."

"Well except Chase," Vance continues.

"I don't mind. I used to pick up your ass every day until you got your car." I remind him.

"Yeah, but that's when we were *in* school."

"Shut up, Vance," Veronica snaps at him. "Chase is being nice. Stop making it a big deal." She looks at me and simply says, "Thank you."

"Yeah sure, have some coffee ready for me," I joke trying to make the situation a little less awkward.

THREE SUGARS

Veronica

I need to fill in Taylor. After the guys drop me off, I scurry up the stairs to my room to wake my sleepy--and sure to be cranky--best friend. Her blonde locks cover my pillow and she's trying to fight the light that's been slowly seeping into my room by covering her eyes with her forearm. *She looks so peaceful.* Oh, well. I rush forward and plop next to her, causing her body to bounce. I shuffle onto my side, propping my head up with my hand. Her arm moves slightly, allowing me to see her blue eyes; wide and alert. She's awake now.

"What time is it?" she croaks, putting her arm back over her eyes.

"Time for you to brush your teeth."

She huffs and blows more of her morning breath in my face, "Bitch."

I laugh loudly, and her lips crack a smile. "Did you find your parts?"

I shift into a sitting position so I'm looking down at her, "No, so I need to order them...but Chase offered to drive me to school every morning..."

Taylor's eyes reappear, "Say what now?"

I fill her in on *everything*. By the end of retelling my morning, we are both sitting cross legged on my bed. She truly is my cheerleader and is so ecstatic, her excitement makes me so much *more* excited. My jaw feels like It's about to come off its joints--I'm smiling and laughing so much.

Taylor glances at her phone and sighs, "I better get going, I promised my mom I'd help her paint the kitchen today," she spins her finger in a circle, "YAY!"

"Yeah, I need to take a shower."

While Taylor gets dressed and grabs her things I go grab my stuff for that shower. "Text me later," she says moving down the hallway.

Later that evening, while I'm lounging around in sweats watching TV, my phone starts to sing. "Jerrrryyyy!" I answer.

"Hey boo."

"What you up to Jer Bear?"

"I'm in trouble, V."

I sit up, "What? What do you mean? Are you okay?"

"I met the sexiest man *ever*."

"Oh my gosh! I thought something bad happened."

"IT DID! He's not 'out' and he has a girlfriend."

"Are you sure he's gay?"

"It's possible he's bi. Okay, so here's the deets--after I left your place, my friend texted me to come out to Stonewall. They were having an all ages drag night. That's where I met him. He's dreamy, V. We were making out, I got his number before he left. Then my friend broke the news to me. I don't know what to do!"

I blow out a breath, "Yikes Jer, that sounds like a sticky situation."

He whines, "I know, but I really like him."

I laugh, "You just met him though."

"He's so pretty," he cries.

"He cheated on his girlfriend. That's not cool. He may be pretty but he seems like he has a lot to figure out."

"Ugh! You're right. I hate it when you're right," he sighs, "Hey! Did you get your parts!?"

He swiftly changes the topic which I entertain. I'm hoping to get his mind off the dilemma he's faced with and tell him about my morning. We gush about Chase for a while.

That's when I hear it...the faint hum of a vehicle. It's definitely coming closer so I rush to the window to take a quick peek. It sounds familiar. Right on cue, Chase's truck pulls into our driveway; but instead of pulling up to the door, I see him park in front of the garage. Both Vance and Chase exit the truck and stroll to the entrance near the garage that connects to the kitchen.

"Oh no, Jer. They just got home, and Chase is coming in the house."

"Oh! Oh! Are you presentable?" he asks. I glance at myself in the floor length mirror propped near my closet and sigh. Sweats, a band shirt, and wild hair.

"That bad, huh?"

I laugh, "Eh, he's seen me at my worst."

"That's right boo! If he can like you at your worst, he deserves you at your best!" He encourages.

"Yeah!" I agree. "I love you Jer Bear."

"I love you too. Thanks for talking. Now, go get 'em, tiger,"

"Riigghhtt," I laugh. "See you tomorrow."

"Toodles."

I hang up, toss my phone on my bed, and look at myself in the mirror again. I'm comfy, and it's not in my nature to change myself so others will like me. Despite that, I throw my hair up in a pony and shrug. If he likes me in sweats and looking like a hot mess, that speaks volumes to me.

I whip open my door--the salivating smell of dinner invades my nostrils--and head down the stairs. Vaughn and Vin are lounging on the couch. Dad is in his recliner. None of them pay me any attention so I continue into the kitchen. I hum my approval. "Yum. What are you making?" I ask my mother, who is pouring milk into a large pot of steaming potatoes.

"Meatloaf is in the oven."

The garage door opens and in walks Vance, followed by Chase. He's changed since the junkyard. He's wearing a simple gray V-neck tee--nice and snug--and some jeans. He looks good, and I look like...*this*. I remind myself of what I said moments before I left my room. He smiles wide when he sees me, and it causes me to smile in return. He is so hot it should be illegal. Mom turns and greets them. Vance informs us that he's gonna go take a shower, and walks out of the kitchen.

"Chase, you staying for dinner?" she asks him.

"I'd love to if there's room."

"Of course!" she waves her hand at him. "Victor and Melissa should be here soon."

"Victor's coming?" I ask excitedly. I miss him dearly. The house isn't the same since he left, and some days I hate Melissa for stealing him away. I don't look forward to the day when all my brothers leave, even if they're cavemen sometimes.

"Yes. Veronica, can you set the table," she asks me and starts to smash the potatoes. I move about the kitchen grabbing plates and getting the forks out. A body moves close, and his deep voice slightly startles me, "Let me help." His hand covers mine gently taking the forks from my hand. To anyone else, it looks like he's simply taking the forks from me, but it was so much more. Warmth spreads throughout my body, and I take a deep breath before turning around. He's placing the last fork down when I approach the table with the plates. I don't look up, and he doesn't move away. It's not until I round the table to the last place setting that I'm forced to look up. He still hasn't moved. His blue eyes connect with mine and we are mere feet apart.

It's moving in slow motion, like a corny movie scene where everything else drops away, and it's just the two of us. If this were a movie, I'd drop the plate and let it shatter into a million pieces. He'd grab the front of my pants, pulling my body roughly to his, and allow me to feel every solid inch of him. His hand would slowly move across my hip, leaving little goosebumps from his touch to my side then upward, grazing my breast. His hand would continue until it was in my hair, grabbing a fist full then gently pulling. My head would tilt slightly back and after his eyes scanned my face, his mouth would be on mine.

"You okay?" My daydream disappears, and I can feel my face redden. This wasn't a movie, and that would never happen under this roof, with my brothers in the next room. He looks amused.

"Yeah," I mumble, placing the plate on the table.

"You sure? You look a bit flustered. What's going on in that pretty head of yours?"

"Nothing," I say quickly.

"You're a terrible liar." He smirks, watching me for a second before turning his back to me and walking out of the room--through the kitchen--into the living room. I gather myself and one thought dawns on me. He called me pretty.

I walk the short distance into the kitchen, "Mom, I'm gonna go get changed."

If it were just a few of us, I'd just wear what I have on, but with Victor and Mel coming, I don't want to look like a *complete* slob. I run up the stairs just as Vance is coming out of the shower, with a towel wrapped around his waist. When Vance was in school, he was a full-on jock, and always at the gym. I know he still goes to the gym, and even does workouts at home but not nearly as much as he used to. I like to pick on him about slacking on his physique. He's still in great shape, but it gives him a complex, and I find that extremely funny. "Better lay off the beers Vance, you're starting to look like dad." I smile knowingly.

His stomach goes in slightly as one would when sucking in. I laugh and rush into my room before he tries to do something to me. I switch out my sweats, and band shirt for black leggings and a nice red tee with lace capped sleeves. I slip my feet into my black flats and skip out of my room. Just as I reach the bottom step, the front door opens, and in walks Victor and Melissa.

"Victor!" I yell and rush towards him. I jump up and he catches me, hugging me while my feet dangle.

"Has someone missed me?" he asks.

"Yes!"

He sets me back on my feet, and I step back taking in his professional appearance. Movement behind him catches my eyes and Melissa comes into view.

"Hi Mel!" I say to her and give her a polite hug.

"Hi V. How are you?" she asks as I move away from her.

"I'm good."

They move further into the living room and greet everyone. I watch their retreating backs. Victor was always tall; he's the tallest of all my brothers. Melissa isn't much taller than me, so she only reaches his shoulders. Victor keeps ahold of Melissa's hand as they greet everyone, and I find it completely endearing. I glance around the living room, and there's a space beside Vaughn, so I make my way over and plop myself down.

"Who's playing?" I ask looking at the game on the TV

"Seattle and Pittsburgh."

"Cool," I say, but it's really not. I watch ten seconds of it before I'm bored and declare, "This is boring."

"Shut up, V!" Vance yells at me.

"You shut up," I say lamely and look toward him. Chase is to his right, eyes on me, and Vance isn't even paying me any attention. Chase smiles. 'What?' I mouth to him.

He points at me. I shrug, and his smile widens.

"Dinner's ready!" my mom yells.

Dad pauses the game and jumps up from his recliner. We all follow behind him. The food is spread out among the table, and she's placing the big pot of mashed potatoes in the middle. With such a big family, we've always had a very large table, but they didn't take into consideration that future girlfriends would eventually be coming to dinner. There's a fold-out chair at the corner of the table and guess who has the pleasure of sitting there.

"Veronica, honey, you can sit at the corner," Mom informs me even though I already knew. I sit between Mom and Victor. Chase is on the other side between Vance and Vaughn. We're not a super religious family, and I haven't been to church in a couple of years now.

However, when the whole family is together, my parents like to say a small prayer before digging in. Our father says a prayer of thanks, and we all jump at a plate of food and then pass it on to the person to our right. There's a lot of light chatter amongst the table, but it ceases when Victor clears his throat like he has an announcement to make.

"I have some pretty great news," He informs us then pauses, keeping us waiting.

"Melissa's father has offered me the job of lead accountant at his firm!" He smiles widely, proud.

I sigh in relief, smile wide, and rub his back. "Congrats bro!"

"Thanks, sis."

My brothers and Chase all praise him in congratulations. Mom is overjoyed. "Oh honey! That is wonderful! I am so proud of you!"

"That's great news, Victor," Our father agrees. "You'll still cover the family businesses?"

Dad. No bull. Victor nods. "Of course. Greg knows how important that is for you--and me."

"Greg, he's a good man!" Dad continues eating.

"That's quite a drive. Isn't his firm located in the city?" Mom is quizzical. I look at Victor as he looks over at Melissa, then back to Mom. "It is," he agrees. "That's why we've decided to move."

Everyone gets quiet. We have small surrounding cities, but the major city in which is being referred to here is a good hour and a half drive. While it's not in another state or across the country, it's still a bit devastating to know that he'll be so far.

Vance is the first one to speak. "Nice! Now we can go to the city and have a place to stay."

Victor laughs and looks at me. I muster up a weak smile, that he obviously sees through because he puts his arm around me and squeezes me to him. This makes me want to cry, but I hold the tears at bay.

"It's okay, V. I promise to visit, and you can come up anytime. There's a lot to do. You and Melissa can go shopping." I grimace. I'm not a huge shopper, and he knows this. He chuckles. "They have lots of shoe stores," he whispers. I smile. I *do* like shoes. Maybe not heels or platforms; anything stylish. I like my Converse and kick-ass boots. I nod, not daring to talk.

"I am so happy for you," Mom says. "But it's going to be hard with you so far away."

"I know, Mom. I know." Is all Victor says.

We all finish dinner, and my tummy is full. I rub my belly. "Mom, that was so good," I tell her. She pats my leg. "Thank you!"

"I have pie!" Mom informs everyone as she stands up, taking her plate, and then my empty one in front of me.

"I think if I eat anything else, I'm going to explode," I say and stick out my protruding belly. I glance up and catch Chase laughing at me. I quickly suck in my stomach and sit up straight. I forgot he was across the table. I look everywhere but at him. I'm totally embarrassed.

"Yeah, we better get going. We're going to go look at some condos tomorrow," Victor informs us.

"Oh okay," Mom says, a bit deflated, "How about some to go?"

"That'd be great," Melissa says politely. Mom goes about getting them some pie to take with them.

"I'd love some pie, Vivian," My father says.

"Of course, my love." Although my parents are old, they are still *very* much in love. I am thankful to have grown up in a household full of compassion. Many of my friends haven't been so lucky.

"Me too, Ma!" Vin speaks up.

"Vaughn, can you please get the dishes?" Mom asks as she places the pie in a container and a slice on a plate for dad. Vaughn sighs and grumbles to himself.

"Vaughn Joseph!" My dad says loudly which quiets Vaughn. I smile wickedly finding it amusing when my brothers get scolded.

"Chase, would you like some pie?" Mom asks him.

"Um no, ma'am. I'm pretty full yet," he tells her.

"Some to go then?"

"Love some!"

She brings small plates with a nice sized slice of pie for Vin and Dad. Then turns and walks back to the counter, bringing back two containers for Victor and Chase. Victor and Melissa stand up and move around the table saying goodbye to everyone. I give them both hugs as they leave.

Chase stands up and announces he is going to head out. "Thanks so much for dinner." He hugs Mom. The scene before me fills me with warmth. It's comforting to know that Mom already likes Chase. I think about confiding in her about my feelings for him, and his possible feelings for me.

"It's a pleasure, you know you're always welcomed here."

"Thank you," he says sincerely.

He turns to me, "Hey can I talk to you?" he asks.

I'm surprised, so I simply nod and follow him to the front door, and out into the dark sky. Nightly creatures are making themselves known with their chirping and clicking.

"I just wanted to talk to you about this week."

"Oh okay."

"I'll be by around seven. School starts at seven-twenty right?"

"Yeah."

"Do you have a ride home?" he asks.

"Yeah, Tay's gonna drop me off."

He nods. "Okay. If you need anything, you have my number."

"You don't have to do this, you know. I appreciate it, I really do."

"I know I don't have to. I *want* to."

This makes me smile. "Okay. Thank you."

"No problem. I'll see you in the morning then."

"Okay, see you." I turn to leave but stop when he says my name. I look back at him, curiously. "Yeah?"

"Three sugars."

My face crinkles in confusion, which makes him chuckle. "I like my coffee with three sugars."

"*Oh!*" I blurt out, getting what he means. "Alright!" He winks before getting in the truck. That wink is my downfall. HE is my downfall. I float into the house. My brothers and dad are back in the living room, finishing the game. Vance glances at me and his eyebrow arches. I know he's dying to know what that was, but I keep walking and take large steps up the stairs to my room. I change into my pajamas and crawl into bed. My phone is blinking, indicating there's a message. I unlock my phone to find a message from Chase.

It simply says,

'Sweet dreams'.

DATE

Veronica

I wake up before my alarm goes off, too anxious to get this day started. All because I get to spend a little time with Chase. *Alone time with Chase.* I try to shower quickly, then dress in my favorite jeans and pair them with a cute button-up plaid shirt. Downstairs, the house is quiet, except for some movement in the kitchen. Vin has already left for work and Vaughn is already at school. Vance most likely still asleep, and Dad off doing...whatever retired people do.

"Morning honey," Mom's greeting is cheerful.

"Morning'."

"You're up and ready early."

"Yeah." I sigh.

"Waffles?" she asks me from the stove.

My stomach is a nervous wreck, and I don't want to push it. "No, I'm good." I start a pot of coffee, and my mother looks at me suspiciously. I don't normally drink coffee. I grab a granola bar from the cabinet, and the OJ from the fridge and pour a glass. I move to sit on a stool at the middle island.

"Is Taylor coming to get you this morning?"

"Uh, no. Actually, Chase is."

"Oh yeah? That's very kind of him." She says nonchalantly, questioning without pestering, and I know this is my time to talk to her. I remain quiet, listening for any movement from upstairs or elsewhere. "No one's home and Vance won't be up for at least another hour...or two. Who knows with him." My mom is now facing me, her back to the countertop.

"I really like him," I rush out.

She smiles. "And I presume, he really likes you?"

"I think so."

She smiles even bigger, making the wrinkles at her eyes deeper. "Hmm," she hums. "I think so."

"Please don't tell them," I motion upstairs, "They will destroy any chance of *anything* happening."

"Do you think this is wise, honey?" she questions. "He *is* your brothers' friend."

"Probably not...no. But I can't help it. I *really* like him. They can't know, they can't." I'm becoming a bit desperate. "It's so new...it may be nothing."

"And when it becomes something?"

I shrug and take a bite of my granola.

"They're not trying to ruin your life. You know your brothers love you and want the best for you."

I nod. "I know, but I'm eighteen. I'm going to be graduating, and I haven't even been on a date! I haven't even had a boyfriend!"

"What about that boy Bobby?"

"Bobby?" I ask. "What? Who? Bobby Fisher?" She nods at the name. "Mom that was in, like, the third grade, and Vance scared him so bad he cried and never spoke to me again."

Mom found it amusing, "Ah, that's right. He had detention for the week. Brenda wasn't too happy."

"Why couldn't you have more girls?"

"I don't know Hun, ask your father."

"Ugh."

"I won't say anything to your brothers, but please be careful. I don't think they'd appreciate the lying and sneaking around. I wouldn't. If it becomes something more, I don't think hiding it will have a good outcome."

"I have no idea where it's going. I just know I like him, and I think he likes me. I'll play it by ear."

Mom doesn't say anything else, and I finish my small breakfast. The kitchen smells like fresh coffee, and I go about making Chase a mug with three sugars. He never mentioned creamer, but he doesn't seem like a creamer kind of guy.

Mom is watching me. "What?" I ask.

"Nothing," she muses.

My phone pings, notifying me of a message. I quickly put the lid on the mug and rush to the island.

"He's here," I say out loud. I kiss my mom on the cheek. "Thank you."

"I'm always here if you need me."

"I know. Love you."

"Have a good day, sweetie. Love you more."

I slip on my Converse and grab my bag, slinging it over my shoulder and hurry out the front door. Chase's silver truck is parked right in front. I open the door and fling myself in.

"Hey," I say a bit out of breath. "Here."

"I was kidding, V!"

I shrug. "It's the least I could do." I didn't want to admit that I thought he was serious. "I didn't know if you liked cream, so it's just three sugars, like you said," I ramble on.

He laughs and then takes a sip. "Ah. Hot." He places the mug in the cupholder. "It's great! Thank you!" I take notice of his appearance--it's something I'm not used to. He has on a nice, wrinkle-free, button-down long sleeve shirt and he's wearing black slacks. Slacks! He looks older, professional, and it's like a look into the future. I definitely wouldn't mind seeing this every day, even though he's admitted he doesn't want to work with his father.

"What?" he asks.

"Ah. Nothing. You just look different."

He laughs. "Yeah. Welcome to adulthood." He puts the truck into gear and starts slowly maneuvering towards the end of the driveway.

"I can't imagine having to dress all professional," I say while looking out the windshield.

"I'll take this over my uniform any day. That shit's heavy. Those boots are no joke." I picture Chase in his uniform and I think I'd prefer him in that ensemble over his professional one.

"I'll be honest, I couldn't picture you at a pencil skirt and a button-up kind of job." He pauses, and rubs his chin, "Not saying that wouldn't be a great look for you.." That makes me smile, and I bite my lip to hide it.

"I don't think you ever said what you were going to college for. What are your plans?" I look over at him as he looks both ways before pulling out and starts heading in the direction of the high school.

"Umm...Liberal arts?"

He chuckles. "Really?"

"Yeah, why is that funny?"

"Not funny, just amusing."

"Because..."

He glances at me and shrugs. "It's just a typical major for college-bound students."

To be honest, I have no idea what I want to do. I thought maybe I would follow in Victor's footsteps, doing something business-related but I'm not sure. I turn to face him, feeling comfort in him, therein, feeling comfort in us. "I have no idea what I want to do," I tell him honestly.

"That's normal."

"Is it? I mean Tay knows what she wants to do, I thought I'd also know by now. I don't like this feeling of...unsettlement. I want to KNOW what I want to do with my life. Did you know you wanted to go into the Army?"

"No, but the decision didn't come lightly. My father wanted me to follow in his footsteps. Part of me joined in resentment; I didn't want to do what he wanted me to do. Obviously, it's more than that...the Army isn't something you do for fun. The drill sergeants aren't easy on you. They're in your face. You're crawling through mud and barbed wire. But it felt right. I'm still figuring out what I want to do. The Army has provided me with options. But I'm still following my father's path."

"I would never last in the Army."

"You'd be surprised what you're capable of."

Sadly, our drive was over way too soon, and I was pretty bummed that I had to get out of our makeshift cocoon.

***

School was school--mundane and dreadful--although something very unexpected happened. While sitting at lunch with Taylor and Jerry, a very cute senior--who transferred from another school at the beginning of the year--approached our little booth. Devin Watts slid in next to Taylor, across from me and

Jerry, and started up a conversation with us. After a couple minutes he *asked me out*. Me! I, Veronica Russo, was asked out by another senior! I still can't believe it. He is cute, athletic, and has great hair. But he has nothing on Chase. My enthusiasm disappears at the thought of Chase, and even thinking of saying 'yes' to this Devin floods me with guilt. Everything between me and Chase is so new, I still have no idea where it's headed. I don't really want to mess it up when it's had no chance to begin. So while I declined, I did tell him that maybe we should get to know each other better before going out; become friends. He flashed me a wide smile, and spent the rest of the lunch period with us. He is funny and nice, and we have a lot in common.

As I hop into Taylor's Jeep, she is gleeful and excited from lunch. "Oh my gosh!" she keeps repeating it, making me laugh.

"It's not that big of a deal."

"Uh, yeah! It is." She starts up the Jeep but doesn't move to go anywhere, except grab her phone. Her fingers are furiously flying over the screen of her phone.

"Jeez, are you writing a book?"

"You'll thank me later," she says, then put her phone in her bag.

"What are you doing?" I ask, nervous, and on edge.

"Nothing," she sings.

"Oh my gosh! What did you do?"

"Just shut up!"

"Tayloorrr!" I whine.

She pulls out of the school parking lot. "I'm taking you to the garage, right?"

"Yeah."

"Kay!" She says excitedly, and then turns up the radio

preventing any further conversation. Not long after, she pulls into the lot of Victor's Garage. She gets out and that makes me curious. "What are you doing?" I ask her as I grab my bag from the floor of her Jeep.

"Gonna wait with you until Wes is done."

"Good, you can do my homework," I tell her while pulling open the front door, causing the bells to ring.

She laughs, "I have my own but nice try."

Mark comes from the break room, "Good, you're here! The phone has been ringing off the hook."

"And have you answered it?" I ask, dropping my bag on the floor.

He scoffs. "No, that's your job."

His response makes me roll my eyes. "You do realize that while I'm at school, it is *your* job to answer the phone."

"They left messages," he says then returns to the break room.

"Why doesn't your dad hire another receptionist?" Tay asks.

I shrug. "Who knows? Because he has me? He doesn't want to pay another person who will probably ask for more money than what he pays me. And I'm part-time. Plus, he has this system in place and most people know how it works."

I go about checking the messages on the machine, returning calls, and writing in appointments. Taylor is very quiet while she does her homework.

It's almost five, and I'm surprised she's still sitting here until the front door bursts open, making both of us jump.

"You have a *date*?" Vance booms.

"What?" I look around. I didn't even hear his car pull

up.

"Well, that's my cue to leave." Tay starts packing up her things.

"YOU!" I point to her.

"Seeyoutomorrowbye!," she yells and runs out the door.

"TAYLOR!" I scream.

"What the hell!?" Vance yells.

"What?" I ask, exasperated.

"Who is this kid?"

I sigh, "He's no one. I don't even know him."

He looks at me like I'm crazy. "And you're going out with him?" His voice has risen dramatically.

"No!" I yell. "I told him no for that *very* reason. Where the hell did you hear this at?"

"Who is he?" He ignores my question.

"Why? It doesn't matter."

"I want to talk with him."

"No, Vance. No!"

"You like him!" He accuses me.

"For real? What is wrong with you? I don't even know him."

"I'll find out who he is."

"Whatever. Is there something else you need to yell at me about? Or you just like being a crazy lunatic?"

He huffs and walks out into the garage bay not saying another word to me. I pick up the phone and immediately dial Taylor.

"I'm sorry," she blurts before I can even suck in a breath.

"What. The. Hell." I grit out.

"I told Wes, who must've told Vance...but I have a good reason."

"And what reason would that be?"
"I can't say."
"Taylor!"
"You'll just have to wait. Look I gotta go...love you!"
The line goes dead before I can get a word in. What the hell just happened? I am *so* confused. "I need new friends *and* a new family," I mumble to myself.

An hour later, I have finished all the shop details and start looking up parts I need to get my car fixed and back on the road. I figure I'll probably have to work every day for the five or six months to fully pay off my bill. I put in my order and place it on the shops' account--a small perk. Thankfully, I won't have to pay for labor.

My phone rings and I groan. I can only imagine who's calling me now. But when I see my big brother's face on the screen, I answer it excitedly, "Victor!"

"Hey, peanut!"

"Really?"

He laughs. "You'll always be *my* little peanut."

"Oh my gosh!"

"You love it. Anyways, what are you doing?"

"Just finishing up at the shop--why? What's up?"

"We found a place!"

"You did!? That's great!"

"It's amazing, V! I'll send you a picture after we get off."

I'm sad at the reality of him leaving our small town and leaving us all behind to be a 'hotshot' accountant.

"V? You there?" Victor questions in my silence.

"Yeah. I'm here." My voice is melancholy.

"You okay?"

"Yeah...it's just really setting in that you're leaving."

"I'm not leaving. Don't think of it like that. It's not that far and you can come to visit anytime."

"Yeah, okay," my response comes out harsher than I intend.

"I promise."

"Okay."

"Let's make plans for next weekend."

"Okay, yeah!" My mood lifts dramatically. "I'm so excited!"

"Awesome. Well, I gotta go call Mom."

"You called me before Mom?" I ask, surprised.

"Well, yeah, but don't let her know that!"

My heart swells. "Cross my heart," I tell him.

"Okay. Love you, peanut."

"Love you too!"

After we hang up, I send Chase a message about ordering my parts, and I let him know when they should be arriving. My phone dings not long after...but it's not the response I'm expecting.

McSwoony: I heard you have a date.

SLIDERS
Chase

It is five-thirty when I'm finally walking out to my truck. Work was long, and boring, and I'm trying not to think about it when my cell rings. I answer too fast.

"What's up, dude?"

"Meet me at Sliders," Vance says without a hello.

"Alright...What's going on?" I ask as I approach my truck, pushing the unlock button.

"Some douche bag asked out V today."

I stop dead in my tracks, "What?" I'm taken completely by surprise! I mean, I'm not shocked that someone asked her out--she's gorgeous and vibrant--but shocked that someone *dared* to. I haven't even thought about this happening. This is *so* not good.

"Who?" I question.

"I have no idea who. She won't tell me."

"Did she say yes?" *Please say 'no'. Please say 'no'.* My thoughts are selfish.

"She told me she didn't, but I don't believe her. I think she's lying to protect him." There's a beep on my phone, and I pull it away to look at the screen. I have a text message waiting.

"So, what's your plan?" I ask, putting the phone back to my ear and picking up my pace.

"I don't know. Just meet me at Sliders." He hangs up before I can even agree.

Looks like I'm going to Sliders tonight. I hop in my

truck and turn over the engine. Sitting idle, I check the message I just received. It's from V. Simply telling me she ordered her parts, and I can't help the surge of jealousy that takes over me. I send a response, toss my phone in the cup holder, and drive.

Fifteen minutes later, I make my way into the bar. I have yet to check my phone; not sure I want to know V's answer, even if she told Vance that she wasn't going out on a date. I don't even know if she'd be honest with me considering I'm one of Vance's closest friends. Is she scared that I would rat her out? It isn't very crowded inside, so I immediately spot Vance's head at the bar. I roll my sleeves up to my elbows. *Damn, it's hot in here.* I can't tell if it's hot in the bar or if it's my blood boiling.

I pat Vance on the back. "Hey man."

Vance's black hair is disheveled. He places the beer bottle in front of him. "Dude, this is stressing me out."

You and me both, man. "I'm sure it's nothing."

The bartender--a guy this time--approaches us. "What can I get ya?" he asks, throwing a rag over his shoulder.

"Just a Miller, on tap," I respond, and he moves away to pour my drink. I turn to Vance, "So how did you find this stuff out?"

The bartender places the glass in front of me, "Thanks, man." He nods and moves down to the other side of the bar. I take a hefty swig.

"I was with Wes and he got a text from Taylor. He said she seemed excited about it. "

I can feel my body heat up, "V was excited?"

Vance shrugs, "I think so."

"She didn't say who it was?"

"No," He sighs and takes a swig of his beer, "I'm going

to figure it out. V knows I will, and when I do... I'm going to break his legs, and then beat him with them."

Damn. This is not good. Vance is damn near scary right now. I feel my phone vibrate in my pocket. I pull it out and unlock it.

Nic: Nooo. I was asked on a date, but I do not have a date.

I exhale a long breath and glance over at Vance, who's peeling at the sticker on his bottle.

Me: You turned him down?
Nic: Yes.
Me: Good.
Nic: Why's that good?
Me: Because it is. For you...and this guy. Your brother is freaking out.
Nic: I can always change my mind. Vance is stupid. Let him freak out.
Me: Who is this guy?
Nic: Who's asking? You or my brother?

I stare at the message before trying to write my response. I don't get too far because Vance leans into me, "Who are you texting?" I quickly push the power button to darken the screen, then put it in my pocket and clear my throat. "Just Nic."

"Ah, the infamous Nic. When do I get to meet her?"

"Uh. I don't know." I need to change the subject--and quick.

"C'mon. Though, she may just take a good look at me and dump your ass."

I laugh, "Your brother said the same damn thing."

"We Russos are studs."

I shake my head at him. "I can't wait until a girl knocks you on your ass."

"That'll be the day..." he mutters. "We have to find out

who this punk is."

I feel my phone vibrate in my pocket. I itch to look at it but refrain.

"It's obvious that Taylor tells Wes everything...so why not wait to see what she tells him?"

He looks at me for a beat, "That's the weird thing. She doesn't always tell him things. Actually," He pauses and touches his chin, "She never does...because he doesn't care. He found it weird, and I think that's why he told me." I think about that for a minute. Taylor is one sneaky chick.

"Man," Vance puts his hand on my shoulder, "I'm so glad you got my back. We have to keep these grimy assholes away from girls like V." I look down to hide my face and cringe.

Fuck.

INTOXICATING
Chase

I hang out with Vance for another hour before leaving. We didn't drink much more so I knew we both were okay to drive. My feelings for Veronica are heavily weighing down on me; the happiness and thoughts of pursuing something with her have evaporated. Seeing Vance stressed out over some random guy asking out V...I can't even imagine what he'd do if he knew about how I felt. I can't do something like that to my friend--to a friend I consider a brother. I'd, more than likely, be creating a fall out to people who are like family. Even more than my own.

Speaking of my family, the white Mercedes parked out front of the house indicates that my parents are home from their vacation. An involuntary groan slips past my lips. I do not want to deal with their shit, on top of the shit storm of feelings for someone I shouldn't even have feelings for. After parking my truck behind said Mercedes, I head inside, pausing in the foyer to listen for any sounds within the house. It remains quiet.

"Hello?" I yell out.

"In here," I hear my mother's voice call from the back of the house. I walk straight down the hall, passing the staircase and into the large open kitchen. My mother looks up when she hears me enter, disregarding the stack of mail she's sorting on the center island in front of her.

"Chase, honey?"

"Hey, Mom."

A large floppy white hat sits upon her head, even though she's indoors where the sun can no longer reach her. She rushes towards me. A wide smile forms on her lips, exposing her white and perfectly straight teeth. Her reaction to seeing me seems genuinely happy. I'm surprised. The anger I've felt for the past two weeks has momentarily subsided. I allow her arms to wrap around me--not even caring that her hat is poking me in the neck--and pull me into a hug.

"I am so sorry that we weren't here for your homecoming," She pulls away but keeps her hands on my arms, "It's so good to have you home."

I bite my tongue, knowing it won't make a difference, and just smile. "It's good to be home. Where's Dad?" I ask.

She backs away swiftly. The question seems to annoy her for some reason, and she goes back to her pile of mail. "He went to check in on everything at the office."

"But you guys just got home," I say incredulously.

"Yeah," she waves her hand. "You know how your father is."

I grunt. "Yeah. Well, I'm going up to my room."

My mother doesn't say another word. I watch her for a second, sorting through the mail before turning my back, and head towards the stairway. Skipping two steps at a time, I unbutton my shirt as I walk down the hall to my room. I rip it off my body, then toss it into the laundry basket just inside my closet. I pace my room until I settle on the edge of my bed--no longer thinking about the unexpected arrival of my parents--but the girl who takes up most of my thoughts anymore.

The effect she has on me, the fact that I cannot stay away from her, and the primal urge to claim her. I'm experiencing feelings I've never felt before. I feel like a damn caveman right now; possessive and jealous. *Shit.* I just remembered I never responded to Veronica's messages. I pull my phone from my pocket and see that there are three unread messages.

Nic: Helloo?
Nic: Did you fall asleep on me?

That makes me smile.

Nic: Just let me know you're okay. Please.

Her last message hurts my heart. *She's worried.* I absently rub my hand across my chest. "Damn it," I whisper to myself. The last thing I want to do is cause her to worry. I send her a quick text letting her know I'm okay, and I'll see her in the morning. I toss my phone on the bed. My chest hurts no matter how much I rub it, so I stand up and stretch my coiled muscles. I rub the back of my neck and acknowledge that I need to let off some steam. My father has a make-shift gym in the basement that he occasionally uses and urges me to use as much as possible.

The Army kept me in great shape, but I haven't worked out since coming home. Switching out my slacks for some sweats, I head down the two flights of stairs and into the furnished basement. The gym is situated in the far back so I have to pass through my father's man cave--a typical room including a bar, a pool table, a poker table, a large leather couch, and massive TV hanging on the wall. One would think that this would be the place to hang out *but* my father would never let me have any friends down in his cave in fear that we would ruin something. Ironically, he's okay with me using his gym. *Whatever.*

I make my way to the closed door and push it open. Immediately turning to the left, I open the cabinet that holds the surround sound receiver. The room is engulfed in hard rock music that's coming from the speakers in every corner for the room, as soon as I push the power button. I use my foot to close the door and walk straight to the weight bench. The loud music is successfully wiping anything troubling from my mind. I check the weights on the bar before laying down on the bench. I go hard for about an hour but bench press less than my normal weight since I don't have a spotter. *Safety first.* I do one last set; exhaling as I push the bar up onto the rack and drop my arms. The burn I feel in my biceps and triceps is a welcoming feeling. I sit up and allow my breathing to slow, grabbing a nearby towel, and clean the sweat from my forehead. Powering off the receiver, I leave the room and snatch a bottle of water from the small fridge under my father's bar. I down half of its contents then make my way back upstairs; beaten and tired. My shower lasts five minutes. I'm in bed before I know it--so tired that I don't even think about anything else before letting my body drift to sleep.

My alarm startles me from my deep slumber. I instantly reach out an arm to turn it off, wincing at the soreness. In the quiet room, I force my eyes to open and rub them with my fingers. I don't even recall falling asleep. It was probably the best I've slept in a *long* time. I stare up at the white ceiling before sitting up in my bed-- my hand hits something hard. My phone. I swipe it open, and there's another notification.

Nic: Oh, okay. See you.

 Just reading her message...I know she feels dejected. The same pain I felt in my chest yesterday returns, but I don't bother to try and subdue it; nothing will help. I place my phone on the side table and stumble to my closet. My closet contains more button-up collared shirts and polos--all purchased by my mother. The thought alone makes me laugh. My *mother* buys my shirts. I sigh while pulling a shirt off its hanger, then remove a pair of slacks from another hanger. I know this is something I don't see myself doing for the rest of my life; I don't envision wearing polos and button-ups every day. I remember Veronica saying that she doesn't know what she wants to do, and she doesn't realize how much I can relate to that.

 At Twenty-one, I thought I'd have my life more figured out. The Army has given me amazing opportunities but I know that's not something I want to do forever, either. Once I'm finished dressing, I grab my phone off the nightstand and shove it into my pocket. *Damn*. I've been looking forward to spending these next few mornings with V, but now I'm dreading it--dreading knowing that I can't make this into the relationship I thought we could have. I must put a stop to this. I'm just not sure how.

 I drudge down the stairs and come to a stop at the presence of my father. I'm a couple feet from the entrance of the kitchen. He's dressed perfectly in a suit;

sipping his coffee while scanning the newspaper. I move further into the kitchen, grabbing a protein bar from the nearby cabinet.

"Ah, Chase!" my Dad greets me.

"Dad." It's the best greeting I can muster.

"I've heard you've done well while we were gone."

"Yeah, well...I learned from the best."

He beams at the compliment. "You'll do well once I retire."

I stifle the laugh with a cough. "Yeah. I better get going."

"Look at you!" he says with pride as I walk out of the kitchen. I pat myself to make sure my wallet, phone, and keys are all accounted for.

The early morning air bites my skin as I stroll to my truck. I start it up and leave my driveway, heading in the direction of the Russo's home. My nerves begin to make me queasy. I force myself to take a couple of deep breaths as I turn into the driveway that meets a modest two-story home. I park in front of the door knowing she might be a few minutes because I'm a bit early. "This is for the best," I say to myself. "You know it's for the best."

I see movement out of my peripheral vision and my head shoots towards the front of the house. My heart picks up at the sight of Veronica. She has another silver coffee mug in her hands...and that makes me unconsciously smile. Even though my messages were short and dismissing, she still made me coffee. Her hair is pulled back into a ponytail high on her head, exposing her long neck, and making her features stand out. Her large hazel green eyes, slim nose, and plump lips.

This is going to be harder than I thought. She opens

the door and hops in. I immediately look forward, hoping she didn't see me looking at her.

"Hey," her soft feminine voice is like music to my ears.

"Hey," I say back, trying to stay neutral.

She hands me the mug, and I place it in the center console. "Thanks."

"Did my brother keep you out late?" she questions as she buckles her seat belt.

"Not really," I say, simply and start to drive.

"Oh."

I feel so bad for being short with her. We were always friends before, but I don't know if I can ever go back to being *just* friends. The thought alone causes me physical pain. This is becoming a mess, and it's all on me.

"My parents came home." I share.

"Really!? How was that?" she asks genuinely concerned.

I shrug, "It was okay. No welcoming home party or anything."

There is a pressure on my arm, which causes me to look away from the road. Her hand is on my bicep. She's concerned for me. I look away quickly.

"I'm sorry, Chase," she says her voice low. Her touch is intoxicating.

I clear my throat. "No need to be sorry, V. You didn't do anything."

She removes her hand and places it in her lap. Neither of us say a word. I don't think we know quite what to say. I shouldn't say anything more, though. I'm lost inside my own mind--on autopilot until I pull up to the school.

"Okay, well...thanks," she says weakly when I don't

say anything. She pulls on the handle of my truck and hops out, closing the door behind her. I watch her as she walks away with less pep in her step since coming out of her house just ten minutes prior.

    I hate to see her go, but I love to watch her leave.

WHAT IFS
Chase

With my father back, the work atmosphere has become full of tension. He's not an extremely mean guy, or even too demanding, but his presence radiates power. He started this company from the ground and, rightfully so, he is a very proud guy. It's not a massive company--it's quite small considering--but it's one of the best investment banking firms in the county; possibly the state.

His clientele comes all over the Northeast and even as far as out West. He's made a name for himself. He's honest, loyal, and straight forward--all qualities that are needed in this kind of business. It doesn't hurt that he's extremely good looking and that his young son is to be the heir of the prestigious company.

The day is dragging and I can't wait to leave, even though I have no plans for the rest of my night. I think about stopping by the garage, but I'm not sure if Veronica will be working. I conclude it'd probably be best that I don't. While walking out to my truck I decide to call Vance.

"Yo, man," He answers.

"What's good tonight?" I ask him.

"Come over. We're working on Wes' car."

"Over where?" *Please don't say your house.*

"Wes'."

"Alright, be there in a few."

I pull the phone away from my face, about to push

the red symbol.

"Yo, Chase, wait!" Vance's yell stops me from hanging up.

"Yeah?"

"Stop and grab a six-pack, will ya?"

"Will do." This time he doesn't keep me from hanging up. I jump into my truck and drive towards the nearest beer distributor.

Ten minutes later I'm parked in front of Wes' garage where the door is lifted, and his car is parked inside with the hood open. I remove my shirt, leaving me in my tank and slacks. Not ideal but I don't need to ruin a shirt--Mom would have a fit.

Wes and Vance both greet me with slaps on the hand, and I take a seat on an old beat-up couch off to the side. "What you guys got going on?" I ask while I pop open a beer. Vance strolls over and pulls one out of the pack too.

"Got a race this Friday," Wes says.

"Oh, yeah? Anyone good?" I ask.

"Yeah. One of Dixon's goons. Five-hundred bucks."

I whistle, impressed at the stakes. The thought of Dixon brings on thoughts of Veronica, and if she'll be going to the track with them even though she doesn't have her car.

My phone vibrates and it causes my heart to pick up. I'm caught wondering if it's Veronica. I slip it out of my pocket and steal a glance. It's not V. It's Shannon.

Shannon: You busy right now?

I stare at her text blankly for a moment. I know exactly why she's texting me. She would be a distraction. She would take my mind off of someone I shouldn't be thinking about, but I have no interest.

Me: Yeah.
Shannon: What about later tonight?

Vance joins me on the couch, sitting on the arm with his feet on the cushion. "That Nic?" he asks. I find it slightly twisted that he's saying V's nickname, and he doesn't even know.

"Nah. Shannon."

"Nice, dude. What does she want?"

"Not sure. I didn't ask."

"She wants the D."

How poetic. I laugh, "Probably."

"So, what about Nic?"

I sigh and lean my head back on the couch.

"Uh oh. She crazy?"

"No. I don't know if that's gonna work," I tell him.

"Ah, we're too young to settle down anyways. We gotta have our fun before the ball and chain locks on."

Wes laughs from under his hood. "You'll never find any chick to put up with your bullshit."

"Less stress that way."

"Better start collecting your cats now," Wes suggests, and I chuckle at the thought of Vance being a 'cat man'. I can picture him sitting in his recliner with cats perched all around him while he watches TV.

"No way. Maybe I'll get some fish and like a cool saltwater tank. Chicks dig that shit."

"Where do you get this crap?" I ask.

He points to his head, "It's all up here."

I shake my head. "Little do they know how much of a loser you are."

"The less they know, the better."

I unlock my phone to respond to Shannon just as Vance asks, "You gonna meet up with her?"

"Nah. Not feeling it." It's the honest truth, he just doesn't know that his sister is the reason why. I send Shannon a text, and exit the conversation only to look at the last interaction I had with Veronica. I close my messages before doing something stupid like texting her.

"Any info on V's mystery dude?" I ask curiously, slipping my phone back in my pocket.

"Nope. She was pissy today. I didn't stick around for that."

"Taylor was pissy today too."

"Huh..." Vance grunts. "Maybe they have their monthly visitor. If that's the case, I'll be avoiding her for the next week."

"Dude," I deadpan.

"What?" He shrugs.

The sun has set by the time I leave the garage and head home. I spend another night in the gym; this time I work my legs until they feel like jelly. I feel myself start to drift the second my head hits the pillow, but my thoughts are busy. Visions of a certain brunette cloud my mind and--instead of trying to stop them--I let them play out until I'm fast asleep.

I pull up in front of the Russo's house right on time. Veronica comes out of the door with less enthusiasm this morning. Her dark hair is in a braid that hangs over her shoulder, coming to rest right on her chest. I take a deep breath and then exhale when she opens the door and hops up on the seat. She hands me another mug.

"How many of these do you have?" I ask, slightly humored, while taking it from her hands.

"A lot. Dad has one for every day of the week."

"I washed the other two." I point towards the bag near her feet. She picks it up, mumbles a thank you, and looks out the window. She is visibly in a bad mood, so I leave her alone. The quiet is deafening.

"Are you okay?" I ask, carefully.

I hear her sigh, and a very faint, "Yeah."

I'm not quite sure what else to say, so I drum my fingers on the steering wheel and continue driving towards the school.

"Yanno what?" She interrupts the silence, "No, I'm not okay." Her voice is hard, and I hear her movement. I glance her way, noticing her body has turned towards me--her knee is bent up on the seat. I look back at the road but it's her face that has me looking back. Her eyes are narrowed into slits, and she's glaring at me. "What is going on?" she asks, tired and defeated.

"I don't know what you mean," I say, not entirely sure what she's referring to.

"Since you've come home, you've been flirty and making me think you like me. No. Scratch that. Not *think*. You've made it pretty apparent that you like me. Your messages, your stupid cute comments, letting me drive your car, comforting me, driving me to school…" she pauses to take a breath because she's talking so fast, "I think I've made it pretty apparent that I like you. I thought this was actually going somewhere and then it's like a door was slammed shut. You blow me off. Then you're cold and distant." She sighs, and when I think she's done, she continues, "That hurt!"

I pull up to the school, "I'm sorry. I didn't mean for all that to be bigger than what you thought." I chance a glance at her, and immediately regret it. The pain is all over her face.

She's quiet before sputtering, "That's it?"

"Yeah." *No.*

"So, this whole time...you were--what? What *was* that?"

"I'm not sure what you mean. " I play dumb again.

"UGH!" She yells, completely frustrated, "I am *so* stupid." She shakes her head, and her eyes bounce back to me, "No! YOU are stupid!" She opens the door and jumps out, turning to grab her bag. She stops when our eyes lock. "Don't worry about picking me up tomorrow."

The slamming of the door startles me as I sit and watch her quickly disappear into the sea of students.

Damn, that sucked. It sucked real bad. I'm straight-up an asshole--and even worse, I'm a coward. A horn beeps from behind me. I'm holding up the line, so I reluctantly put my truck into drive and head to work.

At work, time stands still. I can't focus. The heaviness I felt last night has returned full force. I am constantly zoning out and I'm not able to get any work done. I know this day hasn't been beneficial to my clients, my father, or me. I'm not ashamed to say I did not want to deal with my clientele. Without a second thought, I canceled all my appointments this morning and decide to cut out early.

With no real agenda or place to go, I head home to change out of my clothing, and get out the Z. Something about driving aimlessly is comforting and calming. I head north toward the mountains, recalling a thrilling hike that takes you up the mountainside.

There's an amazing area that looks out over the countryside and, even better, the drive up is full of windy back roads. *Perfect.* I'm hoping that others aren't playing hooky and I can take advantage of the hike.

It's been years since I've been up to The Knob. I don't remember the drive being so tranquil. Large trees on either side merging above the road create a shadowed canopy and the air drops dramatically, but it feels good against my skin.

The road becomes rough and rocky. Not good terrain for the Z, so I downshift to slow the car as I steer it over a wide dirt lot with a couple of other cars scattered about. I park the Z a few spaces away from another car and cut the engine. A glare from a water bottle sitting on my passenger seat blinds me. I'm not sure how long it's been in the car, but water doesn't go bad right? I don't know how long I'll want to wander, so I'll be needing it. Warm water is better than no water. I grab the bottle before getting out of my car.

Walking to the mouth of the mountain, an older couple strolls out with their dog on a leash; they wave a hello as they pass. I smile, return the greeting and continue on my way up the dirt trail.

With nothing to entertain me, other than the surrounding wilderness, this morning floats to my thoughts. Her pain--something that was caused by me-- was heartbreaking. I never in a million years would have seen this coming. My feelings for her crept up on me; fast. I find myself in more of a predicament than before. I hurt her. She could easily come clean to her brothers and they would be out for my blood. I'd like to think that she won't do that. Veronica is unlike any girl I've *ever* met, but no matter who, a scorned woman is someone you don't want to mess with. "Hell hath no fury like a woman scorned." Something my dad once said.

The path becomes rugged, which makes me refocus on not slipping and breaking my neck. For the next hour, I hike the rocky incline until I make it to the top. I throw my hands up victoriously while my breaths come in deep and quick. I bend over, putting my hands on my knees, to help catch my breath.

Once I'm breathing at a slightly normal pace, I move out towards the edge of the mountain and take a seat on a large rock that's easily twenty feet long. It allows my legs to dangle off the edge. The beauty laid out in front of me has left me speechless. I had forgotten how amazing this view is and for a fleeting second my thoughts shift to V, and how I want to bring her up here to experience this with me. I exhale slowly. Subconsciously, she keeps coming to my mind. What this means isn't lost on me, and I'm left even more conflicted than before. I enjoy the slight breeze licking my sweat covered body--despite the sun shining. It causes goosebumps to form upon my skin. I twist off the cap of the bottle and take a long swig of water.

"What do I do?" I whisper to those below me, to those above me, and to myself. Do I risk a life-long friendship or risk losing a potential life-long relationship? What if it doesn't work out? It would be awkward, and things will never be the same. I could lose a family that is more of a family to me than my own. There's so much at risk here. I don't know what to do.

Playing hooky yesterday only set me behind at work. I'm slightly frustrated with myself, but after disappearing from everyone and everything, I went home to work out. I pushed myself to my limits again, which resulted in another early night. I awoke with a sense of clarity. There was no way around the lecture I just received from my father; I listened as he called what I did 'childish and irresponsible'. I could only apologize with promises of making it up to the clients and headed into the office early to get a jump start on the day--which was filled. The packed schedule allowed me to immerse myself into my job and forget about the issues of yesterday.

It's close to six o'clock when I leave the office and I'm scrolling through my messages from Vance-- he's inviting me to come to hang out at the house. I decline and give him the excuse that I'm working late. The phone lights up in my hand with an incoming call from a number I don't recognize. The area code tells me it's a local number, so I answer it--not without some reluctance.

"Hello?"

"I'm going to kick your ass!" a female voice shouts through the line.

"What? Who is this?"

"I cannot believe you pulled this stunt after I *warned* you that I'd break your face."

"Taylor, how did you get my number?" I ask even though I'm sure it wasn't hard for her to get.

"Where are you?" she asks, dodging my question.

"Why, so you can break my face?" I ask jokingly.

"Yes."

I laugh at her.

"Don't you *dare*. I'm serious."

"I'm not going to tell you where I am. I happen to like my face. I don't think you have that kind of force, anyway."

"Tell me where you are so we can test your theory."

"What do you want, Taylor?" I question, despite already knowing why she's calling.

She huffs, clearly annoyed, "What happened? You hurt her when you said you wouldn't. Why?"

"It's complicated."

"Don't give me that weak bullshit. You are turning out to be like just another asshole, just like the guys her brothers try to protect her from."

"And that's why it can't happen," I say simply.

"Keep telling yourself that. Just so you know, she won't be single forever."

A second later the line clicks; then silence. Removing the phone from my ear, I look at the screen to confirm that she did, indeed, just hang up on me. I exhale and glance around the lot. *Fuck.* This is messing with my head again. Taylor called me out on my decision in doing what I think is best for us, and everyone else--my resolve is starting to crack. The fucking thought of Veronica being out with someone other than me is causing intense jealousy. I have no right. I tried doing what was right. I stopped anything that could have been before it even began. I run my hands across my head, gripping my hair out of frustration.

"I need a damn drink."

Fifteen minutes later, I'm sitting at the bar waiting to be served. Jade, hot bartender from last weekend, is working and currently strutting my way.

She leans on the bar top across from me, sporting a welcoming smile. Her top is cut low, exposing her cleavage in another neon-colored bra. "Hey there," she says cheerfully.

"Hey," I say weakly, simultaneously noticing how her dark hair is pulled back like V's was the other morning.

"You're Vin's friend right?" she asks.

"Yeah."

"I thought so. Miller?"

I nod. She gets a glass from under the bar and pulls a beer from the tap. "A man of few words," she says playfully, grabs a napkin, and places the beer on top. "I don't recall you being so dejected the last time I saw you," she says, her arms stretched out on either side of her with her palms on the bar.

"Yeah, I guess things seemed a bit...better then."

"What's got you so down?" she implores, "I'm a great listener."

"I'm sure you always come to work wanting to listen to everyone's problems," I joke.

"You'd be surprised. I'm the bar's shrink," she laughs, "Lady problems?" she continues prodding.

I snicker. "Is it that obvious?"

"It's usually always lady problems"—she smiles and leans back—"and you're in luck. I'm a lady. What better person to talk to?"

"Eh...I don't know."

She holds up her finger, "Hold on," she walks away and disappears into, what I assume is, the kitchen. I shrug and take a sip of my beer. Jade reappears a minute later to my right. "Told them I'm taking my twenty...or thirty," she says with a smile, and places a glass of dark liquid on the bar. She hops up on the stool next to me.

"You don't have to waste your break on me," I tell her.

She waves her hand at me, "I won't lie--I like the drama when it comes to other people. Kinda takes me away from my own. Makes me feel like I'm not alone. I know we all have problems, but sometimes you get so immersed in your own, hearing other people's issues can make you feel like yours aren't so bad...or it could be the other way around." She ponders that for a second. "But if you're having women problems, this should be good. Lay it on me."

I cringe. "I can't."

"And why not?"

"It involves people you know."

"Well I know a lot of people, so that's not surprising. But I promise to not repeat anything you say. I'm a vault of secrets. You'd be surprised what some people confide in me."

"Like what?"

She waves her finger at me, "Nuh huh," then points at herself, "vault of secrets."

I mull it over. I could use an opinion. What would it hurt to talk it out with someone, especially someone from outside? "Okay," I relent and she beams triumphantly, like she won a prize. "This stays between you and me," I point at her; completely serious.

The smile quickly disappears and she puts her pointer, middle, and ring fingers up in front of her. "Scout's Honor," she says seriously.

I arch a brow. "Were you a scout?"

She feigns shock. "Of course! You don't throw out the Scout's Honor in mockery." She smiles then leans in to whisper, "Troop thirty-four."

It makes me laugh, and I realize I genuinely enjoy talking with Jade. There's a fleeting thought of how different it would be if my feelings for Veronica didn't run so deep.

Explaining the whole situation to Jade doesn't seem as complicated as I remember, until the memory of how protective her brothers are comes into play. She doesn't interrupt me once and lets me explain it all until I feel like I have it all out there.

"Ehhh," She makes a face, "I don't wish to be you."

"Thanks."

She chuckles, "Okay, in all seriousness...why now? You've known her for, almost, her whole life. You come back from the military and--what?"

"I can't explain it. It was almost like a punch in the gut. She took my breath away. Seeing her that night at the Field, I saw her in a way I never did before. She was always Vance's little sister, I always cared for her like that as well. We all protected her from the guys at school, but now it's like I need to protect her from me."

"But protect her from what exactly? Are you intentionally planning on hurting her?"

"No, but I'm sure I have."

"So fix it," She shrugs like it's common sense.

"I don't think it's that easy, and her brothers will kill me."

"It *is* that easy. You fix it with her, and then you talk to them. Be upfront and honest. I'm sure they won't like it, but they may just surprise you with how they respond. You never know."

"What if they don't? Vance wanted to murder this guy who simply asked her out. What if she doesn't accept my apology?"

"What if they do, and what if she does? Isn't life just full of 'what-ifs'? You don't want to live your life on 'what-ifs'. They end being nothing but regrets."

"I don't want things to change for the worse," I confess.

"Well...haven't they kind of already?"

Yes. Yes, they have. I don't know if things between V and I will ever be the same, so that's already botched. Jade is right though, I'll continue to wonder what would've happened had I owned up to my feelings for her. She could be the girl that I end up marrying--not that marriage is in my near future, but she could be it for me.

My phone vibrates on the bar and the screen lights up with a message notification. Even though I didn't save Taylor's number, I recognize it.

As soon as I open it, the regret hits me. A guttural groan leaves my mouth and I instantly want to throw up and punch something at the same time. The clatter of my phone dropping on the bar has Jade on her feet.

"What's wrong?" she asks. I pinch the bridge of my nose with my left hand and turn my phone, so she can see the image of Veronica laughing with some guy sitting next to her in a booth. It looks like a diner. *Like our first date.*

"I think this puts it in perspective, yeah?"

I simply nod. She pats my back as she walks behind me, "Good luck."

She's already halfway down the bar. "Jade!" I yell to grab her attention and she turns slightly, pausing where she stands. "Thank you!" She gives me a thumbs up and continues on her way. I throw some cash down on the bar, then pull out my phone to send a text message to end the 'what-ifs'.

DISTRACTION

Veronica

The past twenty-four hours have been a whirlwind of emotions. If this is *exactly* what my brothers were protecting me from and, now, I'll gladly let them continue to do so. All I know is that I never want to feel the way I've been feeling ever again. Foolish, naive, inexperienced, and heartbroken. Of course, Taylor has my back. Her anger is enough for the both of us.

This morning, the hopeful and innocent part of me expected Chase to drive up to my house, disregarding my seething words from yesterday. He'd grovel for forgiveness, apologizing profusely, explaining how stupid he is for throwing away a good thing. That was not the case. He never showed, and I don't even know why I hoped he would. I also never heard from him. By the end of the school day, I'm emotionally burnt out.

After school, Taylor takes me to the garage and insists she'll stick around until I'm done. I promise her we won't stay long because, truthfully, it's the last place I want to be. She pushes that we are gonna have a much-needed girls evening even if it was even though it's a school night. I am sincerely grateful to have her by my side.

"Okay, where to?" Taylor asks me.

"Anywhere but Chrissy's," I tell her. Sadly, I may not be able to step foot into Chrissy's diner for a long time. The thought alone upsets me. The pie...

"Okay, I think I know just the place!" Tay interrupts my longing for the crusted dessert.

"Drive onward!" I point forward.

It doesn't take long to get where we were going--a popular burger joint right outside of town--that I've never been to. Since Chrissy's is a local diner, and a friend of my mother, I always felt obligated to go there. It doesn't hurt that Chrissy's has some amazing food. Taylor finally finds a parking spot towards the back of the lot.

"Well, it's packed. So, that's a good sign, right?" she says, turning her keys in the ignition.

"Very," I respond and glance around. There's a group of kids standing off towards the left, just hanging around.

"I've always wanted to try their burgers. Everyone's been raving about it since they opened."

"Seems like everyone else had the same thought tonight."

We both exit her Jeep and head inside the busy restaurant, I follow behind her but nearly run right into her back. "Tay, what are you doing?" I ask, stepping around her.

She glances around and shrugs. "Just seeing if there's anyone we know..." Then swings her head to the front of the building. "Looks like we're supposed to order first."

Following her line of sight, I see a guy standing behind the counter wearing a red shirt with a large rocket on the front. The name is written across his chest and a red visor upon his head. He's watching us with a less than enthusiastic expression. I smile in an attempt to make him feel...I don't know, appreciated? It doesn't work, his eyes only shift from me to the person standing in front of him. I didn't even realize Taylor left my side. I move through the makeshift line, coming to stand next to her.

"It's on me," Taylor says, and the bored employee looks at me.

"Tay," I whine.

"Zip it." She warns. Her voice is stern. With that, I know there's no use in arguing with her. I quickly give him my order and watch his hands move over the screen in front of him.

"Twenty-four dollars and ninety-five cents," he says, his deep voice void of any emotion.

"Chatty, aren't ya?" Taylor says, handing over her debit card. He glares at her slightly before sliding her card through the machine. She leans to me and whispers, "He has 'promotion' written all over him." I turn away in hopes that it hid my laughter well.

"Someone will bring it out to you," I hear his deep monotone voice from behind me.

"Thanks," Tay says, then joins me a second later, "See an open spot?"

I scan the large room. Booths are lining the perimeter, and the tables with chairs are scattered throughout the middle. There's so much commotion that it requires me to stand on my tiptoes to look over some of the people who are standing, instead of sitting. A rowdy bunch of guys are occupying most of the tables in the middle. I'm assuming they're jocks because of the varsity jackets they're wearing.

"Hmm..." Tay hums. "Maybe we should sit next to them," she suggests and points in the direction of the jackets.

"Let's not." I object, an empty booth in the back corner catches my eye. "How about over there?" I point.

"Really?" She asks scrunching up her face.

"Yep," I say and start walking towards the table without even waiting for her response. I slide into the booth with my back towards the restaurant and a second later Tay slides in across from me.

"Well, at least I can stare at something appealing."

"Why, thank you," I jest, knowing she was not talking about me.

She laughs at me. "You are the hottest piece of ass in this joint, besides me of course."

"Of course. Hey, thanks for buying."

"Just trying to get into your pants." She winks. "Is it working?"

"Oh yeah, it's working!"

"You slut!"

"Only for you, baby!"

Taylor's eyes glance at something to my right, causing me to look over my shoulder. A young girl, wearing the same ensemble as the guy behind the counter is approaching us carrying a red tray with food upon it.

"Hey girls," she greets with a smile, opposite from the guy at the register. They should switch positions. We both smile back. "I have one Rockin' Burger and one Deluxe Bacon Burger."

"Yep," Taylor confirms. The young girl places the tray in the middle of the booth between us. "Great. Enjoy your meal!" She turns on her feet and walks away. Taylor doesn't hesitate to dig in. She grabs the large burger with both hands and takes a massive bite. She groans her approval, "V, this is so good."

I grab mine and follow suit. The burst of flavor on my tongue has me moaning my approval. There's isn't much talking while we devour them, and what seemed like seconds--that were most likely minutes--fries were the only thing left on our plate.

"We have to come back here," Tay suggests after sipping on her drink.

"Definitely," I agree.

"Oh my gosh, look who's here!" Taylor says with a fry hanging from her mouth.

"Who?" I twist in my seat to look towards the door behind me. A group of kids just walked in, but I don't recognize any of them, so I don't understand what Taylor is talking about until my eyes settle upon the last guy walking through the door. I turn to Taylor, eyes wide, "Did you plan this?" She smiles mischievously but says, "I *may* have mentioned that we were gonna check out this place."

"And if I wanted to go elsewhere?"

She shrugs, "I'd text him."

"Wait, what? How do you have his number?"

"I have my ways."

"Why Tayyyy," I drag out her name in a whine.

"Because I love you, and if it's not going to happen with Chase, I don't want you to miss out because he's an idiot."

I sigh. "I'm going to kill you."

"You'll miss me too much."

The noise of moving tables and screeching chairs pulls our attention to the commotion. The jocks from earlier must have left and we didn't even notice; too immersed in our burgers to care. Devin and his friends have taken residence of the, now empty, table. I'm shamelessly watching Devin as he pulls a table closer to the other. It's causing his lean muscles under his shirt to flex. He laughs at something his friend says, then his mouth falls in a lingering smile--a smile he's shown me a lot since Monday. It would be *so* easy to crush on someone like Devin if Chase wasn't in the picture. Devin is good looking. He's funny, nice, smart, and all-around a good guy. Even though Chase has basically put an end to this whole thing, I can't help but still be hopeful, and that thought alone makes me feel so dumb. My appetite has disappeared as I stare down at my uneaten fries.

"Stop. Finish," Taylor says across from the table, pulling my attention to her.

"I'm full," I lie.

"Woman, I paid for your meal, you better damn well eat it *all*"

A smile forms on my lips involuntarily, "I love you, Tay."

She rolls her eyes, "You're giving me whiplash. One minute you're planning to kill me, the next you love me."

"It's just you. I'm surprised Wes has stayed with you for as long as he has.You must have a magical vagina." This causes Taylor to burst out in a loud boisterous laugh and now everyone around us is looking our way. "That's a good one, I'm going to have to take a mental note of that."

"I know," I flip my hair over my shoulder, "I'm hilarious."

A figure approaches our table and grabs our attention. My eyes connect with warm brown ones. "Hey, Devin!" Taylor greets him cheerfully.

"Hey, Taylor...Veronica," he greets her without looking her way.

"Hey!" I greet him. I'm not sure what else to say. I'm taken off guard--this was a setup, and I wonder if he's aware of it.

"May I?" he asks while gesturing next to me in the booth.

"Oh yeah...of course." I scoot over so he can sit. He slides in close, his leg brushing mine, and I feel the warmth spread all over my body. Taylor is smiling so big she looks like the Cheshire cat from Alice in Wonderland.

"How were the burgers?" Devin asks us, "I've been meaning to come to try this place out."

"Yeah, us too. My burger was amazing," Taylor says from across from us while I remain quiet. Devin leans into me, bumping my shoulder with his arm. "What did you think?" he asks, looking at me and scanning my face. I'm not sure what for. I squirm under his gaze. "Good, really good," confirming what Taylor said. He smiles.

"What?" I ask, slightly intimidated at his smile.

He shakes his head, "Nothing, you're just cute."

His compliment causes my breath to whoosh out of me. I feel all kinds of awkward. I've never taken compliments very well, "Thanks, you're cute too," I say lamely.

He chuckles, "Good to know you think so."

"Who are your friends?" a male voice interrupts us, pulling all our attention towards the imposing tall brunette boy with his arms crossed over his chest, standing at the end of the table.

"Oh. Hey Mason, this is Veronica and Taylor." He gestures to us, then explains, "Mason is my knucklehead cousin."

"Holdin' out, Dev."

"Taken." Tay holds her finger up.

"Shame," Mason retorts.

"Yep," Taylor agrees, and that makes us all laugh.

With permission, he takes a seat next to Tay. We hang out with Devin and Mason for a while, talking about everything. They even eat with us and most of their friends have trickled over, too. We learned they all attend the nearby school that Devin transferred from. They're a funny bunch, and my ribs hurt from laughing so much. It's a much-needed distraction. Tay is quiet in her corner of the booth. It pulls my attention away from the conversation for a second. Her features pinched as her fingers moved over her phone.

"Hey, what's wrong?" I ask her in a low voice. She quickly looks up at me and replies, "Nothing."

"You sure?" I ask curiously, "You looked in deep thought."

She shakes her head. "All is good."

"Okay."

We don't leave the restaurant until they have to kick us out to close down. I'm engulfed in a large hug by Devin and a promise from him to see me at school. After everything, I find myself smiling on the way home.

"I had fun," I say, mindlessly, on a slight high. Devin is nice.

"Good, I'm glad," Taylor says.

My phone pings, and I assume it's one of my brothers inquiring about my whereabouts, but it's not. It feels like my heart stops, and a gasp leaves my mouth.

"What?" Taylor asks quickly, "Who's that?"

"Chase."

"What'd he say?"

Taylor rolls to a stop at a red light, and I flip my

phone towards her so she can see.

"Well damn..." she says.

I stare blankly at my phone, totally taken aback by the message displayed on my screen. This is all I wanted to see all day, but since Devin arrived, Chase hasn't crossed my mind...until now.

STUPID OVER YOU
Veronica

I stare at his text, torn at the emotions singing through me. This is what I was hoping for, yet at the same time, I'm angry with him. I had a nice enjoyable night with Devin. It's almost like he knew that I could have something with someone else.
I glance at it again.

> **McSwoony**: I'll be at your house at seven AM.

I push on the power button, making the screen turn back to black. "*Who does* he think he is?" I say, to no one in particular. Taylor remains quiet. The light turns green and she presses on the gas pedal, making the Jeep move forward. "Like, seriously? I don't hear from him in what...two days? And now he thinks he can just text me like everything is peachy keen?" I huff, "I don't *think* so."

"Are you going to respond?"

"Yeah," I swipe open my phone, "I'm gonna tell him to go to hell."

Tay laughs lightly, "Calm down."

"Stupid. He's so stupid," My ranting continues.

"Yeah. Stupid over you."

"Isn't that a song?"

"Stuucckkk on sttuppiiddd for yyoouu." We both bust out in song, stare back at each other, and then burst out laughing.

"Damn. I needed that." I say wiping away the tears

from my eyes. I grab the phone from my lap to send him a response.

Me: No.

"What did you say back?" Tay asks, making the turn onto my street.

"I told him no."

"Really?" she asks, surprised.

"Yep."

My phone pings, and I'm slightly surprised he responds so quickly. My heart rate has kicked up a notch.

McSwoony: Yes. I will be there at seven to take you to school. We need to talk.

He's not leaving it up for discussion--this I can tell. I sigh. "He wants to talk," I tell Tay. I look over at her and ask, "Should I talk to him?"

She smirks, "Well, do *you* want to talk to him?"

"No," I pause, and a puff of air escapes my lips, "Yes. Kind of?"

"You do," she confirms.

"I do. I just don't wanna be this yo-yo. He either wants me, or he doesn't...yanno?"

She pulls into my driveway, "Then you tell him that."

Instead of pulling up to the front, she parks towards the garages. Her phone lights up in the cup holder and she quickly glances down. "It's probably Wes." I watch her unlock her phone, a small smile playing on her lips when she reads whatever's on her screen, "oh shit girl...he *really* wants to talk to you." She flips her phone my way, and I snatch it from her hand whether she intended me to or not.

Chase: Do not pick her up tomorrow.

"Oh my gosh!" I groan, handing her the phone back with wide eyes. She doesn't even hesitate. Her fingers moving over her phone at high-speed, "Wait, what are you saying?" I lean over the center console to peek at her screen, but I can't see the messages. I sit back in the seat.

"I'm not gonna make it easy for him." She smiles at me and says, "Let's see what he says first."

"Oh no." I laugh, covering my face with my hands. Her ringtone chimes and I uncover my face to watch her reaction.

"Ohhh. He's *good*."

"What! What? What is going on!" I hunch over again, but she pulls the phone away. "Why are you doing this to me?"

This goes on for another minute--her fingers moving and the phone pinging, I'm biting my fingernails to the quick. My nerves are eating at me. There's a tap on my arm so I swing my gaze to Taylor's face. She smiles and hands her phone over with a shrug. "He's picking you up." I take the phone from her hands and take a deep breath before reading their conversation.

> **Taylor**: I don't think she wants you to.
> **Chase**: Taylor, you will not pick her up tomorrow.
> **Taylor**: Or what?
> **Chase**: I don't want to play dirty with you, but I will.
> **Taylor**: Hasn't Wes told you? I like to play dirty.

That makes me laugh. "Oh my gosh, Tay!" but I don't look at her, I keep reading.

> **Chase**: Not going there. I think it would be quite difficult to pick her up in a missing vehicle.
> **Taylor**: And how in the world would you manage that?

Chase: It's a secret--one I doubt you want to mess with ;)
Taylor: I knew I liked you, Chase Daniels.
Chase: Right back atcha, Taylor Sullivan.
Taylor: She's all yours.
Chase: I hope so.

My heart sores at that last text. *Oh my*. I place her phone back into the cup holder and turn to look at her, "I guess he's picking me up tomorrow."

She nods.

"I am *so* nervous."

"Go get some rest. Don't be nervous."

I take a deep breath, "Okay. Yeah. Thank you."

"Anytime doll face. Now bring it in."

I giggle and lean in to hug her.

"I wanna hear *all* about it tomorrow."

"Duh." I pull on the door handle to let myself out and hop down onto the pavement. Once I reach my front door, I wave to Tay as she drives away before heading inside. My parents are in the living room. Dad's passed out in his chair and Mom is doing a puzzle on the sofa.

"Hey, Mom." I sit next to her, laying my head on her shoulder.

"Hey baby, have a good night?"

"Of course, I was with Tay."

She laughs lightly. "She was always a wild child. I mean that in the best way possible."

"Yeah," I agree, "I'm heading up."

"Is Taylor picking you up tomorrow again?" she questions.

"No, uh, Chase is."

"Hmm..is everything okay?"

"I don't know." I sigh.

"I'm always here if you need me. I may be old, but I was young once. I may understand better than

you think." I wrap my arm around hers and squeeze. "Thanks, Ma. I love you." She reaches her hand up and pats my cheek. "Love you too, honey."
 "Kay, well I'm going up."
 "Goodnight."

GOOD SURPRISE
Veronica

I wake up way before my alarm clock, but instead of laying in bed and allowing my nerves to take control of me, I get up and keep myself busy. I take a long hot shower and shave my legs until they are nice and smooth. I dress in some black leggings and a cream lace top. It's a rare occurrence when I take the time to blow out my hair, but I have time to kill and a mind to occupy.

When I'm finished my hair looks gloriously shiny and straight. I dust my face with some light makeup--nothing crazy--and do my usual eyeliner. I take a quick glance at the clock and sigh. Looks like I still have a good forty-five minutes yet.

The butterflies are starting to take flight in my stomach. It's so intense I feel like they're going to fly out my mouth. I take a deep breath, flip my hair over my shoulder, and peek at myself in the mirror before heading downstairs. Vance is sitting at the island, which takes me by surprise. I walk around him. "What are you doing up so early?"

"I got shit to do," is all he says. Mom turns, giving him the stink eye. "Sorry. I got *things* to do," Vance repeats. He turns to me and asks, "Chase picking you up this morning?"

"Yeah."

"He's been acting weird lately. He say anything to you?"

"No, why would he say anything to me?" Nervous laughter escapes me.

"I don't know. He mentioned that girl, Nic, the other day. Things didn't seem to be going so well, and he's just been off since. You're a girl...some days. Just thought he might ask your opinion or something." I smack his shoulder and grunt, "No, he hasn't."

"Okay," He knocks on the table and stands up, "I'm off." He struts out the kitchen and, only seconds later, the front door slams.

"You're on your own this morning. I didn't make anything," Mom informs me, but I already guessed that. There didn't seem to be anything cooking, and the kitchen didn't smell like yummy goodness.

"That's okay. I'm not that hungry." I reach for a banana laying in the wire basket in the center of the island. "This will work," I say, peeling it and then taking a bite.

"I'm going to go out on a limb here and assume that *you're* this 'Nic' your brother just mentioned." My chewing slows, and I glance up at her. "Why would you think that?"

She arches her eyebrow. "So, has it gotten serious now?" she questions.

"No. Actually, I'm not even sure. He played it off like I was misconstruing things. Like I was some dumb young girl. I haven't talked to him in two days," I tell her.

"Baby, put yourself in his shoes. I can't imagine that being an easy situation for him."

"What do you mean?" I ask, slightly annoyed. "I didn't put myself out there, he did! He went out of his way to flirt with me, to get my number, to text me, then BAM I'm just some little girl who *misunderstood*?"

"He got scared," She pauses and then laughs a little. "Did I ever tell you about what your uncle did to your father?"

"No, I don't think you have."

"Chase reminds me of your father." I make a face at that comment. "Stop," She scolds and continues, "Your uncle Tommy threatened your father. He avoided me for a couple of days until I approached him and made him talk to me. He was scared. And I only have one brother. You have four, whom Chase is all friends with. Look at it from his way."

"I get that, I do. But he made me feel so childish and I do *not* appreciate that."

"Be honest with him. No one said you have to make it easy on him. A little groveling is good. Your father bought me flowers for a week straight. I forgave him the second I found out what happened--what your uncle did--but he didn't have to know that."

I laugh. "Thanks, Mom."

There's a knock at the door and both our heads turn, slightly confused at who would be knocking now. I look at the clock. It's not quite seven yet. I slide off the stool and move toward the door and peek out the side window. Chase's truck is parked out front. *Hm. He's early*. I pull the door open to reveal him standing on my doorstep, looking way better than I last remember. He's wearing a maroon button-down shirt and black slacks. I scan his face as a small smirk plays on his lips, his blue eyes shining brightly.

"You're early," I point out.

His smile widens. "I am, for good reason. Can I come in?" I move back, allowing him to cross the threshold and close the door behind him.

"Grab your bag, please. I'd like to talk to your mom quickly. Privately."

"What?" I question, clearly confused. "About what?"

"You'll find out soon enough. Go get your things," he says moving past me into the kitchen and I watch as Mom pulls him into a hug. I want to eavesdrop but I realize I left my bag in my room, so I rush up the stairs, and back down. They're talking too low for me to hear, and his back is facing the kitchen's entrance. I huff to myself, and take a seat on the stairs, anxiously playing with my hair until he appears in front of me.

"Ready?" he questions, putting out his hand.

"Yeah." I place my palm in his warm one, and he gently pulls me forward until I'm standing.

"Okay, let's get going then." He keeps a hold of my hand, pulling me along behind him. It seems like a friendly hand holding, not the intimate kind where your fingers are threaded together. "Bye, Mom!" I yell before closing the door behind me.

Chase opens the passenger door for me, helps me up into the truck, and closes the door before heading around to his side. He's never done that before. This is...different. He hops up, and starts the truck before looking at me. "Thank you for letting me take you to school."

"It's not like I had much of an option, you told Taylor she wouldn't have a vehicle if she didn't agree to your terms," I retort.

"Yeah, I did. I don't regret it." His eyes move away from mine.

"What did you say to my mom?" I ask as he steers the truck down my driveway.

"I'll get to that. But first, I'm sorry." He pauses. I don't know if he's waiting for a response--or if he's going to say more--but when he doesn't say anything, I decide to.

"You made me feel stupid."

"That was never my intention. At all. I hate myself for that. You are not stupid, you are one of the smartest girls I've ever known. I'm the stupid one. But look, I've done a lot of thinking these past two days. One thing that *is* for certain are my feelings for you."

His admission causes my breath to hitch. I definitely assumed...but he never confirmed them. To hear the words straight from his mouth is almost like a shock. He glances at me and places his broad hand on his chest, "They're here." My anger instantly melts away. He looks back at the road. "I tried to push them away, to turn these feelings off, but there's no off switch. What I feel is real, and they're not going away."

"Why would you try to fight it? You have to know that the feelings are mutual."

He nods with a smile. "Yeah, and that made it harder to try and do the right thing."

"The right thing?" I question.

"You know Vance has been one of my closest friends since....forever. He is so protective of you--and rightfully so. We're guys, and guys are looking for one thing." I cross my arms over my chest, somewhat annoyed by his admission. "But sometimes a girl will take you by surprise, and they're all you think about. They can start as a friend, and you just want to be around them all the time. Slowly, the feelings evolve until it's so much more than sex."

He pauses to look at me, so I dare to question, "And I'm that girl?"

We're a block from the school when he abruptly pulls over to the side of the road. Putting the truck in park, he turns to me. His eyes scan my face. He reaches out to pull my hand from my lap and I allow him to infuse his fingers with mine. There's a 'zing' in my heart that's touching me to my very core.

"You are. You definitely are. I've been pretty miserable the past couple of days. Your family is more like a family to me than my own. Your brother is like a brother I've never had. He's always had my back. I felt like my feelings for you were betraying him. I was afraid of what my actions in pursuing something with you would cause. I don't want to lose you *and* your family, but my pushing you away was doing just that."

"Okay."

"I'd like to take you out tonight, will you let me?" he asks full of hope.

I'm quiet and shocked at these turn of events. I've been silent too long, so he squeezes my hand. "V?"

"Yes," I agree. His face lights up. His beautiful smile is on full display. The fact that my agreeing to go out with him has him this happy makes my heart soar. He uses the hand that is holding mine to pull me forward and uses his unoccupied arm to wrap around me in a warm hug. He holds on tight, seeming to be breathing me in.

"I haven't been this happy in a long time. Thank you," he whispers. I'm speechless at his heartfelt confession. He pulls away, but his face is close to mine, and his eyes are scanning me. His arm that's wrapped around me moves to my arm, rubbing up and down in a comforting gesture. "You alright?" he questions. His eyebrows have furrowed.

"Yeah," I say low, and give him a smile. "You've just

taken me by surprise this morning."

"A good surprise, I hope." He pulls away when I nod. "Let's get you to school." He keeps our hands intertwined and uses his left hand to awkwardly put the truck in drive. I try to pull my hand away, but he squeezes my hand and looks over, "No."

"Kay."

He's successful using only his one hand to maneuver the truck back on the road. We're mere feet away from the school entrance when he drops the bomb on me.

"I'm going to speak to your brothers later."

"What?" my response is loud, "You can't." The joy I was feeling has turned to fear. He glances at me then back at the road. "I don't want to go behind their backs."

"They won't allow it, Chase…they just won't," I say worriedly. "Please can you just…wait?" He sighs as he pulls up in front of the high school. I can tell he's having an internal battle with himself. "What are they going to think when we both turn down going to the track tonight?" he asks.

"We'll think of something, just please don't say anything yet," I beg, squeezing his hand. I have to get out of the truck but refuse to move until I hear him agree. I don't even care if there's a string of honking cars.

"Alright," he agrees, reluctantly.

I lean over and kiss him on the cheek. "Thank you," I whisper, then swiftly jump out of his truck. I feel like I'm on top of the world. I'm sporting a smile so large I must look like a clown, but I don't care. Chase Daniels confessed he's 'in-like' with me and is taking me out tonight. *I have a date with Chase Daniels!*

YOU'RE BEAUTIFUL
Veronica

"Well, well, well...look at you. All sunshine, rainbows, and shit," Taylor says as soon as she sees me approach her in the senior hallway. "I assume Mr. Daniels had a lot of nice things to say?"

"That, he did!" I confirm.

"Well, do tell."

I don't hesitate in telling her every little detail, unable to wipe the permanent smile from my face. I never realized how many muscles you use to smile. "Jeez, my face hurts," I muse while rubbing my cheeks.

"It's about damn time he got his head out of his ass," Taylor chides, "You do realize that Wes races tonight, right? How are you going to get out of going?" I ponder on it but my excuse of hanging out with Taylor won't work, as she'll have to be at the track to support her man.

"Damn," I whisper, "I don't know." I pull my phone from my back pocket and send Chase a text. My smile returns in full force.

> **Me**: Hey, Wes has a race tonight. We're gonna have to go.

I know that he's at work, so I don't expect him to text back right away. I tuck my phone away and notice that Tay is watching me with a peculiar expression on her face. "What?"

"Nothing." She smiles then wraps her arm around my shoulder, gently pulling me down the hallway with her.

Taylor's blonde hair is swinging back and forth as she bobs her head to the song playing on the radio, also occasionally belting out some out of tune lyrics. We're a couple of minutes from the garage when my phone rings. My hand instinctively reaches forward to turn down the music, and a muttered, "Hey!" comes from Taylor. Glancing down at the phone in my hand, I see Chase's nickname displayed on the screen. My heart takes off in a wild rhythm that's beating out of control.

"Oh, lover boyyy," Taylor sings.

I laugh and answer the phone. "Hey,"

"Hey, you. Sorry I didn't text you back. Work has been pretty hectic. I finally have a moment."

"Wow, that sucks."

"Yeah," He agrees. "It's so good to hear your voice."

A giggle escapes from my mouth, surprising me. I clear my throat. "We spoke this morning," I point out.

"Yeah, almost eight hours ago. That's too damn long. How was your day?" he asks. *I love that.*

"It's school. So yanno...it sucked."

"So, no guys asking you out? No one I have to beat up?" he jokes.

I snort. "No."

"Alright, good," his voice goes soft, "I can't wait to see you."

It's so weird to hear this confession coming from him--his deep voice expressing his need to see me. It fills me with warmth.

"Me too, but about that...what's the plan? Wes has a race tonight."

"Yeah, we'll have to go. Maybe we can go to Chrissy's after, so it won't be much of a date. I'm sorry."

"As long as I get to spend time with you I don't care where we go," I confess.

"I feel the same, but I still want to take you out."

This makes me smile, but it's short-lived when I hear gagging coming from my left, and I glare over at Taylor who is sticking her finger in her mouth. I roll my eyes.

"What is that noise?" Chase asks.

"Taylor is being gross."

"That's not surprising."

"Nope."

"Are you on your way to the garage now?"

"Yeah, are you going to stop in?" I ask, hopeful.

"No, probably not. I'm not sure when I'll get done. I'll see you at your house. What are the chances that you'll be able to ride with me?" He asks.

"I don't know." I sigh and look at Taylor. She's focused on the road, but I know she's listening.

"We should try and talk to your brothers, V."

"I don't know, Chase." I look out the window. "I want to focus on us before getting them involved. Like, what if we don't work out?" I ask.

"And what if we do?" He retorts.

"Then I think we should tell them one by one. Telling them all in a group is just a bad idea." I can see Taylor nodding in my peripheral vision, silently agreeing with me. "They feed off of each other."

"I'm not so sure," Chase sounds uneasy.

"Please, can we just figure *us* out first?"

"Okay," He sighs. "But for the record, me and you...it's

gonna work out."

"Yeah?" I question, totally infatuated with the future of us.

"Definitely," he confirms.

"Okay, whatever you say," I sing.

"See? You keep that up and we'll be golden."

I laugh. "Don't count on it."

"Good. I love that sass of yours."

"Noted."

"Okay, I'll see you in a couple of hours."

"Can't wait!"

"Me either. Bye, babe."

"Bye," I whisper, feeling warm at his term of endearment. I squeeze my phone and lean my head back on the headrest, allowing myself to bask in the warmth he brings all over my body. I look over at Taylor, who is smiling wide.

"What?" I ask.

"That was so *sickly* cute."

"It was." I nod.

"I am so happy for you."

"Me too." I bring my feet up and kick them wildly while screaming my excitement for a solid five seconds. Taylor laughs at my unexpected outburst. I collect myself and then turn to face her, bringing my legs up under my butt.

"You agree that we should wait to confront my brothers?" I ask.

"Yeah. Your brothers are cray-cray, especially Vance. And you're right! You guys are so new. What if you guys don't mesh, or get along or ...whatever the reason. You guys can part and no one would be the wiser."

"He doesn't want to sneak around," I tell her.

"When you guys decide that it's becoming serious, then you let them know."

I subconsciously nibble on my bottom lip. This is starting to stress me out. "How will I know?" She looks at me, her smile growing wide. "You'll know."

"What if it takes too long?"

She shrugs. "By then, your brothers not agreeing won't matter. You guys are already in it, they'll see it, and they'll get over it."

I think it over. I don't want to worry about what they'll think because what they think doesn't really matter. I may have known Chase for a long time, but I've never gotten to *know* him. This is on a whole different level, and I'm excited to explore this with him. I snuggle into myself, feeling all kinds of giddy.

Taylor drops me off at work and I, unfortunately, spend the next couple hours filing customer invoices. After clocking out, I catch a ride home with Vin. Wes, Vaughn, and Vance are already hanging out in the garage.

"Hey!" I greet them as I walk inside with Vin close behind me.

"Hey, V." Wes is the first to greet me, followed by a head nod from Vance, and a wave from Vaughn.

"Whatcha doin?" I ask, halting beside Vance at Wes' car.

"Just doing a quick tune," Vance offers.

"Nice. I hear you got a money run tonight?" I turn my attention to Wes.

"Yeah. Easy money," Wes states, calmly. There's not

an ounce of nervousness emanating from him.

"Oh, yeah?" I laugh.

"Definitely. They ain't got shit on me."

"Should be a good one then. I'm gonna go up to my room. When's Tay coming?"

"Not sure. She should be here soon," Wes responds.

"Alright." I turn and walk through the door of the garage, through the kitchen, and into the living room where Mom is lounging.

"Hey!"

"Hey, honey."

I take in her appearance. "Where are you going all dressed up? And where's Dad?"

"We're going to bingo!" she says excitedly, "He's upstairs getting dressed."

"That sounds like fun."

"A five-hundred-dollar pot? Yeah, that's fun!" Dad speaks from the top of the stairs. He's wearing a 'Victor's Garage' shirt. He's never one to *not* advertise his business, even though everyone in that bingo hall is most likely already a customer.

"Hey, Dad."

"Hey, sweet pea," he says, opening his arms as he reaches me. I move into them so he can pull me in for a big hug. He squeezes me and leaves a kiss on the top of my head. Moving back, I take a couple of steps up. "Well, you kids have fun! Good luck."

"Be safe!" Mom yells.

"Of course!" I respond, head down the hall to my room, and drop my bag near my closet. I take a whiff of myself, knowing that I'll be seeing Chase soon. I don't want to smell bad.

I *definitely* need to shower. I rid myself of clothes,

toss my hair in a bun, wrap my body in a towel, and rush to the bathroom. I quickly wash until I feel certain I no longer smell like a grease monkey. Turning the water off, I grab the towel and dry off my body as much as possible before I wrap it around myself. I peek my head out the door, making sure the coast is clear before running to my room. I burst through the door and turn around to lock it.

"I could get used to this."

I scream at the unexpected male voice, whirling around to find Chase sprawled on my bed. He looks completely comfortable with his socked feet crossed at the ankles, hands behind his head, and a large smile on his face. His eyes are on me. His blue shirt is riding up, showing a bit of his toned stomach.

"Holy shit! You scared me," I grab at my chest, my heart pounding. Chase swiftly moves so he's sitting at the side of my bed, his feet now on the ground.

"What are you doing?" I question.

"I wanted to see you."

"What about my brothers?" I ask, worriedly.

"I told them I was going to the bathroom." He stands up and approaches me, reaching me in three strides. He pulls me to him and embraces me in his stronghold. I love the feel of our bodies so close together--his warmth is so caressing.

"Okay. I need to leave this room, and you need to get dressed." He releases me quickly, moving me so my back is to the bed, and he's closest to the door. I hang on to my towel as his eyes sweep over me. "Yes, I need to go." He quickly unlocks the door and leaves me standing in the middle of my room.

I stare at myself in the mirror in front of me, pleased. The cute jersey top fits my frame nicely, as do the dark wash skinny jeans. I wore shorts to the track *once*--against Vance's advice--and learned why pretty quickly. My legs had a nice, thick layer of dirt on them by the end of the night and my socks looked way more gray than white. Vance found it hilarious while I definitely did not. I chalked it up to just his disapproval of me wearing anything *remotely* revealing. I remember telling him to shut up before he could even explain why. Lesson learned. Now, I'm amused when girls wear skirts or shorts.

My door bursts open, and I'm ready to yell at whoever's entering without knocking, but the words die on my lips when I notice it's Taylor.

"Hey, girlfriend." She comes to stand next to me and we look at our reflections in the mirror. Our outfits are eerily similar. We burst out laughing.

"Cute," I tell her.

She taps my temple lightly, "Great minds think alike."

I grab my boots from the closet and slip them on. I usually wear my Converse since they're good when racing, but I know I won't be doing that tonight.

"Did you just get here?" I ask her.

"Maybe a couple of minutes ago. Chase is looking *mighty* good tonight."

"He always does," I point out.

She ponders on that for a second. "True."

"He snuck into my room earlier."

"Say what? Did you guys get it on?" She sits next to me on the bed, waggling her eyebrows. I reach over to smack her on the arm. "No!"

She rubs the spot on her bicep. "I was kidding! Jeez."

"I didn't even hit you that hard," I muse.

"Anything good happen?"

"No, no way. We just started. I don't even know what we are. I was in a towel. He was pretty adamant about getting outta my room."

"He wanted to ravish you."

"Who wants to ravish you?" Vance asks, violently pushing through my door.

"No one! What are you doing?" I stand up crossing my arms over my chest.

"Who the fuck are you talking about?"

"Are you guys ready to go?" I ask, dodging his question.

"Yeah. I'm riding with Wes. Vin's not going. So you can go with us, or Chase said you can ride with him."

"Vaughn?" I ask curiously.

"He didn't offer." Vance cracks a smile.

I shake my head. "Go figure."

"Where the hell is Vin going?"

Vance shrugs, "Not sure, just said he had plans."

This is a no brainer, but I'm really surprised that Vance even gave me the option to go with Chase. It's almost so easy it's scary. I glance at Taylor while putting a pout face into play. "You okay if I ride with Chase? I'll get shotty."

"Ugh, you're gonna leave me with *this* one?" she asks, pointing to Vance.

"Wes already said you got shotgun," Vance puts in.

"Damn straight. He knows better," Taylor says.

"Whatever...let's go," Vance says, then turns to walk out my room. I give Taylor bug eyes.

"Holy shit. That was close!" I whisper-yell to her. She nods wildly.

I grab my bag from where it lays on the floor, then follow behind Taylor. We make our way downstairs, through the kitchen and into the garage. Wes' car is no longer inside but all the guys are standing around. They all turn to look at us and my eyes immediately meet Chase's. I quickly look away in hopes that my attraction to him isn't as obvious as I think it is.

"Alright, now that the girls are ready, we can head out," Vance announces.

We all head in different directions. Chase is parked further back, allowing us to walk together. "You look nice," he whispers, "But I definitely prefer the towel look."

I bite my lip at his compliment and innuendo. "Maybe it'll make another appearance one day," I flirt.

He groans and I laugh as I round the front of his car to the passenger side door. He unlocks it and we both get inside. I grab the seat belt to buckle up as I hear him say, "You're going to be the death of me, woman!"

I look at him as if I heard him wrong, but he's looking at me as if I'm the best thing on this planet, a small smile playing on his lips. "But I'll die a happy man," he adds. My eyes stay on him, watching him as he starts his car. I can confidently say I haven't ever felt the way I'm feeling right now. Chase has caught me by surprise in more ways than one. I never, in a million years, would have thought that Chase would say these things to me--that he would be the one to risk the wrath of my crazy brothers. At the same time, though, it couldn't feel more right. Like this is exactly what was meant to happen.

We drive in comfortable silence as I watch the streetlights zoom by. I startle at the touch of Chase's hand flipping my hand over--so my palm is facing upward--and his long fingers thread through mine, weaving them together perfectly. I look at our joined hands and feel a smile creep over my lips. My heart swells at the small gesture. It reminds me of all that happened this morning--our conversation. A small squeeze of his hand pulls my attention to him. "Is this okay?" he asks.

"Yeah, of course. It's perfect."

"Okay good. It's going to be hard not to touch you all night."

"I never pictured you as a touchy-feely kind of guy."

"I'm not. Not really. It's just you."

This guy. He has all the right words to say, and I'm beginning to feel inexperienced.

"I bet you say that to all your girlfriends," I joke.

The light turns yellow but Vaughn's car precedes to run through it. It quickly turns red and causes us to stop while my brothers keep going. Chase doesn't release my hand as he downshifts. Another pull on my hand has me looking at him in question, the light shadowing reflects his features in red. His brows are furrowed as his eyes scan my face. "No," He says, sternly. "It's just *you*." His admission causes my breath to catch. I am so surprised. But, at the same time, I'm so relieved to hear this. "Understood?"

Nodding, I exhale. "Yeah."

"Good."

Chase's face is now showcased in green. He uses our joint hands to shift, continuing until we're in his last available gear, then places them on his lap. This causes me to lean closer to him with my arm resting on the center console. I'm overflowing with emotions. I feel like I could cry. I push them aside--feeling overwhelmed and slightly embarrassed. I'm not a very emotional kind of girl, but this is all so new to me.

I lean my head back on the side of the headrest since I'm too far over. I take in his features quietly from the side--his perfectly shaped ear, his sideburns that reach his ear lobes, his eyelashes that seem insanely long, his sharp nose, and his *perfectly* kissable lips. I cannot believe that I am lucky enough to be sitting in his car, holding his hand, and that I will one day get to feel those lips on mine. I'm too busy studying him to notice that the car has stopped until he looks at me.

"What are you doing?" he asks. I glance in front of us. We're stopped at the stop-light right outside the small town near the track. I smile wide. I'm slightly embarrassed, and for the first time, I'm *sure* I'm blushing. He smiles, "Well?"

I peer up at him. His face has moved much closer to mine. "Do you have any idea how handsome you are?" I ask.

"Well, I do now. Thank you. I could say the same about you."

"I'm handsome?" I joke.

"You're beautiful." His eyes are moving between my eyes and lips and without even realizing, I'm moving closer until we're a mere inch apart. I can feel his breath on my face and I know without a doubt, I want to kiss him more than *anything*. I decide not to hesitate one more second. I move in to close the gap and our lips are touching in a soft, tender kiss. It's innocent until our mouths are moving sensually together. His hand is tangled in my hair, while I have no idea where my hands are. I feel this kiss down to my toes. All of a sudden his tongue traces my upper lip, asking for permission to enter. It causes an unexpected moan to escape my parted lips.

A loud noise startles us apart--the light has turned green, and the car behind is honking. Chase quickly pulls himself together and puts the car into gear, gunning it. I rub my face. I am completely flustered. There's a pressure on my leg and I look down to find Chase's hand the source. I look over at him, "I'm sorry. I wanted to wait until a good moment to do that but you were feeding me compliments, all while looking gorgeous."

"Don't apologize," I tell him. "That was everything," I confess.

"Now, now. That's just gonna go *right* to my head."

"It's true. I'm jealous of every girl who's ever kissed you."

We reach the entrance for the track and he grabs my hand, placing a soft kiss on it. I feel it down to my core. "Don't. I don't want any other lips to touch mine and anyone before you doesn't matter."

"Okay," I whisper because he has rendered me speechless. I don't think I'll ever get used to this.

SEVEN TWENTY-FIVE
Veronica

The line for entry into the track is about as long as to be expected. I spot Vaughn and Wes' car not that far ahead of us. The line moves smoothly, and when we reach the pay booth I pull out my wallet to pay for my way in.

"Put that away." Chase pushes my hand aside.

"You don't have to pay for me," I tell him.

"I know, but I want to."

"Thank you," I say with a smile.

"Racing?" asks the young guy standing inside the doorway of the booth.

Chase takes a second to think about it before giving an answer, "Yeah, just one."

The man grabs the window marker and steps out from inside, "Number?"

"Seven, twenty-five." I watch as the worker writes the number on the side window, and the top front, then steps back into the booth.

"That'll be thirty."

Chase hands him the money. "Good luck," The guy says, handing Chase the track rules and regulations. He hands me the paper, and I place it in my lap.

"Seven twenty-five?" I question.

"Yeah. My birthday."

"Ohhh. Right! I knew that." I play off the fact I actually forgot his birthday, despite the fact we've always celebrated during the summer

He puts the car into first then drives towards our usual spot near the chain-link fence. Vaughn and Wes' car are parked--they're already standing around with their hoods popped up. There's an orange Subaru parked on the other side of Wes. "Is that the guy he's racing?" I ask.

"I'm not sure," Chase says, shutting his car off. As we both get out, I catch Taylor looking our way and wiggle her eyebrows, making me laugh. I come to a stop next to her and Chase moves over towards my brothers and Wes, putting some space between us.

Vaughn is talking to the guy I don't know, so I can only assume that he's a friend of his. He introduces Chase but doesn't even bother to acknowledge me. *Okay.* "Aren't you going to introduce me?" I ask, annoyed that I'm being ignored.

"No," Vaughn says, and I catch Chase's eyebrows rise. So I move towards them and put out my hand to the unknown guy. "Hey, I'm Veronica,"

"Brandon. Nice to meet you." He smiles, showing nice white teeth. He has a head full of hair--not in any particular style--and black glasses. His shirt says 'Gamer'.

"Are you done hitting on my friend?" Vaughn barks.

"I am not hitting on him!"

"Hey, she can hit on me any day," Brandon says, playfully.

"Uh. No," Vaughn says, as another voice adds in, "Get the fuck outta here," from behind me. I look over my shoulder at Vance who's glaring at me and glance at Chase who just looks amused.

"I was being polite!" I throw my hands out, shake my head, then stalk back over to Taylor. "They're so freakin' stupid." She shrugs and laughs. "Psychos."

"For real," She leans in and asks, "so how was the ride?"

A large grin breaks upon my lips. "That good, huh?"

I just nod and she loops her arm around mine. "Let's go for a walk," She whirls around and yells, "We're going to the bathroom!"

As soon as we're far enough away I can't help but squeal, "He kissed me!"

"Ah!" She squeezes my arm.

"Come to think of it, I think I kissed him."

"Who cares who kissed who first--it happened! More importantly, how was it?"

I sigh dreamily.

"That good?"

"Yes."

"I knew it!"

I scrunch my face, "You knew he'd be a good kisser?"

"Uh, yeah? You've seen his lips."

I laugh. "True."

"And now you've tasted them."

"Uh Huh!" I say, enthusiastically.

"I am so happy for you."

"It seriously just feels so…*right*. Perfect, actually. He still makes me nervous, but at the same time, he eases me. Isn't that all kinds of contradicting?"

"Nope," she says with a large smirk.

We walk around for a little before we decide we've been gone long enough. We start to head back to the group.

"Ugh. Looks like they've gained some friends." I squint my eyes at my brothers, Wes, Chase, and Brandon. Our group has grown--a few other guys are standing around Wes' Evo--but a handful of girls have joined them, too. I can't help but feel the pang of jealousy at the girl standing a little too close to Chase, but his arms are crossed, and he doesn't seem to be giving her one bit of his attention. Wes and another guy are talking and Chase seems to be engrossed with their conversation. He's listening intently. I wish I could go wrap my arms around him to make the girl move her way along to someone else, but that definitely can't happen. I settle on leaning against his car and look everywhere but at him. Vance is too busy flirting to notice anyone else around him.

Vaughn and Brandon have the attention of three girls, and everyone within town limits knows that Wes isn't available, so most girls don't bother with him anymore. Taylor is a feisty chick you don't want to mess with. Regardless, she wraps her arms around Wes and pulls him in for a kiss. He gives her what she wants and continues talking. Their antics are amusing, to say the least. Taylor joins me again and we make fun of my brothers behind their backs; it's my favorite past-time. A dark-colored car abruptly pulls up behind Chase's and Wes' car. A short, muscular, tattooed man gets out and approaches our group.

Everyone stops their conversation as this bulky dude walks up to Wes. "Who the hell is that?" I whisper to Tay.

"You ready to get your ass handed to you?" the deep voice barks out.

"I don't know, but he looks like a mini hulk," Taylor whispers back, making me laugh. Wes towers over the guy and a sly, cocky smirk emerges on his features, "Not going to happen, but nice try."

"Prove it."

Wes just nods and the beef-head walks back to his car, peeling out aggressively.

"That was unnecessary," I mumble.

Wes moves towards Tay. "Give me my good luck kiss." Taylor, of course, complies. Their simple kiss quickly goes from G to PG-13. I leave them to it and walk over to Chase. The same girl is still trying to engage him in a conversation, but his eyes are on me and following my movements as I come to stand next to him. His back is now facing her. If that's not a silent dismissal, I don't know what is. I am internally cheering, but the smile on my face is apparent.

"Why are you smiling like that?" he asks.

"No reason."

"Uh-huh."

Out of the corner of my eye, I see her retreat to her friend group that's surrounded Vaughn and Brandon. Her arms are crossed over her chest and there's an ugly scowl on her face.

"Seems like she wanted your attention," I point out.

"Did she? I hadn't noticed. There's this cute brunette that I can't keep my eyes off of," he flirts, and the feeling of lust replaces the jealousy. Wes' car starts up just as Taylor joins us.

"Let's rock," she says. Wes backs up his car and drives off to the line of waiting cars.

"That's the guy he's racing for money?" Chase asks Taylor.

"Yeah, I think so. He didn't mention who it was, so I'm not even sure I know who that is."

Vance and his 'flavor of the moment' join us. "That's John. He's from a couple of towns over. I think he heard about Wes through the circuit. If Wes beats him, it'll be a big deal and could get Wes tons of exposure."

"Is this a good thing?" I question, glancing at Tay. I can see the slight worry register on her face.

"Hell yeah! Bigger races and more money," Vance says excitedly.

"Why didn't you bring your car?" the girl asks.

"I'm going to make some modifications to it," he tells her. She pinches her face, not grasping. "Try to make it go faster," Vance explains further. *What the hell is this girl even doing here?* I roll my eyes and turn to look at the track. Two cars go zooming down. I hear their exhausts popping as they hit the rev line. I move towards the fence and leave the group. Hands suddenly grasp the fence next to me. It's Chase.

"I don't understand. Why come to the track if you're going to try and pick up guys? Isn't that what a bar is for?" I ask annoyed.

"What if you're not twenty-one?"

"I don't know, go to parties then? You come here to race or talk cars, meet other car enthusiasts...not pick up guys. Especially guys like my brothers."

"The guys come here to pick up girls," he points out.

"It's a vicious cycle."

"Wes up yet?" Taylor comes to stand on the other side of me.

I squint towards the line. "Don't see him."

"I see his car! Two cars back!" She jumps excitedly.

The rest of the group joins us, including the girls. The same girl that tried to get Chase's attention before squeezes in between us, making me take a step over. Her perfume is heavy and overpowering; it makes me sneeze. I was pretty confident after his complete disregard of her earlier she'd take the hint. Now, I'm annoyed. I'm two seconds away from telling her off, but at the same time, I want to enjoy watching Chase turn her down. Again.

Another set of cars zoom down the track, leaving Wes and John one set away from their race. I can hear the girl ask Chase something, but her voice is too low for me to decipher. *Damn.* I lean over nonchalantly trying to pick up some conversation, but the surroundings are too loud for me to make out any words. The reeving engines at the starting line drown out anyone trying to have a conversation. Movement in my peripheral vision has me turning my head and Chase is leaning towards the girl's ear, causing me to hold my breath. His head comes up and his eyes are on me. She looks at the track in front of her. Her glossed lips purse and then she abruptly moves away. I watch her walk away from us completely, also leaving her friends behind. I can't help but smile.

Seconds later, two more cars are speeding down the pavement. Chase closes the gap when the cars have passed, and I lean in. "What did you say?" I ask, my curiosity getting the best of me.

"I told her I wasn't interested."

"WHOOOO!" Taylor yells from my left, starting me.

"Jeez!" I cry, causing Chase to laugh, "She always does that!"

She's jumping up and down as Wes' and John's cars meet the starting line. I'm finally able to see what John is driving--a black or maybe dark blue old body Honda Civic Si. You can see he's put a lot of work into it, the large front mount is on display. They're both revving the shit out of their cars, the backfiring from the exhaust popping loudly. The body of their cars are lifting upfront as they take off. It's a close call. They are neck and neck. They zoom by our position at the fence, and I can't help but scream my excitement. The further they move down, the harder it becomes to see who's in the lead.

I can hear Vance on the other side of Chase yelling. He's shaking the fence wildly, making me release my grip so my arms don't rip out of their sockets. The times light up on the board at the end of the track. I suck in a breath. Wes has the lead by two seconds. Taylor is jumping up and down next to me, flailing wildly. Vance's hoots and hollers are so loud that everyone is looking our way. He picks up the girl next to him by her waist and seemingly throws her around in celebration.

"Oh my gosh," I whisper, eyes wide.

Arms wrap around my neck as Taylor grabs me and she's pulling me into a wild, messy hug. "He won! He won! He beat him by two seconds!" I join in with her excitement, celebrating Wes' super close win. I can only imagine that John is not going to be happy. Wes' car pulls up to our spot and he jumps out of the car, throwing his hands up in the air. He catches Taylor quickly as she runs to him.

Chase and I are the calmest of the group. "We're friends with a bunch of monkeys!" I say to him. He laughs lightly. Everyone's congratulating Wes on his close win with high fives, hugs, and pats on the back.

"Where's that asshole?" Vance asks as he's looking around at the crowd. I can only assume he's talking about Wes' hotheaded opponent. Wes only shrugs. "If he doesn't pay it won't look good on the circuit. I'm not worried. He'll pay. He's just embarrassed." He turns to his car, lifting the hood, and then propping it open.

"I'll be right back," he tells the group before jogging away. We are all lingering around chatting when Wes returns with a bag of ice to place on top of his intercooler, so he can get back on the track.

"Yo, Chase, you wanna run one?" Vaughn yells to Chase, who is standing close to me.

"Yeah man, any chance to embarrass you," Chase yells and the group laughs. Vaughn looks a little annoyed, especially with the girls around him. I can't help the smirk that's forming.

Our group has gathered some more people--including more women--no doubt wanting the attention of the guys. Another girl slides in next to Chase and I eye her hands grabbing at his arm. He looks down and removes her hands almost subconsciously. I like that, but it doesn't go unnoticed. She pouts and turns to her friend standing next to her.

"More action, less talk," Vaughn says, trying to be tough.

Chase walks towards Vaughn. "Ladies first," Chase says while waving his arm in front of him. Ohh's and more laughter emerge around us. I watch Vaughn interact with the group he's assembled. Each of them kiss him on each cheek, then giggle. Chase looks at me before walking to his car. I throw my fist up and yell, "'Kick his ass, Sea bass'."

He laughs hard at my 'Dumb and Dumber' reference, his head thrown back. As a kid, my brothers and Chase would watch this movie repeatedly, the phrase becoming a staple. "That was a good one!" I watch him climb into his car with a wide smile on his face.

"Yo, Brandon!" Wes yells to the kid--who's sur-

rounded by girls--seeming to be in his glory.
Brandon's head whips up at his name, "What's up?"
"You wanna get one in?"
"Yeah, sure."
Wes kisses Taylor before walking back towards his car, removing the now watered-down bag, and closing his hood. Brandon and Wes both drive off leaving me, Taylor, Vance, and a handful of girls. Taylor and I move towards the fence, not really caring to be near Vance.

"Did you see him *totally* diss that girl?" Taylor asks, low. "I was mentally cheering."

"It was great," I tell her with a smile.

"If that's not a devotion of love, I don't know what is."

I look at her and scoff. "You're nuts."

"Maybe a little, but that boy be lovin' you."

"It is *way* too soon to be throwin' that L word around, okay?"

"Okay. He be likin' you," she pauses, "a lot."

"Who likes you?" Vance chimes in.

"Where the hell did you come from?" I ask, perplexed. He seems to keep appearing out of nowhere, lately.

"Your mom," Vance responds. "Are we talking about the guy who asked you out?" he presses.

"Yep," I agree to just shut him up.

"I'll kick his ass."

"You will not! Shut up." I push on his shoulder.

"Vance, what's with your friend? Is he like...gay?" I glance over Vance, noticing the same girl that Chase turned down. This causes Vance to burst out in laughter. "Who, *Chase*?"

She nods her head, "He totally blew me off."

"No, sweetheart, he's not gay. He's pussy-whipped."
I scrunch up my face.

"The only girl I see him with is her," her finger is pointed my way, "and he's definitely not with her." *What?* The anger in me flares up, and I want to break her finger off.

"No, he's definitely not," Vance agrees. "But he's been talking to some girl."

"Well she's not here, so what she doesn't know won't hurt her."

I can't help the bitter laugh that bubbles out of my throat. "You've got to be kidding me," I mumble. "What was that?" she sneers at me, peering around Vance.

I smile at her. "You," I point my finger at her, "are exactly what's wrong with people today. Have a little respect. If someone is taken, don't be a snake. You don't go after another girl's man. It's pathetic."

She crosses her arm, seemingly unaffected by my words. Her smug smile is making her, once pretty, face ugly. She laughs bitterly. "If he bites the bait, he obviously doesn't care." I shake my head, completely baffled. "Exactly! Chase isn't interested in you, so move along."

"We'll see," she says before throwing her long blonde hair over her shoulder and sauntering away. I throw my hands up and glance at Vance, who shrugs his shoulders, but is clearly amused by the whole exchange.

"Vance, I'm sorry bro, but you need to stop slumming." My words cause the blonde to stop in her tracks, and she whips around.

"Um, *excuse* me? Slumming? Take a good look in the mirror, sweetie."

Two cars zoom by, pausing our intense conversation. I'm about to respond when Vance's loud voice stops me. "Enough!" He barks, eyes on her, "You do realize that's my sister, right?" Her full attention is on Vance now, and her face is becoming pink.

"And?"

"And? You want to hang with us? Then you respect the people I hang with, *especially* my family. If you can't do that, then you can take your ass elsewhere."

Without another peep, she stalks away. The remaining girls standing on the other side of Vance glare at me, but follow their blonde friend, like obedient pups.

"Buh-bye." I wave.

"Knock it off, V," Vance says annoyed. His voice is raised because of the loud exhausts from the cars behind us.

"What? That girl was a bitch," I point out.

"Bitch or not, she was hot."

I groan. "She wasn't even interested in you!"

"I could have swooped in and healed her wounded ego when Chase turned her down." I take notice of the two girls standing not too far away from us and point at them. "Go talk to them."

He eyes up said girls, "Good idea." And walks over to them. I watch as they openly invite him into their conversation. Another set of cars whirl by.

"I cannot *believe* I'm related to him," I say to Taylor. "You were pretty quiet, by the way." I look towards her.

"You were handling yourself!"

I rub my nails on my shoulder, then laugh at myself. The times from the last race flash up on the board at the end of the track.

"You're such a nerd." Taylor bumps my shoulder. I just shrug. There's definitely no denying that. Taking my place back at the fence, I notice the familiar car pulling up to the starting line. "Oh! Chase and Vaughn are up next!" The feeling of pride erupts within me, and I'm jumping on the tip of my toes. I guess this is what Taylor feels like every time she watches Wes run. Seconds later, they're off. Chase getting a good jump off the line. I scream out loud, not able to contain my excitement.

Taylor slaps at my arm, "You scared me!"

"Good! That's just for *one* of the many times you've scared me!"

Chase gains the lead by almost half a car length. "He's got him!" I yell, "Yes!" Their score flashes on the board.

"WHOO!" Vance yells beside me. The two girls have followed him over, "That was a great run!"

"I'm gonna go see Chase," I tell Taylor.

"Okay, I'm gonna stay here and wait for Wes." I nod, just remembering that Wes is running again. I glance behind at the starting line and spot his Evo, but it's about two cars behind.

"I'll be right back," I tell her again, and move away from the fence. Vance does the same, but the girls remain at the silver linking. Chase's silver Z pulls up as we're walking towards the pavement. His smile is enormous and contagious. He removes himself from his car, throwing up his hand in a victory salute.

"Yeah, buddy!" Vance yells.

Vaughn's gray VW pulls up shortly after, but rather than the smile Chase is sporting, Vaughn looks aggravated--like the sore loser he is. Chase moves to Vaughn with his hand out, and Vaughn takes it. We come to stand before the cars. Vaughn is looking around and when he doesn't find what he was looking for, his eyes land on Vance, and asks, "What happened to Sabrina?"

I can only assume he's asking about one of the girls who stalked off not long ago. I just shrug, and no one else seems to pay him much attention. The focus is on Chase's victory. I hold my hand up for a high five since I can't plant a 'winning kiss' on him. "Nice run!"

He's amused at my lame attempt but precedes to slap my hand with his, "Thanks."

"Yeah man, that was great," Vance agrees. He turns his attention back to Chase.

"Pure luck!" Vaughn cuts in.

"Whatever makes you feel better, dude." Chase laughs.

Vaughn crosses his arms, "Seriously, where did the girls go?"

"Rocky here chased them off." Vance nonchalantly points his thumb at me.

"For fuck's sake, V!" Vaughn throws his hands up.

I huff. "What? That girl was grimy!"

"Don't worry, I found replacements," Vance cuts in as he turns to look at the girls who are still standing at the fence.

I shake my head back and forth. "Those poor girls."

"Wes is up!" Taylor yells from behind us.

Our group moves to watch Wes and Brandon go at it. Vaughn wastes no time in chatting up the new girls, and I watch their interaction. The brunette seems a bit quiet. It's a complete contrast to her friend and from the girls who were just here. She honestly doesn't seem half bad. I guess it's people's intuition. Sometimes you can just feel a vibe and you know they're a bad apple-- the gut feeling that somethings not right? But I wasn't getting that from these girls. Good energy.

The loud exhaust pulls my attention away from the girls and back to the race at the end, just missing them jumping the line. The orange Subaru is leading and I'm *shocked.*

"Holy crap!" Taylor says from my left.

"Yo!" I hear Vance, "What!"

Wes pulls in, but Brandon is leading by the nose.

"Damn, B-Rad shoulda put some money down," Vaughn says.

The lights flash on the board, and we're all completely stunned.

"Did *not* see that coming," Chase puts in.

"It's almost a good thing he didn't put any money down," Taylor says.

"Yeah, really."

Seconds later, Wes' black Evo is coming down the parking lot, followed by the Subaru. They pull in next to Vaughn and Chase's car and as soon as Wes gets out, he's over at Brandon. "Dude!" They do that whole 'slap hands and chest hug' thing that men always do, "That was insane!"

We all agree, and the chatting among the group is in high gear with excitement. A male's voice yelling breaks up our conversation pulling our attention to him, especially the brunette at Vance's side.

"Riley!"

The closer the tall athletic kid comes to our group, the easier it is to make out his familiar appearance. He walks straight to the brunette. "Riley! I've been looking for you everywhere," Devin says to her, almost protectively. He glances at the group, his eyes landing on me.

"Veronica!" He moves towards me and pulls me into a small hug.

"Devin, hey!"

"Hey, Taylor!" He greets her then stands next to me. I smile awkwardly because everyone just witnessed the whole exchange.

"Guys, this is Devin. He just transferred to Western," I look at the group, taking a chance to look at Chase. He's watching Devin, almost like he's trying to place him. I look at Devin. "These are my brothers, Vaughn." I point towards Vaughn, then to Vance, "And that's Vance. My two other brothers aren't here." Devin leans in to shake their hands, which they both do without issues. "That's Brandon." I point to the 'Gamer' and then to Chase, "and Chase."

"Nice to meet you all!" Devin says politely. "Guess you guys already know my sister and her friend, Ashley--who are minors by the way. " He gestures to the brunette, who seems a little embarrassed, and her friend. Vance shuffles away from Riley.

"Devin," she hisses, her face pinched in anger.

"What? I'm sure you didn't let them in on that information, and Dad wouldn't hesitate to throw any of these guys in jail if they so much as touch you."

Oh, Boy. Devin's a protective brother, and I can instantly relate with her.

"Relax, Devin." I put my hand on his shoulder. "Nothing was going to happen."

"You two seem pretty chummy." Vance points out, grabbing our attention. His eyes are narrowed.

"Yeah, we're *friends*," I stress the word friends, knowing that my brothers are about to interrogate him.

"You wouldn't happen to be the same friend who asks out their friends?" Vance inquires.

"No, Vance." I point at him, "Devin, it was great to see

you," I tell him. "But maybe you and your sister should go."

Devin nods. "Yeah, okay. C'mon Riley." Riley glances at me and gives me a weak smile before turning to walk away with her brother. Ashley reluctantly trails behind them.

"He's a douche," Vaughn mutters.

I place my hands on my hips. "You're one to talk!"

This night just went south, and I'm ready to go. I'm somewhat stranded since I didn't drive, but I risk asking anyways, "Chase, would you mind driving me home?" I ask.

"What?" Vance asks. "Chase doesn't want to leave."

"Thank you for speaking on behalf of Chase," I respond, sarcastically.

"No, it's okay." He looks at me, then towards Vance. "I have to get up early and check-in with my sergeant anyway"

"Didn't you *just* do that?" Vance asks.

"Yeah, but I have to every so often."

"Bummer."

"You sure you don't mind?" I ask Chase.

"No. It's fine." He smiles.

"Well then, I'm gonna go find me some fun." Vance's remark makes me roll my eyes.

"So glad I'm leaving," I mutter. "Hey, make sure they're legal." I poke fun and Taylor laughs at my side. Vance gives me the finger.

"Love you too, bro."

"I'll see you later," I tell Tay. She pulls me into a hug, "Have fun," she whisper sings.

Chase and I move to his car and the butterflies already start taking flight at being alone with him again.

Keeping my cool in, I'm aware of every movement. I hop inside the Z as Chase sits in the driver's side. He starts up the car moments after buckling up.

"Ready?" He asks.

"Yep!"

He backs up the car and drives out of the lot slowly past the pedestrians. I take in the scene: the number of cars and their drivers. The diversity of vehicles is amazing--old, *older*, and newer. Some have massive noticeable modifications, some only minor, and others that are completely stock. I love this, and I cannot wait until I have my car back. I sigh and lean my head back on the rest.

"What's wrong?" Chase asks, keeping his eyes ahead.

"I just miss my car."

He laughs lightly. "Said like a true enthusiast. Hear anything on your parts?"

"Not yet. Hopefully tomorrow."

"I won't lie, I hope it takes a while."

His response has me looking his way. "Why?" I pout.

"Don't give me that face," He smiles. "I like starting my days with you."

Those words make me melt. "Oh," I lamely respond.

"You up for some diner food?" he asks, pulling onto the main highway.

"Hell yeah." I'm excited at the thought of some yummy food. "Wait, don't you have to get up early?"

"I do," he answers then shrugs. "Not worried about it."

"Are you sure?"

"Definitely."

"Okay! What do you have to do, anyway?" I ask.

"Just take some tests to make sure I'm settling back

into civilian life okay."

"Oh. That's good then."

"Yeah. Sometimes he'll take us out to lunch afterward."

"That's pretty nice of him."

"It is. They become your extended family."

It's easy to forget that he's part of the military and that he could be called away again. He was just gone for so long...I can't imagine them taking him so soon. The memory of our last conversation comes to my mind, and I hope that he'll be staying for a long time. I push the thoughts away, not wanting to taint our time together with my unease.

"I'm gonna have Taylor keep me updated on the bros." After sending her quick text and getting her simple response, I put my phone away. Chase holds out his hand towards me, palm up, silently waiting for me to place my hand in his. I comply, gladly.

"What are your plans for tomorrow?" he asks.

I press my lips, "Work, then probably just hang out with Tay...like we do every Saturday. Why?"

"I'd like to see you, even if it's for just a little."

"Hmm. Maybe I can make that happen."

Chase looks my way. "That'd be nice." His smile is aimed at me.

"It would," I agree. "Aren't you hanging out with Vance or something?"

He shrugs. "Not till later I guess."

"I was gonna catch a ride home with Vin, but maybe I can get Tay to pick me up instead. She can bring me over to your place?" I ask.

"Yeah, that'll work. Let me know for sure."

"Another reason I need my car back," I point out.

"You'll have it back before you know it," He says to appease me.

"I hope so. Maybe we can check the junkyard again on Sunday?"

He looks at me. "Aren't you coming to the lake Sunday?"

"Ohhh, right! Of course!"

"Good. Though being around you in nothing but your bathing suit is going to be hard."

"Oh, yeah?"

"Yeah." He pulls the car off the highway, slowing at the yield sign, but comes to a halt. Confused as to why he stopped, I look at him just as he leans over the console. "Gimme some sugar." He puckers his lips, I do as he asks, giving him a quick peck. Followed by another. "One more," he asks, causing me to laugh, I give him another peck. He hums his approval, and moves back towards his seat, maneuvering the car towards Chrissy's.

The diner is busier than the last time that we were here. We make our way inside, letting the hostess know a table for two would be perfect. She leads us to a booth located more on the nice dining side, rather than the side we sat on last time.

"Enjoy," the hostess says. We sit across from each other.

"Are you going to get the soup, again?" Chase asks me, picking up his menu to look over it.

"Hmm maybe. It's *sooo* good," I say excited. My enthusiasm causes him to chuckle lightly.

"You're cute," He mumbles. The look on his face makes me feel warm and fuzzy all over.

"And you're sweet, Chase Daniels."

"Just sweet?" His brow arches upward, a cocky grin

forming on his lips. He looks sexy as sin.

"Well, you're cute too," I say, playfully.

"Chase!" a female voice pulls our attention towards the girl approaching our table.

"Hey!" she sits in beside him. "What are you up to?" I immediately remember her face. I've about had my fill of blondes for the night.

"Shannon, hey," Chase greets her. The tone in his voice alerts me to his unease. "Just getting some food."

She glances at me. "Oh! You're Vance's little sister, right? Hi!"

"Yep."

"Are your brothers here?" she looks around as she asks.

"Nope."

"Oh." She turns her attention back to Chase, easily dismissing me. "What are you doing after this? I can come over."

Chase is clearly uncomfortable, and it's honestly the first time I've ever seen him in distress. He handled the other girls earlier tonight with ease, but this girl, not so much. This has me curious, and extremely jealous. They clearly have a bit of history.

"Uh, no. I have an early morning, I'm just gonna go home and crash."

Her hand moves towards his chest. "What a shame." Her bottom lip juts out. "We had such a good time."

"Yeah, well..." He removes her hand. "It's not gonna happen."

She moves away, but her gaze follows me. "Wait, are you two...together?"

"No," I jump in.

Chase's expression doesn't escape me. It's one of

slight disappointment.

She laughs a bit. "Yeah, of course not."

A waitress approaches the table. "Hey guys, can I get you guys something to drink?" She looks at the blonde. When Shannon finally notices the waitress looking at her, she speaks up, "Oh! I'm just leaving." She slides out from the booth. "I'll talk to you later," she tells Chase.

His eyes are on me instantly, and I can't help but feel hurt, even though I have no reason to be. He didn't exactly *do* anything, and I told her we weren't together. It's never a nice feeling to be in the company of a person who had any intimate memories with the guy you are hopelessly in-lust with.

"Anything for you two then?" the waitress asks.

I look up at the middle-aged waitress and smile. "I'll take a Sprite."

"Iced tea, please." Chase orders.

"You need some time to look over the menu?" she asks looking between the two of us.

"I think so."

"Sure thing!" She leaves us, and I'm looking everywhere but at Chase.

"Hey," he whispers while leaning forward. His hands are reaching out for mine atop the table. He pulls them apart, tugging me forward. "Vern," he jokes and my resolve cracks a bit at the nickname.

"Who was that?" I ask looking at his blue eyes filled with anguish.

"That was Shannon."

"And she...you guys?"

He doesn't look too thrilled. "Yeah, when I first came home."

My eyes become unfocused as the memory of her

hanging on his arm that night comes back to me.

"Hey, I'm sorry. If I would have known what I know now, it would have never happened."

"You don't have to apologize," I tell him, my eyes focusing again. "I mean, it's nice to hear that, but you don't owe me anything. It just sucks to run into your ex or flings at any place we may go. You don't have to worry about that because I don't have any."

"I do owe you. I care about you, and I don't want my actions to hurt you. I don't think you realize the number of heads you turn when you walk around."

I scoff, "Yeah, right."

Chase tugs on my middle finger. "Yeah, I am right and for the record I haven't been with anyone else since. It's you that's been on my mind. I'm sorry that we may run into an ex, but as I said earlier, you're the only one that matters. You're all I see."

Those last few words trigger another memory we had of the conversation from his car. *I'm* all he sees. This whole moment has tarnished our time together. I have to learn from this and not allow it to affect me. I'm the one sitting here with Chase...not any of them. I smile weakly at him. He pulls my hand to his mouth, pressing a small sweet kiss to the top which causes my smile to turn genuine.

He intertwines our fingers, our arms stretched across the table, resting atop. Using my unoccupied hand, I pick up the menu only to put it down again. I already know what I want. Chase is muttering to himself, reading the options, and thinking aloud. "Hmm, that sounds good."

I laugh lightly, and my sight moves towards the others seated around us, taking in the busy scene.

Across the way, Shannon sits in a booth among her friends, glaring our way. When our eyes connect, a skinny brow arches upward in question. My heart instantly drops into my stomach.

LIKE IT OR NOT
Chase

Veronica removes her hand from my grasp, which causes me to look up. Her skin is lacking color and her lips are in a tight line. *What the hell?* I sit up straight in the booth and ask, "What's wrong?"

Her face whips my way. Both fear and worry are written all over her expression. "What?" I repeat, louder this time. I find myself looking around the booth, but I'm not seeing anything out of the ordinary, "V, you're worrying me."

"Shannon," she says softly.

"Don't worry about her," I dismiss. I don't want to touch on that topic again.

"No. She was just staring at us."

"So?" I don't see the problem.

"*So*, she may have seen what you just did."

"And?"

"What if she tells my brothers?" she asks, nibbling on her bottom lip.

"Well, then we should tell them before she does."

"Chase!"

"What?"

She huffs and shakes her head. "How can you be so calm over this? You know how they are!"

I nod. "I do. Look, I can talk to Vance. He's a lot of talk, but he does care for you."

She's not entirely satisfied, "Can you at least wait

until after the weekend?"

"Yeah. Let's have a good time at the lake. Maybe I can get together with him after."

The waitress returns. "Ready?" she asks, smiling at us both. I look at V, and she nods. I wave my hand for her to order first. She orders very light-- a soup and salad--and I put in an order for their 'Cowboy' burger.

"Victor invited us all up to his condo afterward, but I think he forgot I have school," She laughs lightly, "So, maybe, we can go up the next weekend? Together?"

"Yeah, I'd like that."

Her posture goes from stiff to relaxed, and she smiles. We have a very easy conversation, and I find myself thinking about how our whole relationship has moved to a different level. It doesn't feel awkward or unnatural; it feels almost perfect. I've never dated anyone that I was friends with beforehand. Maybe that's what all my previous relationships were missing, or maybe it's just Veronica. They weren't her.

Taylor comes through and informs Veronica that her brothers--in true Russo fashion--have secured new conquests and most likely won't be home until late. We take our time at the diner and stay until we are some of the last customers. A yawn escapes her--and as much as I never want to take her home--I know she has an early morning ahead of her and it'd be selfish of me to keep her out all night.

"Are you ready?"

A sleepy, happy smile spreads across her beautiful lips. "No. I don't want this night to end."

"Neither do I, but we'll have plenty more."

"Promise?" she rasps.

"Promise," I confirm.

"Okay," she whispers, "Take me home."

I stand up and move towards her side of the booth, reaching out for her. She places her small dainty hand in mine, and I help her out of her seat. "Such a gentleman," she teases.

"Only for you," I respond without hesitation. She smiles shyly and looks away. "After you, madame." I wave my hand in front of me with a slight bow, trying to make her laugh.

I succeed as a small laugh escapes her, "You're *so* cheesy."

We stop at the counter to pay for our meal and Veronica can't help but grab a sealed mint from the bowl stationed in front of us. The hostess kindly greets us and asks us how everything was as I hand her my credit card. Meanwhile, V seems to be struggling with opening the little wrapper. I watch her, slightly amused, until she gives up using her fingers and places the candy's wrapper in the corner of her mouth. It rips open easily, but the mint flings out and falls to the floor. Her body sags, her lips pout, and whimpers. She looks so incredibly cute. I grab another one from the bowl, open it without any problems, and hold it out to her. Her eyes meet mine, "Thanks."

The hostess places the receipt on the counter for me to sign. I grab myself a mint for the road and open the door for Veronica to walk through. I place my hand on her lower back as we walk to the car. I make sure to open the door for her as we reach the Z. She turns around swiftly, surprising me. "Thank you, Chase."

"You're welcome," I tell her, assuming she's thanking me for dinner.

"I mean, for like, everything. You make me feel...,"

she pauses. "You make me feel special."

"You are special and you really shouldn't think otherwise." I kiss the tip of her nose, watching her face light up. "C'mon, let's get you home."

Once we pull into Veronica's driveway, the lack of cars confirms that her brothers are still not home. She seems hesitant and nervous as she unbuckles her seat belt. I don't want her to be nervous around me for any reason. I grab her hand with a, "I'll see you tomorrow?" She only nods.

"Text me," I tell her.

"Okay," she whispers, her eyes scanning my face. "I really want to kiss you," she confesses.

"I wouldn't object."

Her lips meet mine a second after the words are out of my mouth. The feeling of her hand at the back of my neck gives me goosebumps. My hand slides to the base of her throat, and then into her hair. This time it's Veronica who deepens the kiss. She takes me by surprise when her mouth opens slightly, allowing our tongues to meet. A moan escapes her, and my hand tightens in her hair. If only I had more room, I'd pull her over the console and into my lap. *Damn it! Should have brought my truck.* She sucks on my bottom lip--it's so *hot*. If I was a pubescent boy I'd probably be...unloading already.

Subconsciously, we both slow our movements--the kisses turning soft and slow--until it ends in a sweet peck. Our foreheads rest together as we allow our breathing to return to a normal pace. I open my eyes. Her eyes remain closed, but the smile on her lips tells me she enjoyed our make-out session.

I squeeze her waist. "You better go inside," I advise. Her eyes flutter open, staring into mine. She slowly moves away and widens the space between us.

"Yeah, I better," she agrees. Her hand blindly fumbles for the door handle until she finds it and pulls. I grab her chin. She visibly shivers before I kiss her inviting lips once more. "Good night," I whisper. She smiles and removes herself from my car. I watch her until she disappears safely behind the door and allow myself to calm down before pulling away from the house.

Driving home, my phone dings. The thought of it being from her, even though we just separated, has me smiling. Once I'm parked and inside the house, I check my phone, and kick off my shoes. My smile drops as I read the text--it's not from Veronica.

Shannon: So. You and the little Russo sister?

I type out my message as I head up the stairs and into my room. I sit on the end of my bed.
Me: What do you mean?
Shannon: You guys seemed quite cozy.
Me: We're friends, Shannon.
Shannon: Fuck buddies then?
Me: No. Not that it's any of your business.
Shannon: Then why do you keep blowing me off?

I pinch the bridge of my nose. I do *not* need Shannon running her mouth and telling Veronica's brothers before we can. I know I need to squash this quickly.

Me: I'm sorry, I met someone else. I should have just told you. But no, it's not V.

I really hate lying about Veronica.

Shannon: So you take all your friend's sisters out?
Me: We were at the track. She doesn't have her car and she wanted to leave. She asked me for advice, so we stopped for some food, and I gave her advice. I really don't even need to be explaining

this to you.

Shannon: So if I happen to just run into Vance, he would be okay with you and Veronica going to diners late at night?

This chick just doesn't quit.

Me: I'm no longer entertaining this conversation. Have a nice life, Shannon.

Shannon: Whatever. You're an asshole with a tiny dick.

I burst out laughing. The girl's got *jokes*. I toss my phone aside, turn on the TV, and get ready for bed. In nothing but my briefs, I make sure my alarm is set before plugging in my phone and climbing under the sheets. Thoughts of Veronica--along with the sounds of the TV in the background--lull me to sleep within seconds.

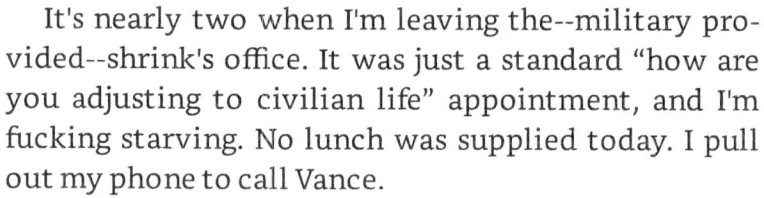

It's nearly two when I'm leaving the--military provided--shrink's office. It was just a standard "how are you adjusting to civilian life" appointment, and I'm fucking starving. No lunch was supplied today. I pull out my phone to call Vance.

"What's up, bud?" he greets.

"I'm just leaving now. Where are you guys at?"

"Garage." Seconds later, I hear some power tools confirming his answer.

"Alright man, I'm gonna grab some food and head over. Anyone want anything?" I ask.

Vance yells around the garage before answering, "Nah. We're good."

"V?"

"I don't know. She's in the office."

I laugh. "Alright, see ya in a bit."

"Later."

Ending the call, I pull up the garage's number. It rings twice before I hear Veronica's melodic voice, "Victor's Auto."

"You hungry?" I ask.

"Wh-Chase?"

"Yeah, you hungry?"

"Hmm, a little. Are you coming to visit?" The hope in her voice is obvious, and I like it.

"Yeah, just talked to your brother. Gonna stop for some food, you want anything?"

"Yes!" She rattles off her order and adds, "Don't forget the barbecue sauce!"

"I won't."

"Vance always does."

"Well, I'm not Vance."

"Thank goodness for that."

"Uh yeah, that'd be a *bit* weird." I laugh. "I'll see you in a few."

"Can't wait!" she squeaks.

"Awe. Does someone miss me?"

"Yeah, right! I just want the food."

"I'm feeling a little used right now."

I pull into the parking lot of the fast-food joint.

"I'm joking," she says.

"I know, I'm about to pull up to the order window. I'll see you in a bit, babe."

"Okay," her voice has softened.

"Bye."

We hang up and I rattle off the decently long order. You'd think I was buying for the whole garage. As soon as they hand me the bag I pull out a burger, quickly unwrap it and take a large bite. It couldn't wait. I groan. *So good.*

The drive to the garage doesn't take long, but I've already demolished my second burger and fries. After parking in front of the office, I make my way inside. Veronica jumps from the desk eagerly. Her long brown hair is pulled up neatly, it swings behind her as she walks to me. "Thank you so much!" She takes the bag from my hand. "I'd kiss you if I could."

"You can make it up to me another time," I wink.

"You bet," she says with a wicked smile. She saunters back to her desk, and I take a moment to check out her ass and long legs. The jeans she's wearing enhance her behind. She moves behind her desk, effectively cutting off my view. "I can't eat all this!"

"The nuggets and fries are yours. The rest is mine."

Her eyes widen. "Piggy!"

"I spent all morning at the base. No food. I'm *starving.*" I rub my stomach.

She pulls all the food from the bag and lays it on top of the desk. I swipe the second box of nuggets, opening it, and biting into the breaded meat.

"How's your morning been?" I ask.

"Not bad. It's been pretty busy." She pauses, "Oh! My parts shipped!"

"Already?" I ask, a little saddened by the news, "That's great!"

"It could take a little bit until the radiator is in though. So you're still stuck with me for a minute." She flashes her teeth at me.

"Good."

Vance comes bursting through the door. "Dude, your parts came in. You know what we're doing tonight!"

"Nice!" I respond.

Vance moves behind Veronica and steals a nugget from her open box. She slaps his hand away. "Get your own!" she yells.

"Come out when you're done," Vance says then walks out of the office.

Veronica shoves a couple of fries into her mouth. "I love their fries," she says with a mouth full.

It makes me laugh. "I can tell."

"Looks like you're going to have a busy night."

"It might be here for a week or so. I doubt it'll be finished tonight. May have to come over after work to get it finished." I throw her a wink.

"So then we can't hang out for a little." Her lips turn down.

I shake my head. "No, probably not. I can talk to him tonight?" I offer.

"No, no." She's adamant. "Let's enjoy the lake. We'll spend next weekend with Victor and talk to him first, then we'll work on the rest of them."

"Alright." I sigh, finishing off the last of my nuggets. "I better get out there." After cleaning up my mess and throwing it into the trash bin near the desk, I lean over and bring my face close to Veronica, who is intently focusing on the computer. "You look nice today." Her head turns, and she's staring at me. "Thank you," she whispers. Her breath fans my face.

I move away--I revel in the effect that I have on her--and wish *so* badly that I could kiss her. I knock on the top of the desk. "Well, have a good night with Taylor." I leave her and walk into the garage towards Vance. At the other end I see Vin, and greet him as he's working on a Jeep.

"Yooo," Vance says, stretching out the word when I near him, "I am so stoked!" he exclaims, bouncing on the balls of his feet. I notice the stack of boxes off to the side--boxes of all shapes and sizes.

"That's all mine?"

"Sure is. Go get your car and bring her in so we can get started."

My engine bay is ripped apart. The old stock pieces are laying in a pile while the shiny new, smaller pieces lay on top of a flattened box. We've only been tinkering for an hour, but we've managed to do a lot in that time. I guess with the two of us, things move along at a faster pace. We may be able to get more finished tonight than I previously thought.

The click of a door has me moving away from under the hood, stretching out my back. Vance does the same. I hear her voice before I see her, "Wow. You guys made some massive progress." She comes into view when she steps over the flattened box of parts. She's looking down and around at the parts, "I am so jealous."

Vance grabs a towel from the counter behind us, and wipes his greasy hands on it. "No worries V, your car is next."

She smiles wide, "You need a hand?"

I want her to stay, but I have a feeling that Vance is going to dismiss her. It surprises me when he doesn't.

"Actually yeah, we could probably use your small hands to get in the tight areas. You all done in the office?"

"Yep," she says, popping the last letter. "My tiny

hands are all yours for a couple of hours."

"A couple of hours, then what?"

"Taylor's going to get me, and then we're *totally* going college rager," her voice rising with excitement. I can't help but chuckle.

"What? Not without me, you're sure as shit not! " Vance barks. He watches intently as she tries to control her lips from moving upwards, "Veronica Marie Russo, you *better* be joking." She's now smiling so hard, her eyes are squished. "Yeahhhh, maybe."

"V, so help me, get your ass over here and help me get this bolt out."

She stands up, amused, and with a roll of her eyes replies, "Yes, Dad."

Vance sighs long and hard, "I pity the guy who ends up with you."

"You'd have to allow that to happen first," She deadpans.

"Yeah, that's true," He pretends to think, "You're gonna be single forever."

His words change my whole demeanor--carefree to tense. I feel incredibly guilty. Not only that, but his words of never letting her date have me worried.

"I'm off to college next year, Vance. Lots of parties, and *lots* of boys."

"I'm going to kick your ass so hard V, you won't be able to walk."

"Uh-huh. I'll tell Mom."

They continue to bicker while my mind wanders. I know I need to talk to him soon. Maybe Veronica and I should back off a bit. But I've already tried that, not to mention that would be way too hard. My eyes have found their way to Veronica's rear end. I can't help it, she's bending over the front of my car. *What a sight.*

"Chase!" My name is called, instantly snapping me out of my thoughts. I look up at Vance, who is staring me down. "Dude, you alright?"

"Yeah. Just zoned out."

"Let's get back to work."

The three of us work together, but Veronica and Vance are in a constant state of bickering. I remain quiet; lost in my thoughts. By the time Taylor and Wes arrive we're close to being finished. I'm surprised.

Veronica washes her hands at the sink, then announces their departure. "Thank you for your help, V," I say to her before she walks out of the garage. She waves and throws me a sexy smile. To Vance it probably just looked like nothing out of the ordinary, but to me...everything about her is sexy. Wes joins in and I'm now feeling like this baby will be running tomorrow night after some final tuning. This has me elated!

"I don't know what I'm gonna do when she does find someone who wants to date her," Vance confesses, watching her walk out of the garage to Taylor's Jeep. Even though I want to speak up, I don't.

"Well, while she hasn't found that someone yet," Wes articulates, "you may want to back off a bit. She needs to learn. She may get desperate and end up jumping the first guy at college who shows her an ounce of interest. *That* will be even worse." I blanch at the thought. "You think I'm too tough on her?" Vance's question is to me this time. I shrug. "Wes has a point." I hate that point, but it's valid. I hope she's not just desperately wanting to date me because I've shown an interest in her. I want her to like me for me.

"So you think I should let her date?" I'm about to

say something--not even sure what--but Wes beats me to it. "Honestly, dude? Yeah. She's home, where you're around if she needs you. Who knows when she's off at college? You won't be around, and I doubt she'll tell you anything."

"When the fuck did you become Dr. Phil?"

"It's just common-sense man. Plus, Taylor talks and *sometimes* I listen."

"And what does Taylor say when she talks?" Vance asks.

"Mostly, that you're holding her back from normal teenage experiences. Funny coming from you, because you're the most experienced of anyone."

"*Exactly.* I'm a guy!" he says annoyed. "I know what they want! It's all they want."

Wes looks at him. "I get what you're saying, I do. But dude, you just haven't met the right girl."

"And Taylor is your 'right' girl?" Vance says, quoting Wes.

Wes shrugs. "I love Taylor, and I have no desire to look at another girl. Am I going to marry her? I don't have a clue, but as of now, I'm happy."

Vance stares at something across from the garage. He's obviously in thought. "I don't like that."

"Like it or not, she'll meet someone eventually...and he may think she's worth the risk."

"You're awfully quiet over there," Vance says to me.

"I don't have sisters. I'm not sure what to say," I lie. I like everything Wes is saying, and if Vance is more open to Veronica dating, this may help me.

"But V's *like* a sister to you so what would you do?"

I cringe. I try to hide it by looking down. "I have no idea, honestly," I shrug my shoulders, "I care about

V, but she's not my sister." Vance doesn't say anything so I continue, "Wes, man, you're the next Dr. Phil. Soon you'll have your own talk show." I joke, trying to lighten the mood. Vance doesn't laugh, but Wes cracks a smile. Vance turns around and starts working on the car. He remains quiet for a long time.

TOGETHER

Veronica

The light breeze causes me to shiver, then I'm suddenly being shifted. The feeling is frightening. I grab onto the closest thing next to me, it's fluffy and soft like a blanket. *What?*

"Wake up!" I hear the words, but don't see anyone as I try to remain upright. *Don't fall*--the last thing I think before I'm unexpectedly thrown into the air.

My eyes snap open to find the familiar surroundings of my bedroom. I have an iron-clad grasp on my comforter. You'd think I was hanging on for dear life, and I guess in my dream state I was. My body is airborne again causing me to yell out in surprise.

"Wake up! Wake up!" Vance and Vaughn chant in unison while jumping around my bed, causing my body to bounce. But it isn't until they both bounce at the same time that my body goes completely airborne again.

"You guys! You're going to send us through the floor!"

Bounce.

Bounce.

Vance hops off while Vaughn continues to jump.

"You're going to make me throw up." Those words cause Vaughn to stop immediately, then step down off my bed.

"Let's go, you sleeping troll," Vance says.

"It's sleeping *beauty*," I correct him before sitting up. I can feel my hair sticking out all over.

"Not you." He laughs.

I glare at Vance.

"Definitely not you," Vaughn says, and I turn my glare towards him. He's sitting in my desk chair spinning around in circles. I grab a small pillow next to me, throwing it across the room. It nails him right in the head, catching him by surprise. He falters a bit.

"That wasn't very nice!" He throws it back at me, but I duck, and it sails over me landing on the floor.

"Since when am I nice?"

"You used to be. What happened to you?" Vaughn questions.

"PMS." I smile wide.

"Gah! I don't want to hear this shit." Vance covers his ears. "Let's go, get out of bed you lard!"

"Jeez, *you're* being mean now!" I look over at the clock on my nightstand. It's seven-thirty. "Hello! I thought we weren't leaving until nine."

"Change of plans, we're going out for breakfast."

I make an unpleasant noise. "You're an asshole," I mumble.

"Yeah, yeah. Nothing I haven't been called before. Hurry up." Vance turns and leaves my room, Vaughn does the same.

"Close my door!" I yell, but it's no use because they're already running down the stairs. I get up and slam the door. "Bunch of animals." After getting dressed and do my bathroom routine, I go downstairs to the whole family waiting for me in the living room, including Mom and Dad.

"Finally!" Vance stands up. "Let's get going. I told Chase to meet us there at eight."

"Oh, the whole family's coming?"

"We are." Mom smiles as she walks by me. I slip on my flip flops and follow everyone out the door. The early morning air nipping at my skin. We all settle in my parent's Yukon. "Are Victor and Melissa coming?" I ask.

"Yeah, they're gonna meet us there," Vance answers.

Once my father turns onto the familiar street, I know we're going to Chrissy's, and I smile at the new fond memories.

The parking lot is pretty full, but that's not unusual for a Sunday morning. Chase's silver truck is already parked, alongside Victor's Volvo, but the cars are empty so I presume they're already inside. Dad parks in the nearest open spot, and we all unload. It's kind of like one of those clown cars, other than the fact that our SUV is pretty large, you just never think so many people can come out of it.

As suspected, Victor, Chase, and Melissa are inside waiting for us. They already informed them of our arrival, so while the staff gets our table together, we all greet each other with hellos. Shortly after, the hostess informs us our table is ready and leads us back. Without being too obvious, I try to snag a seat next to Chase, but my brothers end up on either side of him. I'm forced to sit across from Vance.

Breakfast goes smoothly. We discuss an array of things but I don't have much to contribute to the conversation. Our bellies are full, the bill is taken care of, and now we sit in relaxing and easy flowing conversations. The smile on my mother's face is one of true joy and I make a mental note to do this more often with her.

"Alright, I don't know about y'all, but I'm ready for some water action!" Vance stands up, stretching out his limbs. We all follow his lead, stand and begin our way to the front double doors. Once we're outside we say our goodbyes to my parents. I watch them walk away, arm in arm. "It's hard to believe they're still together right?" The voice comes from my right, and I glance over to see Victor watching them as well.

"Yeah," I agree, my eyes back on them as my father opens the door for my mother. Chivalry isn't dead.

"Everyone deserves to find that love."

I smile at his words. "Have you?" I ask, curiously.

"Yeah, I think so."

I look to Victor again, but his eyes are on Melissa. "You will too." His gaze moves to me.

"I hope so."

"Let's roll!" Vance yells out, grabbing our attention.

"We'll follow you," Victor says before moving away. "Anyone's welcome to ride with us," he says before moving towards his car. I'm torn between who to ride with. I want to be with Chase, regardless if we can't show any affection. I just want to be around him but at the same time, I'd love to spend some time with Victor.

"I'm gonna ride with Victor," Vin announces, moving towards the back door.

"When did Victor get rid of the Audi?" I hear Chase ask Vance as I move towards them.

"Not long after he started working for Melissa's father's firm. I guess it wasn't 'professional enough'. Whatever that means." Vance says annoyed, with a shake of his head. "She's got him so whipped. His nose is permanently glued to her ass." I smack Vance with the back of my hand. "Stop. He loves her," I point out.

"Yeah, loves her magical box."

"You are such a pig." I need to walk away, so I turn to

stalk towards Chase's truck.

"Oink. Oink." Vance snorts behind me, followed by his obnoxious laughter.

"Shotgun!" Vaughn yells just as I'm about to grab the handle of the passenger door. I quickly jump in and lock the door, watching him stand right on the other side.

"Not cool, V. I called shotty!" Vaughn yells, through the closed door. I stick my tongue out at him. Vaughn gets in behind me as Vance climbs into the back behind Chase, who's settling into the driver's seat. I pull the seat belt over my torso, and I'm clipping it in when I feel pain on the tip of my ear.

"Ow! That hurt." I turn to glare at Vaughn, who's laughing.

"Yeah? It was supposed to."

"Jerk," I mutter. I rub my ear.

"Alright, *children*," Vance cuts in. "Knock it off."

Chase is struggling to try to contain his laughter.

"I hate you all," I say, crossing my arms, and keeping my gaze out the window.

"Hey Chase..." Vance voices behind us, but doesn't continue. His lingering pause piques my curiosity, I turn in the seat. His face is painfully close to his phone, fingers moving diligently when they stop, he looks up and scoots forward. "How many people can fit on your boat?"

I groan while Chase answers, "Ten. Why?"

"Because we are getting some company, boys."

"This was supposed to be a relaxing day!" I protest.

"Hush. It will be."

"Who did you invite?" I ask, annoyed.

"Talia and friends will be meeting us there."

Fantastic. I was looking forward to a relaxing, calm

afternoon on the water. "Seriously Vance? You didn't even *ask* Chase."

"Chase doesn't mind, do ya?" Vance looks at Chase, who's busy driving, but he shrugs his shoulders in response. "See?"

"Did you ever think that maybe he didn't want a bunch of random people on his boat?"

Vance laughs a little, "No sane guy will mind a few hot girls in bikinis on his boat." *Why did my brother have to go and ruin such a good thing? Oh, that's because it's what he does.*

"Stop being a baby. Talia isn't that bad. We'll still have a good time."

So yeah, he's right--Talia's not bad. I can't speak on behalf of her friends because I have no idea who they are. Talia and Vance have an odd relationship. I don't know all the details, and I'd like to keep it that way. She is always nice to me, so it honestly could be worse. I just wanted a nice relaxing time with Chase and my family.

After about an hour drive, we arrive at the lake's marina. Chase pulls his truck into the parking space closest to the dock's entrance and Victor's Volvo pulls in next to us.

Without realizing it, I must have a permanent scowl of annoyance plastered across my features. That or Victor just knows me. "Whoa, what's with the face?" he asks after taking a good look at me.

"Vance invited his girlfriends." I use my fingers to quote the word 'friends'.

"Really?" Melissa says as she joins us, then looks at Victor.

"It's not my boat." Victor shrugs and pulls her to him. "Don't worry, those girls have nothing on you," he says to Melissa, then places a kiss on her forehead. It's so sweet. Despite him being my brother, it's swoon worthy. He looks up at me, "We'll have fun." They walk around to the trunk and grab a cooler out, along with some towels and a beach bag.

Loud music grabs all of our attention, causing us to look at the convertible Beetle driving our way before parking behind Victor's car. I instantly recognize Talia behind the wheel. Her eyes are covered by big sunglasses, her honey-brown hair is pulled up into a messy bun, and her tan skin on full display. It goes quiet when she shuts off the car. "Hey guys!" she yells out to our group along with a wave. Her two friends climb out of the back and help Talia close up the top.

Talia has on a cute long tank that dips low on the sides, showing off her bright pink bikini while her cut-off shorts peek out at the bottom. Her friends have nothing but their bikini tops and some shorts on. I hate judging people before I get to know them, but I can't help but be envious of their assets--therefore I hate them. Well, hate is a strong word, so let's just say...I strongly dislike them. I have a mental battle with myself as I watch them work together, admiring their bodies, and wishing I look half as good as they do.

Once they're all finished, they close the circle of our group. Talia comes to hug Vance, although when they pull apart his arm remains wrapped around her shoulder. Talia's face lights up when she sees me, standing across from her. "Oh my gosh! V! It's been forever." She moves forward--out from under Vance's arm--and embraces me in a hug.

"Hey Talia," I respond as she steps back. She pulls her sunglasses off, placing them atop her head. Her caramel eyes widen. "Look at you, girl!" she says as her eyes roam my body, even though it's covered by a white romper. "You're hot!" her voice is loud. It seems as if she's almost shocked by this. I've never had another girl openly admire my body, but I don't find it awkward in the least. It's actually a very empowering thing.

"Thanks?" I say, not knowing how to respond.

She laughs. "Work it girl!"

"Uh, No," Vance chimes in from behind, and she waves her hand at him.

"Oh shut up, Vance." There's a smile playing on her lips.

Talia moves around the circle saying hello to my brothers, stopping to chat with Victor and Melissa for a bit, then ends up by her friends. "These are my sorority sisters, Jenny and Laura." She introduces us all one by one. Laura's eyes linger on Chase a bit longer before moving to me and smiles. This, of course, annoys me. But it's completely understandable because, well, Chase is hot. We all exchange pleasantries with the girls.

"How come you haven't told me you were in a sorority?" Vance asks, surprised.

"Why?" she asks, placing her hands on her hips.

"Education reasons." Vance smiles.

"Uh-huh." She smirks.

"Let's get a move on!" Vin suggests. Vance and Vaughn shout out their approvals. Chase leads our large group out onto the dock towards one of the larger boats parked on the water. Someone whistles. "*Damn*, Chase," Talia's voice cracks, "I am with the wrong guy." she quips, causing Chase to laugh.

"He may a big boat, but *I* have a big—"

"ALRIGHT!" I yell out, stopping Vance from finishing his sentence, and he erupts into a fit of laughter. Chase climbs on and has Vance come up with him to help the girls over. Victor does the same, helping Melissa with their stuff and then bringing her over. I move to allow Chase to help me. I grab his outstretched hand and he pulls me over as if I weigh nothing. When I am safely standing on two feet, his free hand moves to my hip, giving me a slight squeeze. "You good?"

"Yeah."

He laughs lightly following that with a wink, then releases me to help the others. My eyes scan the boat, taking in the seating options. There's seating at the front, a seat across from the driver, and then a bench seat across the back of the boat where Melissa is sitting--looking slightly peeved. I don't blame her. I decide to take the seat next to her, she gives me a weak smile.

Once everyone is on board, Chase goes about getting the boat ready to go. "Chase, you need help?" Victor asks him.

Chase starts the engine and looks at Victor. "Yeah, if you can untie the ropes from the dock and reel them in."

"V." Victor gets my attention. "Can you help?" I nod and get up moving towards the front. He unties the rope, and I pull it up. He moves to the back and then quickly jumps back onto the boat pulling that rope up. Once I've pulled all the rope up into the boat, trying to keep it organized, I yell, "What do I do with this?"

"Here." The voice is closer than I expected, which startles me. I turn around and come up close and personal with a nice set of smooth, tan, muscular pecs.

I look up into Chase's vibrant blue eyes. He's standing really close, and it makes me nervous and excited at the same time. Chase has lost his shirt, and it's making my mouth water.

He gives me a wicked grin and it hits me low, low, *low*. He takes the rope from my hands. "You okay, V? You're looking a little flushed." He smiles wide, giving me a nice view of his, near-perfect, teeth.

I release a breath, "Yeah." It comes out airy. I take a step back, hitting the boat, which startles me again. I hear his laughter and I clear my throat. "Yeah. Yeah, I'm good. I'm good." I move away from him before I do something stupid.

I take my seat next to Melissa, who is now staring at me as well, but I avoid looking her way. I take in the nearby boats, realizing just how big this boat is compared to those around us. My heart has slowed to a normal rate. I glance away, still feeling eyes on me, eyes that belong to Mel. "What?" I ask. Her smile widens then her eyes flick to Chase. I ignore her.

A whining noise comes from behind me, startling me. "What is that?" I quickly look at Chase. He's amused on behalf of my frightened state. "I'm pulling up the anchor."

"Oh. Okay." I settle back into the seat while the boat starts to move away from the dock. More of the lake comes into view--it's stunning. The other side is nothing but a mountain of trees, and it truly looks like something out of a movie. Other boats glide across the glistening water. He's driving slowly, but I still feel a slight breeze. The sun is shining bright, and I bask in the feeling of it on my skin.

When we're a decent distance away from the marina,

Chase yells for everyone to hold on. He slowly pushes the throttle down, and while the boat picks up speed I grab onto a handle on the side. I'm so glad I sat in the back because sitting at the front looks frightening. The girls up front squeal out as the tip shoots upward.

My eyes move to Chase, taking in his muscular back rippling as he moves. I've never thought a broad back would affect me like this, but Chase's back is sexy as hell. I can't tear my eyes away from him. His body twists, and now his abs are facing my way. That's when I realize the breeze has stopped, and we're no longer moving. My eyes move upward to a very amused Chase staring back at me. His posture and cocky smirk tell me he knows exactly what he's doing to me. I look away, because I have to--for my sanity.

I take in the surroundings and realize we've made it to the cliffs. Multiple boats are floating nearby. There are people laying on rafts connected to their boats, and others swimming in the water.

My eyes crane upwards towards the highest cliff, and even though we're still a decent distance away it still requires me to look up. A guy is standing at the edge, looking over while his friends are waving their hands in gestures that I can only assume mean to support him. He walks away until he's out of sight, then seconds later he appears running. He runs until he reaches the end and launches himself off, falling headfirst into the water. His friends yell atop the cliff, and some shouting comes from a nearby boat.

"Oh my gosh," Melissa whispers next to me.

Someone else throws themselves off, but they've done this before because unlike the first guy. This guy shows off--he does a flip in the air, then dives in perfect form into the water.

"Do you do that?" she asks me, and I look at her. Her eyes are wide.

"I haven't," I tell her, "but the guys do."

"How high is that?"

I shrug. "I'm not sure."

"Victor, how high are the cliffs?" I called out to Victor, who is standing near the front, watching the people jump from the cliffs.

He turns to me. "I'm not exactly sure, but I'd say roughly eighty feet." His attention goes to Chase who asked him something. Melissa's eyes widen. The worry is evident on her face.

Vance jumps down from the front of the boat. "Who's jumping?" he asks, rubbing his hands together.

"I'm in!" Talia yells, jumping onto Vance's back. He easily catches her.

"Hell yeah!" Vin yells.

"That is *high*," Laura says.

"No way." Jenny's shaking her head back and forth.

"Oh, you chicken shits!" Talia calls to them. "C'mon V, let's show these girls how it's done!" She jumps off of Vance and walks to me. Vance's laugh is boisterous, "V won't jump."

The last time we came here, which was two years ago, I chickened out. I couldn't jump off the highest cliff and opted to jump off the smallest one. Even *that* was terrifying. For some reason, Vance telling me I won't jump makes me want to even more. I stand up defiantly, untying the knot at the back of my neck.

"Oh, shit." I hear Vin. "She's gonna do it!"

"She'll get up there and choke." Vance dismisses, which only adds more fuel to my fire. I completely remove my romper, leaving me in my bikini, and toss it on the seat. Loud coughing comes from Chase, whose face is red, and he's hitting his chest. Vaughn, who is closest to him, hits his back, "You alright, man?"

"Yeah..." He coughs and sputters some more, "Just..." he points to his throat, another cough. "Spit went down the wrong tube."

"Alright!" Talia shouts, grabbing my hand and pulling me towards the rear. "Let's do this!"

I wasn't prepared to jump, so when she jumps in while holding my hand, I don't land in the water gracefully. Thankfully I managed to turn on my side to avoid doing a big ol' belly flop. As soon as we're both under the water, we release hands and swim upward, breaking the surface. The water is surprisingly refreshing, so I allow myself to float and enjoy it.

"C'mon you pansies!" Talia yells, laughing.

"Pansy?" Vance rips off his shirt and walks to the back. He dives into the water and surfaces next to Talia. She yells and squeals as he pulls her to him. His head goes to her neck and I look away.

Vaughn and Vin both do the same but flip off the back, creating a massive splash. We're all treading water but my arms are quickly becoming tired.

"Let's go, Daniels!" Vance yells. My eyes move to Chase, who looks up at his name being called. "I'm coming." He slips off his shoes and dives in off the back, surfacing behind the group a second later.

"You comin' Victor?" Vaughn shouts.

Victor shakes his head. "No, I'm gonna stay with Melissa."

"Fucking pussy whipped pansy," Vance mutters low enough, but I still catch it. "You hush!" I splash him which he returns a bigger wave in my direction.

"Race?" Vaughn questions pulling Vance's attention away from me.

"One. Two. Three. GO!" Vance shouts, right before taking off.

We all race to the side of the cliffs. Vance gets there first and makes sure everyone knows it. The guys climb up, leaving me and Talia in the water. There's a thick rope hanging from a rock above, so I move to grab it when a hand shows up in front of my face. My eyes travel up the muscular arm, connecting with blue eyes, and a beautiful smile.

"C'mon," He says, shaking his hand for me to grab. He pulls me up easily, then helps Talia.

"Thanks, honey bun." She walks ahead while ringing out her hair. I follow, which leaves Chase behind me. I follow the makeshift path, created by the years of people coming up the side of the cliff. I try to stay confident, but I can't help when my ass is practically in his face as we climb upward.

Reaching the top, the area is massive and most of it is flat. Towards the back are all trees. Moving towards the middle, you can see the wide expanse of the lake and all the boats moving along. It's a beautiful sight.

Vaughn is standing at the edge of the cliff, and yells out, "WHOOOOO! I'm the king of the world!" The shouts and whistles come from down below. He backs up a good distance and then runs forward, launching himself out in the air. My heart is in my throat, and I'm not even the one jumping. My nerves are getting the best of me. A second later, he screams out, "Clear!"

Vin is pumping himself up to go next when Vance sprints by him and jumps off yelling, "pussy" on his way down. A second later, we hear him yell, "Clear!"

My heart is pounding, and my eyes are focused on Vin before he darts and disappears. I don't even hear him call out after hitting the water. My vision is becoming tinted around the edges, and vaguely I can hear my name being called.

Talia's standing in the middle of the vast area, getting in position to run and leap off. *We're crazy. This is crazy! Who does this?* She takes off and soars into the air-- her scream can be heard down until it's suddenly cut off.

"V!" I'm jostled. I look over at Chase whose hand is on my shoulder--his face just inches from mine. "Are you okay?" I can feel his breath on my cheek. I nod. I'm really not, though. Internally, I'm freaking out. Heights are *not* my thing. I'm terrified, and it must show on my face, because Chase offers me a sympathetic, "Do you want to go back down?"

I shake my head. I shouldn't care what the hell Vance thinks, but I know he'll give me so much shit. I take a deep breath. *I can do this.* I take another deep breath.

"I can jump with you." Chase breaks my concentration, and I just stare at him.

"What?" I finally speak up.

"I can jump with you," He repeats himself. "We can jump together."

"Together?"

"Yes."

"Okay."

He holds out his hand. I take it, but he moves my hand so our fingers are interlocked, "It's not that high, you can do this." His face is so close to mine. He's looking right at me. There's so much intensity in his expression. I move forward and kiss him. The kiss is gentle and sweet but could easily lead to so much more.

"Let's go, V!" a yell comes from below. It startles us apart despite the fact that we know no one can see us. Chase lets out a shaky breath. "What was that for?"

"For being you."

He smiles and kisses my nose, "You ready?"

"I think so."

"We run on three."

"Okay."

"One."

I take a deep breath.

"Two."

I release it.

"Three!"

We take off. The edge of the landing is nearing closer by the second. I blink, and then the cliff is gone and we're airborne. For a split second, it feels as if we're flying. My stomach is in my throat and then gravity beckons us down. A scream erupts from my mouth, and I quickly pinch my nose seconds before we crash into the water, which causes our grasp on each other to break apart. I sink like a rock, but quickly move my limbs until I break the surface. I'm rapidly pulling in air. My heart is racing, and when I open my eyes I'm feeling disorientated. Yelling and screaming comes from behind me. I splash around to see everyone yelling for me--for us. I throw my hand out.

"See, it wasn't that bad. Was it?" Chase's voice is beside me. I turn to face him. We're both treading water.

"That was scary," I confess, "But *so* amazing!"

He smiles. "Wanna go again?"

"Yes!" I shout.

We race to the rocks--he beats me, of course. We climb up, and it seems to go faster this time. I wait off to the side once we reach the top, expecting him to want to go by himself. But he surprises me when he grabs my hand and pulls my body flush to his, wrapping his free arm around me. He's warm and cold at the same time; it causes goosebumps to break upon my skin. He leans down and kisses my shoulder. "We jump together."

"Together?" I ask.

"Together." He confirms.

YOU'RE MINE
Chase

I am *completely* enamored with Veronica. Her body is amazing. I could barely keep it together when she took off her clothes, revealing the leopard printed bikini top that was hiding underneath.

After the second jump, we swim back to the boat and rejoin the rest of the gang. Vaughn has a screaming Jenny in his arms, but her pleas fall on deaf ears as he jumps into the water with her.

"You asshole!" Jenny yells as she comes up from under the water. Vaughn just laughs with no remorse. She huffs and treads back to the boat, purposely stomping to the front where her friend lays sunbathing. Veronica relaxes on her back, drifting on the water. I can't help but admire her physique until Vance jumps in the water--scaring her out of her peaceful float. She splashes him. "Jerk."

"What happened up there, Vern?"

"I have no idea what you speak of," she fires back.

"Did Little Vern need someone to hold her hand to jump from the big ol' cliffs?" He speaks as one would to a child.

"Shut up."

"Make me." Vance is already next to V and before she knows it, he grabs her leg and pulls, causing her to go under. She comes up sputtering and wiping the hair from her face, "I hate you!" Vance is already swimming away, laughing loudly.

"I'm hungry," Vance announces. "What food do we have?"

"We packed some sandwiches, but there might not be enough. We didn't know more people were coming," Melissa says from the boat.

"No worries, girl. We stopped at the sub shop," Talia says, waving Melissa off.

Vance and I are the only two stil in the water, so we move to the boat and climb on board. I grab my towel from my seat, drying off my short hair and then moving down my body. Melissa hands out sandwiches and I thank her for thinking of me, in which she thanks me for allowing her to come out. We all sit around, enjoying our sandwiches with light conversation.

"What time is it?" Vaughn asks.

"Two o'clock." Victor informs us, looking at the watch on his left wrist.

"Wow, already?" Veronica says.

"Time flies when you're having fun," Vance responds.

"What time do you guys want to head out?" I ask.

"Four?" Vaughn says, more like a question.

Victor nods. "Yeah, that sounds good to me."

"You guys wanna do some tubing?" I ask.

"Can we just lounge?" Talia asks.

"You girls are no fun," Vance says.

"We just ate!" she whines.

"We can hang out for a bit and let our food digest. I don't need anyone getting sick," I suggest.

"Can I use a tube?" Talia asks me.

"Yeah." I move towards the back of the boat, opening the compartment that holds them and their ropes. I hand them over to Talia.

"Thanks, I'm gonna float. Can you hook me?" she asks,

smiling. I nod and hook her to the back. She places the tube into the water and eases herself on.

"Oh! I want one!" Laura says on my left. So I do the same for her, then turn to see Veronica moving towards the front of the boat. She makes a spot for herself, then lays on her back.

Melissa and Victor get up. "I'm gonna show Mel the cliffs," he says.

"I'll go with you!" Vance says, getting up. Vin and Vaughn agree. "You coming?" Vance looks at me.

"Nah. I'm gonna stay here."

"Suit yourself." Vance shrugs then dives off.

I watch as they all swim off. Jenny sits at the end of the boat, her feet in the water. That leaves me and Veronica practically alone.

Against my better judgment, I move towards the front of the boat, completely soaking up the view of her body that's only being covered by little strips of fabric. I grab my phone from the compartment by the steering wheel and snap a picture because I don't think my mind will ever *really* do this justice. I slip my phone into my, now dry, shorts and move to sit across from her.

Her eyes are closed, and I notice the white cords leading to the buds in each ear. I glance towards the back of the boat to make sure we don't have an audience and move forward, getting on my knees next to her. The sinful images of what I want to do to her floods my mind. I shake them off, knowing it's too soon and not something that can happen right now. I settle for trailing my finger gently down the side of her torso. She visibly jumps, and her eyes flash open. "What are you doing?" she whispers.

"Admiring you," I tell her softly.

"Why?"

"Because you're meant to be."

She seems to have lost her speech because she doesn't say anything. Speechless. I smile at the thought of me being able to leave her in that state. I lean forward and press my mouth to hers. *There. Now she can't disagree with me.* Kissing her is my new favorite thing. I don't think I'll ever get enough of her lips. There's a simplicity of two mouths meeting to show expression of affection, and yet, there are no words that can properly describe it.

I move back on my heels. "What was that for?" she asks.

"Because it's my new favorite thing," I tell her with a wink. "So, get used to it."

She bites her lip, and it damn near kills me. I groan, "I'm going for a swim." My skin is on fire, and I need to cool down. Before moving towards the back of the boat, I remove my phone from my shorts, then proceed to the stern and dive off. The cool water is much-needed relief. I swim underneath before breaking the surface.

"Chase!" My name is yelled out, and I turn to look at Talia and her friend on the rafts, who are wiping their bodies down.

"My bad," I yell. *Whoops.* In my peripherals I can see Vance swimming our way. His head disappears under the water, and I already know that those little droplets I splashed them with won't matter anymore. Talia shrieks out as her raft is abruptly flipped over.

She reappears, shouting, "You *asshole!*"

"I'm ready for some tubing!" Vaughn calls out.

"Yes!" Vance punches the air.

"Alright. Where's Victor and Melissa?" I ask.

"They're coming," Vin informs me.

Vance pulls himself onto the boat's pad. "Let's go, ladies, pack it in!" He begins to pull in both tubes--including Jenny--but when she gets close, he tugs hard and sends her flying into the water. He *is* an asshole, and the girls still flock to him. Vaughn and Vin climb on, then help the girls up. Victor and Melissa rejoin us.

"Hey, we're gonna do some tubing," I inform them, swimming towards the boat.

"Nice," Victor says to me but pulls Melissa to the ladder at the end of the boat. "Babe, you gotta try it," he directs this to Melissa.

"I don't know," she says, looking uneasy.

"I won't go fast on your turn, I promise," I tell her, and she gives me a weak smile.

We tube for a good two hours, and I'm sad it's over. It's always a really fun time. Vaughn quit after slamming into the water so hard that a glob of wax came out of his ear. Melissa surprised me by trying, and as promised, I took it easy. So easy that she tells me she found it relaxing. Jenny managed to lose her bottoms and give everyone a full moon. Vance lost his trunks but wasn't as embarrassed as Jenny about it. V and Talia had a full-on battle that lasted a good while until V hit a huge wake and flipped off. My protective instincts wanted to make sure she was okay, but I had to reel it in and fortunately Victor made sure she was all good.

Everyone is officially beat and ready to head back to the docks. Once everything is put away, we make our way back. It's extremely hard to focus with Veronica sitting in the front this time. My eyes keep roaming to her on their own accord. It becomes easier once we hit the no-wake zone, and I can only go so fast. I need to focus. "V?" I ask, and her head snaps in my direction. "Can you move towards the back and help guide me in?" She looks at me quizzically. "Yeah, sure."

I don't need much help. I've done this a million times since the age of fourteen, but I need her out of my line of sight. I throw out some questions to her, in which she responds to the best of her knowledge.

Once we are feet away from the assigned area, I allow the boat to idle into the slip, not touching the throttle. When I feel it's parked perfectly, I shut off the engine and drop the anchor before hurrying to remove the ropes. I quickly jump off the side and onto the dock. "V, throw me that rope!" She does as I ask, and I catch it, pulling the boat closer and fasten it to the cleat.

I move to the front and ask her to throw me that rope as well. "Perfect," I tell her, climbing back on the boat. "Thank you for your help."

She smiles and nods. I maneuver around the boat, making sure there's no garbage and put away anything that was pulled out. "All good?" I hear a deep voice ask, causing me to look up at Victor. "Yeah, seems good," I tell him.

Melissa hands Victor their things, and then he helps her off. Vance helps Talia then slaps her ass as she steps onto the dock. They wander away, and Vance is mauling her like she's his last meal. Vaughn and Vin help the remaining ladies off, and they walk away. This leaves Veronica by herself, who moves to jump off. I grab her arm before she steps up.

"Wait, I'll help you."

I jump off and reach out for her. She grabs my hand

and jumps down. Her body's close to mine--just the way I like it. She looks up at me with a smile, her green eyes shining brightly, "Thank you."

Her head just reaches my chin. I love that she's so small but so amazingly tough. A walking contradiction, this girl is.

"Yo! What the fuck you guys doin'? Let's go!" I hear Vance's voice yelling from down the dock.

"Damn. I guess we need to get moving," I tell her.

"Yeah, I guess so. Or, maybe, we should tell him to fuck off?"

I groan.

"What?" She laughs and moves past me.

"You said fuck."

"Yeah? And?"

With my head thrown back, I sigh loudly. Hearing her curse like this is doing something to me. Anything she does makes me all kinds of crazy. I have to think of my grandma in her underwear to keep my excitement from showing.

Veronica looks over her shoulder, a small smirk forming, "You coming?"

"Evil. Evil, sexy woman," I mumble to myself and catch up with her.

Victor and Melissa thank me again for a fun day, and head home after Veronica tells them she won't be able to come out because of school. She promises to call and set something up for the following weekend. Vance keeps us waiting in the truck while he has a five-minute make-out session before jumping in the cab.

"Finally," Vaughn mutters.

"Don't hate."

"Please. I got Jenny's number."

"Don't you three look cozy." Veronica jokes at the three brothers sitting closely together because of their size.

"Yeah, what the hell, V? Why do you get the front?" Vance complains.

"Because I'm your sister and a lady."

Vance scoffs, "Since when do ladies burp and fart the way you do."

"Shut up," she grunts, and hastily turns forward.

"Yeah. She can clear out a room," Vaughn chimes in.

"Kill me now," she mutters, covering her face while her brothers pick on her.

I listen while the guys talk about their plans for tonight. Vance is planning on meeting back up with Talia...leaving my night wide open. My thoughts instantly turn to Veronica. We may be able to spend some time together, without worries, after all.

My tank is near empty, so before getting on the highway, I turn into the gas station near our entrance. The guys head inside, and Veronica remains in the truck. When I have the nozzle in my gas tank, I lean over the seat to tell her, "Don't make any plans later."

She looks up at me, "Why?"

"Cause, tonight, you're mine."

BEST DAY EVER
Veronica

I can't stop myself from smiling. I can't even find the right words to describe what I feel like. I'm so happy I could burst. His words replay in my head. *Cause, tonight, you're mine.* Today turned out to be so much better than I could have imagined, and I feel slightly guilty for judging Talia's friends-- they weren't bad at all.

I fall asleep on the drive home. Vance has the grand idea to scare me during the middle of a dream, and I definitely almost pee myself. I instinctively slap his arm as he's cackling like a hyena. Chase drops us off and informs Vance--after being asked--that he's going to stay in and relax at home. I hop out of the truck and skip off, knowing that he'll be with me.

I take a relaxing shower, scrub all the lake crud off of me, and wonder what he could possibly be planning tonight. *Will we go out or stay in?* The thought of staying in sounds very appealing and the butterflies form low in my belly. I feel flushed as I finish standing under the stream of hot water--I turn the knob--and dry off. The nerves stay with me as I get ready and become even worse as I'm driving Mom's car to Chase's. I pull into the driveway that leads to the large white house and park off towards the far side. Chase instructed me to since then Mom's car won't be visible from the street. I am so nervous I could vomit. The feeling is such a drastic change from earlier this afternoon.

I take a couple deep breaths before stepping out of the car, leaving its much-appreciated warmth. I dressed casually, but still cute; I have no idea what we're doing. I nervously shuffle towards the front door, glancing around the house. The door swings open as I move up the porch and Chase appears, wearing a knit sweater with some faded jeans. He looks amazing. He smiles at the sight of me, and I can't help but mirror it back. He moves forward, wrapping me up in his strong arms. He smells like fresh laundry, and I breathe him in.

"Finally," he whispers, and my insides melt. I shiver as he pulls away. "Let's get you inside." His hand moves to grab mine, and he pulls me along with him.

"Are your parents home?" The butterflies are flapping wildly in my stomach.

"No." He closes the door behind me, and I take in the massive foyer.

"I don't think I've ever seen your house," I admit, "It's beautiful."

"It's not that special. It's just a house."

"So, what's on the agenda tonight?" I ask him, the curiosity getting the best of me.

"Are you hungry?"

"Famished."

"Good. I made dinner."

"You cooked?"

"Yeah. Don't get too excited, it's nothing extravagant." He pulls me deeper into the house--towards the back--where a large white kitchen comes into view. It's gorgeous, but he doesn't stop there. He continues into another room, right off the kitchen, that's adorned with a large oak table and a crystal chandelier hanging above it. It's...lavish. I notice the two-place settings are set across from another at the left end. He moves me to the seat that faces the kitchen opening and puts on a show by pulling out my chair for me.

"Wow. Chase, this is beautiful," I say, almost at a loss for words. "Thank you."

"Don't thank me yet. I just hope the food is edible. I'll be right back."

He moves out of the room and returns a moment later with two plates filled with baked ziti. He places them down at each setting. First thing I notice is the amount of cheese on the top, then the two meatballs off to the side. Amazing. "I have garlic bread. Do you like garlic bread?" He asks in a rush. *He is so cute.*

"Yes," I tell him and watch him leave the room again, returning with a tray and a pitcher of, what looks like, lemonade. He sets them both on the table between us, then takes his seat across from me.

"This is the nicest thing anyone has ever done for me," I falter, almost becoming emotional.

"Get used to it. You deserve everything good."

I can't help but stare at him. There is a beautiful man sitting across from me, who's made me dinner--just because. He provokes things in me that I never thought possible. In the very short time that we've spent together he's managed to make me feel special, cherished, bold, and brave. I am so full of gratitude that I don't even hesitate on my next move. I push my chair back, stand up and move around the table to him. His eyes are following my every step. He pushes his chair back and allows me to climb into his lap. I wrap my arms around his neck, laying my head on his shoulder. His arms encase me.

"Aren't you hungry?" he questions.

"Yes, but I don't think I have words to express how much this means." I kiss his neck and as I notice his breath hitch slightly, I do it again--and again. I'm kissing my way up to his jawline when he moves his head to capture my lips with his. It starts sweet until he deepens the kiss with his tongue, and I happily allow its entrance. His hand moves to the back of my head, cradling it. *I love this.* I love the way he makes me feel by just kissing me. I whimper when he slows the kiss, removing his tongue from my mouth, and ends it with small pecks on my lips.

Small puffs of his breath flutter upon my lips as he rests his forehead against mine. It's a couple minutes until he speaks, "As much as I love this form of gratitude, we have to stop."

I pout. But, I know he's right. He pats my thigh, and I remove myself from his lap. He tugs me back for one more kiss. "Okay. Go sit."

I take my seat across from him again. I pierce a couple noodles with my fork, and make sure to get a fair amount of cheese in with them. Chase is watching as I place the food in my mouth. The burst of flavors on my tongue is surprising; it's sweet and spicy all at once. I chew, making sure not to look like a pig when I'm finished. I wipe my mouth before I speak.

"Chase, I know you said it's nothing special, but that's the best sauce I've ever tasted!"

"Really?"

"Yeah, that's no jarred sauce."

"No, it's not. It's my grandma's recipe. So are the meatballs."

"So you made them all from scratch?"

"She always says," he clears his throat and when he

continues it's in a much higher pitch, "'Don't be lazy. You show someone you care by taking the time to cook for them, and none of that boxed crap.'"

"Smart woman," I muse.

"She is."

I am so impressed, and completely awed by him. Again.

"So, can I look forward to more tantalizing recipes created by grandma, cooked by you?"

"I think I have a better idea."

"Better?" I question, and then a thought occurs to me. "Oh! Do I get to watch while you do it?"

"Watching me would be better?"

"Definitely" I nod excitedly, "Even better if you're *shirtless*."

"I'll keep that in mind." He seems to be blushing. It's adorable. "But that's not what I was thinking."

I draw out a dramatic sigh. "Darn."

He smiles, showing me his white teeth. "I'll take you to have her cook for you herself. She'd love to meet you."

Okay, I was *not* expecting that. "You want me to meet your grandmother?"

"Yeah, she'll love you. She lives a couple of hours away. We can make a weekend of it."

"Okay," I say slightly dazed.

"We don't have to. It's purely selfish, really. Spend time with you and Gram's cooking...win-win."

"No. That actually sounds really nice."

We talk about his grandmother for a while, in between our bites of food, and it's really sweet how much he adores her. I learn that he spent the summers with her when he was little, and that he never got to meet his grandfather because he passed away before he was born. She never remarried. I'm curious about so much more, but don't pry. If he wants to offer up more, he will. Plus, I hope we have more times like this to learn even more about each other.

Our conversation moves to other topics, and I find that I enjoy learning about him immensely. I am an average school student, but anything to do with Chase, I soak in like a sponge. My plate is empty, as is his, and yet we still sit and talk. There is absolutely no pressure to do anything else, and I'm more than content.

His eyes move to my empty plate, and it seems to spark something. "Do you want dessert?"

"You made dessert too?"

He laughs. "As much as I'd love to take credit for it, no."

I stretch and rub my belly. "I'm still full."

He gets up from his chair, grabbing his plate, and moves to grab mine. "Well then, let's go relax and watch a movie," he suggests and turns to walk out of the room. I get up from my chair, and follow behind him, watching as he places the plates in the sink. He turns to me. "I'll clean up later." He moves towards me, easily slipping his hand in mine and pulling me towards the massive living room. He sits down on the gray couch and tugs me down next to him, grabbing the remote off the coffee table in front of him.

"What are you in the mood for? Comedy? Thriller? Horror? Romance?" he asks while scrolling through the guide.

"Whatever," I say, pulling my feet up underneath me.

"Hmm," he hums. He drapes his arm around my shoulder and lets me lean in against his chest. I have no choice but to snuggle into him--not that I'm complaining. *He's so warm.* Without even realizing it my arm lays across his stomach, and my head rests right above his pec. Everything about this has come naturally.

"Oh, I've wanted to see this! Is this okay?" he asks me, and I can feel his head move as if he's looking down for my approval. Moving my head back, so I can look up, our eyes connect. My forest to his ocean.

"It's perfect," I tell him. He smiles; it's heavenly. He leans down to give my lips a sweet kiss. I sigh happily.

He turns his focus back to the TV, putting on the movie that he's settled on watching. I could care less what we watch--just being here with him is good enough for me. Occasionally, I feel him play with my hair, or rub my shoulder; always touching me in some fashion. It's as if he can't get enough. We remain like this throughout the movie; comfortable and at ease. When the credits start rolling, I slowly move away, but he holds me to him.

"Where are you going?" he asks, his voice low. I don't know, actually, it just felt like the right thing to do. "Well, I can't stay here forever," I say, playfully.

"Oh but you could." I look at him in surprise. He has a wicked smirk on his face.

"You're right. The brother brigade would come banging on my door, and we don't want that, so let's go eat some pie," he suggests.

"Pie?" I perk up.

"Pie," he confirms and moves to stand up, pulling me with him.

"What kind of pie?" I ask.

"You'll just have to come to find out." He moves out of the room and into the kitchen. I follow close on his heels. *Pie!* He quickly tries to conceal it when I come up behind him to peek.

"Back up, woman." he jokes, keeping the pie tucked to him. He then smoothly starts moving to the island that's located in the middle of the kitchen.

"You can't tease a girl with pie!" I huff.

"Ta-daaaah!" He reveals the crumb covered shoofly pie, and my mouth waters.

"Oh, Daniels, you sure know the way to a girl's heart."

"Only yours." he replies with a wink.

He grabs a fork and digs right into the middle, a nice sized bite on the tip, then moves to me. This surprises me, but I open my mouth and allow him to slip the fork inside. Closing my mouth, he pulls the fork out, and I subconsciously move my hands to cover my lips. I hum my approval, and he suddenly looks like a starving man.

He clears his throat. "It's from Chrissy's."

After swallowing my bite, I can speak, "*That's* why it's so good."

I watch him as he goes for another fork full but placing the food into his mouth this time. He hums. "So good," he says, not caring about covering his mouth. It makes me laugh. He still looks hot. We continue this back and forth until I can't possibly eat any more.

His phone goes off, but he doesn't bother to look at it. Instead, he pulls me to him wrapping me up into a cocoon of his strong arms, and rests his head atop mine. I allow my arms to wrap around his waist. My head is against his chest, and his voice rumbles as he speaks, "I don't want you to leave, but I know it's probably best if you did."

I just nod, remaining silent, and completely enjoying this moment. I sigh. "I know. Thank you for tonight. I don't think this will top any date you may have planned in the future."

He laughs lightly, "Cheap date...this will definitely work."

I pull back. "I don't need anything but you."

He likes that response because his lips are on mine in an instant, and it's unlike any kiss we've experienced so far. It's needy and it's rough. His tongue doesn't waste any time asking for entrance, and I happily oblige. He presses me to him, and I'm positive he can feel my heart hammering in my chest.

The kiss deepens quickly and his hands move to my backside until he's lifting me up. My legs wind around his waist. I can feel his excitement, the slight friction entices an unexpected moan from me. My hands move up his back and claw at his shirt. My fingers evoke a low groan from his throat.

His movements become hasty, and his hands are traveling to my sides, exposing my skin. His touch feels so good, I'm barely aware that we are still in the middle of his kitchen. *I want to feel his touch everywhere.* He places me on the kitchen island when the unexpected ringing of his phone causes us to rip apart as if we've been caught. Our breathing is ragged and uneven. He starts to laugh as he's placing his forehead to my chest. He reaches into his back pocket and moves his head away from my chest to look at the screen.

My curiosity gets the best of me, I am instantly doused with imaginary cold water--my heart is hammering for another reason now. He sighs, and answers the phone, "What, Shannon?" His eyes lock onto mine. I can hear her voice, but I can't make out the words she's saying.

"No, I'm on a date."

Pause.

"I answered because I thought I made it clear before."

Pause.

"Shannon, are you drunk?"

"Whoa. Whoa. No. Look..." His eyes never leave mine, "Yes, I very much like this girl."

His eyes widen.

"Shannon, stop. Don't cry. Is there someone with you?"

Pause.

"Yeah, put her on."

Pause.

"Damn," he whispers. "Mandy, make sure she gets home okay...and erase my number from her phone, please."

Pause.

"Thank you."

He ends the call and slips it back into his pocket. Well, that was weird, but hearing his words were kind of nice at the same time.

"I am so sorry, V."

"It's okay." I shrug and look away.

He gathers my face in his hands. "No, it's not. I only answered because I don't want you to think that I'm keeping secrets."

"Okay," I say. "So you very much like me, huh?" I chirp.

"I do."

"Good, because I happen to very much like you, too."

"You better."

He leans forward and kisses my nose. "Let's get you

home."

I pout.

"Don't do that. I'm trying to behave here."

I nod, "Fine." He's right.

We walks me out to the car, and before opening the door I spin around, "Thank you so much for tonight."

He flashes his teeth, "You're so welcome."

He helps me into the car and doesn't go back inside until I'm down his driveway. I am bubbling with euphoria.

Best. Day. *Ever.*

IT'LL BE OKAY
Chase

My eyes continue to wander to the large clock hanging on my office wall, and I'm having a hard time focusing on the work that needs to be done before leaving for the day. I'm filled with anxiety at the night ahead of me--of us. In just a couple hours, Veronica and I will be heading to Victor's, where we will confide in him about our relationship. I can only hope he'll be accepting and understanding. I'm freakin' *praying* he is.

Veronica seems to be taking it well. She's always reassuring me that it'll be fine but, to be fair, she's also not the one who would get their ass beat. I had to make up a lie for tonight--Vance wanted to hang-- so I told him that I was going to visit Nic at school. Vance slapped me on the back and told me to get some pussy. *Typical.*

Every morning, I pick V up and take her to school since her parts still haven't arrived. I don't mind, even in the slightest, *especially* since our mornings now include an intense make-out session in the front seat of my truck. Plus, the coffee she continues to give me is a bonus.

Veronica has also fabricated a clever story about tutoring someone after work. It isn't much but it allows us to have a little time together. The rest of our time apart is spent on the phone, whether it's vocal or through texts. We avoid certain conversations that, unfortunately, still really need discussing. We both knew this when we began, but we didn't want to face the reality that our time together could come crashing down if her brothers found out about us before we could let them in. I don't want to fight with her about it, but I still feel extremely uneasy with us sneaking around. Victor is our first step and I truly hope the rest will follow.

I habitually glance at the clock again. I still have an hour to go. The plan is to pick Veronica up from school and head down to her brother's right after. Our bags are already packed and sitting in the back of my truck. Her parents are well aware that she is going to be away for the weekend. Victor knows Veronica is bringing a friend, he just doesn't know that friend is me. She told me she would handle her brothers if a problem arises.

I let my eyelids drop and pinch the bridge of my nose--I need to focus and get this paperwork finished.

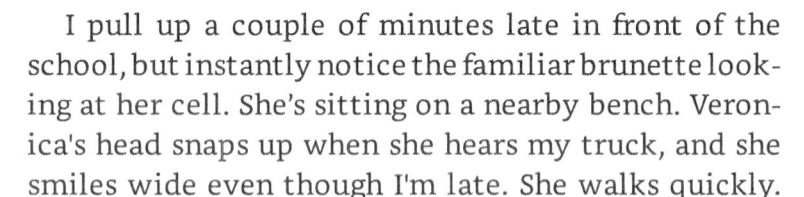

I pull up a couple of minutes late in front of the school, but instantly notice the familiar brunette looking at her cell. She's sitting on a nearby bench. Veronica's head snaps up when she hears my truck, and she smiles wide even though I'm late. She walks quickly. She's radiating with excitement.

As soon as she has the door open, she throws herself into the cab, and her arms snake around my neck. I breathe in her familiar cocoa butter smell. Before her, I had no idea what cocoa butter was and now it's my *favorite* scent.

"Hey, babe." I laugh at her enthusiasm. She pulls back and plants a quick one on my lips.

"Hi," She smiles, "I'm so excited."

"I can tell." I laugh.

"Aren't you?"

"Somewhat."

"It'll be fine, I promise." Her hand moves to the back of my neck, lightly scratching at my hairline. I love when she does that..

"I guess we'll find out."

Veronica gives me Victor's address, and I plug it into the GPS on my phone. "In five-hundred feet, turn right on Chestnut Lane," the robotic female voice speaks from my phone.

"Ready?" I ask, looking towards Veronica, who is curled up on my seat.

She smiles at me. "Yep."

Twenty minutes into the drive and Veronica has passed out, her head resting on the arm between us. So it's just me, the road, and my nerves. The closer we get to the city, the heavier the traffic becomes, and soon we're moving like snails. Constant stop and go. I could never live in the city, even though the tall shiny buildings do look cool. Veronica stretches her arms and sits up, drowsily taking in the surroundings. "We there?" she asks, rubbing her lash line.

"Almost. Looks like it's about two blocks away, but it says it'll be another sixteen minutes."

"Wow, this is so cool. You can walk to everything! Oh, look, a Starbucks!" she says excitedly as she presses her face to the window.

After what seems like eons, we finally make it to a massive building. We pull into an underground parking lot, and I have V scanning for the closest space to the elevators. With both our bags in one hand, I round the back of the truck to meet V and she grabs my hand as we walk towards the lift.

"Okay, I let him know we're here."

The doors open almost instantly after she pushes the button, and I'm hesitant to get in. Veronica walks forward but stops short when I don't move with her. She looks back at me and takes the two steps to stand in front of me, grabbing my face with her free hand. It forces me to look at her. My eyes connect with her viridescent ones. "It'll be okay," she reassures. With a light squeeze of her hand, she steps backward and tugs me with her. I move, slowly, into the elevator. *How is she so confident? This could end badly.*

I'm so lost in my head I don't even realize we're standing in front of a gray door, labeled with gold numbers. It's almost like everything is in slow motion as Veronica lifts her hand and knocks on the door. Less than a minute later, the door opens to reveal Victor who looks at Veronica, then to me. His expression goes from happy to shock in less than a second.

ACTIONS SPEAK VOLUME
Veronica

The shock on Victor's face makes me falter for a second, but I move forward to hug him, releasing Chase's hand in the process. I move back and slip my hand back into Chase's. Victor's eyes move down to our connected hands, a look of confusion as he looks at the both of us curiously.

"This is a surprise. I thought you were bringing a friend?"

"Yes," I say slowly, "I wanted to introduce you to my *boyfriend*."

"Boyfriend?" Victor chokes out. "What?" His eyes move between the two of us. "Chase is your boyfriend? When the fuck did this happen?" His voice is loud, but not necessarily angry.

"It's very new," I tell him.

"Uh, I'd say. I don't recall anything being said last weekend when we were all together," he points out. "I can't imagine Vance is taking this well."

"We haven't told Vance."

"What?!" he barks.

"Maybe we can take this inside?" Chase speaks up.

Victor seems to notice that we're still standing out in the hall and moves aside to let us in. I stroll through the door and move through the condo without waiting for my brother, taking in its modern and sleek appearance. The kitchen is immediately on the right, full of silver appliances, and past the kitchen is a dining room with a small table that fits four. Beyond that is the wide-open living room. My eyes take in the floor-to-ceiling windowed wall.

"Victor, this place is amazing," I tell him before moving towards the windows, looking down at the bustling city lights below.

"Yeah, it's great but back to you and Chase," Victor's voice is stern, causing me to whip around. His posture says anything but relaxed as he's standing with his arms crossed over his chest. Beyond Victor, Chase stands awkwardly, still holding our bags.

I notice Melissa isn't around. "Where's Melissa?"

"She'll be home soon. Stop evading the question."

"Victor," Chase speaks up. He releases our bags at his feet and looks at my brother. "We're sorry to spring this on you. It wasn't our intention. "

"What are your intentions?" Victor cuts Chase from finishing his sentence. Victor's facial expression is one of concern, and I'm starting to doubt our decision. I thought he would be the most understanding out of all my brothers.

"I have no intentions, other than making her happy." His words make my heart skip a beat. Chase's eyes move to mine, in silent understanding, and he strides across the room to me. Despite my brother standing feet away, Chase looks confident. His arm wraps around my shoulder when he reaches me, pulling me into his side. I stare at him in awe, momentarily forgetting my brother. Chase smiles and looks towards Victor. I dare to glance at Victor, afraid of what I'll see exactly, but his posture has visibly relaxed. I exhale, the nervous dispersing. *It's going to be okay.* This time, I believe myself.

The front door opens. "Vic?" the female voice calls

out. A second later, Melissa appears in the dining room looking fresh from work. She places a brown bag on the table. "Oh hey," she pauses and looks around, "Everything okay?"

Victor's face lights up when he sees her. "Yeah, everything's good. V and Chase wanted to share some news with us." He holds out his arm for her, and she moves into it, her head tilted back as she waits for a kiss, which Victor readily gives.

Her gaze moves to us. "Oh, yeah?"

I smile at her.

"So, it's official then?" she asks.

"You knew?" Victor says loudly, looking down at Melissa.

"No, not officially." She shrugs her shoulders, "But I noticed at the lake. They're smitten." She smiles wide towards us.

Victor shakes his head. "I don't know how I missed it." He sighs, "Well then..." He looks at us, and takes a step forward, causing Melissa to do the same. His hand moves out to Chase, who returns the gesture. "If she's going to be with anyone, I'm glad it's you. I know you're an honorable guy, and you know that I'll kick your ass if you hurt her."

I move forward quickly and wrap my arms around Victor. From behind me, Chase speaks up, "If I hurt her, I will come to you, so you can kick my ass."

It's all okay.

The tension completely evaporates, as Melissa moves from the room and into the kitchen. "I bought some food for tonight, but we can save it and go out instead?" she yells.

Victor looks at the two of us. "Let's go out."

I feel so elated like I'm on top of the world.

"So, why haven't you told Vance yet?"

And just like that, I fall right off that world.

I move into the living room, taking a seat on their brown leather couch. Chase follows, and sits down next to me. Victor's sitting in the love seat across from us. "Well," I start, "out of you all, Vance seems to be the most protective. You're not around as much, and you have Melissa. I thought you'd understand the most," I tell him honestly.

He nods and glances towards the kitchen. Melissa is visible through the pass-through opening. "I'll admit, I probably wouldn't have been so understanding had I not met Melissa. I get how telling me was such a big deal." He looks at me, "You know her father's my boss. We took a risk by being together, too. I could have lost my job. She walked into the office, and I instantly wanted to get to know her. She is so different from any girl that I've ever known. I immediately asked her out," He starts to laugh, "I didn't even know that she was Greg's daughter! It wasn't until weeks later when I found out. She didn't want to tell me. She was scared to." Melissa came to sit next to Victor, I watch him grab her hand and look at her. It was a side of Victor I've never seen. It made me admire him so much more than I already did. "It worked out for the best." He kisses the side of her head gently. I look away to give them their moment only to find Chase looking directly at me.

"What?" I whisper. He doesn't say anything, just continues his staring, but his mouth slowly spreads into a beautiful smile. He moves forward to capture my lips. I gasp in surprise at this bold move in front of my oldest brother.

"This is weird." I hear Victor say, and Chase laughs. "It's going to take some getting used to."

"It's so cute." Melissa gushes and I can feel myself blushing.

"Oh my gosh." I cover my face. "Anyways, let's move onto another topic."

"I'm gonna say one last thing," Victor speaks up, "You need to tell Vance as soon as possible. He most likely won't take it well, but it needs to come from you two before he finds out from anyone else. We live in a small town, and people notice the smallest things." I look at Chase worriedly, and he nods because I know he agrees with Victor. "Okay!" My brother claps and stands up. "Enough of that shit, let's go out!"

"You guys like sushi?" Melissa asks, "There's this amazing sushi bar not far from us."

I shrug, "I've never had it."

Her eyes bug out of her head, and she looks at Victor who shrugs, "We come from a very small-town Mel. Sushi bars aren't common."

"Well then, it's settled!" Melissa says

We all gather our things and head out the door, walking into the elevator that delivers us to the lobby. I can feel Chase's hand on my lower back as we exit the elevator into the beautifully massive lobby.

"Have you had sushi?" I ask Chase as we walk through the lobb. It looks more like an expensive hotel, rather than a lobby of a condo building, but then again, this is the first time I've ever been in one.

"I have." Chase answers.

"Did you like it? Is it really raw fish?" I cringe at the thought.

He laughs lightly, "It's okay. There are all kinds, not

all of it is."

"Okay. Good."

True to Melissa's words, the Sushi Bar isn't far. It's at the bottom of a massive building and it's pretty busy. The place is actually called Sushi Bar. We walk inside, and surprisingly, it doesn't smell all fishy like I expected. There's an actual bar at the front, and it seems to be moving. I watch guests sit in front and pick up the sushi with their sticks from the moving plates.

"This is so cool," I whisper to Chase. A hostess greets us then leads our group to a table for four. Settling in, Melissa explains, "Normally we'd sit at the bar, but it's usually just the two of us."

"So you just pick from the plates of what you want?" I ask, and look back at the people sitting on the stools.

"Yeah, they're made fresh and placed on the moving bar."

A very small young woman approaches the table with a smile, "Hello." she greets us with a slight bow, "Welcome. What would you like to drink?" Her accent is noticeable, but she speaks English well. We place our drink orders, and she walks away from the table.

"Since this is your first time, are you okay if I order?" Melissa asks.

I shrug, "Sure."

"They have this amazing platter, it'll feed all of us, but it has all different kinds of rolls."

"Okay." I agree, then look at Chase to see if that's alright with him. He says, "Whatever you want, babe." I smile, feeling shy at this term of endearment. His hand moves to my thigh and squeezes.

"*So* weird." I hear Victor mutter from across the table. I laugh happily.

"You know he's sleeping on the couch, right?"

"What? No!"

"I may be okay with you guys being together, but there's no baby making happening under my roof unless it's me doing the baby making!"

"Victor!" I shout, causing those around us to look. Chase is laughing so hard next to me, while I glare at Victor. Melissa smacks Victor lightly with the back of her hand. I turn to Chase, who is still laughing. "It's not that funny!" He wipes his eyes, then pulls my head towards him, placing a kiss on my temple.

"It's fine, Victor," Chase assures my oldest brother.

I huff my disapproval. To be honest, I hadn't even thought of our sleeping arrangements until Victor mentioned it right now. I wanted nothing more than to be cuddled with Chase in a bed. He really doesn't have to worry; there's no way my first time is happening in my brother's spare bedroom.

The waitress returns with our drinks and Melissa places the order for the platter she's been gushing about. The conversation between the four of us flows easily; I'm grateful. Chase's hand remains on my thigh, occasionally drawing patterns that cause me to break out in goosebumps. I want to visit here as much as we can because we're free to be us.

I know we need to talk with my remaining brothers, and my resolve is slowly crumbling. I can only hope that they'll be as understanding as Victor, somehow, I doubt it. Even so, it seems that Chase is serious when it comes to making us work, but I don't want to be the reason behind a fallout between friends. I focus back on the conversation happening around me, pushing the thoughts away to be in the here-and-now. Victor and

Chase are talking about the Z. "I'm hoping to get it down this weekend," Chase says.

"V, did your parts come in?" Victor asks me.

"No, not yet." Earlier in the week my parts shipped out and, when I checked the tracking, it said they should be here within the next couple days. Not long ago I wanted my parts, so I didn't have to rely on anyone to give me rides and now I'm saddened at the thought of not having Chase pick me up in the mornings. But on the flip side, slipping away any time I want won't be so difficult.

A long wooden plate, covered in a colorful variety of rice rolls, is placed in the middle of the table. Our waitress bows slightly and walks away. Across from me, Melissa wiggles in her seat. "This looks so delicious!" She picks up her chopsticks and selects a roll. My brother joins her, but I don't know where to start.

"Here, try this one," Chase suggests, picking up the small circle and putting it on my plate. "Do you want wasabi?"

"I don't know," I whisper.

He smiles amused, "It's a bit spicy, but it's good."

"Okay." I watch him as he scoops a little dab of the green mush on the end of his stick. He shoves the green glob in the middle of the roll.

"Do I stick the whole thing in my mouth?" I ask him quietly.

His smile widens. "That was hot," he says low.

I smack him with the back of my hand. "Perv."

He throws me a wink and grabs himself a roll, popping the whole thing in his mouth. *Alright then.* I grab the roll and shove it in my mouth. At first, the taste is bland until I slowly start to chew. The flavors come alive.

"Well?" Melissa asks.

I chew some more, covering my mouth, so I don't look like a total slob. "Not bad," I say after finishing. Melissa picks up another circular roll, "Here try this one!" I look at it a little unsure. "Just try it!" I pick it up and pop it in my mouth. "Ohhh...this one is *really* good!" I say. I end up trying every different type of sushi, not favoring the one with the raw fish. It was a great time, and I'm proud of myself for trying something new.

Victor ended up paying after refusing Chase's many attempts at trying to put money in. Once stepping out onto the sidewalk outside the restaurant, I immediately went to Chase's side for some warmth.

"Wow. It got cool out" Victor says, wrapping his arm around Melissa.

"So, where to next?" I ask excitedly.

"There's a neat little coffee place up the street. They sometimes have poetry readings," Melissa suggests.

I've never been to anything like that, and while I'm not huge on poetry, I thought it'd be fun to try something new. I look up just in time to see Chase's cringe, and it makes me laugh. "Not a fan of poetry?" I ask.

"Not really, but I'll do whatever you want to do."

"Thank you," I whisper, stepping up on my tippy toes to give him a sweet kiss. We walk a couple of blocks until we come to an old-looking brick building with a large front window that's painted black--the door is a cerulean blue. Upon entering, I'm instantly hit with the delicious aroma of coffee beans and baked goods. The building is deceiving. The room is much larger than it looks. There are small tables scattered around the center and high top tables near the edge of the room.

The coffee bar is located near the front, my eyes instantly spot the display case of cupcakes, pies, cookies, and other delicious looking baked goods. Near the back of the place is a small stage where a young woman is speaking passionately about...fairies.

"Oh shit," Victor mumbles says he tries to contain his laughter.

"We can just sit back here," Melissa whisper-yells to us, and we follow her, sitting around the nearest open table.

"You want something?" Chase asks.

"Yeah. Surprise me."

He kisses me on the nose and walks the short distance to the bar. I can't help but admire his muscular figure. He's so sexy, and all *mine*. I smile to myself, looking away back towards the front stage, noticing Victor's eyes on me. My head cocks in curiosity, he leans forward in his chair, resting his arms on his knees. "I never thought that this day would come, Vern."

"Neither did I," I agree.

"He cares about you. His actions speak volumes."

His words are comforting. "I care about him too."

Victor reaches his hand out, covering mine in a reassuring gesture. "I know, it shows. All I want for you is to be happy."

"Thank you." I lean forward and engulf him in a hug. His large arms wrap around me.

"Tell Vance," he whispers. I only nod. Chase returns with two cream cheese cupcakes and two hot drinks. I clap my hands excitedly. "You did good!"

We don't hang around for too long, getting bored with the entertainment. Poetry isn't for us. "Tomorrow we have all day!"

Melissa says excitedly. "I love living here."

"I don't think I could," I admit.

"Me either," Chase agrees. "Not sure how you do it, Victor."

"You get used to it." He shrugs.

We walk back to their building and make our way back up to the condo. Once inside, Victor announces they're turning in. "No funny business!" He wags his finger at us.

"Stop," I whine.

"Leave them be," Melissa tells Victor while pulling him into their bedroom right off of the living room. Before the bedroom door can close Victor pokes his head out, his eyes moving between me and Chase. "I'm watching you." He narrows his eyes and points to the both of us, then disappears, the door closing a second later.

"That's so embarrassing." I plop down on the sofa. Chase takes a seat next to me.

"It's not. He cares about you." Chase grabs the remote from the side table, turning on the TV.

"I know." I sigh. "Do you want to go to bed?" I ask, silently hoping he doesn't so we can spend some more time together. This has been such a fun night.

He shrugs. "I'm good." He grabs my legs and places them over his, and I snuggle into him. His hand moves, drawing circles on the outside of my jeans. My mind starts to wonder about Victor's comments about funny business and while this may not be the most ideal moment to bring it up--sitting on my oldest brother's couch--I know I need to get this out.

"Chase?" I ask.

"Yeah, baby?" he murmurs.

"You know..." I trail off, not exactly sure how to say it.

"I know, what?" he prompts.

"Um. That, I--what my brother said earlier? About having sex?"

He shifts, and I can feel his eyes on me. There's no way I can look at him. Maybe I'm not ready for this conversation. "V, look at me." My eyes slowly move to his. "You know that this"—His finger moves between the two of us—"is not what it's about, right?"

"You don't want to have sex with me?" I ask, a little confused.

He laughs, "I do." His head falls back, his eyes on the ceiling, "Very, very, very, very much."

"Oh." I suddenly feel hot all over. His head lifts and his eyes are on me again. "But I'm not with you for that reason. This is so much more."

Wow.

"Okay...but you know you're my first boyfriend, right?" I confess. "This is all new to me. I haven't done anything. Like *that*." I stress.

"I won't lie. I thought you haven't, considering I know who your brothers are. There's no rush. When you're ready, you let me know. We can take this as slow as you need. I'm just happy to be in your presence. I'm with you, for you."

Be still, my heart. There's this weird feeling in my chest. I can easily fall in love with Chase Daniels. In fact, I'm sure I'm already falling. "Okay," I whisper.

I feel so relieved--and so glad to have this off my chest--that he took it so well. It brings me back to the conversation I had with Taylor. Talking with him is like talking to my best friend. *This is how it should be.*

I shouldn't be afraid to talk to my boyfriend about my concerns or feelings. Having already confessed something so deep I know, without a doubt, that I can talk to him about anything. He leans forward and captures my lips with his; a gentle kiss followed by a nip.

Victor's bedroom door opens causing both of us to look away from each other, but not out of fear because kissing isn't 'doing anything wrong'. Victor strolls out in a white tee and boxers. He eyes us as he walks to the kitchen, returning shortly after with a glass of water. He then disappears back into the bedroom. I can't help but laugh. "He's so crazy." I snuggle into Chase, and we fall into a comfortable silence. Every moment I spend with him is perfect. Before I know it I fall fast asleep.

TO FAMILY

Veronica

The low murmuring of voices seeps into my unconscious state, rousing me awake. Slowly, my eyes open. The whiteness of the room combined with the sun peeking through the windows makes me squint until they adjust to the invasive light. I'm lying on an amazingly comfortable and fluffy bed, covered by a purple comforter--completely alone. Last I remember, I was with Chase on the couch. I notice I'm still wearing my shirt from yesterday, and I can feel the scratchiness of my jeans. Chase must've carried me to bed.

The faint smell of bacon has me up and out of the bedroom door. Chase and my brother are sitting in the living room watching some game on the TV. They both look towards me, and I smile weakly. "Good morning, sleepy head!" Victor greets me first. I mosey around the couch and plop down next to Chase, snuggling into his warmth and close my eyes.

His chest moves as he laughs. "Good morning," his voice is low.

"Morning," I croak. I feel a slight pressure on my head from his kiss.

"Sleep well?" Victor asks.

"Uh huh. I smell bacon."

"Melissa's making breakfast," Victor informs me, "Maybe you should go take a shower?"

"Do I smell?" I ask.

"Maybe a little," Chase jokes.

My eyes pop open. I didn't even think about my morning breath. I cover my mouth and sit up quickly which causes him to laugh. My eyes narrow in a glare, but that only makes him laugh more. "Oh stop," He pulls my hand away, places a kiss on my lips, "I'm kidding."

"I think I'm gonna take a shower anyway." I walk back into the spare room noticing that the bed is rumpled from my sleep. Realizing I never brought my bag inside, I turn to leave only to notice it sitting on the dresser.

After a nice long relaxing shower, I slip on a tan oversized sweater and some maroon leggings before drying my hair. Chase and my brother are no longer on the couch, but sitting at the table eating. My stomach rumbles at the sight of food. Melissa's head peeks through the pass over, a big smile on her face, "Hey! What do you want to eat?"

"Whatever they're having is fine," I tell her. "Thank you so much."

Melissa puts a plate on pass through, and it smells *so* good. I grab it and dig right in. A phone goes off. "Oh! I have to get that." She rushes into the bedroom, and I look at Victor curiously.

"Probably work. She's always on call."

"Really? Even on a Saturday?" I ask. I know Melissa does some promotional business event type stuff, but I never really cared for more details.

"Yeah, I just hope she doesn't have to go in," he says, shoveling eggs into his mouth. My face drops...that wouldn't be fun.

We're all finished eating and Victor takes our plates into the kitchen. Chase and I move back into the living room, taking a seat back on the couch and Melissa returns from the bedroom looking flustered and annoyed.

"You look pretty." Chase compliments me, pulling my attention away from Melissa. I lay my head back to look at this handsome guy. I smile wide. "Thank you." He throws me the sexy wink that I love so much, then pecks my lips.

"Everything alright?" I ask as Melissa and Victor come into the room.

"Yeah, clients can be *such* a pain. I had to firmly explain that I'm unavailable today," she huffs annoyed, "Anyways, are you guys ready to go out?"

"Yep!" I said excitedly, "What's on the agenda?"

"Well, what do you guys want to do? There's the park, the museum...we can shop. Tonight, we're taking you to one of our favorite restaurants, but that's not until later."

I bounce in my seat and exclaim, "I want to do it all!"

Our whole day is spent out in the city, but by nightfall my feet hurt and I'm ready for a nap. Experiencing all this with Chase by my side makes everything *that* much more exciting. He was enthusiastic about everything, and the day was so much more enjoyable knowing he was having as much fun as I was.

We all agree that a nap sounds perfect before we head out for dinner. The place they want to take us is a more upscale restaurant, and I'm excited to dress up a little. Our reservations are for eight, which gives us plenty of time for some much-needed rest. As soon as we enter their condo, I pull Chase into the spare bedroom that I slept in, alone, last night.

"V!" Victor shouts, "What do you think you're

doing?"

"Taking a nap!" I yell over my shoulder, pushing Chase aside and closing the door. Surprisingly, Victor doesn't come bursting into the room. I kick off my shoes before jumping on the bed, and pull up the sheets to crawl underneath the fluffy comforter. Chase stands near the door, watching me. I pull the covers up, "You gonna join me?" His lips form a wicked grin that spreads warmth throughout my body. In two strides, he's under the comforter, wrapping his arms around my waist and pulling me to him. When we're comfortably spooning, he pushes his leg between mine and intertwines our fingers. I sigh happily. I don't think I'm going to ever want to sleep alone again.

I'm startled awake by a deafening bang, "Are you guys decent?" Victor shouts through the closed door.

"Of course!" I yell, wiping the sleep from my eyes. I move to lay on my back, and Chase's eyes are on me. He doesn't move away even with Victor opening the door.

"Rise and shine, lovebirds!" Victor's boisterous voice is booming, especially now that the door is open.

"Must you be so *loud*?" I groan.

"I do." He comes further into the room, taking a set at the edge of the bed. "Let's go!" He claps, "You got..." he trails off to look at his phone, "forty-five minutes!"

"Alright. Alright." I grumble. Victor turns to leave, not bothering to close the door. Chase's hand grabs my side and pulls me to face him. His face is sleepy, and he looks so beautiful my breath catches.

"You sleep okay?" He asks, his voice rough.

"I don't think I'll ever be able to sleep alone again."

He smiles wide, and it's such a sight. He leans forward, half his body covering half of mine then presses a kiss to the tip of my nose. "The feeling is mutual."

He's rendered me speechless, something he's been very good at doing more frequently. His eyes are scanning my face--for what I'm not exactly sure--and I find myself doing the same. His blue eyes are vibrant and I notice the slight dusting of freckles on his nose. "You have freckles." I blurt.

"Do I?" his face is one of amusement. I nod. Neither of us bother to move, completely comfortable with how we are, and a small part of me wants to remain in bed with him for the rest of the evening. *Who needs to eat?* But Victor has other plans.

"You guys are still in bed? Get up, ya bums! Let's go, we have to meet Melissa in.." he pauses again to look at his phone, "forty minutes." I lift my head to look at my brother standing in the doorway. Chase lays his head on my chest.

"Melissa left?" I ask, curiously.

"Yes, she had to take care of some work stuff. Chase, get your head off my sister's boobs."

"They're comfy," Chase mumbles and nuzzles in. His response makes me laugh, causing his head to move up and down, which is even funnier.

"I don't want to hear that!" Victor leaves the room.

"Now we know how to get rid of him," I say, sitting up, which causes Chase to move off of me and onto his back. He places his hands behind his head, and I don't even think before making my next move. I swiftly swing my leg over his torso to straddle him. His eyes widen for a fraction of a second then turn hungry--his hands are instantly on my hips. I lean down and press my lips to his.

"What are you doing?" he whispers against my mouth. I shrug. He tugs on my hips. "You are a tease." He picks me up and tosses me onto the plush mattress. The force causes my body to bounce, making me laugh. I move my hair away from my face to see that Chase is standing next to the bed looking down at me, incredulously. He bends down, "One day..." His voice is low and husky, "We'll do that again. Without clothes."

I suck in a breath. The words make my body hot and Chase just smiles wickedly. *Who's the tease now?* He is too sexy for his own good. He stands up tall, "I'm going to leave so you can get dressed now," and he does just that. He also leaves me a dizzy mess.

I take a few minutes to pull myself together. When I was packing my bag, I tried to pack for every occasion. A girl's gotta be prepared. I actually managed to bring a dress. It's not super fancy but it's blue cotton, with long sleeves. *I can make this work.* I find my black tights to go underneath, pair it with my favorite black booties and *Voila!* Comfy and fashionable. I apply some make up-- not a lot, but enough--to make the green in my eyes pop.

"Okay! I'm ready." I announce to the guys. They're both lounging on the couch, already dressed and ready to go. Chase in a gray button-down shirt while Victor is in a maroon button-down. They're both sporting black slacks.

"Finally!" Victor huffs.

"Oh, shut up!" I tell him. "We're taking a car, right?"

"Yeah. It should be here soon, so let's head downstairs." Victor turns off the TV and gathers his things from the coffee table. Chase moves around the couch and to my side, kissing the side of my face. "You look beautiful," He whispers, "I am so damn lucky."

I could get used to this.

Chase and I leave the condo hand in hand, and I'm busting at the seams with happiness. I've always wanted this--a relationship. It's sad to think of what I've been missing, but you also can't miss something you never had. I hope this never has to end. I shake off the forlorn thought. It only ends if we want it to. I'm so wrapped up in my thoughts. I'm on auto-pilot until I'm suddenly being guided into the car and Chase is climbing in behind me. My body instantly shivers from the change of environment. Warm to cold, then to warm again.

Victor gives the driver the name of the restaurant, Blue. The young driver merges into traffic, and I stop to imagine how crazy driving in the city is. I don't know how he does it. I soak in the city life and buildings. Coming to a stoplight, I watch the people crossing the street--people laughing, lovers holding hands--they're all on their way to somewhere. It doesn't take long to get to Blue, but it's far enough that I'm very glad we didn't walk. The car pulls into a white-stone paved driveway that leads towards the side of the tan building. I assumed that Blue would be bluer, but it seems to be the opposite.

Trees surround the restaurant, which gives a feeling of isolation, although the steady sounds of cars and horns can be heard. There's even a beautiful outside deck. I'm sure it would be amazing to dine at when the weather is nice. It's empty, of course, due to the arrival of the cool fall weather. Melissa is waiting inside the foyer when we walk in. She smiles at our arrival. Her short brown hair is curled, and she looks lovely in a red, cinched waist dress. "Perfect timing! Our table should be ready soon."

"Wow," I whisper, looking around. The foyer is dim, but beyond that it's lighting is done in tasteful colors of blue. There's an illuminated bar in the middle of the restaurant, surrounded by bar stools, and a tall tabletop beyond them. The section is divided by, what looks like, streams of gems and tubes of bubbling water on either side. It's mesmerizing. The middle section has a more casual feel to it while these separate, more private, sections have more of a fine dining one.

"Russo?" is called from the hostess at the front. I instinctively look. The pretty hostess is smiling scanning for the Russo party. Victor moves forward, "Party of four?" She asks. Victor nods, "Okay, right this way!" She's delighted and full of enthusiasm, leading us to a smoke-tinted glass table on the right side. The high back chairs match the tables but have blue plush cushions. It all looks so *fancy*.

We each take a seat. Chase sits next to me, followed by Victor, then Melissa on the other side. "This is so neat!" I squeal. "Do you guys come here often?" I ask Melissa and Victor.

"Every once in a while," Melissa says, "My father holds his company's parties here."

"Nice," I say, impressed, "Victor, how is your job going?"

"Good. Great, actually!" Victor beams, "Working with Greg is an amazing experience. I'm learning so much."

"I'm so happy for you!" I'm full of pride. At the same

time, Chase says, "That's great!"

"Thanks, it'd be better if I didn't have to work with this one asshole. He's probably one of the biggest douche bags I've ever met. He walks around the office like he's the only one who pulls in new clients." Victor complains, "I don't understand what your dad sees in him." he directs to Melissa who's looking at the menu.

"I don't know, Victor. You know I don't pay any attention to my father's business," she brushes his comment off, effortlessly.

"How come you don't work for your father?" I ask, curiously.

She smiles, "Not my thing. Believe me, he wanted me to, but I want to do something I enjoy and...it's nothing he provides."

"V's going into business." Victor says proudly, then looks to me, "Right? That's still what you're going to major in?"

"I think so," I shrug, "I'm still a bit undecided."

"Uh oh. Does Dad know?" Victor eyes me warily.

"No. It's not for sure."

"Wait, do Mom and Dad know about you two?" Victor points his finger between the two of us.

Chase smiles, "Your mom knows."

"And Dad?" Huh. Dad's so wrapped up in work, even though he's 'retired', I hadn't even thought of him. Surprisingly, Dad isn't as protective as my brothers, and maybe that's because my brothers are like guard dogs.

"I may have done it backwards but honestly, I'm way more afraid of your mom than your dad." Chase answers. "But I had a conversation with Vivian. She approves." This makes me laugh a little.

"Yeah, Mom definitely wears the pants." I joke.

"I think Dad likes that." Victor puts in.

"Gross. Moving on, what's good here?" I implore before picking up the menu to take a look. Even the menu is fancy and there are no prices to be seen anywhere. I lean forward, "There's no prices." keeping my voice low.

"Don't worry about that." Melissa offers. My gaze turns to Chase, who shrugs and grabs my hand, so I return to looking over the menu. Roasted Salmon, Prosciutto-Wrapped Pork Tenderloin, Filo Wrapped Vegetable Wellington...I have no idea what this stuff is. I lean into Chase, "I don't know what half this stuff is." I whisper.

"Me either." He laughs.

I am definitely a product of small-town living.

A waiter approaches the table. He's a tall, thin, and clean shaven young guy. "Good Evening, my name is Andrew. Any special occasion we're celebrating tonight?" He glances around the table. Melissa speaks up, "New condo." she points to Victor and herself, then gestures to Chase and I, "New Relationship." she smiles at us, "And good life."

"Wonderful!" Andrew gushes, "Can we start with any house wine?"

"Yes, please!" Melissa happily agrees.

"Fabulous! White, or Red?"

"White."

I watch the whole exchange and can't help but think that I'm the only minor sitting at this table. He doesn't bother to ask for ID.

"I will be right back with your wine." He smiles then saunters away from the table.

"What are you having?" I ask Chase.

"The Filet," he answers simply. I should've guessed.

Steak always has been the way to his heart. "What about you?"

"I don't know." I sigh. Ordering food's a big deal and it's stressful especially when you don't know what half the menu means. "The scallops sound good, but I don't know if I want seafood." I ponder my options. Chase laughs lightly.

The waiter, Andrew, returns to the table with a bottle, tucked into a silver bucket, in one hand and four glasses between his fingers in the other hand. *Impressive.* He places the flutes on top of the table along with the bucket. I continue to watch his swift movements. It's like he's done this a million times, and presumably, he probably has. He expertly removes the cork with a 'pop' and pours wine in each of the glasses, then distributes them around the table while everyone mumbles a 'thank you'. I meekly take a sip, almost afraid that he would know I'm not of drinking age, and my face cringes from the taste. Thankfully, no one notices.

"Have we decided yet?" Andrew asks.

Victor looks around the table, and we all confirm that we are ready to order. Andrew, the waiter, removes his pad and starts with Melissa. He moves to each of us, happily writing in his pad. I like him. Once he leaves, Melissa excuses herself to the bathroom, and when she's out of sight Victor pulls out a maroon small box.

"What is *that*?" I ask, knowing my eyes are bugging out of my head.

He smiles and opens the box to reveal a beautiful, massive diamond ring. "Whoa." Chase says, while I let out a little squeal, "Victor! Seriously? Are you doing it tonight?"

"No, no. Mom would kill me, but I wanted to tell

you."

"Why are you carrying it around? Let me see!" I stretch out my hand to take it from him, he obliges surprisingly. It's *so* shiny and sparkles with even the tiniest of movement. The massive diamond is surrounded by smaller, sister diamonds that then stretch out into the silver band. Chase leans into me, glances at the ring, and then lets out a whistle. "Nice man. This *had* to have cost a fortune."

He shrugs, "She normally cleans on the weekends, so I keep it on me. Can't have her accidentally finding it. Then, I put it in my sock drawer the rest of the week." He doesn't say anything about Chase's comment.

I close the velvet box and hand it back to Victor, "When are you planning to do it?"

"Melissa wants to have a 'post-Christmas, pre-New Year, condo housewarming' party, or something. Her father already knows. I've mentioned it to Mom, so I think it'd be a good time with all our friends and family there."

"That's so sweet!"

"Incoming," Chase informs us, causing Victor to quickly tuck the box away.

"Okay. What'd I miss?" She takes a seat and scoots her chair closer to the table.

"Ah, nothing." Victor dismisses with a large smile, and I can't help but smile knowing the big secret.

"Why are you all smiling?" I look at Chase who looks amused.

I shrug my shoulders, "This is just exciting." I gush, and then lower my voice to a whisper, "I've never had wine!"

"Are you tipsy?" Melissa asks.

"No, I've only had one sip."

"Our V doesn't drink." Victor says with sarcasm and I give him the stink eye which makes him laugh, "Don't even, you're about as scary as a cute little puppy."

"Did you seriously just compare me to a dog?"

"A puppy, there's a difference."

"Not much," I grumble.

"Hush."

"Anyways..." Chase cuts in, "I wanted to thank you guys for having us this weekend, and for being so accepting. I-" He stops, corrects himself and smiles at me, "We appreciate it."

"Let's do a toast!" Melissa suggests, then picks up her glass. We all follow suit, "To new adventures." She says, then nods to Victor who clears his throat, "To new relationships." He looks at me then to Chase and it warms my heart. "To the future," Chase says, causing my gaze to move to him. He's staring intently at me, the smile still upon my lips. I know he means to *our* future. It's my turn to say something now, so I raise my glass a little higher, "And to family." Looking around this table I know that each person-blood or not--is my family.

BAR BRAWLS
Chase

"Here ya go, handsome." Jade places the bottle in front of me on the bar top. "It's been a bit since I saw you...I assume things went well?" I smile, thinking about the past week. Things have been incredibly great. "Yeah, things have been good."

She claps her hands, "Yay!" She leans forward and glances around, "Do the brothers know?" her voice is just above a whisper.

"One down, three to go!"

"Really?" She asks, surprised, "I guess it didn't go *too* bad, then? I mean, you're still here in the Land of the Living." She laughs at her own words.

"Yeah. It could've ended horribly, but Victor was surprisingly welcoming after the initial shock wore off."

"Ohh, Victor! How has he been? I haven't seen him in forever!"

"He moved out to the city and got himself a condo with his girlfriend."

"Girlfriend? No shit! That's a damn shame, I always had a thing for him."

This is news to me. "Really?"

"Oh yeah, he was way out of my league."

"No way." I find that hard to believe. Jade seems right up Victor's ally--more so than Melissa.

"I wasn't always this hot." She jokes then waves her hand, a way to dismiss the conversation. She places another beer bottle on the bar just as a hand clamps down on my shoulder, causing me to turn to my right. "My man," Vance greets me.

"Hey, buddy!"

Vance has been bugging me all week about going out for a drink, and naturally, I've blown him off to hang out with 'Nic'. He's blown me off for chicks before, so it's not like he can get mad about it, other than for the fact that it's his sister I'm really with. Obviously, Vance is still in the dark.

"The pussy snatcher let you out? I'm surprised."

I cringe.

"She's a freak, eh?" He nudges me while grabbing for the bottle and I shake my head. The irony.

"Dude." I laugh.

"Ah c'mon," He razzes, "When do I get to meet this elusive chick?"

"I don't know man, we're just seeing how things go. She's pretty focused on school," I lie.

"Whatever, man." He takes a sip of his beer. "So, since last night was rained out, we moved all the races to this upcoming Friday. You're in, right?"

"Yeah, definitely. I wanna test out the Z." He nods. Looks like he already knew my answer already. I pick up my bottle and take a swig.

"I think V's got herself a boyfriend," He relays the information calmly.

I choke on my beer and end up coughing my head off. When the fit ceases, I manage to croak out a mangled, "What?"

"Yeah. She claims she's tutoring someone, but she comes home all like, bouncy and shit." He picks at the corner of the beer label on his bottle. "I'm not sure what to say. I try to come up with something. "I don't know man, maybe she enjoys it?"

He laughs. "No one enjoys tutoring."

"Do you know where she goes?" I ask, curiously.

"She says the library. I thought about following her," Vance confesses.

"Dude, that's a bit much." There's no fucking way he can follow her.

"I know. That's why I haven't." He sighs, "I don't like it, but I don't know if there's much I can do about it."

"Really?" I'm shocked at the thought he may just let it go. "So, you're okay with it? If she is seeing someone?"

"Fuck no!"

Loud commotion pulls our attention away from the conversation when a group of, maybe, five guys walk into the bar. They're rowdy and loud, obnoxious, and probably already intoxicated.

"What the fuck they doin' here?"

"Who're they?" I squint at the group, who seems to be moving our way.

"Dixon and his cronies."

They end up on the other side of Vance, who doesn't seem thrilled. I vaguely remember him from the track a while ago as the douche who was hitting on Veronica.

"Vance!" Dixon barks loudly in greeting.

Vance swivels his stool to face him. "Dixon," he responds. Not too nicely, either.

"Oh man, I just ran into your sister. *Fuck*, she's hot. I don't know how she's related to you."

"Shut the fuck up, Dixon," Vance growls.

"She must get it from your mom." Dixon laughs at his jab and before I can fully comprehend what is happening, Vance has Dixon pressed against the bar by his shirt, in a vicious grip. Vance is speaking low, almost growling, but I can't hear what he's saying. Dixon doesn't seem fazed by it. A cocky smirk spreads upon his lips.

I slowly come up next to Vance, "Dude, it's not worth it," I mention low into his ear, my hands on his shoulders trying to pull him away. Vance slowly releases Dixon's shirt and takes a step back. Dixon rights himself. I can see the mischievous glint still in his eyes, and I realize he's clearly not done baiting Vance. Possibly me.

"Chase, man, you've been spending some time with Veronica, right?" I glare at him, wondering what the fuck is going to come out of his mouth. "Tell us, is she as good in the sack as she is on the track?"

It happens so quickly. Dixon goes flying; he's bouncing off the bar and falling into the stools. The pain from striking him goes up my arm, but I shake it out. I'm ready for him to retaliate when his friends are at his back.

"Hey!" a strong female voice yells from down the bar. My eyes stay on Dixon as he picks himself off the floor, slapping the hand of his friends away. "Take this shit elsewhere!" Jade comes to stand between us.

"He hit me," Dixon spits, rubbing his jaw while glaring at me.

"I'm sure for a good reason, but this isn't a gym. You want to continue the sausage fest, take it somewhere else!"

Jade looks at me, placing her hands upon my chest and pushing me until my feet move backward. She leads me towards the other end of the bar, and Vance follows behind her. "What was that?" her hands move to her hips. I flex my hand, which captures her attention, "Do you need ice?"

"No. I'm good," I tell her and my eyes remain watching Dixon. "He just needed to stop talking."

Jade laughs. "Well, that's one way of making him stop."

"That was epic!" Vance praises, "You almost got me too, but man, he flew like a sack of potatoes! The Army did you good." I laugh. "Man, I'd pay to see that again." Vance carries on. Jade just shakes her head.

"Are you guys going to behave? Or do I have to kick you out?" she eyes us, wearily. I glance up and over to the spot we were once sitting. Dixon and his group are no longer there.

"We should be fine."

"Okay," She sighs, "I'll be watching you two." Jade moves back behind the bar, and we take the nearest open stools.

"Oh, but sweetheart, I'll be watching you. My damn, the ass on that one," Vance says watching Jade with interest. "Anyway, man, I'm glad you got my back. Maybe you can strike up a conversation with V and ask her about the tutoring thing."

"Sure, but I don't think she's gonna tell me much."

"It's worth a shot. What do you guys usually talk about anyways?"

I laugh, mentally thinking about what we really do. This is so fucked, "Nothing crazy. It's a short drive. School stuff, teachers, college, the Army."

"Sounds boring. I guess it's a good thing you won't have to worry about it after this weekend, but thanks for helping her out!"

I'm taken back by what he just said. *What?* "What's happening this weekend?" I ask, pretending to be casual.

"Didn't she tell you?"

"I wouldn't have asked if she did, dude."

"Oh. Well, the parts for her car came in. They're going to be working on it, so hopefully by Monday she'll be driving herself again."

"That's good," I try to sound happy, and I am, just bummed at the same time, "I know she really wanted her car back." He backhands my shoulder. "Ah! Now you can sleep in that extra five minutes."

"Yeah, but now I have to make my own damn coffee."

Vance laughs. We continue bullshitting and putting back beers. I have no idea how long we're there. I have to admit I miss Vance, but I know putting space between us until Veronica is ready to confide in him is for the best.

"Last call," Jade yells loudly, her voice carrying throughout the bar.

"Oh shit, dude." I look at my phone, "I can't believe it's already that late." I throw my finger up to get the attention of a bartender. Jake, who occasionally works the weekends at Sliders, approaches us, "What can I get you, man?"

"Can I get water?"

"Sure thing."

"Water?" Vance bellows. "Pussy."

"Hey Jake, make that two," I yell.

"Fuck you, man." Vance laughs.

"You need it."

"Whatever," he grumbles.

"You want me to drive you home?" I offer.

"Nah, I'll be fine." He waves me off. Jake places the waters in front of us. "Thanks, man." He nods and walks away. I grab both cups, handing one to Vance. "Drink up." We spend another half an hour at the bar until Jade *literally* has to push us out the door. "Damn woman!" Vance jokes.

"Shut up. Drive safe," she says before disappearing back inside.

"She's *so* hot," Vance mumbles.

I pat his back. "I know, man."

"She turns me down every time," He says, suddenly sullen. I chuckle.

"Can't have them all."

"Gotta catch them all," Vance sings, and I burst out in laughter.

"You sure you're good, man?"

"Yeah. I think I'm gonna see what Talia's up to."

"It's almost..." I pull out my phone, "Dude, it's almost two am."

"Even better." As we both approach our vehicles a shadowed figure appears out of nowhere, followed by a few more. "What the fuck?"

Dixon takes a hit of a cigarette, inhaling and slowly releasing the smoke from his nostrils. "Did you think I'd let you get a hit on me, and I'd just let it slide?"

Well, shit. It looks like we've just walked into a jump. "So, what? You just decided to wait outside with your little buddies so you can jump me?" I ask.

He shrugs. "Well, yeah," he replies nonchalantly, throwing down his butt, not bothering to step it out. The tip is still burning and causes a small trail of smoke to rise upwards.

"You have nothing better to do?"

"Nah, kicking your ass is on the top of my list." He smiles mischievously, "Second on my list: getting your girlfriend on her back."

"The fuck you will," I bark.

"Ah, touchy," he baits.

I'm about to lose my shit, but I know that if I move first, his goons will be on me. The best thing for us right now is to get out of this. Dixon is full of shit. There's no way he knows anything, and he's baiting us. He knows that talking crap on Veronica is a good way to aggravate Vance.

"How the hell does he know Nic?" Vance asks from my left.

"Vance knows you're fucking his sister?" Dixon's dark eyebrows move up in surprise. "Nice. Wanna send her my way when you're finished with her?"

"What you fuckin' say?" Vance rushes forward, but I quickly reach out my hand and manage to grab the back of his shirt.

"I mean, I usually *hate* sloppy seconds but Veronica's a special girl."

The rage I feel in myself is bubbling out of the surface, but I won't allow him to get the best of me--of us. Vance fights against me, "Stop, Vance. He's just saying shit to rattle you. It's not worth it." I look at Dixon. He's loving this, his face is lit up with excitement. "Dixon, you're drunk. Go home, asshole." I pull on Vance's collar again. "Let's go." I tug once more, and he allows me to pull him away. I push Vance in front of me to make sure that he keeps walking.

"Where are ya going, ya pussies?!" Dixon yells. I notice Vance's hands ball into fists. "Keep walking," I tell him.

"Fuck you, Daniels!"

We manage to take a few more steps before I'm unexpectedly shoved forward. It nearly knocks me to the ground. *Nearly.* I manage to stop myself from eating asphalt, but Vance is off before I can stop him. He dives for Dixon and slams him to the ground. I catapult towards them, but a hand grasps my shirt, causing me to jolt backward. Instinctively, I turn my body. My arm swings outward before connecting with the side of some guy's head. He flops onto the street like a dead fish. With that guy out of the way, my eyes move towards my friend. Dixon is now on top of Vance and he's getting a couple of good punches in. The wail of sirens causes us all to freeze.

"Fuck! Cops!" One dude yells and takes off towards the back of the lot. He's followed by the rest of Dixon's goons. *Some friends.* I rush towards the grappling men. Vance gets a blow to Dixon's head which causes him to fall over. Vance scrambles off the ground and sits on Dixon's torso. He's throwing down punches left and right--the sickening sound of skin on skin is loud.

"Speak of my sister again, and I'll fucking kill you!" Vance has lost all sense of reality, and I have to stop him before he *does* kill him. In seconds I'm at Vance's back, grabbing his arms and pulling them behind his back, "Dude, stop!" I yell, trying to break through the trance he's in. The wailing sirens are coming closer, and he struggles against my hold. Dixon's face is covered in blood "Vance, we need to go!"

Vance's chest is heaving, a groan passes through Dixon's bloody lips, giving me a bit of peace. "We *have* to go!" I repeat, and this time, I'm yanking on him with all of my upper strength. Red and blue lights approaching seem to get Vance moving, he pushes himself up, and we both take off towards my truck. Within seconds, we're peeling out of the parking lot and into the alleyway. I glance in the rearview mirror just in time to see Dixon's body being tossed into a car. I don't turn on the lights until we come to the end of the alley. Vance is quiet despite his heavy breathing.

"Dude you okay?" I ask.

"Yeah," his voice is rough.

"What the *fuck* were you thinking?"

"I wasn't."

"No shit!"

"What the fuck was that?" He goes on a coughing fit, "Ah. Fuck."

"You wanna go to the hospital?"

"Nah. This isn't my first brawl, cowboy." Vance laughs. "Ah. That hurts."

"What?"

"You've been gone a while."

"Where am I taking you?"

"Talia's. She's expecting me. "

"Dude, you'll scare her. You're looking gnarly."

"She's studying to be a nurse. She'll baby me and then fuck me silly."

I laugh. "Alright, man. Just tell me where to go."

After about twenty minutes we arrive outside of Talia's dorm, where she waits outside in her robe. "I am going to kill you, Vance Michael Russo!" I hear her stern voice as she helps him from the truck.

"Oh baby, you love me. Plus, this is practice."

"Thanks, Chase." Talia waves and then shuts the door, leaving me to the silence of the cab. The clock on my dash says it's nearly three am, and I know this is not the smartest thing for me to do, but the adrenaline has me wide awake. I unlock my phone, and select the phone icon, pressing on the second name in my history.

"Hello?" her voice is just above a whisper.

"Hey, you. Did I wake you?"

"Yes, but I don't mind. Is everything okay?"

"Yeah, I want to see you."

"You miss me?"

"Yes." She laughs breathlessly, and it's such a hypnotizing sound. "What time is it? Where's Vance?"

I cringe a bit. "It's almost three, and I just dropped him off at Talia's."

"Three?" she groans.

"I'm sorry. I shouldn't have called you. It was a crazy night, and I just wanted to see you. I'll call you in the morning."

"No, No!" She sounds more alert. "Park down the block and I'll meet you out front."

"Really?"

"Yeah."

"I'll be there in fifteen," I tell her.

"Okay, see you soon."

I end the call and speed towards my dream girl.

LATE NIGHT
Veronica

I jump out of bed, throw on a sweater and rush to my bedroom door. I pull open the door, slowly, only to be met with darkness. *Just what I wanted to see.* I peek my head out, looking at each door for any signs of life, but all is black. I creep down the hall, avoiding the creaky spots that I've memorized. I know that sneaking Chase into the house is insane--my heart is pounding wildly--but this is also *so* exhilarating.

I pace the front foyer and wait for any indication that he's near or here. After an *agonizing* seventeen minutes my phone chimes in my hands and a squeak of excitement passes my lips. The light from my phone blinds me as I look at his text. My legs begin to dance, and I have to remind myself to be quiet. I excitedly move to the door, whip it open, and wait upon the threshold until I see a figure walking down the driveway. I jump in place until I can't keep myself together any longer. I rush towards him, throwing myself in his arms. He laughs into my neck, "Someone *did* miss me."

I pull back to look at this face, and I'm greeted by his beautiful smile. "I did."

He gives me a small peck on my lips. "We should probably head inside."

I nod in agreement, and he releases me onto my feet. We make our way into the house and up the stairs.

"Stay towards the wall," I whisper. Once we reach my bedroom, I hurry in and lock the door behind us. That's when I notice the blood on his shirt. A gasp escapes my lips, I rush towards him and grab onto him. "What happened? Are you okay?"

He looks down confused but, strangely, his face relaxes when he sees the blood. He places his hands over mine. "Yeah, I'm fine. Vance is a bit roughed up though."

"What?" I gasp, my jaw going slack.

Chase pulls me to my bed, sitting down, and having me sit next to him. "He'll be fine. There was an incident at Sliders."

"An *incident*?" I ask sarcastically.

"Dixon."

"Oh no." I sigh.

"V, he was talking a lot of shit."

"About what?"

"You," he pauses, "Me. Us."

"Us? What do you mean?"

"I don't know. I don't remember exactly what he was saying, but he was referring to you as my girlfriend. I managed to get Vance to walk away until Dixon shoved me, and Vance went nuts. Dixon looks a lot worse off than Vance."

"Oh no." I'm repeating myself.

"V," he breathes heavily, "We have to talk to Vance soon. He never questioned what was said, thankfully, but if he did...I don't think I could lie to his face." I can see the internal struggle I'm putting Chase through, and I let out a lengthy sigh. I *know* he's right. I'm terrified of what may happen when he does find out. I lean into Chase, needing his comfort, and he doesn't hesitate to wrap his arms around me. "It'll be okay, no matter what happens. We will be okay."

We're quiet for a while, and I'm just enjoying his

company until he breaks the silence. "I should probably go."

"No!" I say, panicked. "Stay."

"Are you sure that's a good idea?"

"Yeah, we'll figure it out tomorrow. I'll go get you a new shirt." I move out of his hold and leave my room again, making sure to be unheard as I head into Vance's room--adjacent to mine. I turn the knob and start pushing the door open quietly. I flick on the light and tiptoe across his room to his dresser. It takes three different drawers until I find his sport shirts, but I grab the first one I see and quickly leave his room. I make sure the door is shut and lights are off--just how he left it. I hurry back to my room, close the door, and lock it.

My eyes move to Chase, who is still sitting where I left him, but he's removed his shirt. My heart kicks into overdrive when I catch sight of him. I grasp onto the shirt, and pull it to my chest.

"You okay?" Chase asks with a smirk.

I nod.

"You want to give me that shirt?" He laughs.

I shake my head.

"No?" he questions.

"No," I whisper. Something I have never fully experienced takes over me. *Lust.*

Out of nowhere, confidence drives my body forward, and I can tell it even takes Chase off guard. He leans back as I approach him, and without any warning, I place my knees on either side of him. When I'm straddling him, his hands instinctively move to my backside, and his playful expression is instantly replaced with desire. His breathing has become labored, and I know I'm affecting him as much as he affects me. *I love this. This rush.* I have never felt more powerful and desired in my life.

"V," Chase whispers, our mouths inches apart. "What are you doing?"

"Something I've only dreamed of," I reply and move forward to connect our mouths, hungrily. He groans as soon as our lips touch, and I revel in it. His hands are all over--they're on my lower back and then they're gripping my butt until I'm pushed forward against his hardness. The friction is right where I need it. I moan into his mouth, and he does it again. It feels *so* good.

I've never felt this way before but all I know is that I need more. Without his hands guiding me, I continue to move, and grind my body down onto him. He moans into my mouth this time. His hands move further up my back, causing my shirt to lift higher and I suddenly need it off of me. My skin is burning up. I remove my sweater without breaking our kiss and lift my arms, signaling him to remove my shirt.

"You're sure?" and I nod at his question. His hands move slowly up my sides, causing goosebumps as he lifts my top up and over my head. He flings it somewhere behind me and now I'm bared to him--something no other person has seen intimately. His muscular hands rest on my hips while his beautiful blue eyes bore into mine, "You are so beautiful," he whispers. I feel it. I *feel* beautiful.

Steady palms are roaming my body, until they rest just below my breasts, almost if asking for permission. I place my hands over his and guide them until they're cupping each breast. "Fuck," he hisses. "Beautiful, V. You're fucking *beautiful.*" My head involuntarily falls backward as he massages them and then I feel his mouth. He's placing kisses and light licks upon my clavicle. The various sensations hit me deep in my core. His mouth moves down, slowly, until his mouth reaches my right breast--lightly sucking--causing my back to arch forward. *I want more.* My fingers scrape through his hair as I continue to grind myself on him; his dick is much more prominent than before. He releases one nipple and moves to the left, sucking lightly.

"Chase," It's a whisper. The throbbing has become intense and I need a release. He hisses and frees my breast from his mouth. I'm overcome with emotions; feeling wild. My mouth instantly connects with his, our tongues dancing around each other. "Pants," I gasp, "*Off.*" He doesn't move at my request, and I lean back to look at him curiously. Our chests are heaving and his lips are plumped--flushed--from our intense kisses.

"Trust me, this is more than I ever dreamed of. But we don't have to have sex right now."

"You've dreamed of this?" I ask playfully, moving my hips. His eyes roll back. I treasure his reaction, and I do it again. He halts my movements with his hands on my hips and grins.

"Many, *many* times." He hugs me to him with my breasts pressed against his chest. The skin on skin contact results in a shiver that's sent down my spine. He wraps his arms around my waist; I can feel him so close to where I need him. He places a light kiss on my shoulder--a gesture so sweet-- and I feel a *zing* in my heart.

"We should wait," he says, rubbing his nose up the side of my face. He seductively nips at my ear.

"*Wait*?" I ask. I'm so confused and so turned on at the same time.

"I don't want a secret relationship with you. Until

we're out in the open...we should wait."

"But..." I start to whine but he cuts me off with a kiss, sucking my bottom lip.

"Don't worry. I'll take care of you." He flips us over; his body is covering mine. Our lips meet with a sensual kiss, and he's deepening it--ravishing me like it's his last meal. I can feel him at my center and, instinctively, my knees drop. He grinds down, causing my body to arch up. His lips leave mine, and I whimper. I miss the feel of them. He places little wet kisses onto my throat, down the middle of my chest, and to my left breast. His fingers slide down my stomach--making me quiver--and they continue down, under the waistband of my shorts until they're skimming over my clit. I cry out. He nips and sucks at my nipples, giving each the same amount of attention as he circles the most sensitive part of me, over and over. He speeds up then, agonizingly, slows down again. It's a tease; a ride, and one I don't want to end. He knows just how to prolong these intense feelings.

My vision starts to blacken, and I release a moan unlike any other; the pleasure quickly spreading throughout my body. "There you go, baby," Chase whispers, his fingers still working magic. *Stars* explode behind my eyes and I yell out. Chase's mouth covers mine to conceal my outburst. I struggle to catch my breath and open my eyes to see Chase hovering over me with a wicked smile.

"*Oh,*" I say, breathlessly.

"You can say that again. That was the single most sexiest thing I've *ever* witnessed."

We lay together for a while, neither of us wanting to move from our comfortable position. Eventually, we do get up to dress, but then we settle underneath my covers. Chase lays on his back, allowing me to nestle into his side. I rest my head upon his chest. His breathing evens out quickly, and I sigh in contentment before I drift off to sleep.

THREE DOWN
Veronica

In my subconscious state I hear a loud bang followed by an even louder male voice. "What the *fuck* is going on?" I jolt up. My eye-sight is trying to adjust from sleep. Vaughn is standing at my open door. "And *who* the fuck is in your bed?!" he shouts. Chase becomes startled at the yelling and jumps up faster than I've ever seen him move before. He's standing behind me at full alert; ready to fight. My eyes widen. Oh, *shit*.

"Get out! Why are you even in my room?" I scream and dash for the door.

"Chase?" Vaughn questions, and his mouth drops open in disbelief. "What the *fuck*?" He looks at me as I run to him. I place my hands upon his chest and push, he moves backward a bit, but not as much as I would like.

"Get out! Get out! *Get out!*" I chant while trying to shove him out of my room.

"What the fuck is he doing in your bed, Veronica?" Vaughn's voice is still so loud.

"Shut *up!*" I hiss.

I hear Vin's bedroom door whip open. *Great.* "What the hell is going on!?" He's rubbing his eyes. "*Some* people are trying to fucking sleep."

"*Chase* is-" Vaughn starts, but I place my hand over his mouth to stop him from finishing his sentence. Vin moves out of his doorway, and Vaughn fights to remove my fists.

"V," Chase says, behind me.

"Who the fuck is in your room?" Vin barks. He's wide awake now and stalking towards us.

"Stop! You're going to wake Mom and Dad!" I cry.

Vin is now standing next to us, leering into my room, curiously. Vaughn's managed to rip my hands away but keeps them in his grasp. "They're not home," He informs me. I relax a bit, except for the fact that my two brothers are standing before me, staring daggers at Chase.

"Whoa, what the hell is happening right now?" Vin yells. "And why is Chase in your room? In his fucking boxers?" Oh, no. *Oh, no.* I want to crumble at the repeating questions. I start to panic. I start trying to search for any plausible reason. Who am I kidding? There aren't any.

Hands land on my shoulders and ease me backward. "Guys, why don't you come sit down?" With Chase's guidance, I retreat slowly. Vin and Vaughn follow. Vaughn takes the seat at my desk, but Vin is stoic.

"I'll stand, thanks." Vin remains near my closet with his arms crossed over his chest.

"Veronica and I are-"

"Fucking?" Vaughn puts in.

"Vaughn!" I hiss.

"That's what it looks like."

"Shut up, Vaughn," Vin reprimands.

"No, we're not. I know what this looks like. But, we are...together."

"*Together*?" Vin questions.

"Yes. We're seeing each other."

"I thought you were seeing Nic?" Vin asks, calmly.

"Veronica *is* Nic."

"You've got to be fucking kidding me." Vin's arms

drop to his sides. "You're serious?"

"Yes," Chase confirms.

"What the--," Vaughn mumbles.

"Wait a minute. How the hell did you get in my room?" I interrupt.

Vaughn moves to grab something from his pocket and pulls out a small screwdriver. He holds it up, "I was trying to get you back for that stunt you guys pulled." I laugh, remembering the prank Taylor and I pulled on him just last night when she was over. Even though our girls' night usually ends with her staying the night, she left around eleven to meet up with Wes.

"And Vance knows you guys are together?" Vin asks. It ceases my laughter.

"No," Chase responds, grimly.

"That's fucking *great*," he spits, "and why the fuck not?"

"I was scared. I didn't think he'd approve," I put in.

"Ya think? I'm sure he'd be just *peachy* with his best friend and his baby sister hooking up."

"We're not hooking up!" I retort, becoming annoyed.

"Then what do you call this?" He gestures to the two of us in our nightwear. I look away, not exactly sure how to answer. We slept together--yes--but we didn't have sex, even though I really, *really* wanted to. I'd never tell my brothers that.

"We were hanging out and we...fell asleep." I sound guilty even though it's the truth.

"Right, and he just *magically* lost his pants in the process," Vin says, sarcastically. Point for Vin. "Look, I know you're getting older V, and we can't stop who you see, but sneaking around with our friend isn't the answer."

"Vin," Chase is sincere, "I can assure you that wasn't our intention. This just...happened. We wanted to be sure before confiding in you all."

"Well, you better be fucking sure. You're already practically sleeping naked together," Vin says harshly and stomps out of the room.

Vaughn whistles. "Well, then." I glare at him. This is all his fault. "I'll be honest. This was a surprise, but I don't care what you do, V." He shrugs and gets up from the chair, walking towards my door. I watch his back as he leaves my room, completely baffled. I quickly move forward, close the door and face Chase. His eyes are on me, "Are you okay?" he asks.

I move to him, "Yeah, you?"

"I'm fine."

"That's three down." I joke. He doesn't crack a smile.

"We *need* to tell Vance."

"I know." I sigh.

"I better get going."

"Yeah, that's probably for the best," I agree. He grabs his pants from the end of my bed, and steps into them; one leg at a time. He pulls off Vance's shirt and replaces it with his bloodied one. The sight of his muscular back brings memories of the intimate things we did last night to the forefront of my mind. "You alright, there?" He's now standing in front of me, amusement etched upon his face. *There's a smile.*

"Yeah." I relax.

"Okay. I'll talk to you later." He kisses my forehead and leaves me standing in the middle of my room.

Not long after Chase leaves, there's a knock on my bedroom door. "Come in," I groan from my bed. The door opens to reveal Vin, who slips through. He looks pensive, and his features squished together.

"What's up?" I ask. My nerves are at large; I can only imagine what he's going to say to me. He remains quiet as he moves to sit at the end of my bed. I place my phone to the side and watch him. He finally speaks after what seems like forever, "How did you two happen?" That's not what I expected him to ask, to be honest. He was pretty harsh earlier, so I thought he'd come to berate me some more.

I shrug slightly. "I don't know. It just did. He didn't come after me and he tried to stay away. We spent some time together, and we just...click. We really like each other, Vin."

"Okay," He abruptly stands up, "Let's go finish your car." He leaves me alone, and I change into some old clothing. I send Chase a text just to let him know that I'll be at the garage.

McSwoony: You forgot to tell me about your parts.

I cringe. *I did.* I hid the packages for about a week until Vin found them and questioned me about it. I made up some lame excuse about the packages arriving sporadically, and that there was no use to start it until they all arrived. I didn't want my mornings with Chase to end.

Me: Sorry.
McSwoony: You're forgiven. I'm going to miss our mornings together.

I grin, quickly typing a response back.

Vin and I have been working on my car for a couple

of hours and while he hasn't mentioned anything about Chase, he seems to be incredibly focused--putting all his effort into this build. It's almost robotic.

"Vin?"

"Hmm?"

"Are you okay?"

"Yeah," he answers immediately.

"You seem off."

He's quiet as he tightens up a bolt. There's only the sound of the ratchet twisting. His muscles bulge when he finishes with one last twist then stands up straight. He places the tool on the bench behind us and wipes his hand on his pants.

"I think it has hit me that things are changing," he says quietly, and that surprises me. "Victor is starting his life with Melissa; they'll get married, and have kids. I've taken over the garage. You're going off to college next fall. Then we find out you're dating behind our backs," he rambles. I know he's not done, so I remain quiet. "What can we really do about it? Seriously? I'm a bit disappointed that you couldn't confide in me. I know we're protective of you. We only want the best for you. Is Chase the best?" He shrugs. "I don't know. He's not a bad guy. He's an honorable one. I mean, he joined the Army instead of following his father's footsteps and living a cushioned life. There's a reason we've been friends with him for so long."

"I'm sorry," I blurt out. He nods and runs his hand through his black hair.

"Let's finish this, yeah?"

I smile. "Yeah."

The wind is whipping my hair around my face, but I can't help the ecstatic laugh that escapes my mouth as I take the corner at an alarming speed. Man, I missed this car! I want to go to Chase's, but I know it's probably for the best if I don't--especially after such an eventful morning. I park next to Vance's car and bite my lip in worry. Chase and I had never asked Vaughn or Vin to remain quiet about us, so I can only hope they didn't spill the beans.

I cautiously walk into the house and everyone, including Chase, is sitting in the living room. I stop dead in my tracks. "Oh hey. I didn't see your truck out front," I say, stupidly.

"Hey, V. Vance picked me up," Chase responds, nonchalantly. I glance towards Vance and gasp. His face is all swollen--his lip is busted, his right eye is all black and blue, and his eyes are bloodshot. "Holy shit!"

"Don't worry, the other guy looks worse," Vance jokes.

"Who's the other guy?" I ask as I move around to sit on the other side of Vance. Although I already know the whole story, Vance doesn't know that. It seems like the right question to ask.

"He's not important." He waves me off and continues to watch the game. I notice my dad isn't in his chair.

"Where's Dad?" I ask then glance out in the kitchen.

"They went out to eat. We just ordered pizza," Vin informs me. "You go for a nice ride?" he asks with a smile.

"I did. It drives amazing. Chase looks like you're free now. Thanks for your help."

"No problem."

"Well I'm gonna go upstairs. Call me when the pizza arrives," I say to the room. I glance at Chase as I walk by him. While he's watching me, I catch Vin's eyes on the both of us. It makes me a bit nervous, so I hurry up the stairs and once I'm in my room, I release my breath.

I pull up Tay's number and hit the dial button. It rings twice before she answers, "Hello my bestest friend."

I laugh. "What are you up to?"

"Just hanging at Wes'."

"Okay. Give me a call when you're alone, then."

"I can be alone, just give me a minute." I hear rustling through the phone and Wes' voice. "I'll be right back," she tells him. "Okay, I'm alone. Spill."

"Wellllll..." I drag out, happily.

"You had sex!" she whisper-shouts.

I laugh.

"You did! You little slut!" she jokes.

"No, no. I didn't. Wes isn't near you, right?" I ask.

"No, I'm in the bathroom. He doesn't care anyway."

"Okay..." I say low into the phone. "I will just say this, Chase has very talented fingers."

Taylor screams into the receiver. I have to pull the phone away from my ear, "Oh my little Veronica is growing up," her voice becomes weepy, "Did you..orgasm?" she whispers the last word.

"I did. I *definitely* did."

"Did you see his penis?" she blurts out.

"Tay!" I shout.

"What?" she asks innocently, "It's big, isn't it?"

"I mean, I don't have anyone to compare it to but it *felt* big."

"I *knew* it." she yells, causing me to laugh out loud.

There's a light knock on my bedroom door. "I gotta go," I inform Tay, then quickly end the call before she protests. "Yeah?" I yell out. The door opens slowly, revealing a head of dirty blond hair. His blue eyes find mine as he moves into the room.

"Hey, what are you doing?" I whisper.

He smiles as he moves towards me, "Vin told me to come get you. Pizza's here."

"Did he really?" My hands move to my hips.

"Uh-huh." He closes the gap between us, and his lips meet mine instantly--like it's something he's been wanting to do all day. It's greedy, yet sweet, and it ends way too soon. He pulls away, but his arms remain wrapped around me.

"I doubt he meant for you to do *tha*t," my voice comes out low.

He shrugs with a smile that lights up his face, and it's beautiful. "I'll take what I can get."

"You're something else, Chase Daniels."

"Veronica Russo, you're *my* something else."

Those words cause my lips to break into a wide smile; a smile so big it hurts. "My own personal McSwoony," I whisper. His head falls back as laughter bursts from his throat. "What?" I ask, "The name is quite fitting."

"Is it now?"

I nod.

"I'll make you swoon."

"Hmmm sounds naughty," I say playfully, but his gaze quickly conveys pure lust. His face moves forward and my eyes close, expecting another wonderful kiss, but instead there's a quick sharp pain on my neck.

"Ow!" I yelp, my hand rubbing the area. My free hand swats at his shoulder.

"Love bite," he laughs and releases me, "We better get out of here before they come searching for us."

"You better not have left a mark!" I whisper shout as I walk after him out of my room.

"Nah."

"Finally," Vin says as we walk into the kitchen, where the rest of my brothers are gathered around the center island.

"She was on the phone. I felt rude interrupting," Chase shrugs off, coming up with the half-lie quickly.

"Uh-huh," Vaughn laughs.

"Pizzzzaaaa," I sing and move towards the pizza box. I don't even bother with a plate, I just pick up a slice and take a hefty bite.

"So, you gonna race this weekend?" Vance asks, and I turn around to see his eyes on me.

"Oh, me?" I ask. "No way. I just got her back on the road."

Vance's head bobbles up and down. "I figured."

I move to take a seat at an open stool, tuning out the conversation that the guys are having about this upcoming Friday night. My eyes wander to each guy as I munch on my slice of pizza--they linger a bit longer on Chase, rightfully so. As I do, it occurs to me that everyone in this room is aware of the secret relationship between Chase and I...except Vance. Vaughn and Vin probably wouldn't have known if it hadn't been exposed this morning, but it's almost a relief that it's out. It gives me the confidence I need to move forward with letting Vance know. I can only hope it goes smoothly.

LUCKY
Chase

My knee bounces as I wait for my sergeant. I'm racking my brain to find a reason why they've called me in this morning. The only thing I can come up is that they're deploying me again. I'm hoping not, but I don't see any other reason for this impromptu meeting. The door opens behind me and I stand to attention. "Daniels," he says, as a way of greeting.

"Sir."

"At ease." He moves behind his wooden desk and takes a seat, placing the manila folder in front of me. I return to my seated position in the chair in front of his desk.

"Well, Daniels, I won't drag this out. I'm sorry, but I gotta tell you we have to send you out. We have a situation at the border, and we need some more soldiers on staff. Job is classified, you'll be notified when you arrive but they need all the men they can get. I know you just returned not that long ago, but you'll be within the states. I don't have a timeline for you but I'll try my best to have you back home in a timely manner."

Damn.

"When do I leave?" I ask.

"Wednesday."

Shit. That's less than a week.

"Any questions, Daniels?"

"No, Sir."

"You are dismissed."

"Thank you, Sir."

I leave the office and know that the first thing I have to do is tell Veronica. The last time I left it wasn't nearly this hard; it was pretty simple. I had no one here that cared enough whether I stayed or not. The thought of leaving her makes my heart hurt. We are just beginning, and now we have to put us on hold. *Would she even want to wait for me?* Even with me being as selfish as I am--I want her to wait-- I'd never ask her to. *Fuck. This sucks.* I grip my hair in frustration. The last thing I want to do right now is to go to work, but I have to. I also have to inform my dad of my deployment.

The drive to the office doesn't take long, and I'm sitting at my desk before even realizing I walked up here. My mind is in an entirely different world. I better get this shit over with. I pick up the phone and dial my father's secretary.

"Mr. Daniels office, June speaking." My father's secretary answers.

"Hey June, it's Chase. Is my father in?"

"Yeah, but he has a meeting in ten."

"I won't be long," I tell her simply and hang up. I want to get this over with. I approach his office on the other end of the building. June is sitting at the open desk before his. "He's right inside."

"Thanks, June." I open the door, my father seated behind his desk looking over papers pauses to look up. "Chase," he says in greeting and continues moving papers. "I have a meeting, let's make this quick, yeah?"

"Yeah, no problem. I'm being deployed," I tell him, bluntly.

This news actually makes him still, his blue eyes

meeting mine. "You *just* returned."

"Yeah," I shrug, "I'm needed elsewhere."

"What about the company? You're needed here!"

"Unfortunately, they own me. I have to go."

"I still don't understand why you joined the Army when you have a promising future here. I'm going to have to fill your position until you return."

"Yeah, I figured that." I ignore his first comment.

"You don't seem to be saddened by that."

"I understand. You have to do what you have to do."

"Alright then. When do you leave?"

"Wednesday."

"Wednesday? That's in five days!"

"Yeah, I'm aware."

"They don't give you much notice, do they?"

"Apparently not."

He curses under his breath. "I'll figure something out." And with that, it seems I'm dismissed. I leave his office, close the door behind me, and make my way back to my own. I sit behind my desk. Telling my father wasn't as bad as I thought, but I'm dreading having to tell Veronica. This isn't what I envisioned. I knew I might've been called again, but I didn't think it would be this soon. I wonder if anyone else from my unit got called out, too. I ponder on it for a minute before snapping myself out of my thoughts. I need to get this work day over with.

I immerse myself with paperwork until it's time to call it quits. I leave the office and try to stay positive. I want to enjoy this night. I've decided to hold off on telling Veronica until tomorrow, or maybe even Monday. Tonight is the last race weekend for the year. The weather is dropping week by week and we're lucky winter held off this long into October. It could also be my last Friday with Veronica, and I don't want to sullen the night with my impending departure.

Ideas of how to tell her run through my mind on the drive home, which is depressing. I decide to stop thinking of it altogether and embrace the night. I quickly change out of my clothing, and get into something more comfortable than my pressed shirt and slacks. I jump into the Z. I shoot a text to Vance, who informs me he's not home yet. He thinks the rest of the guys should be, though. I smile and select Veronica's name. She answers immediately.

"Hey!" she answers enthusiastically.

"Hey, you." I put the phone on speaker and start the car.

"What are you doing?" she asks, "You driving?"

"Yes ma'am. I'm on my way to you."

"The best thing I've heard all day."

That makes me smile. "I'll do you one better when I get there."

"Can't wait."

"Me either. I'll see you soon."

"Kay."

The call ends, and I press on the gas to get to her faster. My heart is beating wildly, and there's a tickle in my stomach. *I'm turning into a goddamn lovesick fool.* I laugh at myself. I haven't been this happy since...well, since *ever*. The thought that I have to leave her slams into my happiness like a fucking meteor. Damn.

Minutes later, I'm parked next to Veronica's RSX. The front door opens as I step out of my car. V comes running toward me, and I brace myself for her enthusiastic greeting. She doesn't disappoint as she lunges herself at me, her long legs wrapping around my waist. "Well, that was quite the greeting."

"I missed you," she mumbles. I kiss her forehead and move us towards the house.

"I missed you, too."

I climb the few steps to the front door and pause as she releases her legs from around my torso. She stands on the top step, which ends up making her level with me. I scan her beautiful face, committing it to memory--every single feature. "What?" she whispers.

My hand moves to her cheek, feeling her soft skin. "I am the luckiest guy in the world," I breathe, and her lips break into a smile before moving to capture my mouth into a hungry kiss. This only confirms what I just told her; I am most *definitely* the luckiest guy in the world. Her hand moves to the back of my neck and her touch causes my body to quiver.

"Get a room!" someone shouts from inside the house, causing our kiss to falter. We break apart.

"Sorry." She smiles.

"That's nothing to be sorry about," I tell her. She only sniffles and grabs my hand, pulling me inside behind her.

"That looked painful," Vaughn says from the couch. Veronica smacks him in the back of the head while passing behind him.

"Ow!" he shouts, his hand instantly moving to rub at the spot. Veronica continues to pull us past the living room and into the kitchen. She pauses and turns to me, pressing a quick kiss to my mouth. "Last one." I smile, knowing what she means. Vance will be here soon, and we have to keep our cool. That was something else I momentarily forgot about, but I know I need to talk to

Veronica first, then tackle the Vance issue.

Within the next twenty minutes, everyone arrives and we're lounging in the living room talking about Wes' bets while Vance changes.

"Easy money," Wes dismisses a rumor Vin heard. My eyes move to Veronica, watching her sexy lips as she speaks with Taylor. I love those lips. Heavy footsteps descend from the stairs as Vance moves down them. "Alright, let's roll," he announces. We all move to stand and make our way out the door. "V, you driving?" Vance asks as she slips on her jacket.

"Yeah, why?" her eyes glance towards me while he shrugs on a hoodie, then moves back to her brother.

"No reason, just wondering."

She shrugs and moves out the front door behind him. I'm curious as to why she felt the need to look my way. Does she think I'd be mad that she's driving? Veronica is a car girl, through and through, and I already knew that about her. It's no surprise that she'd want to drive her car--she's been without it for so long. Sure, I'd love for her to ride with me, but I get it. She lingers outside the door and moves with me as I exit. "It's okay if I drive?" she asks low.

"Of course." I wink at her, which causes her sexy lips to widen into a beautiful smile. Damn. *I'm so lucky,* I think for the millionth time tonight.

LET'S RACE
Veronica

As usual, Taylor sings loudly and horribly the entire way to the track, but I barely notice because I'm enjoying myself. I've missed driving my car so much, and a small part of me wants to run tonight. I've been having a mental battle with myself--to run or not run. The chances of something breaking are slim, since so much has been repaired, but there's always a chance. It's the last night to race for the year, and the track won't be open again until late May. I pull up next to Chase's Z and put my car into park. I guess I'll see what the night has in store.

As I exit my car, a thunderous roar erupts from behind and my head snaps towards the source. A trail of classic cars are pulling into the parking lot; there has to be at *least* ten of them. There's all kinds of beautiful, old school muscle. Chase appears next to me. "Damn," he mutters. I nod because it's a glorious sight. I glance towards my brothers who are also watching with appreciation. The muscles park about three rows behind us and take up almost a whole row. My eyes zero in on the yellow Camaro--it's just like the one at the junkyard. The rumble ceases as each car is shut off and their drivers exit the cars.

Our group gathers in front of our cars, and it slowly grows. Like flies on shit, the girls appear out of nowhere. Some familiar, some not. Chase pays no mind to any, and it's extremely satisfying. I lean against the front of my car and listen to the guys talk. A few others have joined us to ask Wes about his build. The announcer welcomes everyone to the last race of the season, thanking all for the support.

"This yours?" a male voice scares me, and I about jump out of my skin. He laughs and apologizes. I glare at the stranger to my left.

"Yeah," I answer him while taking in his appearance. A hat is resting upon his head, but I can see his dark hair peeking out on the sides. He's tall--taller than me at least-- and slightly built, but not bulky. He's cute in an unconventional way. If I had to guess, I'd say he's in his twenties but I've never seen him before.

"Nice. Don't meet many legit car chicks. What does she run?" He nods to my car.

"Just had some stuff done. Last I ran in the high fifteen's." I shrug.

"Not bad. You going to run tonight?"

"Not sure. Just got her back. I don't know if I wanna risk it."

"Now is a perfect time! You gotta break her in." He smiles, his eyes move above my shoulder towards my right, and I feel a presence at my back. "Hey man," the kid greets.

"Hey," Chase's voice is deep, "Who're you?"

"Oh," He laughs a little and puts out his hand. "I'm Kyle."

Chase reaches around me to shake his hand. "Chase. This is V."

"Nice to meet you guys! Which is yours?" He asks Chase, whose hand is now on my arm.

"The Z."

"Nice man, she's sexy! What do you run?"

"I'll find out tonight."

Kyle nods.

"So, where are you from?" I ask him. "I've never seen you around."

"Ah. I just moved here, heard about this place and thought I'd check it out."

"Oh that's cool. What do you drive?" I ask curiously.

He points over his shoulder. "I have the Camaro." I glance around him at the new generation, black Camaro parked a couple of spots down.

"Awesome. Have you run it yet?"

He rubs the back of his neck, "Nah, not yet."

"Yo. What's goin' on over here?" Vance joins us. "Hey man, who're you?" he asks Kyle. The pressure of Chases' hand leaves my arm. I'm saddened by the loss.

"Hey, just chatting with Chase and V here. I'm Kyle." He reaches his hand out to Vance, who obliges and gives him his name. They get on about the track, cars, and the local area; seeing as Kyle is new in town.

"Why don't you and Chase go for a run?" Vance suggests.

Chase chuckles, "He'd destroy me, dude." Kyle beams.

"He's never ran, and you need to test out the Z. Doesn't have to be for competition, just fun." He shrugs. "You in?"

Kyle lights up, "Hell yeah!" It's sweet how excited he is.

Vance looks to Chase for his answer as I look behind me. "Sure."

Kyle moves away towards his car. Vance slaps Chase on the shoulder. "Give it all you got man!"

Chase smiles wide, then moves towards his driver's

side. He glances at me before getting in, and I throw him two thumbs up. I watch him as he reverses out of the spot, then join the rest of the gang when he's out of sight.

Taylor slides up next to me. "Who was that guy?"

"Just someone racing," I shrug, "Says he just moved here. He seems friendly though."

The talking around us seems to cease; their stance has gone from relaxed to on guard and my brows furrow as I take in everyone around me. Vance's face becomes hard as stone, and he mutters a few choice words. A drawn-out 'damn' comes from Vaughn, which causes me to turn at what has grabbed their attention. "Oh *shit*," I gasp. *Why today.*

A group of guys are moving in our direction--Dixon at the front. I haven't seen Dixon around for a while, and though it's been at least a week since his and my brothers' fight, his face is still showing signs of bruising. Vance's face has cleared up, so when Vance said Dixon was worse off, he wasn't lying. Dixon's eyes move to me, and they narrow. He's always been an asshole, but most of the time, he's joking around. This is the first time I'm frightened of him. I take a step back and put myself into the center of our group.

"You should thank me, *Dick*! I think I made your face more appealing," Vance calls out. *Jeez, Vance!*

Dixon's eyes move from me to Vance. He cracks a smile and it's *not* a friendly one. He stops a couple feet away from our group. "What do you want?" Vance asks.

"Your car," is all Dixon says.

Vance bursts out in laughter. "My car? Fuck you. You're not getting my car."

'We race..." he pauses, "for slips." That's pretty ballsy,

and cocky. It's rare when anyone races for slips; it's something you usually only see in movies. So, to say I'm shocked is an understatement. Vance's silence pulls my attention towards him. His eyes are narrowed. He *cannot* be thinking about doing this. He's not that stupid. Dixon has to be up to something.

"I don't want your piece of shit." Vance throws out. "I'll pass." I feel myself relax.

Dixon smiles then turns to the guy next to him. "See Zach, I told you he was a *pussy*." Zach and all the guys around them laugh.

"Yeah, you were right," Zach agrees with Dixon. They're trying to get under Vance's skin.

"You're a stupid fuck, Dixon." Vance spits, "Didn't you learn your lesson?"

"It's easy to overpower a drunk guy. Let's let our cars do the talking this time."

"I think my fists spoke volumes. Get the fuck out of here," Vance dismisses Dixon, whose eyes are still slits; this clearly isn't what he expected. It's not what I expected either, and I'm quite proud of my brother. Dixon moves closer to Vance, who remains on guard. "You'll be sorry," Dixon hisses then continues walking past with his friends following behind, looking smug.

"Jeez," I mutter.

"Yeah, that was intense," Taylor agrees.

"Pussy? Me?" Vance laughs. "I love pussy, but I definitely ain't one."

"Ew," I whine and turn to look down at the lineup. I don't see Chase's Z or the black Camaro, so I tug on Tay's shirt. "I think Chase is coming up." I move towards the fence, allowing myself to see around the bend. Kyle's Camaro is about four cars back.

The car at the line begins to roar as if it were to take off, but remains in place. Smoke pours from the rear tires and within seconds the line is engulfed in gray smoke. The crowd cheers on as the driver continues to let loose and drive down the track; the smoke billowing out everywhere. The smell of burning rubber is inescapable. The track officials clear the track and start hosing it down.

With a little bit of time to spare until Chase and Kyle race, Taylor and I decide to move back to the group. Vance is occupied with the girl he has pinned against his car. Vaughn's arm is wrapped around another chick, and I can see his mouth forming words into her ear.

I lean into Tay. "This is like an opening of a bad porno."

Taylor laughs. "Those girls may be your saving grace tonight."

"How so?"

"They occupy your brothers and then you're free to be with your man."

I grab her arm in excitement, "Oh shit, Tay. You are so right!"

She throws her blonde locks over her shoulder, "I know, I'm a genius."

"You so are!"

"Are what?" Wes asks when we join him and Vin, along with some others.

"A genius." Taylor smiles at Wes and leans into him.

He smiles down at her with a, "You are, baby," and leans forward to capture her lips with his. And then there's tongue. *Looking away now.* So while they add to the whole 'porno' vibe, I move back to the fence to wait for Chase. I grab onto the chain-linking and once I reach it, a little Honda Civic, and a BMW 3 series lineup. I scoff. *This* is an easy win. Seconds later the BMW is off, but the Civic remains at the line. No way. I blink once and then the Civic is off; catching up the BMW easily.

"Whoa," I whisper to myself. Watching the little Honda fly down the track and pass the beamer was insane! The numbers flash up on the board above. The Civic ran a low nine; quite impressive. I glance back down at the track as another set moves up. Chase is one set away. I turn towards the group and wave my hands to grab their attention. A small gust of wind rushes by as the next set of cars move down the track. Wes notices me first. "They're coming up!" I yell.

It takes him a few tries to get Vance to part from the girl he's with. I cringe, but remind myself it's a good thing. I turn away when he pulls her back to his front, but not before I catch him nip at her ear.

The next two cars zoom by and Chase's Z moves forward, along with Kyle's Camaro. I bounce with excitement and a small smile spreads upon my lips at the thought of Chase racing. *That's my man!*

The group joins me at the fence just as they take off. It's only seconds until they're off the line. Their exhausts are roaring as they press on the gas, only pausing as they shift gears. Chase is off the line first--giving him a good lead--but the Camaro catches up easily. The Z jolts as Chase shifts. He's losing ground but not by much. They're neck and neck as they zoom by us. Vance is yelling, "Yeah, baby!" The cars disappear until they're specks, and then their times appear above.

"WHOO!" Vance yells.

"Damn, that is an awesome time!" Wes comments.

I glance back at them both. Vance is all smiles and

Wes looks impressed. I think we're all shocked at how well the Z did. We all move to greet the guys, who pull up just as we make it back to our cars. Kyle comes bounding from his car as soon as he's parked. There's a massive smile on his face; it's contagious. "That was fucking amazing!" He holds up the time slip. "I want to do it again!"

Chase exits his car and joins up.

"Did I win?" Kyle asks excitedly. It's pretty adorable; looks like we've nabbed another one. Vance moves towards Kyle. "Chase had you off the line, which gave him a better reaction time. That's what you need." Kyle's smile falters slightly, and he looks down at his slip.

"But I was faster?"

"In the end? Yeah," I tell him, and his smile returns.

"Sweet!" he looks up, "I wanna go again. Who's with me?" He looks around and ends on me. "C'mon, V!"

"What? For real?"

"Yeah, I'll even let you win," he says playfully, and I roll my eyes.

It takes me a second to answer. "Alright. I'm in."

Kyle jumps up, and he takes off towards his car. I laugh at his eagerness. Taylor pats me on the back, and everyone else throws out words of encouragement. I allow myself to steal a glance at Chase, who gives me two thumbs up. I know that he's mimicking me but he adds in his signature wink. *Oh.*

As soon as I get in my car and start the engine, my heart begins to pound. "You got this, V." I repeat the words as I reverse out of my spot. Thankfully, I wasn't hurt when my car broke down, but it was extremely traumatic. That shit stays with you.

Kyle's Camaro is idling ahead; he's waiting for me to

line up next to him. We move up into the queue line and wait. In my peripheral vision I can see a lot of movement, so I look to my right, thinking that Kyle is trying to get my attention. Nope. Kyle is full-on headbanging, and I burst out laughing. He smiles, and I just shake my head. *This kid.*

One by one we move up until we're next. I put on my face mask and then my helmet. I glance back over at Kyle who now has his hand out of the window with his pointer and pinky fingers up in the 'rock 'n' roll' sign. The cars ahead of us take off down the track. The officials motion us forward, so I give my car some gas and coast up until the front tires align perfectly into the duvet. Kyle moves a little too far up, and the guy waves him back. I giggle a little then get myself into focus. *Deep breath.*

In.

Amber.

Out.

Amber.

In.

Amber.

Out.

Go!

Without thought, my hands and feet move on their own. My engine roars, and I slam it into second. It howls in each gear until I've hit my last. I focus ahead--even though I can see Kyle has the lead--I'm right on his ass. This is extremely satisfying.

We cross the finish line, and I remove my foot from the gas, allowing my car to slow and downshift. I made it! My car didn't break, and it ran amazing! I yell out in excitement. I move the car around the bend at the end of the lane and pull up behind Kyle at the booth to grab my time slip.

"Nice run!" the guy tells me, and I thank him.

I pull up beside Kyle's Camaro and jump out once I pull my key out of the ignition. Everyone greets me, and Chase pulls me into a hug but breaks away quickly--to my displeasure. Vance pulls me into his side. "That was great! How did it feel?" he asks.

"Awesome!" I gush.

"I'm so proud of you!" he squeezes me, then releases me from his grasp. Even though I initially had no intention of racing, I'm so glad that I did it.

"That was so *hot*!" Kyle says and everyone stops to looks at him. "What?" he puts his hands up in surrender.

"You seem cool, but she's off-limits," Vance informs him.

"Oh, is she with you?" he looks between me and Vance. I begin to gag as Vance yells out, "Fuck no." He moves away from me at record speed. "No, bro, no. V's my sister."

"Oh," Kyle laughs, "My bad."

A loud car pulls up behind my RSX and Kyle's Camaro and all our attention turns to the car as the tinted window slides down. "Yo man, let's do this." The guy yells out. I glance back at my brothers, and it's Wes who's moving into action. This must be his first race of the night.

Wes rushes off and the group lingers around. Kyle gets Vance to go for a run and--just after they leave--I feel hands upon my hips. "I have to agree with Kyle. That *was* hot," Chase says in my ear, causing me to bite my lip.

"Oh yeah?" I turn around to face him and his hands

fall to his side.

"Oh, yeah," he confirms. His gaze moves from my lips to my eyes as he takes a step closer. "If we weren't standing here surrounded by all these people, I'd show you."

I clench my legs together. *Yes, please!* My expression must tell him what I'm thinking because he pulls me flush to him. My hands instinctively go to his chiseled chest and his breath tickles my ear as he whispers, "Later. I promise."

My hands pull his shirt into tight fists. He laughs as he tries to remove them. "You have to let go." I loosen my grasp, and he takes a step back. I pull myself together and look around quickly; everyone has moved to the fence.

"You can't make promises like that. Now I'm all excited." His eyes widen at that, and he shifts on his feet. *Ha! Two can play this game.* I flash my teeth at him.

"Fuck." I hear him mutter.

"I know..." This time I move to him, getting super close and personal to tease him.

"What?" he asks.

"Let's race..."

COSMO
Chase

Veronica smiles wickedly before turning to run to her car. I am *definitely* looking forward to 'later'. My mind begins to wander but, thankfully, the sound of the car's exhaust pulls me from my thoughts. I bound to my car and quickly jump into the driver's seat, turning over the ignition and reversing out of the spot.

As soon as I pull up next to Veronica's RSX, my eyes find hers. I can't help but think how beautiful she is. She blows me a kiss and then her car moves forward. *Such a tease*. I cannot wait to get my lips on her. Also my hands...and my tongue. My pants are becoming tight. I guide my car up until we're beside each other again.

Slowly, set by set, we move forward until we're up next. I'm super stoked to be doing this, and not just because it's racing--it's racing with *my* girl. There are two kinds of girls; one that sits with you, or one that cheers you on. Both are great, but V? She's a unique kind all her own, and it's quickly become my favorite kind.

Movement in front of me snaps me out of my thoughts--a man is waving me forward. I quickly comply. V's engine roars next to me just as the first light on the tree flashes. Then the second blazes, followed by the third. In milliseconds, it's green and I'm on the gas. The car launches forward. I shift into second as soon as I hit the rev line and quickly glance to my right. I don't see V's car.

The gentlemanly thing to do is to let her win, but she'd know. She's very competitive and she would never be happy with it. So, I give it my all and make it my goal to do better than the last time. I shift into the fifth and final gear and press my foot down on the gas pedal without removing any pressure until I cross the finish line.

Once my car crosses the line indicating the end of the track, I let off the pedal and apply the brakes--shifting down into each gear until I approach the booth. I glance up into my rearview mirror and Veronica is right behind me. I move around the bend and drive up towards our spot and park my car next to Vance's; V does the same.

We get out at the same time, and the whole group moves towards us, giving us words of encouragement. I move closer to V, "Could you see?" I ask, teasing her.

Her eyebrows furrow in confusion. "What?"

"With all that dust I kicked up? Could you see? I smoked you!" I joke.

Her eyes instantly narrow at me, and she pushes my shoulder. "You jerk," Her hands go to her hips, "I'll have you know, I was right next to you!"

"It's okay, we can't all be winners." I continue to poke at her.

"Keep it up. You'll be going to bed alone tonight." Her eyes scan our surroundings as if she forgot herself. I barely care anymore.

Lowering my face to hers, "You're up here," I point to my temple, "I won't be alone."

Her face softens, "I hate you," she whispers with a playful smile.

I wink at her, "Whatever you say." then move away

from her as Taylor comes to her side.

She purrs, "What are you two up to?" Her eyes move between us.

My gaze remains on Veronica as I answer, "Nothing, yet." I smirk and join the guys standing towards the front of Wes' car.

The night continues smoothly, and it's a great time for us all. Wes wins money, I kill Vance in a race, and V is all smiles--that's my favorite part. "Alright folks, it's been a great season," The male voice speaks to the crowd from the call box, "Again, we appreciate your support and hope to see you next May. Y'all don't have to go home, but ya gotta get up outta here! Goodnight!"

People begin to scatter out, walking to their cars.

"We going to the diner?" Wes looks around as he asks.

Vance is busy sucking face with the girl that's been on his arm all night and he breaks away for a second to answer. "They don't have anything I'm hungry for." He bites at the girls' lip.

Kyle walks around the group and shakes hands with everyone. He hugs V, and my eyes catch something he slips into her hand. She looks down as he moves away to his car, and I move up behind her. There's a number written on the slip. I laugh low in her ear and reach around to grab it from her. "You won't be needing that." I crumble it up and shove it in my pocket.

"I don't know," she says turning around to face me. "The guy I'm dating is being a jerk."

"Hmm, I think he will make it up to you."

She smirks. "He better."

"I'll meet you at my place," I whisper in her ear.

Forty minutes later, I pull into my driveway. V's car appears not long after and I'm already out of my car and leaning against my rear bumper. As soon as she's within reach, I pull her to me and my lips crash onto hers. Our tongues meet, and it's oh-so-sweet. She shivers, and I don't know if it's from us or the cool night air. I rub my hands along her arms, hoping to bring her some warmth. Our mouths slow, and I reluctantly break away from her. "I've wanted to do that all night," I tell her, "Let's get inside." I grab her hand and pull her with me to the front door.

"Are your parents' home?" she asks.

"No idea." I don't notice any cars, but I'm sure some could be tucked away in the garage. I fucking pray no one is home because I want to hear V screaming my name. As we enter the house, all seems quiet, and I can assume no one is present. "Doesn't seem like anyone's here."

We move up to my room, but just before entering, I turn and pick Veronica up. She squeals out in surprise, "What are you doing?!" I waltz into my room and close my door with my foot before crossing to my bed. I toss V onto my mattress, and the sight of her on it instantly has me hard. She leans up and grabs me by my shirt, pulling me to her. I place my arms on either side of her, not wanting to completely suffocate her. She doesn't give me any time. Her mouth is on mine. Her kiss is searing. Her legs wrap around my waist which rubs her groin right against my dick. A soft moan vibrates through V, and I can tell she enjoyed that as much as I did. She does it again, and I can feel everything tighten. If she does that a couple more times, I may end up releasing early. This is something I've never experienced before. I pull my lips from hers and move down her jaw, and even lower onto her neck. She rolls her hips again, and this time it's me who's moaning. "Baby," I whisper.

"Yeah," her voice is soft.

"You gotta stop doing that, or this will end sooner than I'd like." The wicked girl does it again and laughs. "You *evil* tease." I lift my weight off of her and my dick is throbbing. She tightens her legs around me and pulls me back to her but her lips nip at my ear.

"I want to make you feel good," she whispers. It's so fucking sexy. My head drops onto her shoulder. Her hands move down to my pants. Before I know it she's unzipping them and reaching inside. Her hand reaches around my shaft, and I groan at the contact.

"Fuck." I hiss.

Her legs loosen from around my waist, and with her free hand, she pushes me until I'm on my back. She pulls my pants and boxers from around my hips, down my legs, and throws them on the floor. Her eyes widen, and then she licks her lips as her hand grabs my shaft again. She begins to stroke me, the immense pleasure causes a moan to slip pass my lips.

Without warning, my dick is in something wet and incredibly warm. I glance down at the most glorious sight I've ever seen. I am two seconds away from exploding--and I warn her--but she doesn't stop. My hand moves to the back of her head, while my other grasps at my bedsheets. I try to hold off as long as I can until she begins to move faster, and I fall. Once I come back to earth, I open my eyes. Veronica wipes her lips and smirks at me. "That okay?" she asks.

"Fuck, baby. That was amazing." She smiles wide and proud. I sit up quickly, surprising her, and pin her onto her back. "I thought you'd never done that," I ask her, curiously.

"I haven't," she whispers.

"Where the fuck did you learn how to do *all that*?"

"Cosmo."

I glance up at my ceiling. "Thank you, Cosmo!" She laughs beneath me, and I look back down at her beautiful face. I capture her mouth with mine and explore it with my tongue. My hands move to her jeans, and she lifts her ass off the bed, allowing me to move them down her legs. I kiss my way down her throat and sit up to pull her jeans off. "Your turn."

FANCY SCHMANCY
Chase

It's well into the afternoon when I finally wake up, unfortunately alone. Can't say I didn't try. A smile spreads across my lips of the memory of how I tried to convince her to stay. She struggled with that, but in the end, she was right. She had to go, for numerous reasons. Though now I'm wondering how she's functioning on the amount of sleep we *didn't* get.

I press the screen on my phone to see the time. Twelve forty-five. Veronica's shift is half over, but this gives me plenty of time to make some calls and plan something special for tonight.

Taylor is a damn pain in my ass. Being polite doesn't get you anywhere, but then trying to explain why it's important that I have this Saturday with Veronica without a legit reason doesn't fly, either. She's too cunning. I didn't want to tell anyone before telling V, but now Taylor knows. She promised to keep it a secret, and finally agreed it was a good enough reason to let me have Veronica this *one* Saturday. She even went out of her way to help me out with something else but...she's still a pain in the ass. With that being my last phone call, everything is finally set in place. I send Veronica a text.

Me: Tonight, you're mine babygirl.

My phone vibrates shortly after.

Nic: Correction: Tonight I'm Taylors.
Me: Nope. Already spoke with your girlfriend.
Nic: You did? Why am I the last to know?
Me: Because you weren't supposed to know. Be at my house by six, dress nice.
Nic: Who's the tease now?

I send her a wink emoji and leave it at that. An imaginary night seems to play out in my mind. How do you tell someone you care about that you're leaving? And what's more, that you hope they'll wait for you? I sigh and try to push that to the back of my mind. Tonight we enjoy our time together, and tomorrow I tell her. With things to do, I grab my keys and head out to my car to run some errands.

I make it back home with *just* enough time to spare. The house is empty; just the way I'm used to. I rush up the stairs and get myself dressed in some nice shit I have hanging in my closet, then quickly make something of my short hair. From the bathroom, I hear my phone go off at the same time I hear the exhaust of a car coming up the driveway. I slip on my shoes and quickly make my way back downstairs to greet her at the front door.

She's just reaching the door as I open it. I stop dead in my tracks at the sight of her. Her face lights up in the most beautiful smile. My eyes drink her in. "Well, don't you clean up nice," she jokes, but I'm still speechless--my lack of response causes her smile to drop.

"What?" she asks, panicked.

She's wearing a snug red dress that stops right above her knees; it showcases her sexy figure and long, *long* legs. "You look amazing." I move towards her, picking up a dark curl and wrapping it around my finger. "I like your hair like this." Her megawatt smile returns.

"You better," She pouts, "It took forever to curl." I

smile at her and notice she's wearing makeup. It's not a lot but just enough to emphasize her natural beauty.

"As much as I want to take you up to my room and peel this dress off you, we need to go." She bites her lip, and it's my undoing. In a second, I have her flush to my body and my hands are roving all over as my tongue does the same to her mouth. If it weren't for my phone ringing, we would never have left. Reluctantly, we break apart and I pull my phone from my pocket.

It's a short call from the restaurant confirming my reservation. I put my phone back in my pocket and take Veronica's hand in mine. "We gotta go."

"Where are we going?" she asks as I pull her behind me towards my car.

"You'll find out soon enough." I open the passenger door for her and wait to close it until she's safely tucked into the seat. She graces me with a grin just before I close the door and make my way over to the driver's side to get behind the wheel. The car starts with a purr. Once we're on the main road, and I'm cruising in fifth gear, I reach over to grasp Veronica's hand in mine. I quickly glance towards her and the light from my head unit allows me to see her smile in the dark.

"So…" she drags out the word, "*Now* can you tell me where we're going?"

"Nope."

"Pleassseee," she begs.

"Nope." I gently squeeze her hand.

"You're mean."

"Well, that's not very nice."

"You not telling me where we're going isn't very nice."

"No, it's called a 'surprise'. Maybe you've heard of

them?"

I hear her huff in annoyance. "Well, are we almost there?"

"Kind of."

"What? How long till we're there?"

I glance at the clock. "Hmm, twenty minutes give or take."

I pull her hand over to my mouth, and place a kiss on the top. "Stop it. Please, let me do this for you." I scan her face as it softens.

"Okay," she responds, quietly. I place our intertwined hands on my thigh.

I smile. "Thank you."

"So how did you get Taylor to agree to give up her Saturday with me?"

"It wasn't hard actually. She agreed pretty quickly. She was claiming she needed a break from you, or something along those lines."

"Uh-huh," she murmurs. "Did she ask to see your penis? I told that bitch it's mine." I cannot contain the laughter that erupts from my mouth. "What?!"

"She's obsessed with penises." I see her shoulders shrug in my peripheral vision.

"So, my penis is yours?" I joke. "I'm *pretty* sure it's connected to me."

"And you're mine. So yeah, it's mine. Like I'm yours."

I won't lie, my penis liked hearing that just as much as my heart. "Damn right, you are," I growl. The sound of her laugh causes my lips to widen.

The large green metal sign hanging above the overpass reminds me that our exit is next. I shift lanes and Veronica hums next to me, grabbing my attention. Her eyes are narrowed and the tip of her finger tapping her bottom lip. This damn girl.

"Stop it," I scold her. "I should've blindfolded you."

"Do you want me to close my eyes?" she asks amused.

"I think I have a shirt somewhere in here, I can pull over and blind you with that," I tell her while steering the car onto the exit ramp.

"I have no idea where we are, so I'm clueless."

"Good."

"Have you been here before?"

"I have."

"With…?" she asks, a slight hesitation in her voice as if she doesn't want to know.

"Family."

I can hear her exhale. I squeeze her hand in reassurance.

"Are we almost there?"

"Yep."

We drive on the main road for a bit--and I let off the gas--allowing the car to slow down as we approach the wide driveway. The massive wooden sign is lit up and the name of the restaurant is prominent in the middle: 'The Glasbern Inn'. I make the right onto the road. The long driveway is surrounded by trees on both sides until it opens into a clearing, and the large stone inn stands tall behind a fountain set in the middle of a roundabout. Veronica's body is turned, so she can look out her side of the window.

"So pretty," she murmurs as we pass the large fountain. I pull up to the front, and two young men quickly approach the car. One's opening my door and the other's opening Veronica's. "Good evening, sir."

I give him a polite 'hello', inform him of our bags and which suite we're booked in, and slip him a tip. Veronica comes to my side, and I place my hand upon her back, gently moving her forward and into the inn. Taylor did me a huge solid by packing a bag without Veronica knowing.

The inside of the inn is all stone walls and wooden beams. Straight ahead is a wooden lobby desk for checking in and to the left of that is a massive grand staircase that leads up to the second floor. The most impressive part is the enormous chandelier hanging from the ceiling. It's far from your average chandelier; it's completely made of antlers.

Bypassing the main lobby, I guide us towards the left where a young girl in uniform stands behind a small stand. I give her my last name, and she smiles wide. "Your table is ready, Mr. Daniels."

I nod, and we follow behind her as she leads towards the back of the dim-lit room. Couples are scattered around the dining area. Tables are spaced for privacy with a large candle set in the middle; there are small candles placed on each side. The hostess sets the menu in front of each chair and leaves us with a polite comment to enjoy our meal. Our table is nearby a large lit fireplace with windows on either side. I imagine the view would be scenic but, since it's later into the evening, we can't see much.

Veronica leans forward while glancing at the candles. She speaks low, "This is so *fancy!*" I smile when she looks around the room again. "Fancy schmancy," she mutters. Her eyes land back on me as she unrolls the utensils and places the white cloth on her lap. "To what is the occasion, Mr. Daniels?" She adds a British accent to her vocals.

"Ah, Miss Russo," I respond in a thick, fake accent

that causes her eyes to widen with surprise. "A beautiful maiden such as you deserves the fanciest of schmanciest of evenings."

She laughs and shakes her head. "That was hot," she admits, somewhat shyly. "This is seriously amazing, Chase. I'm feeling a bit spoiled."

"Good. There's more to come." I smile at her, then she bites her lip in that way I find incredibly sexy. Unfortunately, our waitress takes that moment to approach our table. After she introduces herself, she takes our drink orders and goes over the menu with precision before leaving us to make our selections. Veronica doesn't wait a beat to dive back into our previous conversation. She leans forward. "More?" she prods.

"More."

She hums softly in thought, and I throw her a wink that I know puts her off-kilter. "No fair."

"Don't worry, you'll enjoy it."

"And you're so sure of yourself because..."

"Because it's my job to know you; your likes and dislikes. To fulfill you with your wants and needs and to know your *every* desire...and fulfill those too. I'm still learning, and I plan to continue learning for a long time," I tell her this in complete seriousness. I can tell by her face that I have taken her by surprise. She remains quiet for a while, and I just wait.

"Wow," she says low, but I catch it, "I wasn't expecting that. You better be careful or you'll never be able to get rid of me," she jokes.

I smile and rub my hands together greedily. "My master plan is working then." She smirks and then laughs.

Our waitress returns, and even though we didn't

look over the menu, we both ordered as if we did. Our conversation picks right back up as our waitress leaves us--we laugh and throw playful banter back and forth. I am so happy with Veronica. I feel content to just sit here and talk with her. She makes me laugh and smile with all her quirks. I've known her for so long and never thought that we'd be here together. I wouldn't change it for anything. I want to feel this for as long as I can.

Soon our plates are placed in front of us. My steak to her seafood platter. She wiggles excitedly in her chair. "This looks so *good!*" Veronica doesn't waste any time digging into her food. I like that. She's comfortable enough to be herself with me. She moans at her first bite, groans with her second. With every bite--and with every tantalizing sound--my pants become tighter until I'm sporting a tent. Thankfully my lap is covered by the table, and I'm the only one aware of my problem. She notices that I've barely touched my food, "Are you okay? Is your steak alright?" she asks, concerned.

"It's perfect," I tell her.

"This is so good." She takes another bite.

"I've gathered," I smirk.

"Do you want some?" she asks, covering her mouth.

"No, I'm okay."

She stops chewing, and her face falls into a frown. "What's wrong?" she asks and then, almost instantly, her eyebrows shoot up as if she's come to some kind of understanding. "I'm sorry!" She swallows her food and removes her hand from her mouth, "This is probably so unattractive."

I cut her off before she can get the wrong idea and berate herself further, "Uh, no. It's the complete opposite, actually."

"Huh?" Her expression is one of deep confusion.

"First off, nothing you do is unattractive. Second, if you could see over here right now, you'd notice the tent I'm sporting in my pants."

Her face morphs from embarrassed confusion to a mischievous glint. "Really?" she asks.

"Yes, really. Keep moaning over your food, and I'll take you upstairs to our room and give you something else to moan about."

"You got us a room?" she blurts out.

"Fuck." I hiss and then laugh at my own stupid mistake. I glance up at her, "Is that okay?"

Although she's probably trying not to show it, I can tell she's nervous. That's the *last* thing I want her to feel because while I want nothing more than to sleep with her, I don't want her to think that's why I did this. Internally, I cringe at that thought as well. I place my hand on top of the table, palm up, and wiggle my fingers to indicate I want her hand in mine. She places her small, soft palm on mine, and I intertwine our fingers. "Veronica, I don't want you to think I did this for any other reason than to spend time with you. We don't have to stay. We don't even have to share the bed. You have me so wrapped around your little finger, and you don't even know it." I continue, "Well, now you do."

She smiles shyly and says, "I want to stay."

"Are you sure?"

She nods slightly. "Yes."

I squeeze her hand in reassurance, and her smile widens. "So, do I have a bag or am I going to wear this?"

"*I* prefer nothing," I tell her and add, "but unfortunately Taylor agreed to pack you a bag."

"She knew?!"

"You wouldn't be here otherwise."

Her lips pucker in thought, "True."

It's an hour by the time we finish up our meals--we're in no rush and savoring every bite and every moment together. Here, just us two, there's no stress of the outside world. I wish it could always be like this and I push away the impending news that I'll have to reveal to her.

Veronica rubs her stomach, and the waitress comes to remove our empty plates. "Any room for dessert?" the woman asks us. My dessert is sitting across from me, so I shake my head while looking at the beautiful girl I adore.

"No, thank you," Veronica responds.

The waitress smiles wide. "Okay, if you change your mind the kitchen is open until eleven. We only serve dinner until ten but you can have your dessert delivered to your room. Enjoy the rest of your night."

I thank her before she turns to leave, then look to V. "You ready to check out our room?"

"Is it fancier than this?" she asks.

I shrug my shoulders and unfold myself from my chair. I reach my hand out for her to take, and she obliges. We move through the dining room hand in hand. The room has thinned out and there are only, maybe, two couples still dining. I guide us towards the lobby desk to collect the room key and the clerk informs me that all is ready and our bags have been placed in our room. I thank her and move towards the staircase.

The inn isn't massive, but it's big enough to provide twenty-five rooms. Five of those are suites, and one of those suites is ours for the night. At the top of the staircase, it splits into three hallways, and according to the plaque on the wall our room is to the right. We follow the numbers but regretfully take a few wrong turns. We joke about getting lost and never making our way home. I honestly wouldn't mind. We reach the end of the hall and the last room--smack dab in the middle--is ours.

I place the key into the card slot--a soft click of the lock sounds--and the green light allows the door to open. The room is dim, but there's a source of light coming from a table in the entryway. There's a door that leads to a bathroom on our right. We move further into the room, and I allow Veronica to go first, and come up behind her. There are candles scattered around the small living room that gives the room just enough light for us to see how beautiful it is.

Veronica's attention moves to the open door to the left--the bedroom--filled with candles. They cover every surface of the room. I remain behind her as she takes in the view. She's taking small steps forward until we're both just beyond the threshold. The bed is covered in flower petals and placed in the middle is a tray holding a bucket of ice with a bottle inside. Alcohol? I know. I never claimed to be a saint. We won't be leaving the room for the rest of the night, so there's no harm done.

I allow her one more second before I move forward and wrap my arms around her waist. She lets out a soft breath while placing her smooth hands on mine. She still hasn't said anything so I break the silence, "What are you thinking?" I whisper, moving my head to rest on her shoulder.

"I-" she starts and stops. "Just...wow. You did this all for me?"

I nod my head, and my chin nuzzles her shoulder. "Well the staff did it for me, but I thought of it." She turns around in my arms, the loss of my head rest causes me to straighten my stance. Her eyes are glistening, which catches me by surprise. She's not supposed to cry. Her eyes scan my face before she places her hands on my cheeks and pulls me forward. Our mouths meet in a sweet kiss, and then she's placing kisses all over.

She moves away, but her hands are still holding my face. "Thank you." Her smile seems to make the room brighter, or maybe it's just my life she brightens.

"You're welcome." I move forward to kiss her nose, and her hands move to my shoulders. She puckers her lips when I move back. When my girl wants a kiss I will always comply. I feel her tongue, but I don't allow the kiss to deepen. "I have one more thing to show you," I whisper against her lips.

Before she can respond, I turn her around and walk her towards the right side of the room to stop her in front of dark curtains. Behind the curtains lead out to a balcony outside, but since the curtains are drawn shut--and with the dim lighting--you'd never know. I move forward and push the curtains aside, then open the double doors.

"A hot tub?" she squeaks and moves forward with excitement. The cool night air is welcoming as I follow Veronica out onto the wide balcony. On either side is a privacy fence, and above is a tent-like cover, with lights hung around the entire perimeter. The hot tub is already bubbling, and there's thick steam rising from the surface. "Did Taylor pack me a suit?"

I smirk. "Nope, I told her to leave that out." I'm teasing her; I made sure Taylor did pack her a suit. Veronica surprises me though. Only after a quick thought, she shrugs and smiles wickedly. She turns her back towards me while moving her hair to the side, then reaches behind her to lower the zipper at the base of her neck and slowly--excruciatingly--unzips her dress. *Dammit, I'm trying to be a noble guy here.* That is not what this night is about. Don't get me wrong, I've thought of it a million times. Okay, a billion, but I know that it's important to her.

I quickly shoot forward to stop her from lowering it any further, before I lose myself. Placing a kiss on her bare neck, she shivers slightly. "Taylor packed you a suit." She looks over her shoulder at me and leans back against me. Her hand reaches up to cup my face. "You're so sweet," she says with a smile. Her voice laced with amusement.

"Only for you," I respond.

She moves away from my body. My eyes move along with her and continue until she's left the bedroom. My focus returns to the darkness beyond the balcony. I take a deep breath and fill my lungs with the fresh night air. After a few more peaceful seconds of the wilderness-- and bubbling water--I move back into the bedroom and to the small living room area to grab my bag. A sliver of light shines from underneath the bathroom door. Within seconds my pants are removed and replaced by my trunks. The bathroom door opens just as I'm on the last button of my shirt and the light turns off, but Veronica doesn't move out from the doorway.

"Um..." she says nervously. "I'm not sure whose suit she packed, but it's not mine."

"Okay?" I question, not quite sure what it matters. "Maybe she got you another one."

She steps out of the bathroom, and I see small strips of white covering her private areas. I'm not quite sure what the big deal is until she steps closer and, suddenly, I feel as if I'm choking on air. The bathing suit is teeny *tiny*, only covering the smallest of areas, and allowing all of her curves to be on display. She belongs on a cover of a swimsuit magazine. No doubt.

"Damn," my voice is strained.

"I don't know what the hell she was thinking," she huffs and turns to go back into the bathroom. I lunge forward, engulfing her in my arms. "What are you doing?"

"I'm taking this-this...," she sputters, "this *non*-bathing suit off."

I laugh, "What are you planning to wear? I vote for nothing," I joke. I pull her back against me, and I'm sure my arousal is apparent.

"Oh!" she blurts. "I get it now, she was thinking about your penis!"

I laugh hard. "What?"

"I know what she's doing!"

I begin to move us through the room and towards the balcony. "And what would that be?" I ask her.

"Sex."

"Yeah, she may be doing that," I say amused.

"That's not what I meant."

"I know what you meant." I lean against the hot tub and pull her in front of me. "You look amazing. I'll have to thank Taylor." She smiles and looks away at the compliment. I grab her face and turn it towards me, "But remember what I said earlier? I didn't bring you here for sex. You have control, alright?" She nods and I pull her face to mine, pressing my lips to hers. Her hands wrap around my waist; her body feels so good pressed against mine. "Okay, let's get in this bad boy." I help V into the tub and follow behind her.

As soon as I've emerged under the hot water, I feel my whole body relax. "Ahh," I groan and lay my back against the tub. "I could go for a massage right now," I think out loud. "I think they have a spa. Maybe we can do that before we check out tomorrow." I peek an eye open at the sound of splashing. V is moving towards me. "What are you doing?" I inquire as she moves to my side and pushes my shoulder forward, then squeezes between me and the tub. "I'm gonna give my man a massage." She places her legs on either side of my hips.

"My man." I hum. "I like that." I pull her hand that is on my shoulder to my jaw and kiss the top of it. She returns it to my shoulder and starts massaging. A groan escapes my lips, and my head lolls forward. She moves down from my shoulders to my biceps, then back up to the middle of my back. *It's heavenly.* She's quiet as she works my muscles, and I fall into a haze. I hear her speak, but don't understand the words. "Hmm?"

"Can I ask you something?"

"You just did."

Her massaging stops and she smacks my arm, "Wise ass."

I laugh. "What's up?"

"I want you to know, don't feel obligated to agree just because we're together. I understand if it may not be your thing, and you already probably went to one..." She starts rambling, "So it's okay to say no. I mean, it's not for another..." she pauses and I can hear her counting out loud, "It's like six months away yet."

"V." I grab her calf. "Ask your question."

She takes a deep breath, before rushing out a muttered, "Will you be my date to prom?"

I know I stiffen slightly, and not because I *don't* want to go with her. It's because I don't know if I *can* go. It obviously made her nervous to ask me--if her mumbling on and on had anything to do with it. My posture and lack of response must be a sign of my disinterest because she starts talking again.

"Yanno, never mind," she says, laughing lightly, "I don't even know if I'm going. It was just a thought."

"No, no," I rush to assure her. I didn't want to tell her just yet. I want tonight to just be about us together. It was all going as planned until this moment, and now I'm going to have to break the news to her. I grasp her wrist, "V, I'd be honored to go."

"*But...*" she pushes, exasperatedly. I tug on her wrist and she allows me to guide her between my legs. I lock my feet behind her. As hard as this is, I stare right into her eyes. "I'm sorry."

Her whole face drops. "For what?" she asks, her voice a hoarse whisper.

"I wanted tonight to be special."

"It is! I don't think anything will ever top this. What's wrong?" She moves closer, and I pull her to me, wrapping my arms around her middle. She squeezes me. "Chase..." I nuzzle into her chest; I can hear her heart beating erratically. I'm sure mine matches hers right now. "Tell me what's going on, Chase, you're scaring me," she whispers.

"I'm being deployed again."

"What?" Her whole body stiffens. "You just got back! Can they do that?"

"Apparently, they can."

"For how long?"

"I don't know," I admit, "Sarg is hoping it won't be long, and is going to try to have me be the first one sent back. It's short-term deployment, but there are no guarantees."

"When do you leave?" she asks. *Here goes.*

I squeeze her but don't answer right away. "*When?*" she whispers again.

"Wednesday."

"What?" she yells and struggles for me to release her. I don't at first but loosen my arms, and she moves away. "Chase! That's in four days!"

"I know."

"What the actual fuck? When were you planning to tell me?"

"Tomorrow."

"*Oh my-*" Her lip quivers as she starts to cry.

"Please, please don't cry." I pull her to me. I can *feel* my heart break. "I'm so sorry." I squeeze her, and she wraps her legs around my waist, hugging me back like her life depends on it.

"I don't want you to leave," she whispers.

"Believe me, I don't want to leave either." I kiss her shoulder.

"Will you be able to call me?" she asks.

"Yes, if that's what you want. I'll call you every chance I can."

"What do you mean if that's what I want?" She pulls back to look at my face. "Of course it is!" My body instantly fills with relief.

"I wasn't sure if you'd want to continue our relationship."

"What?" she rasps.

"You're young and beautiful. I can't expect you to wait for me. I don't know how long I'll be gone," I admit to her.

"I don't care about anyone else or about dating anyone else." I like those words way too much. A tear slips from the corner of her eye, and I stop it from traveling down her face with my thumb. "I'm so sad." her lips tremble, and I cup her face with my hands.

"I'm so sorry," I whisper, then place a small kiss upon her lips. "I wouldn't have started seeing you if I would have known this."

"I would have," she says quickly. "I wouldn't change a thing. You are the best thing to ever happen to me."

I smile at her words, "You are the best thing to happen to me," I repeat to her. The tears start to pool in her eyes. "Please don't cry. We'll be fine. We'll be great."

She nods her head and gives me a weak smile. Her arms wrap around my neck and pulls me to her. We stay like this for a while--quiet--knowing there's not much else to say. It has, unfortunately, dampened the mood. I place light kisses on her skin, leaving goosebumps and her body shivers despite us being in warm water.

"Why don't we head inside and watch a movie," I suggest.

"Okay," she whispers but doesn't release me. Chuckling while I stand with her wrapped around me, I slowly maneuver us out of the hot tub, and quickly take us inside the room, closing the doors behind us. Grabbing a towel that's placed on a dresser and wrap it around us both. My hands rub up and down her back, hoping that helps warm her up.

"Do you want to take a shower?" She shrugs at my question. I laugh, "Okay, well let's get you dressed." I move us into the small living area and grab her bag, then walk to the bathroom and place the bag on the sink. I tap her butt, and she slowly removes herself from me. She's sliding her body down mine, and that makes *my* body quiver this time. "Get dressed." With one last look at her in that sexy little bikini, I close the door and grab my bag to get dressed in the bedroom.

WITH YOU
Veronica

Chase leaves me standing in the bathroom and I allow myself to peek at the barely-there bikini. *Freakin' Taylor.* I'm slightly disappointed at the restraint Chase has, but he's made it clear that he didn't make this about sex. I internally laugh at myself. I'm such a contradiction. Part of me wanted him to not be able to keep his hands off me, and the other part is grateful for his respect. I sigh, then decide to take a quick shower. I reach behind the curtain and turn the handle to hot, then untie my bikini and peel it off my skin. I hang it on the hook behind the door.

I step under the stream of steamy water and allow it to bead down my body. To the right is a small inset box; a small basket with little wrapped soaps and bottles sits on the ledge. The soaps are in an array of colors that look like flowers and I decide on a pink one. As soon as I rip open the clear wrapping, the smell of roses engulfs the shower. Rubbing the soap between my hands under the water, I get a good lather and begin rubbing my body. I get my arms, my shoulders, down to my chest, over my stomach, and lower. I do this without thought because my mind is elsewhere. I wash my hair with the provided shampoo and conditioner, thinking about how perfect this evening is. It would have been even better without the news of his deployment. It would have been pure *bliss*.

His deployment scares me--for numerous reasons. A

million and one questions plague my thoughts. What if he's gone for another year? What if he meets someone else? What if he gets hurt? Or worse, what if he doesn't return...*alive*? I don't even want to think of that scenario. The tears blur my vision, and my heart hurts. I rub at my chest; not that it helps relieve the pain I'm feeling. I want to curl up in his arms and never leave them. With that thought, I turn the water off and open the curtain. I grab the white towel that's hanging on the rack and wrap it around myself, pulling another one off to wrap around my wet hair. I take my time drying off, and subconsciously imagine Chase's hands moving over my body. His hands--what they could do to me-- and what they've done.

I wonder if Taylor packed any sexy underwear. I bite my lip in thought and move towards my bag on the sink countertop. For once, I hope Taylor was thinking of sex because I am now.

As soon as I have the bag open, I search through the contents and my hand touches something lacy. A large smile greets my lips, and I pull out the underwear. They're black, lacy and very...cheeky. *They're perfect.* I look back in the bag for a bra or bustier, but I see a black box with gold lettering. Magnum. I lift the box out of the bag and laugh. Condoms. A dark blue box grabs my attention, next. This one reads 'Pleasure Pack'. I laugh and shake my head...freakin' Tay. I silently thank her for this before I dive back into the bag--looking for a top. I feel the lace before I see it, as the black blends in with the bag. I pull it out and stretch it out in front of me. It looks like a halter but has a small keyhole area between the cups; it's all lace. Thankfully, it's simple to put on. I place it around my neck and snap it in the back like a bra. It's sexy as hell and makes my boobs look amazing. I'm euphoric. I can't wait to see Chase's face. I pull on the underwear and turn to look at my butt in the mirror. I am not disappointed--it looks amazing.

I remove the towel from my head and quickly dry my hair with the dryer hanging on the wall. I run a brush through my tresses and look at myself in the mirror. I take a deep breath, grab the condoms, and open the door.

"What are you in the mood to watch?" I hear Chase yell from the bedroom. "Comedy? Action? Thriller?" he lists different genres, and I take slow steps to the bedroom door. It's still dim. I take another deep breath and stand in the doorway, my left hand holding the boxes behind my back. Chase is laying on the bed in sweats and a tee, one hand behind his head and the other holding a remote pointed towards the TV.

"What are you doing?" Chase questions then I hear his intake of breath, "Oh *fuck*," He shoots up in a seated position and puts the remote down next to him. I smile at his response; it only makes me feel bolder. "Wow," he says again, and I move closer, trailing my fingers along the edge of the bed.

"I found these in my bag. I thought you might like them."

"Like them? I fucking love them." He sits up on his knees and grabs my waist as I come to stand in front of him. He pulls me to him and his free hand moves to the hole at my chest, tracing the circle. "I *really* fucking love them."

"I also found these, thought maybe we could put them to use." I pull my hand from behind my back and show him the boxes. I can see his eyes widen even in the dim light and at the same time I can hear his intake of breath.

"Are you sure about this?" he asks, and I nod. His mouth is on me in a flash, and I drop the boxes, hearing them clatter to the floor; not caring about anything but his touch. His hands move down to my bottom, and without warning he lifts me. A gasp passes through my lips. I can feel his smile against my mouth. He sits back and places me on his lap, I can feel him beneath me. My hips involuntarily begin to grind down on the bulge between my legs, and he squeezes me every time I do. It feels *so* right, and so good. He becomes ravenous with every thrust, and after about the fifth time, he growls and swiftly lays me on my back. I squeal out in surprise. His arms pull mine above our heads, and he nestles himself between my legs. His lips are moving all over my skin--my neck, down the base of my throat, and back up to my lips. He grinds himself against my core, and a moan escapes my throat. It becomes muffled by his mouth.

He pulls back abruptly. Both of us are breathing heavily. "Are you *sure*?" he gasps out. I nod again. "I've never been more sure of anything," I whisper. His head falls onto my chest for a brief second and then he looks back into my eyes. Our hands are still interlocked above our heads.

His eyes move over my face. "I love you."

"What?" I gasp, blatantly shocked at his admission.

"I am so in love with you, Veronica Russo."

"I am so glad I waited for you, I love you too."

He smiles wider, then leans down, kissing me deeply. It's slow and sweet, and full of passion; until it's not. He begins his descent down my body while he's slipping the lace down my legs. He begins kissing the inside of my thigh, then moves on to the other leg and I squirm while waiting for him to do something. He chuckles. "I love having you at my mercy." I'm about to speak--call him a tease--but his mouth is on me, and I'm squirming for another reason.

"Oh my God," I whisper. It's followed by a moan, and my hands move to his head. He works his magic as I'm climbing higher and higher until fireworks explode behind my eyes. My body quivers, and shakes. He climbs up my body, leaving a trail of kisses in his path. "I'll never get tired of doing that."

I grin, somewhat shy, even though he just had his face near the most intimate part of me, "I thought we were going to have sex."

He laughs lightly. "Yes. If that's what you still want, I would love to. It's not always comfortable the first time, or so I've heard. I want yours to be good."

I touch his face softly, lean forward, and kiss him lightly. "It will be, because it's with you." At that, he kisses me again, with passion. I pull at his shirt; I want it off. He rips his lips away, and I grasp at his tee, pulling it up and over his head. It reveals his muscular, toned body. I run my hands down his chest and to the top of his waist--the bulge in his pants is very apparent. He doesn't stop me, so I dip my hand inside his sweats and take him in my hands. His head falls backward with a blissful groan. I understand what he means when he enjoys pleasing me because I feel like I'm on top of the world right now. I feel in control and sexy. I will never get tired of this, either.

Moving lightning-fast, he pins me back to the bed, nestles between my legs and grinds down. I twitch, still sensitive from my recent orgasm. His lips devour mine like it's the last thing he will taste. I arch up into him. I *need* to feel him all over my body, and I want him inside me.

Although this is something I've never done, it's like my body just knows what to do. He disappears, and I open my eyes at the lack of his heat. "Remove my pants," he tells me as his chest is heaving. I slide to the side of the bed and all while looking up at him--never breaking contact--I slowly pull his pants down. In front of me a glorious sight, I can't help but touch him. He's soft, and hard all at the same time. It's perfect.

He groans his approval, and with my other hand, I cup his balls. He jerks forward and hisses through his teeth. I love that I can explore him. I want to learn everything I can to make him feel good. Remembering how much he liked my mouth on him, I lean forward and take him deep. His hand moves to the back of my hair, grabbing a handful, and his other hand moves to my breast which is still covered in the lace halter. He tugs it down, allowing both breasts to be free, and I twist into his touch. He pulls away, causing a pop from my mouth, and orders me to lay back. I do as he says.

I'm turned on by the way he looks over my body and his lustful gaze makes me squirm for his touch. He bends down and picks a box up from the floor, ripping it open hastily. Watching him sheath himself with the condom is insanely hot. It's not a want, anymore, it's a need. I *need* him inside me. He kneels before me and he leans down, wrapping his lips around my nipple. My back dips and he gives my other breast some much-needed attention. He continues to do this as he lines himself up with my center, then very slowly, and carefully enters. I suck in and hold my breath as I take in the slight pressure. His tongue that's busy sucking on my nipple brings me immense, distracting pleasure. He slowly pushes forward a little more and lets out a groan. "Just a little more, baby," he pants.

"Go," I whisper back, wanting all of him. He moves forward and it's slightly painful.

"Are you okay?" he asks, then places kisses all over my face.

"Yes," I answer, honestly. I am.

"You have no idea how good you feel," he says. "I'm going to move. I'll start slow, okay?"

"Okay."

He begins to move pulling out then pushing back in. With every thrust, it becomes a little less uncomfortable, and I feel a little less pressure. He's not rushing, and he isn't rough. He continues to kiss me all over my face. "Baby," he whispers in my ear, and I hum in response. "I need to move a little faster. If it hurts, tell me please."

I squeeze his shoulder. "Alright."

His pace begins to quicken, and he buries his face into the side of my neck, leaving light kisses and nibbles. The pain begins to subside as he continues to move and hits something inside my center. Spots start to cover my eyes, and pleasure spreads throughout my body, causing me to moan, light at first. "That's it, baby." His words send me over the edge, and I scream out his name. This orgasm is more intense than the first. His movements become more eager until he's squeezing me tight to his body and releases a muffled moan. I smile and rub my hands down his back.

"That was amazing," he says quietly. He lifts himself

from my neck and looks into my eyes, "I love you."

I smile, "I love you, too."

He slowly removes himself, kisses my nose, and moves away to dispose of the condom. He leaves the room and comes back just as quickly climbing onto the bed and settling half his body on mine. He lays his head upon my bare chest and wraps his arm over my stomach. He begins to draw circles on my hip causing goosebumps to pucker on my skin. "Was it good for you?" he asks, after a few quiet seconds.

"Amazing," I sigh, "and even better because it was with you."

He kisses the side of my breast, and it tickles. "Thank you for trusting me. Are you feeling okay? Do you hurt?"

"A little," I admit, feeling the soreness more prominently now.

"Why didn't you tell me?" His head shoots up, and he grimaces.

"It obviously felt good at the time!" I defend, not wanting him to worry.

"Promise?"

"I promise."

"Do you need ice or something?"

I shrug because I don't know. Is that something you need to do after your first time? He shoots up off the bed and pulls on his sweats. "What are you doing?" I ask, pulling the blankets up. With his body heat gone, I'm cold.

"I'll be right back, I'm gonna get some ice."

I laugh to myself as I watch him leave, his back muscles on full display. I *love* his back. I grab the remote and turn on the TV, scanning the channels settling on the movie 'Thor'. He returns a few minutes later with a small bucket of ice, then disappears into the bathroom, and reappears with a rag. I watch him fill the rag with ice and move towards me. He drops his sweats and crawls under the covers then places the cool rag against me. It's incredibly sweet. "I gotta take care of my girl." He lays on his back next to me and pulls me to him. I snuggle more into his side and without a word, we watch Thor.

BACK TO REALITY
Veronica

There's a light tickle on my back, a touch that moves up and down, and my body shivers. I rouse slowly, my head on a soft pillow. Chase's face is inches from mine. "Morning, beautiful," his voice is raspy.

"Morning," I mumble.

"We have to get a move on."

I groan. "Nooo. Sleep."

He laughs at my stubbornness. "Sorry, baby, I have plans for today. I let you sleep in as late as I could. "

"*Sleeeep.*"

He pats my bare butt. "It's almost eleven. We need to check out and grab some breakfast."

"If someone wouldn't have woken me in the middle of the night, I may not be as tired," I grumble.

"I didn't hear you refusing. In fact, I heard 'Oh my God,' quite often. You're gonna give me a complex." I smack his clothed shoulder, and I can feel my cheeks getting hot. He laughs. "C'mon, get up! Get dressed before I take you for round three." He leaves the bed, and my eyes watch him as he moves out of the room. I turn onto my back, taking the sheet with me to cover myself. *Yeah, not too sure if modesty is a thing anymore after last night.*

I sit up, keeping the sheet pressed against me, and notice my bag at the end of the bed. I pull it towards me, removing pieces of clothing from the bag, and quickly dress.

Chase comes back into the room. "Shame."

I laugh. "You were just telling me to get dressed."

"I know, and it's a good thing. I just like seeing your skin." He moves to me and wraps his arms around my waist. I place my hands on his chest and nuzzles in. "How are you feeling?" he asks.

"I'm good. Perfect." He places a kiss on the top of my head.

"Alright, let's get a move on."

He grabs my bag, zips it up, then tosses it over his shoulder. I follow him out of the room, and he grabs his bag, carrying them both in one hand to open the main door. Once in the hall, he reaches for my hand, and we make our way down to the lobby. At the front desk, he asks if they'd keep our bags while we have breakfast. There's a lot more activity this morning. I watch as guests and staff move around the inn. Chase's tug on my hand brings me back to him. He smiles. "Let's eat."

With our bags tucked safely behind the lobby desk, we move towards the dining room we ate in last night. The tables no longer have the candles set on top. Instead, there's a little tray-like thing with different jellies that are placed in the middle. You can see outside now, and the scenery *is* beautiful. Set back on the grounds of the inn is a large pond with a fountain of water in the middle that's shooting upward. Two beautiful large swans are swimming near a small dock, where two people seem to be enjoying their coffee. Beyond the pond is surrounded by large trees; the trees in various colors of orange, yellow, and browns. It's a gorgeous view, and I'm so glad I was able to see it before we left.

We enjoy our breakfast together, and I feel like I'm floating on air. I'm the happiest I've ever been, and it's all because of the man sitting in front of me. I know the next few days are going to be tough--with having to tell Vance about our relationship, and Chase's deployment. It's hard not to think about, but I don't want it to damper the time we have left together.

Chase takes care of the check, and soon we're leaving; the car moving down the long driveway. I can't help but watch it move further away from the back window. Chase's warm hand lands on mine. "We'll come back," he says, and I smile at the thought. This is forever our place.

The drive back home seems to take less time than it took to get to the Glasbern. I see the familiar stores and signs for our small town, and I'm saddened by that. Until we confront Vance we have to remain a secret, and after yesterday, I don't want that anymore.

"We need to tell Vance," I blurt and look towards Chase.

He nods before speaking, "We do."

"How should we go about it?" I ask.

"I think we should tell him together," he says.

"Okay." I bite the inside of my cheek. "He's not going to like it."

"He may surprise us. I mean, look how Victor handled it. He accepted it more quickly than I thought."

"Yeah, maybe."

"I have something to show you. We can tell him later today, or we can do it tomorrow?"

"Let's do it tomorrow. This is my last full day with you, and I want to spend it drama free."

"Okay. Tomorrow then." He squeezes my hand in a

comforting gesture.

He continues to drive us towards Harry's junkyard, and I'm very confused about why we're coming here.

"Harry's?" I question.

He turns onto the rocky road, taking his time since his car isn't made for this kind of travel. A few cars are parked near the fence since Harry's is open until mid-afternoon today. "What are we doing here?" He doesn't answer me and remains quiet as he parks his car. "Chase?" I ask again.

He smiles at me, "C'mon."

My eyes instantly move to the old yellow Camaro next to the booth. The for-sale sign is missing, and instead 'SOLD' is written boldly in red across the windshield. An older man is approaching us with a Harry's U-Pull It hat on his head. His shirt stretches over a large belly, and his suspenders are connected to his pants. "Chase?" he asks as he nears.

"Yes, sir." Chase reaches out his hand, and they shake as the man stops in front of us.

"Harry. Nice to meet you," he says then continues, "She's all ready for you." Harry holds out a set of keys to Chase. I watch this whole conversation from the side, completely stunned.

"Oh, they go to her." Chase gestures to me.

"Here ya go, young lady. I hear you're going to take good care of her." Harry holds out the keys to me, and I slowly reach out my hand. *Is this a joke?* He releases the keys, and they fall into my palm. I watch this as if it's in slow motion and I dare not make a sound. Still confused, I look back up at Harry then to Chase.

"What?" I finally speak up.

"You are the proud owner of a 1969 Camaro," Chase

tells me.

"What?" I ask again, not sure I heard him right.

"It's yours," Chase says pointing to the car.

"Are you serious?" I yell out.

"Yes." He laughs.

"How? What the hell! I'm so lost right now."

Chase chuckles at my behavior, and Harry leans into him. "She gonna be okay?"

"Yeah, she's gonna be fine."

"Alright then. Thank you." He pats Chase on the back and leaves us standing there.

"You bought this?" I ask. It's the only thing I can think of.

"Yep."

"But it's mine?"

"Yep. Well, it's ours."

"Ours."

"Yes, I thought, well...I was hoping that it could be something we could work on together. But since I'm leaving, I thought maybe you could work on it while I'm deployed. Would give you something to do."

"Really?" I'm shouting in excitement, now. "For real? No way!" I've about lost it. I'm bursting at the seams, and the thought behind this is so beautiful.

"Yes, really. For real." He pulls me towards the car. "I even got a plate for it."

He guides me towards the back of the car, and it's a custom plate that reads "VERNICA".

I deadpan over to Chase, "Really?" and place my hands on my hips.

He laughs lightly, "You'll always be Vern." I can't stay mad at him. Especially with this gesture. I just can't. The thought behind this is enormous, and well planned out. I know it takes time to get a custom plate done. I jump on him, successfully taking him by surprise.

"Thank you so much." My throat becomes tight, holding the tears at bay.

"You're welcome," he responds.

"This is..." I pause. "I have no words. It's so thoughtful. I love this car!"

He smiles. "I know, and I love you."

I grab his face and smash my lips to his, kissing him multiple times.

"So, what now?" I ask.

"A towing company is going to come pick it up tomorrow and drop it off at the garage. I already spoke to your father about it." That surprises me, and he must see it. "Yep. I have it all situated."

"You're good."

He winks at me. "I know."

I squeal in excitement and jump in place; a few guys walk by looking at us strangely. I stop jumping. "This is my car!" I yell at them. Two of them look at me like I've lost my mind, and another says, "Congrats."

Chase laughs at me, "Let's get you outta here, you weirdo."

I giggle with enthusiasm. 'Where to, now?" I ask.

"I didn't have much planned after this. We can go to my house and spend the day together," Chase suggests.

"I don't care what we do, as long as I'm with you."

"Perfect answer," he says kissing my lips, and we part to get into his car.

I buckle up my belt and hit my legs while yelling, "I have a Camaro!" Chase is watching me, amused. "Okay. I'm done. I promise."

He puts his hands up, "Hey, I didn't say anything. I'm

glad you're excited about it."

"I have to learn how to work on the body." I think about it. "I'm pretty sure Victor took a course. Maybe I can look into taking one too."

"That'd be hot," Chase says and starts up the car.

"Yeah, I'll ask him about it."

"Good," Chase responds while reversing from the spot, driving slowly back down the bumpy road. He drives us towards his house.

We spend hours in his room, enjoying our time together, and don't leave until we're both starving. Chase suggests we do some take-out. "Chinese?" he asks.

"Hmm yeah, I could go for some sushi. Does the China House have sushi?" I ask, never having any since visiting Victor, but I could seriously eat some now.

"I guess we'll find out."

We hop into the Z and head to our local China House. We stand back, scanning the menu, and I notice the small sushi bar in the corner.

"Yes!" I point towards the little bar.

Chase laughs, "Alright then. Do you want anything else?"

"Yeah, I'll take some pork fried rice, and some crab rangoons."

The lady behind the counter asks if we're ready. Chase nods then takes a step forward.

"I'll be right back, I have to pee," I tell him and skip off to the side of the small restaurant, and thankfully, the bathroom is unoccupied. I quickly do my thing, wash my hands, and leave. Chase is off to the side, but his back is facing me. His large frame is definitely one to admire, and I know just how sexy those shoulders look without a shirt. I come up behind him, wrapping my arms around his waist. I feel the vibrations of him speaking, but he immediately stops. "What's wrong?" I ask, looking up and removing my arms from around him, so I can move to his side.

I see who he's talking to, and I freeze. *Crap.* Shannon stands in front of Chase, her hand on his pec. She takes a step back when she sees me, her hand dropping to her side. Her eyes narrow on me and then move to Chase. "You *are* screwing little Russo!"

Chase sighs. "If I recall correctly, I told you that's none of your business."

Shannon laughs, and it's not a nice laugh. "Whatever. I don't fucking care." She abruptly turns and stalks out of the restaurant, her blonde hair swooshing.

"Crap," I mutter.

Our weekend has spoiled me; being allowed to grab him without consequences is something I enjoyed. Being back in town, we have to be a bit more discreet until we speak with Vance.

"Don't worry about it," Chase dismisses, then wraps his arm around my shoulder not caring. "What about Vance? What if she tells him?"

"She said something about us awhile ago, too. She never said anything to him then, why would she now?"

"I hope you're right," I murmur.

"Sushi, pork fried rice, crab rangoon, General Tso, and an egg roll!" the lady at the front yells, placing the large bag on the counter. Chase steps forward, taking me with him, and grabs the bag.

Once back in his room, we sit cross-legged on his bed watching one of his favorite movies, 'Iron Man'. He couldn't believe that I have never seen it before and insisted that it be changed, immediately. He "cannot date someone who hasn't been introduced to Tony Stark". I have to admit, by the time the movie was over, I fell a bit in love with Robert Downey Jr. He put in the second movie, and we snuggled up together. I struggled to keep my eyes open halfway into the movie, but I lose the fight.

HURT
Chase

I'm jolted awake by the ringing of my phone, slightly disoriented and confused. The ringing ceases, and I glance around the room. Veronica's head is resting on my chest and her steady breathing indicates that she's still asleep. The DVD menu for 'Iron Man 2' is on constant replay. I must've fallen asleep, too. Our Chinese take-out containers are on my nightstand, next to my phone.

The ringing starts up again, and I know someone needs to speak to me. I don't want to wake Veronica, so I try to tilt my body and slide her head off my chest and onto my bed. I reach over her to grab my phone from the stand, disconnecting it from the charger. My heart rate instantly speeds up when I read the name on the screen. I slide the green icon over, then place the phone to my ear. "What's up, man?" I ask, nonchalantly. *Play it cool, man.*

"I'm out front," Vance says before the line goes silent.

Everything comes crashing down around me, and I feel like the air instantly got kicked out of my lungs.

"What's wrong?" V whispers as she turns onto her back. I glance down at her beautiful face, her eyes slightly squinting from sleep.

"Vance is here."

Her eyes widen at my response. She's wide awake now. "What? No, No!"

"It'll be okay." I kiss her forehead and move off the

bed towards my bedroom door. I rush down the stairs and can see Vance's form as I approach the front door. Taking a deep breath, I open the door, and Vance comes in without a word. He walks into the living room, just off the foyer, leaving me standing with the open door. I run through my options, but I know there are none. It's time to come clean.

A swift push of my hand on the door, and I move towards the opening of the living room. The sound of the door clicks shut from behind me. Vance is facing the fireplace, his back to me, and I allow him to gather his thoughts. After a few seconds--which felt like minutes--he turns to stare me dead in the eyes.

"Why is V's car out front?" he asks, but he doesn't wait for me to answer before firing off another question. "Is she here?"

"Yes," I answer. There's no point in lying, now.

"Veronica!" He screams loudly and unexpectedly; it makes me jump.

I remain quiet but from my position, I can see her moving down the stairs cautiously. When she reaches the middle, a small creak emits from her steps. Vance glares at her. She stops, almost as if he froze her body. A laugh of incredibility escapes him. "Yanno, I ran into Shannon tonight."

My eyes move to him, remembering that we did see her at the China House. Vance continues talking, "She mentioned seeing you two together, and I had no idea what she meant. But she kept mentioning how you guys were *together*. I mean, I thought there was no way. No way that my best friend and my sister would be hooking up behind my back. That's what this is right?" He pauses, and we both remain quiet. I glance at Veronica just as she looks at me. "Right?!" he yells again.

A weak "no" comes from V, at the same time I begin to speak. "Dude..." but his hand comes up, cutting me off.

"I don't want to know and don't call me dude." He points to me. "We are not dudes! Dudes do *not* lie to their best friend, and dudes do not *fuck* their best friend's little sister!" his voice has risen dramatically, his hands have turned into fists, and a small vein is starting to bulge in his neck.

"Vance," V starts to speak.

"No!" He points to her.

"Let us explain!" she tries again.

"Explain what exactly? That you guys have repeatedly lied to me? How long has this been going on?"

"That doesn't matter," V says, "We care for each other," her voice is soft.

Vance begins to pace, and the anger is radiating from him. I look back to Veronica, who shrugs her shoulders and mouths 'do something'.

"Vance," I step forward but pause when his pacing stops, and he looks up at me. His stare is hard, and it's threatening. I've been in tough situations, but never one to have someone who's almost like a brother look at me like I've completely betrayed him. And I have. It hurts.

"What about Nic? I thought you were seeing her."

I sigh, "I am."

"What the fuck?" he shouts, not allowing me to finish and before I can blink, I'm abruptly pinned to a wall. It happens so quickly, it knocks all the air out of me. I'm gasping for breath and seeing black spots behind my eyes. I can hear him yelling but can't make out the words. Vaguely, I can hear Veronica's voice and the fear behind her words.

"How could you?" Are the first words I can make out.

"Vance, let him go! You're hurting him!"

The spots start to clear. He has me by the shirt, hands on both sides. He slams my back into the wall again, "Fucking explain to me!"

"We're trying. You need to calm down!" Veronica's voice is broken by sobbing hiccups, and there are tears streaming down her face. He releases me, and I drop to the ground. V's hands are instantly on my face. "Are you okay?" she whispers. All I can do is nod.

Behind her, Vance is running his hands through his hair. Veronica helps me up, but I keep my body against the wall for support. She turns to face her brother. I've seen his anger quite a few times, but it's always been towards other people. I'll admit, it's scary being on the receiving end.

"I *am* Nic," V confesses.

Vance's head snaps up, "What?"

"I'm sorry, Vance," She moves forward to stand directly in front of him. She reaches just under his chin, and I want to protect her, but I know she's strong. His nostrils flare slightly. It's like prodding a bull--though he'd never attack a woman, let alone his sister. "We were planning to tell you, but his is what we were afraid of. You're overreacting."

"Overreacting?" he scoffs. "I doubt Victor, Vaughn, or Vin will be thrilled to find that you two are hooking up."

"Stop!" Veronica shouts, and it surprises Vance. "We are not just hooking up."

Vance laughs. "That's all Chase is capable of, V! He's

just like me."

"He's nothing like you!" She screams, her breathing is rapid. She takes a moment to collect herself, "He's treated me with nothing but respect. I have yet to see you treat any girl with anything remotely close to that," her voice is strong. "*How dare you*! You've been scaring guys away left and right! I love Chase, and Chase loves me." His eyes widen at her admission. He starts to speak, but she cuts him off, "Shut up! I am *so* tired of this. I can understand why you're mad! I do, I get it. But this--the way you're acting-- is exactly why you've been left in the dark. *I* was afraid to tell you! Chase has wanted to tell you since the beginning, and I told him I didn't want you to ruin the one good thing to come into my life." She pauses then continues, "We were going to come to you tomorrow, and I'm sorry you had to find out from someone else. But how you feel isn't going to change how we feel."

Vance continues to stare at Veronica. He doesn't make a sound. After a very tense staring contest, he grumbles something, walks around her, and moves to me. I stand up, willing to take whatever he's going to dish. I expect a punch or something, but he doesn't even look at me. He walks right to the front, opens the door, and disappears behind it.

I sag in relief and slight hurt. My eyes seek out Veronica, whose hands are covering her face. She pulls them down to look at me. "That went horribly," She moves towards me, "Are you alright?"

"Yeah, I'm fine."

"He'll get over it."

"I don't know. He seemed really pissed."

"You're not going to break up with me, are you?"

"No," I shake my head and pull her to me, wrapping my arms around her small frame, "No. I hate that this happened. I don't want him to be mad at us. Maybe I should go find him."

"He needs space. Let him cool off. I think I should probably head home. I'll try to talk to him. He can't stay mad at you. You're leaving in three days. He'd be a pretty shitty friend if he doesn't talk to you before you leave."

"I'd understand."

"I'll come over after work?"

"Yeah." I squeeze her.

"It'll be okay...he'll get over it. He's going to have to," she says into my chest. My hands mindlessly rub her back, a million miles away. "I'm sorry," she says low. It's quiet, just above a whisper, but I hear it loud and clear.

"What are you sorry for?"

"I should have listened to you."

"It'll be fine," I reassure her. I don't know if it will be, I can only hope.

WHEN YOU'RE GONE
Veronica

Vaughn is laying on the couch when I get home. He looks up when I walk through the door.

"Hey," I greet him, laying my bag near the door.

"Yo."

"Did Vance come home?"

"Nope."

I nod, even though he's not looking at me anymore. "Mom and Dad in bed?"

"Dad went up. Mom's in the kitchen."

I walk straight through and find Mom sitting at the dinner table with her recipe box, and small cards all over the table. She looks up when I approach. "Hey, honey," she greets me with a warm smile. "How was your weekend?"

I can feel the heat rise on my neck. "It was good. What are you doing?" I point at all the note cards.

"Ah, looking for your great grandma's tiramisu recipe."

I pull out a seat, plopping down, and place my head on top of my hands. Mom pauses her movements and looks at me. "Everything alright?"

I sigh. "Not really."

"Can't read your mind, baby. You're gonna have to spit it out."

"Vance found out about me and Chase."

She hums, "And I take it he wasn't happy."

"No. He's really mad. It was a little scary."

"Vance has always been a little hot-headed. His temper's always getting him in trouble. He is also the most sensitive out of you all. Perhaps this is why he reacts to things much more passionately than you or your brothers."

I scoff, "Yeah, right. Vance, sensitive? I find that hard to believe."

"Well, it's true. Just consider how this may have hurt him."

I ponder on that a bit. Mom goes back to looking through her cards. Is Vance mad because of Chase dating me? Or because we went behind his back? Is he scared that I'll take away his best friend? I would never do that. I couldn't imagine if Wes isolated Taylor away from me. I'd be devastated. Vance has always been a pain in my ass; scaring every guy who dares to even look at me. He had to know that I'd meet someone eventually. He knows Chase better than anyone, and his words from earlier come back. "Chase is just like me."

While I know Chase has had his flings, I've never seen him treat a girl poorly. Unfortunately, Shannon pops up into my mind. I don't want to think about her, or what she shared with Chase. There's no doubt they hooked up, he admitted that to me. It was before we started talking, but he pushed her to the side like she was yesterday's dirty laundry. No. I'm not going to go there. He's never treated me badly.

"Aha!" my mom yells out, making me jump, "I found it!"

I laugh, "Great Mom, I'm gonna go up and take a shower."

"Alright, baby. Love you." I lean in to kiss her on the cheek and head up to my room.

After a nice shower, I give Taylor a call and tell her all about the amazing weekend I had.

"No way! He bought you a car?!"

"Well, it's *our* car."

"You must give good head."

"Taylor!"

"What?" she laughs.

"I think your mom has dropped you on your head a few times." I laugh.

"Maybe. I have noticed a flat spot on the back of my head."

"You're too much."

I hear a car pull into the driveway. Thinking it's Vance, I scramble off my bed and rush to the window. Pulling the curtains aside, I see the black beamer pulls up in front of the garage, then the lights shut off. Taylor is going on about something, but I cut her off, "Tay, Vance is home. I need to try and talk to him."

"Kay, good luck. I'll see you tomorrow."

"See ya." I end the call while watching Vance get out and move to the front door of the house. I move back to my bed, sitting on the edge, and anxiously wait to hear footsteps come up the stairs. I think I should approach him before he enters his room.

After what seems like forever, I finally hear his heavy footsteps clamber up the steps. I know their Vance's, he never takes his boots off until he's in his room. I pull open my door just as Vance is coming up the hall, and I step out in front of him.

"Go away," he grumbles and tries to move past me, but I move in front of him, "Knock it off," he growls.

"We need to talk."

He stops and looks at me dead in the eyes, crossing

his arms over his chest. "What could we *possibly* need to talk about?"

"Chase is leaving."

"So?" He rolls his eyes.

"Don't act like a dick. Chase is being deployed!"

"I don't care," he snaps.

"You don't mean that! He's your best friend!"

"Some friend," he sneers. "Friends don't date your sister behind their back, and then lie about it."

"If you want to be mad, be mad at me. He wanted to tell you. I was afraid."

"Whatever." He pushes me out of the way, causing me to stumble back, and stalks to his room. He slams the door right in my face. Stupidly, I try the knob, but it's locked. I knock and call out his name but he never answers. I press my face to the door. "He leaves Wednesday."

The next three days go by way too quickly. Chase and I spent every minute we could together. With approval from my mom, I was allowed to stay the night with Chase. His flight was insanely early Wednesday and I didn't want to sleep our last few hours away. We didn't. We made love and held each other until a little red car pulled into his driveway. The car that was to take him to the airport.

We walk out to his front door and I plaster myself to him. He lifts me up and my legs wrap around his waist. I grip his uniform tight in my hands as the tears well up, and I try hard to keep it together. I fail miserably; they stream, reluctantly, down my face.

"Baby, this isn't goodbye." He holds me tight to him.

"I know," I whisper, knowing that my voice would come out strangled.

"I will call you the first chance I get." He promises.

"Okay." I sniffle.

He pats my butt, and I reluctantly untangle myself from him. He places me back on the ground and his hands move to cradle my face. I close my eyes, not wanting him to see my tears, even though I'm sure it's quite obvious. "Baby, look at me," He begs. His pleading voice has me opening my eyes--and in shambles. "I love you so much. I will see you later." He smashes his mouth to mine, and claims me, stealing my breath from me. When we pull apart, I see the wetness on his cheeks as he wipes away mine. "I love you." He whispers and turns away from me, leaving me standing on his front steps. I watch him toss his bag into the back seat of the car and climb in. The car disappears down the driveway, and an ugly sob rips from my lips. I cry the whole drive home, and as soon as I see my mother, I collapse in her arms.

A few hours later my alarm sounds for school. Mom insists that I go and that it will help get my mind off everything. As much as I don't want to--I know I look awful--sitting at home alone won't help. Vance never went to see Chase, and I was extremely pissed off at him.

As Chase promised, the Camaro was towed to the garage on Monday, but with our limited time, I didn't do anything with it. I wanted to spend *every* moment with him. The gesture behind his gift meant so much more now, knowing that I needed something more to occupy my mind. I looked into classes at the local community college and they taught an auto body seminar for a reasonable price. I called the college and signed up for the most recent class. They start in two weeks.

A week after Chase left, I received my first phone call from him. It wasn't nearly as long as I had hoped but it was all he was allowed at the moment. He gave me his address and told me to write to him as much as I wanted. When he had to get off, I had a really hard time with it. He promised to call me as much as he could. I could hear a man in the background barking orders, I kept it together but cried myself to sleep that night.

Two months later, I anxiously wait for my video call with Chase. It doesn't always go as planned and sometimes, it doesn't happen at all. This has become our new normal but my nerves still tend to get the best of me. I play a game on my phone until the notification that Chase Daniels wants to video chat. After I press accept, his handsome face fills my screen and my heart jumps at the sight of him.

"Hey, baby!" His full smile is on display and I feel my body melt when I hear his voice come through the speakers. "You look beautiful, I miss you so much."

"I miss you, too," I say, getting a little choked up with emotions, "Did you get my most recent letter?" I write to him as much as possible, my last letter included a few pictures of myself.

"I did! I hung the pictures in my bunk. It's nothing like having the real you but I stare at them before going to sleep. You're the first thing I see when I wake up."

"McSwoony." I say low but he hears me.

"Only for you, forever and always." There he goes again...he's proved time and time again that the nickname fits him perfectly. There's some commotion that pulls his attention away for a moment but then he's back. "Sorry about that. So, how are the auto body courses going?"

"Oh! It's *so* awesome! I'm really enjoying it and I think it's something I can see myself doing in the future."

"That's so great, babe! I'm so proud of you. Have you spoken to your dad yet?"

"I haven't, but I spoke with mom and Vance about the chances of expanding the garage to offer body repair and paint. Vance seemed interested so that's a good sign."

He nods, "It is. How is Vance?"

"His temper has calmed down. He's not ignoring me anymore, at least."

"That's good."

"It is. He's stubborn but he won't hate us forever." I reassure him, the guilt of all that happened resurfacing. Vance will get over it. Chase and I love each other, that won't change or go away.

"Let's hope not," He drifts off, "What else is new with you? Tell me. I want to hear everything."

"Oh! Melissa and Victor are having a party next weekend, I think he's going to propose!" I squeal in excitement.

"Damn, give them my best."

"I hope you come home soon. Have you heard anything?"

He sighs and shakes his head back and forth, "I haven't. I'm sorry."

Our conversation lasts for about an hour, and I'm on a high to be able to spend that time with him, even if it's through a screen.

I am running late! I rush into the house and run up the stairs, taking two at a time. I quickly unbutton my shirt and step out of my sweats, tossing them aside. Already wearing my special strapless bra, I remove the long slim red flowing gown from the hanger and step into it, pulling it up my body. I secure the straps around my neck but struggle to zip up the back.

"Veronica?" Mom calls out.

"I need your help!" I yell out.

A second later she comes into my room and sees me struggling to reach the zipper. She smiles and moves to zipping it up to the top. "Oh my goodness, you look beautiful! My little girl." Mom gushes. I turn to look at myself in my floor-length mirror, noticing the glistening eyes of my mom. I chose red because it's Chase's favorite color, and if he wasn't here to go to prom physically, at least he was here in thought. He insisted I go and claimed that it's a thing all high schoolers should experience. Unsurprisingly, Taylor also insisted I go. The top is a beautiful off-white halter encrusted with crystal beads and the back is completely open, exposing everything down to the top of my waist. It is elegant and, yet, very sexy. As soon as I saw it on the bust form in the boutique, I knew it was 'the one'. My hair is up; complete with curls and a million bobby pins. I went and had it professionally done, and it took longer than I expected; it's exactly the reason I'm running super late. I also had my makeup done since I know little to nothing about it. False eyelashes are my new favorite thing.

"I'm so sorry that Chase couldn't be here," my mom speaks quietly.

I turn to look at her. "I am, too," I say, sadly.

"Let's go take a picture to send to him," she suggests.

"Okay. Let me grab my shoes." My heels are an off-white satin to match the top. They're nothing crazy fancy, but they are insanely high. Rather than kill myself by falling down the stairs, I grab them on my way out the door and wait to put them on until I'm safely on the first floor. Mom makes me stand in various places for pictures.

Finally, the rest of the gang arrives. Taylor looks incredible in her off the shoulder form fitting navy dress and Wes is looking quite dapper as well. Jerry whistles when he sees me, tugging Mateo along behind him. "Oh dollface, you look *stunning*." He grabs my hand and twirls me around.

"You guys look so handsome." I gush over their stylish suits. Jerry is wearing a black suit with a maroon tie and his boyfriend sports a deep maroon suit with a black tie. They purposely coordinated and it's so adorable. They fuss over each other, my smile widens knowing after the playboy Jerry met that night months ago is long gone. Mateo mended Jerry back together and I've never seen him so happy.

Vance walks through the door and halts in place, looking at each of us in our formal wear, his gaze stopping on me. His face softens and I think he may finally be seeing me as more than just his little sister. Our relationship has been strained, but lately he's seemed more accepting. Chase asks about him often, and I tell Vance every chance I get. I'm actually surprised to see him standing here, but I'm glad. A small smile graces his lips causing me to smile in return. He moves forward, placing his hands on my biceps. "You look beautiful, V!"

"Thank you," I murmur.

"Man, Chase would be shittin' himself if he could see you now."

I'm taken aback by his comment. It's the first time that he's acknowledged us; Chase and I together. I smile sadly, truly wishing that he could be here. Vance unexpectedly hugs me, and whispers a soft, "I'm sorry."

Before I can respond, he releases me and walks away. My heart expands and I feel like a huge weight has been lifted. *I cannot wait to tell Chase!*

"We better get going," Taylor announces.

"Oh, let's get a few more pictures in the front yard!" my mom suggests.

"Okay, but let's make it quick, Mom."

We all move out of the front door, and start walking down the stairs towards the small yard in the front. I stop as if I hit an invisible barrier and suddenly feel very, very faint. The man of my dreams is standing in my front yard, holding a corsage in his hands, and dressed in his uniform. I pull up my skirt to run to my handsome man--who's here. He's really here!

"Oof!" Comes out of his mouth when I slam into him. "Surprise!" he whispers. His arms come around me, and squeeze me.

"How?" I question, full of emotions.

"I just got in. Vance picked me up."

"Vance? What!"

"Yeah, we had a good talk. It was long, but it was good. Are you ready?"

"So ready," I gasp as Chase dips me low; his hands are at the small of my back and his lips caress mine. He leans up and I take a moment to look into his handsome face, those blue eyes--my future.

EPILOGUE

One Year Later

Veronica

I hear a shout from my left that makes me pause my movements. I shut off the sander and glance over my shoulder at Chase. He's wearing his blue jumpsuit. The front zipper is open, showing his white shirt underneath. I love seeing him in his work uniform. My eyes move back up to his face, which is dressed in a smug smile, and I know he knows what I'm thinking. I twist on my stool to face him and remove my safety glasses, "What?"

He laughs, "Are you about done?"

"Not really." I shrug.

He points at the clock on the wall, "It's almost six, let's go home."

"Holy crap," I hadn't realized how late it was. When I'm working, I become so immersed I tend to lose track of time. "Did everyone leave?"

"Yeah, about an hour ago."

"Wow, okay. Yeah, let me just put my stuff away." I stand from my stool, unplug my sander, and deposit it on top of my workstation. I remove my suit and hang it near my things before I head over to the sink. I turn the water on warm, lather up my arms and wash away the crud. A series of beeps from the alarm signifies the door opening, "I'll be outside," Chase shouts from across the shop. His voice is followed by three beeps, again.

I move throughout the building, checking the

rooms, the paint booth and make sure all major power tools are off and unplugged before setting the alarm and locking up.

The garage side of the now larger building is darkened and deserted, as Chase said, and the parking lot is empty. Only one car remains in the expanded lot, and my beautiful man is leaning against it. He hasn't seen me yet; he's looking off into the distance. I take my time ogling him and the car. The once sad-looking yellow Camaro, now red, is shining bright in all its glory. I worked on it every chance I had when Chase was deployed, and when he returned, we worked on it together, slowly bringing it back to life. Chase and I worked so well together, it changed the course of both our futures.

Chase catches me looking at him, and I move forward until I'm standing in front of him. He pulls my shirt until I'm flush against him, and his arms wrap around my shoulders, "What's going on in that beautiful noggin' of yours?"

I purse my lips, pretending to think, "Just how incredibly lucky I am to have this amazing…" I smile and pause, letting my sentence linger, "sexy," I pause again and grab his butt.

Chase hums his approval, "Go on."

"Car!" I squeal while pulling the keys from his back pocket, duck under his arms, and run to the driver's side. He eyes me over the roof.

"That was *mean*, woman!"

I laugh loudly and tuck myself behind the wheel. Chase quickly gets into the passenger side, "You know, I think you're more in love with the car than you are with me!"

"No way!" I *do* love the car, and it's the best gift I have ever--and probably will ever receive, but she's got nothing on Chase. I try and drive her as much as possible. I start her up, and the loud rumble fills the cab causing my grin to double in size. "She's just so much fun to drive," I yell towards him. He makes a face like he doesn't believe me. "I'll make it up to you, I promise!" I blow him a kiss.

Before I know what's happening, he slips his hand behind my head and slams his lips to mine, kissing me so deeply it makes my toes curl. He rips away from me, but not before the pure lust on his face puts me in motion. I rip out of the lot and speed towards home, arriving at the small yet perfect house in five minutes flat. Chase pushes the garage door opener, and I ease her inside before quickly cutting the engine. We move swiftly--hungrily--coming together at the door leading to the kitchen, and his mouth is on mine again. He lifts me and holds me to him, never breaking our kiss but moving through the kitchen, and down the hall to our room.

Vance arrives home shortly after we finished our shower, with food--it couldn't have been timed any better!

It's just the three of us tonight; sometimes Vaughn and Vin join us. While this isn't my permanent home, I stay here enough to warrant my own closet space. Whatever Chase told Vance in their long talk broke through, though I never did get the details--it was between them--things are good.

We settle with pizza and wings in the living room, and there's some sport playing on the TV. I eat and occupy myself with texting Tay because I could care less about the game. I get together with Taylor as often as possible while she's in her second year of college. I don't regret not going to college with her, I love making cars beautiful again.

When I finish my food, I place my empty plate on the coffee table, and make myself more comfortable on the couch, laying my head on Chase's lap. I'm completely content as Chase idly plays with my hair, and my eyes begin to close on their own accord. Just as I begin to doze off, a knock at the door makes me jump. I roll onto my back and look up at Chase, who shrugs. We both look at Vance, thinking it's most likely one of his lady friends, but he shrugs. "I'm not expecting anyone."

The knock comes again.

Vance remains seated, so Chase taps on my hip indicating me to move off his lap, which I do. I sit up and watch him move to the door. The way the room is situated, I can't see who it is when he opens the door and greets the person. I vaguely hear him ask the person if everything is alright.

Vance looks when he hears Chase's question, most likely wondering who it is. He's on his feet in an instant, moving to the door, his pizza disregarded. I'm beginning to worry, and I'm not sure if I should move, but I slowly find myself standing up.

"Victor?" I hear Vance ask, and at the sound of my oldest brother's name, I move closer to the door. Once Victor comes into view, my steps falter. He's completely disheveled. His hair is wild, his eyes are rimmed with red, and--is that blood on his face? His eyes are vacant, and he remains frozen in place. "What's going on, man?" Vance asks carefully, and rightfully so, I have never seen Victor like this. He looks almost unstable. His stare lands on me, but I don't think he even sees me. I move closer to Chase. "Victor, are you okay?" I ask.

It seems as if he's finally aware that we're standing in front of him. I'm terrified. His lips begin to move, but no words are coming out, but he finally finds his voice, "Can I crash here?"

"Yeah, of course," Vance says. "What's going on? Where's Melissa?"

Victor's eyes turn murderous and it's scary.

"My wife's a whore."

AUTHOR NOTE

If you are reading this right now, I cannot thank you enough for taking a chance on this book and therein, myself.

So much of Labeled stems from my own personal experiences. I truly hope you enjoyed Chase and Veronica's story.

As a brand spanking new author, It would be greatly appreciated if you would please leave a review on Amazon.

All my love,
Jenni

ACKNOWLEDGEMENT

Where do I even begin? This has been quite the journey and I would not have happened if I didn't have these amazing people in my corner.

My very own Taylor, Kayla, who has been there from the very first sentence to completion. Who has continued to be my personal cheerleader. Picking me up when I've doubted myself and this book. I love you to pieces.

Beth and Kelli Flynn, that one conversation in the lobby of a hotel kicked my tush into motion. I am forever grateful of your continuous support and love.

Lauren Anders, your friendship and support have been a godsend in this process. I cannot thank you enough for making this story come to life before my eyes!

Janna, for letting me use your car(and son)! Jakob and Alyssa for bring Chase and V to life. Logan Habermehl, for bringing your beautiful Z out to play!

Darlene Ward and Terri Varady, all of your help, input, love and support. I adore you guys!

To my work family, Jamie, Leigh, and Jodi. Letting me talk to you about the process, sharing my doubts and goals. You guys have been a pillar of outlet and support.

Author M. Mabie, for your guidance, advice, and support. You are my favorite person.

My Wattpad family! Without you, I don't think I

would have gained the courage to publish this. I love each and every one of you. THANK YOU!

Elise, your friendship, advice, and kindness means so much to me. Thank you for being there!

To my family, for all your constant encouragement, support, and love.

My sister Rhonda, for ALL of your time working on Labeled with me, for bringing out the best of this story. It wouldn't be as great as it is without you. Love you Nye Nye.

And last but most certainly not least, my husband, Dustin. Your love and support has no bounds, and your sheer excitement of my writing means more than words. I love you forever and always.

ABOUT THE AUTHOR

Jenni Linn

Jenni Linn is a full-time dreamer and part-time writer. 'Labeled' is her debut novel written with sprinkles of real life experiences.
When she's not writing, she's hanging out with her family--her husband and 2 children--watching FRIENDS, or curled up on the couch with a book and coffee in hand.
Jenni lives in the country, but dreams of blue oceans and believes in being yourself-- her hair is always changing and her skin is a canvas.

You can contact her at JenniLinnWrites@gmail.com or Follow her on social media:
Facebook: https://www.facebook.com/jennilinnwrites
Twitter: https://twitter.com/JenniLinn6
Goodreads: https://www.goodreads.com/jennilinnwrites